ENTANGLED

This book is a work of fiction. Names, characters, places, and incidents either are products of the author's imagination or are used fictitiously. Any resemblance to actual persons, living or dead, events, or locales is entirely coincidental.

Printed in Australia
First Printing: September 2025

Cover design by Jess Chaplin
Typeset by Jess Chaplin

Paperback ISBN 978-1-7638695-3-0
Hardback ISBN 978-1-7638695-4-7
eBook ISBN 978-1-7638695-5-4

Angry Cat designed by Freepik.com

A catalogue record for this work is available from the National Library of Australia

ENTANGLED

ROBERT M. SMITH

Also by Robert M. Smith:

Purgatory
The Price of Justice
The Granite
Shark Bait

For my wife.

PROLOGUE

A desperate and increasingly pessimistic Bowker stared at the latest report on the table in front of him. DNA summaries, mainly, which provided details of their target. Details, but not the name of that person they sought so urgently. The name that could bring an end to their hunt and to the nightmare that was rapidly approaching.

He'd thought he'd found a promising lead, but Erin O'Meara at Forensics had nipped that in the bud. 'Don't get your hopes up, Greg,' she'd said. 'Go buy a donkey and run it in the Melbourne Cup. The chances of it winning are better than those of him being a match. And when I say a donkey, I don't mean a slow racehorse, I mean a real bloody donkey.'

Of all the investigations Bowker had conducted over the years, none came close to carrying the consequences of this one. Success would see a killer taken from the streets, but more importantly, an innocent life would be saved. Failure would shatter his mental state, tear his family apart and see him lose one of the things most important to him. His life would be turned upside down and his career as a police officer finished.

But while there was still a chance, even one so microscopically small, Bowker could never concede defeat.

CHAPTER 1

Showbag Norton had worked for Southern Rural Water and its predecessor since he left Bacchus Marsh High School at the end of Year 11, or Form 5 as it was called back then. His real name was rumoured to be Vincent, but he was known to everyone as *Showbag* – full of shit. And there was no end to that shit – stories that glorified his own abilities, hot racing tips for horses that never won, rumours he insisted were fact but turned out just the opposite. Norton was short, slight of build and losing greying hair from the crown of his head. As a kid, he'd dreamt of becoming a jockey like his well-known uncle, Handbrake Norton, but a severe allergy to horses drew a thick line through those aspirations.

Today the weather was cold, with misty rain arriving in squalls across Pykes Creek Reservoir, an irrigation water source for farmers in the Bacchus Marsh and Werribee districts. Usually abuzz with anglers, swimmers, skiers, or those just seeking a shady picturesque spot for a picnic, the public reserve adjoining the lake had been quiet of late. Signs along the water's edge warned of a blue-green algae bloom. Given that, with the abysmal weather thrown in, most regular visitors had sought alternative venues for their leisure activities. And that suited Showbag just fine. No litter to collect, no arguments with yobbos about the registration of their boats or jet skis, or their licence to pilot those craft.

No futile debates concerning the restrictions shallower water put on allowable activities.

The little man smiled. He could see a leisurely morning ahead. He might read the paper in the warmth of the company vehicle for a while, perhaps have a smoke while he filled in the time he would later log as spent picking up litter.

Showbag unlocked the double steel gates to a restricted area that contained a large building and gave him access to the reservoir's retaining wall. He checked the dam wall for anything untoward and the spillway for obstructions, although with the water level low, he knew the main outlet wouldn't be running. Retracing his steps and locking the gates, he drove back along Pykes Road and into a dirt carpark. He positioned his vehicle between two pine trees, where he knew it was invisible from the Western Freeway above. He wound the windows up tight to shut out the chilly wind blowing off the reservoir before retrieving the morning newspaper from the passenger seat. *Life is perfect*, he thought as he spread the racing guide across the steering wheel, lit a smoke and listened to the garble of magpies in the clump of pines in front of him. A kookaburra laughed somewhere on the other side of the water, and a hawk circled high above.

The cawing of crows interrupted his study of form for that afternoon's Wodonga races. Something near the fence twenty metres in front of his car was of intensifying interest to an ever-expanding coven of crows. *Or is it a murder of crows?* he asked himself. If it was a dead roo or wallaby that had been hit by a vehicle before struggling to its final resting place, then his leisurely morning had suddenly taken a turn for the worst. He'd have to load the bloody thing onto the back of his vehicle and dispose of the carcass before public complaints found their way back to his desk — not that he *had* a desk. He reluctantly folded his paper, climbed from his vehicle, and wandered over to where the crows were aggressively disputing claims over whatever carrion they had located. The murder lifted as one as he approached.

Within thirty seconds, Showbag was leaning on the bonnet of his vehicle, struggling for breath between vomiting up mouthfuls of bile and his breakfast of bacon and eggs. He reached for his mobile phone and hit his supervisor's name from his favourites list. After four rings, the call was answered.

'Showbag. What have you fucked up this time?' asked a gravelly voice.

'There's a dead body at Pykes,' Norton spat out.

'I'm not in the mood, mate.'

'No crap, Sean. It's a woman. Crows are picking at what's left of her. And she's covered with a million fuckin' blowflies and stinks to high heaven.'

'You sure it's not a roo like last time? I take it you've had a good look.'

'I'm spewin' my guts out here, so of course I've had a good fuckin' look.'

'If this is more bullshit, so help me…'

Norton was frantic. 'It's no bullshit, I tell ya. We need to call the cops.'

'I'll do that. Where abouts in the reserve are you?'

'Up on the bank just short of where that road goes up to those houses.'

'You stay where you are, and don't let anybody come close to what you've found. I'll be out as soon as I've given the Ballan police a call.'

'Why not just ring triple zero?'

'We'll let the locals check it before we're all over the news tonight, okay?'

CHAPTER 2

Ballan's Constable Nathan Patterson was about to leave the modern Inglis Street station on a town patrol when he heard the phone ring in the office behind him. He debated whether to let the call go to voicemail or run the risk of spending the next half hour listening to one of his favourite callers reporting another peeping Tom and demanding he visit her house to search for evidence. Patterson knew there *was* no peeping Tom, but even if there was, the last person to attract a voyeur's interest would be the late-middle-aged, morbidly obese widow from Atkinson Street. Patterson was handsome, his dark hair and black-rimmed glasses giving him a Clark Kent look and making him a favourite among local women. Although he was completely aware of the widow's ulterior motives, his professionalism won out and he picked up the phone. He breathed a sigh of relief when Sean Reading from Southwest Rural Water identified himself. That relief was short-lived as Reading explained what one of his staff had reportedly found at Pykes Creek Reservoir.

'Look for a short, skinny bloke in a white vehicle with our logo on the side. He's bald on top and will more than likely have a ciggy hanging out the corner of his mouth. Name's Showbag. Showbag Norton.'

Patterson was puzzled. 'Showbag?'

'Yeah. You know. Full of crap,' Reading replied without a hint of amusement. 'That's why I said a woman's body has *reportedly* been found. A couple of years ago, Showbag claimed to have found human remains in a heap of branches near the Melton dam. Turned out to be a kangaroo. All you could see through the dead leaves was an eye staring up, and Showbag didn't investigate further. He copped a shit-stirring from his mates, so this time I expect he has taken a better look. And he sounded like he was shitting himself.'

Using his flashers and siren to clear his way along the crowded highway, Patterson reached Pykes in less than ten minutes. After a quick scope of the area, he spotted a lone man nervously standing beside his work vehicle, a half-smoked cigarette hanging from his lips.

'Mr Norton?' Patterson asked as he approached.

'Yeah.' He thrust out a hand. 'Call me Vincent.'

Patterson shook his hand, noting the absence of the nickname. 'Constable Patterson. Better show me what you've found, mate.'

'This way,' Norton said as he strode up the rise to the freeway hidden by scrub above. Patterson towered over Norton and took one step for every two of his.

The body of a woman was hidden among the scrubby pines by the boundary fence. Patterson had seen the odd corpse in his short career, but the sight of the young female's decomposing remains still accelerated his pulse. The body was lying face up, fully clothed except for bare feet. Her belt and the fly of her jeans were undone, her high-necked blouse untucked at the waist. Animals, birds and insects had severely ravaged the body, making any assessment of the woman's age difficult, although Patterson guessed she was probably in her late twenties, early thirties. He estimated her height at around one seventy centimetres and thought she must have been an athlete of some description, or at least kept herself in good physical condition. Her face was badly damaged, her eyes were missing – the crows had made sure of that – and the side of her skull was caved in.

Everything that Patterson could see pointed to murder. But his training screamed to keep an open mind. Maybe she had fallen down and fractured her skull, animal damage making it look more gruesome. He scanned the ground but saw nothing that could've caused her head wound. Maybe she had sustained it somewhere nearby and staggered to her final resting place. Maybe she'd had a stroke or a heart attack or some other fatal medical episode. But if that was the case, how did she get to Pykes, in the middle of nowhere? There was no car, and it was too isolated a spot for her to have just been out walking on her own. Besides, she wasn't dressed for walking, and where were her shoes? Then again, if she did suffer a catastrophic medical event, it was possible she may have thrown them off elsewhere before she collapsed and died.

Patterson shook his head and exhaled loudly. Despite alternative explanations, deep down he knew the woman had met foul play.

'Fuck me,' he said softly to himself. He looked up at Norton. 'How long since you found her?'

Norton had his eyes closed. 'Half an hour, tops. I sprinted back to the car and rang the boss.'

'There was no need to hurry. She's been dead quite a while. Several days at least. Perhaps a week.'

'Do you need me anymore?' Norton asked. The whole morbid scene was starting to get the better of him. The crows circling overhead only made things worse.

'Go sit in your vehicle, mate. I'll be over to ask a few questions as soon as I call in the big dicks.' Patterson dragged his phone from his jacket pocket.

* * *

'Been a while since we've been back to the bush, Sherlock,' Detective Inspector Greg Bowker said casually to his colleague and best mate Detective Sergeant Darren Holmes as they travelled up the Western Highway and through Melton. The bitumen was wet, and leaden clouds hung low over the road ahead.

'Melton was out in the scrub a few years ago, mate,' Holmes replied. 'Just a whistle stop on the old highway to Ballarat. Then out of the blue it became a dormitory city for workers in Melbourne, and look at it now – virtually absorbed into the greater metropolitan area.'

Bowker nodded. 'Urban sprawl. Happening on all sides of Melbourne. Look at Werribee, Pakenham, Beverage… they were all out in the sticks once. Flourishing little towns that died in the arse before the city swamped them.' He laughed. 'Australia, the great rural nation where ninety percent of the population lives in cities!'

Holmes chuckled as a Bunnings Warehouse shot past to their right. 'City won't get out to Murrayville in my time, I don't reckon.'

'Probably not to Manang either,' Bowker replied, looking at his partner with a grin.

Both men knew the Victorian Mallee country well. Holmes was born and raised on a farm at Murrayville on the South Australian border, while Bowker had spent more than ten years in the one-copper town of Manangatang in the central Mallee. Both were now senior officers in the homicide squad. Both were tall, well-built men in the second half of their careers – Bowker closer to retirement than Holmes by a few years. Bowker had a strong, handsome face, a full head of hair turning grey at the sides, and a body he'd kept fit even as the years slowed him down. Holmes had a happy disposition that put those around him at ease and wore a bushy moustache that he hoped would balance the reclining hair on his scalp. Despite both officers being past their athletic prime, it would take a brave man to challenge either of them physically.

'Kirsten still enjoying working in Homicide?' Bowker asked as they left Melton's outskirts and the road dropped down to cross the Djerriwarrh Creek. 'She's more likely to tell you than me. Me being her boss and all that.'

'She's like a pig in mud. Found her calling, she reckons.' Holmes smiled. 'Which is kinda lucky when you give up five and a half years at med school to become a copper.'

Bowker kept his eyes on the road. 'You and her still going okay?'

Holmes nodded. 'Yeah. Things are good.' He paused, then shrugged. 'But the seventeen-year age difference hasn't kicked in yet. Give it a decade or so and she'll still be a hot chick while I'm an old bastard.'

Bowker had listened to this fear of Holmes's many times before. Kirsten Larsen was an attractive woman in her early thirties whom they had met working a murder case in Benalla, where she was stationed as a detective constable. Larsen and Holmes hit it off from day one, and with Holmes's marriage already on death row, one thing led to another and the two became an item. Larsen had since been transferred to Homicide. She and Holmes worked a Port Fairy murder investigation together, but their personal relationship had complicated their handling of the case and Bowker had since avoided pairing them.

'Enjoy the sun while it's shining is my advice, Sherlock,' Bowker said as he flicked on his indicator and changed lanes to overtake a B-double loaded with construction timber. 'I think you're selling Kirsten short anyway, mate. I doubt she'll bail just because you lose the Danny Zuko looks.'

Holmes grinned. 'Danny Zuko from *Grease*? That's a joke. More like a six-foot-two Danny DeVito!'

Bowker laughed out loud. 'Cassie still enjoying work on the other side of the ditch?'

'As far as I know. Don't hear a lot from her these days. Any news I do get comes through our kids. She's going out with some Kiwi, apparently. Doing the horizontal haka with him, no doubt, but that's none of my business anymore.' Holmes looked out over acres of fruit trees all covered with bird netting as they dropped down onto the flats where the Werribee and Lerderderg rivers converged on the outskirts of Bacchus Marsh. 'Enough about *my* love life. How's Rachael?'

Bowker's face tightened. Normally, the mention of his wife generated a beaming smile. 'I'm a bit worried about her health, to tell you the truth, mate. She's lost her normal high-voltage energy.'

'We're all getting older, Greg,' Holmes said. He grinned widely. 'Just because you're down to two or three times a week doesn't mean there's a health problem.' When Bowker didn't respond with a clever retort or even the hint of a smile, Holmes knew his partner was genuinely concerned. 'Has she seen a doctor?'

Bowker shook his head. 'Nope. I suggested that when she cancelled a couple of her beloved dance classes. And twice last week, she contemplated not going to work at the kindergarten.'

'Rachael is the most sensible person I've ever met. Why not see a doctor?'

They crossed the Lerderderg River and overtook a line of cars taking the exit into Bacchus Marsh. Bowker shrugged. 'Stuffed if I know, mate. She puts the whole thing down to a virus, probably a dose of Covid she didn't realise she'd caught.'

'What's the harm in getting it checked out?'

'Don't think I haven't asked her the same question a hundred times, Sherlock. She's never had a thing wrong with her all her life, and I think perhaps she's scared that the doc will find something serious. Her mother died of breast cancer, and her old man's grappling with a melanoma that metastasised before they found it.'

'All the more reason to get to a doctor, surely.'

Bowker raised his fingers on the steering wheel. 'You're preaching to the choir here. But some people prefer not to know.'

By now, they were beginning to climb into the Pentland Hills and onto the Central Highlands Plateau. Even though the freeway was easier to negotiate than the old winding Ballarat Highway it had replaced, the incline was still steep, and most heavy vehicles were in a low gear as they made the slow ascent. The rain became heavier and visibility more compromised as they climbed into low cloud, made worse when they overtook trucks throwing up billows of swirling mist. Both detectives chuckled as they passed a sewage tanker with *We transport milk on weekends* painted across its rear.

It was quiet for a few moments as Bowker braked to avoid a BMW sports car changing lanes from behind a slowing semitrailer. 'Wanker!' Bowker said half under his breath. 'Indicator would have been nice.'

'BMWs aren't fitted with 'em, from my experience,' Holmes replied. 'Entitlement is built into the vehicle.'

Bowker smiled. 'What do you know about Pykes Creek Reservoir?'

'Not a lot. Been past a few times on the way to Ballarat, but usually there's no time to take in the view. You come down that steep hill on the brakes, over the bridge near the dam wall, then climb up out of the valley in three lanes. Trucks struggle to make it to the top. My only real memory still scares the shit out of me when I think about it.

Bowker glanced across at his partner. 'I've got a story too. But you go first.'

'A week or so after I moved to Melbourne, a mate and I went up to see Kryal Castle on the outskirts of Ballarat. He was in his brother's Renault and decided he'd see how fast it would go down the hill into Pykes. We got up to over a hundred and twenty clicks. Miles an hour, not kilometres. The motor is in the back of those things, and I could feel the front starting to lift off the ground.' He laughed. 'After I cleaned myself up, I swore I'd never drive with the bastard again.'

Bowker chuckled. 'I nearly filled my undies at Pykes too, and it wasn't my fault either. Rachael and I drove over the bridge and got trapped in the left lane by two cars outside us as we climbed out of the valley. No problems. In no hurry. You might remember the road swings left as you near the top of the hill. Just around that bend was a bloke parked in the left lane with a tyre half rolled off his front driver's side rim.'

'Shit.'

'Yeah, shit alright. I hit the hooks and managed to squeeze around between two cars on my outside.'

'Did you hear if anybody got cleaned up?'

'I parked in the truck stop at the top of the hill and walked back down to where he was removing his spare from under a big load of crap in his boot. I flashed my badge and told him to move the car up the hill to where I was parked. He carried on about how that might wreck one of his fancy mags until I warned him I was about to book him and call a tow truck.'

'He move?'

'Yeah. Didn't do the wheel much good, but better than a heap of people being killed.'

'Driving a BMW, I bet.'

'Porsche.'

'Young bloke spendin' Dad's money?'

Bowker shook his head. 'Nope. Middle-aged with a dolly bird half his age.'

Immediately, he regretted what he'd said. Holmes saw the parallel with his own relationship but said nothing.

Bowker was keen to change the subject. 'I don't like these cases where bodies are found in isolated places. Brings back memories of the first murder I helped investigate as a senior connie. When I was stationed in Manangatang in the eighties. Took months to solve that one.'

'And the one we knocked over in the same place two years ago. Another long, drawn-out inquiry.'

Bowker sighed heavily. 'Yeah. You run into problems right from the start. Usually, nobody was around when the crime was committed or the body was dumped, and there's bugger-all help from CCTV.' He shrugged. 'But I s'pose, on the other hand, stray cars in isolated areas tend to be noticed.'

'That's if someone's there to see them.'

'On the bright side, while Pykes Creek Reservoir is around six k's from the nearest town, the Western Highway runs right beside it. I read a story about a Ballan copper who was on that highway and saw a jet ski doing circles on its own with three people in the water. She swam out in her uniform, climbed aboard the jet ski and brought the three of them to safety. So the reservoir is definitely visible for a few seconds from the freeway, and the road carries a lot of traffic. We might be lucky. Maybe a motorist saw something useful.'

Holmes nodded. 'I guess there's a chance. When we're talking isolation, we're not talking *Mallee* isolation. And we're talking about a widely used recreation area, not a bloody silo out in the middle of nowhere.'

'Not sure how widely it would have been used over the last

day or so, though. The weather has been shithouse across the whole state. I'd hate to imagine what Pykes Creek Reservoir would have been like with a cold southerly ripping across it and those sleety squalls.'

Bowker flicked on his left indicator and took the exit to Pykes Creek Reservoir. He reached an intersection at the top of the rise and turned right onto a bridge over the freeway. They followed Pykes Creek Road until they were stopped by a junior uniformed officer stationed to intercept casual visitors or well-informed rubberneckers. The detectives flashed their credentials and were directed further up the road, where they found a cluster of vehicles in a gravel carpark adjacent to a clump of pine trees. An ambulance was reversed onto the grass, its rear doors open. Alongside were three police cars and two Southern Rural Water vehicles.

Bowker drove to the closest parking spot and pulled in. An older, overweight uniformed officer saw the detectives arrive, broke away from his conversation with Constable Patterson and wandered across.

'Fuck me. That's all I need,' Bowker mumbled.

CHAPTER 3

The older policeman ambled towards the newly arrived vehicle but stopped in his tracks when he spotted Bowker alighting from the driver's side. He rolled his eyes, attempted to hitch his trousers over his beer gut, then traipsed forward towards the figure from his past. Neither man offered to shake hands.

'So, we've hit the jackpot with this one, have we?' the uniformed officer said sarcastically. 'Homicide's golden boy here to solve things for us.'

Bowker didn't take the bait. He looked at Holmes. 'Detective Darren Holmes, I'd like you to meet Sergeant Brian Delaney. He was a great mate of Trevor Flynn when I worked in Ballarat thirty-five years ago.'

'Hard to be Trev's mate now after events down at Port Fairy last year, eh, Bowker? And by the way, it's *Senior* Sergeant Delaney.'

'And it's *Detective Inspector* Bowker,' Bowker shot back.

Holmes quickly gathered that there was no love lost between his good friend and Delaney. The Trevor Flynn to whom they referred was the abusive first husband of Bowker's wife Rachael. Once good mates, Bowker and Flynn fell out badly over Flynn's treatment of Rachael, and Flynn's subsequent behaviour resulted in his dismissal from Victoria Police. The pair clashed again via an accidental meeting in Port Fairy last year. Flynn was murdered a few days later. Bowker found himself chief suspect and was suspended from duties while the homicide investigation took place. Holmes knew that any friend of Trevor Flynn was, by definition, an enemy of Bowker.

'What have we got?' Holmes asked to defuse the fiery reunion.

'Remains of a woman,' Delaney replied as he dragged a notebook from his trouser pocket and flipped through the pages until he found his jottings. 'Discovered by a local water officer, Vincent Norton, doing his normal rounds. Victim appears to be in her late twenties or early thirties, but she's so badly ripped apart by animals it's hard to be sure. The ambos found her head caved in, which is consistent with her being bashed to death, but the coroner will sort that out officially. No ID, no phone, no purse or bag, no keys, no shoes. No car, no tyre tracks except those left by the Southwest Water vehicle.'

'Forensics?' Bowker asked.

'The team have dusted anything close by for prints, although this weather makes things hard. Soil and vegetation samples have been collected. Nothing more of interest around except for a short bit of chrome trim, or more accurately, plastic chrome trim. Techs reckon it's impossible to know how long it's been there or what type of vehicle it came from. Pretty generic stuff, apparently.' Delaney flipped a page. 'Bugger-all people out here for days, by the looks of it. In one of the bins, there were two empty stubbies, a UDL vodka can, and a KFC box, drink container, and wrappings. Forensics have bagged and tagged the lot. Other than that, all the rubbish containers are empty.'

'Any idea about time of death?' Bowker asked.

'More than a few days, according to the forensic team. Norton arrived here reasonably early – the crows tipped him off.'

Holmes folded his arms. 'The shit weather probably kept

visitors away. Explains why she wasn't found earlier.'

Delaney shrugged. 'I'd say so,' he replied. 'But then again, I'm not a swingin' dick, am I? Just a dumb flatfoot.'

Bowker let the jibe pass. Delaney had a chip on his shoulder the size of a redgum sleeper, but Bowker was determined it not interfere with the investigation. He'd deal with Delaney after they got their killer. 'Better show us where she was found.'

Delaney led them to the trees. 'In behind there. No real attempt to hide the body once *in situ.* Not even sticks or leaves thrown over it.'

Bowker slipped his hands into his pockets and inhaled deeply. 'If the killer had been serious about hiding her, the best place would have been in the lake. She might have disappeared forever, or if found, been assumed to have hit her head and drowned.'

Delaney shrugged. 'The killer is maybe cocky and believes he won't be found, or was shit scared and just wanted to get away from here ASAP.'

'You're assuming it's a male,' Bowker said, scratching his cheek.

'I'll bet my left testicle it is,' Delaney replied quickly.

'You're probably right, but at this stage we assume nothing, OK?' Bowker advised with an edge.

Delaney didn't answer even though he was sure the detectives agreed the perp was a male and Bowker was on his high horse. The same high horse he was forced to ride out of Ballarat all those years ago. If he had kept his nose out of other people's private lives back then, it would have been better for everyone concerned.

'Seems like we've got two puzzles to solve here,' Bowker said. 'The obvious one is who killed her; the other is how the hell she got out here in the first place.'

Delaney pulled a hanky from his pocket and blew his nose. 'This bloody weather's not doing much for my fucking head cold.'

He carefully rolled the hanky into a ball, wiped a stray strand of snot from his palm then pocketed the slimy square of fabric. Bowker and Holmes exchanged sly looks. With his nostrils clear, Delaney offered his opinion. 'Obviously, whoever killed her must have brought her here. Perhaps alive or perhaps already dead. No other scenario fits.'

Bowker screwed up his face. 'What if there was more than one perpetrator involved? If she had arrived here in her own car, it could have been stolen after the killing.'

Delaney chortled. 'Are you suggesting she and her killer, or killers, came here in convoy? Breaker, breaker one niner?' He mimicked pulling the cord on an overhead air horn. '*Brrr, brrr.*'

'Probably not,' Bowker replied, ignoring the attempted humour. 'But maybe she drove in here to have a look around, take a photo, break her journey. Maybe the perps arrived after following her, or were just having a look around themselves and the crime was one of opportunity. I'll be interested to know what the coroner can tell us about recent sexual activity.'

Again, Delaney chortled. 'Too many maybes for me, Detective. My bet is the killer brought her here before or after he killed her. The simplest explanation is usually the right one. Occult's razor. Something you probably haven't heard of. I read about it in a book.'

'*Occam's* razor,' Bowker corrected with a smile.

'Whatever,' Delaney shot back, rolling his eyes.

Bowker pointed to Norton sitting behind the wheel of his vehicle now parked in the asphalt carpark. 'I presume he's the bloke who discovered the body?'

Delaney nodded. 'That's him. Vincent Norman. He's pretty shaken up. The ambos gave him some breathing exercises to settle him down. The whole morning's been a bit too much for the poor little prick.'

'Has someone taken his statement?' Holmes asked.

'Nathan Patterson,' Delaney replied. 'He's a senior connie at Ballan.'

Bowker nodded. 'We might have a word with Mr Norman ourselves, I think.'

'Don't trust the uniform boys, is that it?' Delaney asked sarcastically. 'Forgot you were one yourself for fifteen years? Although you made a hash of that in Ballarat. Cost you a decade in purgatory up in some God-forsaken Mallee shit hole.'

Bowker had lost patience and leaned in close to Delaney. 'I'd had enough of your crap in Ballarat, and I've just about had enough of it here. Right now, I'm debating whether to report you for insubordination, or do what I should have done in Ballarat and deck you where you stand.' He stood up straight. 'So let's keep things professional, shall we? In an hour, Detective Holmes and I will return to Melbourne and start work on catching the prick or pricks who rolled this woman. No doubt we'll need to return here more than once if this crime has local connections, and when we do, I will expect nothing but respectful cooperation.'

Delaney saluted sardonically. 'Got it, *sir*.' He then turned and walked off towards where the forensic team was packing up.

'Useless fat bastard,' Bowker mumbled.

'You and Delaney don't like each other? Or is it just my imagination?' Holmes said with a wide grin as they made their way to Norton's vehicle.

Bowker didn't answer, but Holmes could see he was seething.

They introduced themselves to Norton after he climbed from his vehicle. The small man was still shaky, the horror of what he had found escalating with the progressive arrival of emergency personnel. Any inclination to revert to his big-noting Showbag persona had long since evaporated.

'Finding something like that knocks the wind out of you, doesn't it, mate?' Bowker said, staring down into Norton's blood-drained face. 'It still does the same to us, and we see this type of thing as part of our job.'

'I thought I would find a dead possum or a roo when I went over to check what the crows were on about. The closer I got, the more it stunk.' Norton breathed out heavily and steadied himself on the bonnet of the car as a light misty shower passed over quickly. 'I've never seen a dead person before.'

'What time did you arrive at Pykes?' Bowker asked.

'About eight thirty. I check this reservoir every Monday morning. Clean up if there's any mess after the weekend.'

Holmes nodded. 'Anybody else around?'

'Nobody. The weather was worse than it is now, and the lake has blue-green algae, so I didn't expect anyone to be here.'

Bowker slipped his hands into his trouser pockets. 'So, tell us what you did when you got here.'

'I unlocked the gates to our work area and drove in. I made sure the locks on the shed hadn't been tampered with, then walked down to the wall and checked the spillway. No water's going over it at the moment, so I knew there'd be no obstruction, but I always check anyway.'

'And when you finished your rounds?' Bowker asked.

Norton glanced towards his boss, who was in deep conversation with Patterson and Delaney, to ensure he was out of earshot. 'I could have driven straight down to Melton and checked the dam there, but with bugger-all to do here I was a mile ahead of my normal schedule, so I thought I'd find a quiet spot, light a smoke and study the race page.' He took a deep breath. 'If it wasn't for those fuckin' crows I would have been out of here half an hour later and it would have been up to some other poor bastard to find the body. But that's par for the course. If shit's gonna happen, it'll happen to me.' He stared down at the wet asphalt.

'I'd say that woman in the ambulance is worse off than you, mate,' Bowker shot back.

Norton eyed the detective, then looked back at the ground. 'Yeah. Sorry,' he replied softly.

'Where do you live, Vincent?' Holmes asked.

'In Bacchus Marsh. Why?'

Holmes shrugged. 'Being pretty much a local, with your job involving travel around the district, I thought you might know the woman. Or at least have seen her around.'

'Recognise her!' Norton retorted quickly. 'Most of her face is bloody missing.' He pointed to the freeway above. 'Besides, I'd say ninety-five percent of the traffic on that road is just passing through the area. Not locals. Going to Melbourne that way' – he pointed south, then north – 'or going to Ballarat or Adelaide that way. I wouldn't know them from Adam.'

'But not too many non-locals would drive down here, would they?' Holmes asked.

'You'd be surprised. Often see cars with interstate plates. Good place to take a break. Public dunnies, playground if you've got restless kids. There's a Maccas a few k's up the freeway. Not a bad spot to stop and eat.'

Bowker saw he had a point. 'Did you touch anything near the body when you found it?'

'Shit, no. I went back to the car, took a few deep breaths and then rang the boss.'

Holmes raised his eyebrows. 'Why didn't you ring triple zero?'

Norton kicked away a small stone and took a moment to answer. 'Because I thought I'd found a body hidden in some leaves down at the Melton dam a few years ago. I rang triple zero and it turned out to be a kangaroo. I've never heard the end of it, so I wasn't taking that chance again.'

Bowker chuckled, more in disbelief than anything. He pointed to where the body was found. 'Surely you knew it was a woman you found this time?'

Norton held up both palms and shrugged. 'Of course I knew. But I still thought I should ring Sean first and let *him* contact the police.'

Bowker looked at Holmes. *Insecurity gone mad*, he thought as he spotted Delaney approaching with purpose in his step.

'I've just been talking to your boss, Mr Norton. You didn't tell Constable Patterson the whole truth about your movements last week, did you?' Delaney asked aggressively.

'Whoa, whoa, whoa, Senior Sergeant,' Bowker said, holding up a palm. 'Detective Holmes and I are in the middle of an interview here.'

Delaney placed his hands on his hips. 'Has Mr Norton told you that he came out here last Wednesday to take samples of the algae?'

Bowker eyed Norton. 'Is that true? A moment ago, you told us *Monday* is your day here.'

Norton stared down at the ground. 'Yeah. I was here on Wednesday, but for less than ten minutes. Grabbed a few samples from various points around the lake then hit the road.'

Delaney snorted. 'And it slipped your mind to tell the constable?'

Norton looked up angrily. 'If I saw the body here last Wednesday, I'd hardly wait until this morning to report it, would I?'

Delaney moved forward, invading the little man's space. 'Maybe you planned to leave it until this morning to report the remains.'

Norton took a step back but found himself pinned against his vehicle. 'Why would I do that?'

'Maybe you killed the woman last Wednesday, panicked and

left the scene, then decided no one would suspect a bloke who'd made the gruesome find,' Delaney said forcefully. 'Acted the poor innocent who became an unintended second victim of a grisly act.'

Norton shook his head vigorously. 'That's total bullshit.'

'Why didn't you mention you were here Wednesday?' Bowker asked quietly.

'I did a million things that day on top of my normal rounds,' Norton retorted. 'One of the other blokes from work can vouch for that. The visit here was a quick job on the way home.'

'So you took the samples just before knockoff time?' Holmes asked.

'Yeah. On my way back to Bacchus Marsh.'

'Where was the woman when you first saw her?' Delaney said aggressively.

'There was no one here. Just me. And it was cold as shit.'

'From here, you went directly to Bacchus Marsh?' Bowker asked.

'Yeah. Straight home. Didn't stop except to drop the samples off at the depot. Didn't see anyone. I'd been up since sparrow fart the day before, and I was totally rooted. Had a nap soon as I got home. My wife woke me up when she lobbed in about six.'

'Yeah, right,' Delaney replied. He smiled sardonically at Bowker. 'Let me know if there's any other cases I can solve for you.' He wandered back to where Patterson was farewelling the forensic team.

Bowker rolled his eyes at Holmes. 'Okay, Mr Norton,' he said, 'just a few more questions to tidy up.'

Norton stared at the ground, wondering why he hadn't just driven back onto the freeway this morning and left the body for someone else to find.

CHAPTER 4

Detective Senior Constable Kirsten Larsen had been in court most of the morning. When she returned to the Homicide centre, she was still dressed in her navy-blue jacket and knee-length pencil skirt, with matching stilettos and a white silk blouse. Her blond hair was pulled back in a long ponytail, and she dragged a small document trolley with her right hand. She parked the trolley then stood deep in thought, leaning forward over her desk with her hands propped on the back of the chair in front of her. It had been a successful morning, and she was sure that justice would be done by the jury when final arguments were concluded later that afternoon.

Two male detectives sat in discussion on the other side of the room when Detective Sergeant Marco D'Angelo entered carrying a cup of coffee in one hand and a manilla folder in the other. He was short in stature, and height restrictions would have made him ineligible for Victoria Police in earlier times. He displayed the beginnings of a paunch but was otherwise in reasonable physical condition. His hair was receding, and he sported a bushy moustache on his round face to compensate. Today, he wore one of the shiny grey suits that had once fitted him snugly but now strained their buttons. Among his colleagues, he was admired for his tenacity, where hard work rather than detective instincts often saw crimes solved. He caught the eyes of his male colleagues, motioned towards Larsen and feigned fanning his face with the folder. The other detectives smiled and nodded, their grins more to do with how far Larsen was out of D'Angelo's league.

D'Angelo continued to his desk beside Larsen, admiring her backside and long legs as he approached. 'How'd court go?' he asked as he placed the coffee and folder on his desk, careful to give no hint he'd noticed her appearance.

Larsen stood up straight, towering over D'Angelo in her heels, and placed her hands on her hips. 'The bastard's going down, I'm pretty sure. The jury won't take long. You could see the contempt in their eyes.'

D'Angelo nodded. 'Good. All killings are bad, but your wife and three-year-old kid is a step further along.'

'Do you know where Greg and Darren have gone?'

'They took off a few hours ago. Human remains were found at a reservoir somewhere up near Ballarat. That's all I know.'

Larsen nodded but said nothing.

'We've got a new case as well,' D'Angelo said as he picked up his folder and pulled out a few pages. 'Security guard out at Car City in Ringwood. Found bashed early last Thursday morning by the owner of Ando's Pre-Owned Cars, one of the dealers out there. A Mr Samuel Anderson. The victim's name is Jeremy Ralston. Twenty-four-year-old with a partner and two little kids. He was found unconscious by Anderson among the cars in his yard and taken by ambulance to the Alfred hospital. Passed away from his injuries late last night.' D'Angelo looked up from his papers. 'The case has escalated from assault to murder, so looks like we cop it.'

Larsen had worked with D'Angelo since she first arrived at Homicide from Benalla a year ago, except for the Port Fairy investigation, where she was teamed with her live-in partner

Detective Sergeant Darren Holmes. Now Holmes was back with Bowker, Larsen with D'Angelo. Although chalk and cheese, D'Angelo and Larsen worked well together. She was the thinker, he was the work horse. D'Angelo would have given anything to swap places with Holmes, even forfeiting the ten-year age gap between them, but he was a realist and knew working with Larsen was the best he could probably hope for. Conceding the main meal was out of reach, he was resigned to eating crumbs from the table, seeing but not touching. In his more optimistic moments, he hoped that might somehow change. But he wasn't holding his breath.

Larsen pulled out her chair and sat down. 'What do we know?'

D'Angelo took his own seat. 'Severe head injury and bruising to the midriff. We'll get more details when the post-mortem results come through, of course, but that might be a few days.'

'Any sign of a break-in?'

D'Angelo again consulted the notes. 'Nope. No sign of attempted forced entry into the showroom or offices, and the chain fences around the yard itself were untouched.'

Larsen screwed up her face. 'Maybe the assailants were scared off before they could do what they came for.' She thought for a moment. 'Any prints?'

D'Angelo read further down the page. 'Some were lifted from cars in the immediate vicinity of where Ralston was found. Heaps of different ones, as you can imagine with customers and tyre kickers roaming those car yards. Only one print came up on the database, but the owner was in Albury the night the assault took place. Rock-solid alibi. He does admit to looking at cars in that yard two days before the night in question.'

'I think we should take a run out to Ringwood and get the lay of the land, don't you reckon? Talk to the owner of the business where the vic was found.'

D'Angelo nodded his agreement. Larsen looked down at her skirt. 'Perhaps I should change out of these court clothes first.'

'I wouldn't worry about changing,' D'Angelo shot back a little too quickly. 'It's not as though we're doing any hack work. Just a drive into the suburbs, an interview, and a general look around.'

* * *

Car City Ringwood was a multi-dealer pre-owned vehicle complex housing forty independent used car yards on one twelve-acre site wedged between the Maroondah Highway and the Mullah Mullah Creek north-east of central Melbourne. Used car dealers had made the same observation as major fast-food outlets – trade was increased if multiple options were provided for customers at the one stop.

D'Angelo and Larsen located Ando's Pre-Owned Car Dealership on one of the furthest lots from the highway where they'd parked their vehicle. They'd barely set foot in the yard before a snappily dressed man in his early thirties materialised in front of them.

'Welcome to Ando's Pre-Owned Cars,' the salesman said, arms outstretched as if welcoming a long-lost relative. 'I can save you walking the entire twelve acres, because the vehicle you're looking for is in our yard right here.' He looked at D'Angelo. 'Hunting for a car for the pretty lady, sir? We have–'

Larsen had her badge out. 'We're Homicide detectives from the Major Crimes Division. But if I *was* looking to buy a car, I'd do it myself, and you've just scratched this place off my list.'

'I'm sorry, I didn't mean to–'

Before the salesman could grovel further, Larsen again interrupted. 'Are you Mr Anderson, the owner of this place?'

The salesman pointed towards a small, square, glass-fronted building. 'He's in his office.'

'Thanks,' D'Angelo replied, winking at Larsen.

'Is this about the security guard who was bashed here last week?' the salesman asked.

'Is there anything you can tell us about what happened? D'Angelo asked.

The salesman shook his head. 'I only know what the boss told me.'

Larsen spotted a primary-school-aged lad walking into the yard with a young woman in her late teens, early twenties. She turned and addressed the salesman. 'We'll leave you to your job. Seems like a young bloke looking to buy a car for his sister.'

The salesman took a deep breath nervously, and his face wrinkled. 'Listen, I'd appreciate you not mentioning my little faux pas to the boss. I just misread the situation, that's all.'

'You did,' Larsen shot back as she and D'Angelo walked towards the office.

The building comprised a waiting room, a small kitchenette to the side, and a glass-fronted office with a large desk, behind which sat a man in a floral shirt. Two late-model Porsches were parked in the showroom, along with a Holden Monaro V8 racing car from the 1990s. In front of this vehicle was a display of memorabilia from Bathurst 1000 events of the past, including several winners' trophies.

The man stood when he saw D'Angelo and Larsen enter, manufactured a wide smile, and approached the pair, his hand outstretched from the moment he left his office. 'Sam Anderson at your service. I saw through the window that you've met my son. Still has a lot to learn, but he'll get there with experience and a little guidance from the old man. Been in the business twenty-five years.' He looked at D'Angelo. 'I'm sure we have what the little lady is looking for. Something classy, by the way she's dressed.'

'I hope you do have something,' Larsen said edgily. She introduced herself and D'Angelo, both ignoring the car dealer's outstretched hand.

'Detectives, eh?' Anderson said, crestfallen, dropping his hand to his side. 'I presume you're here about the security guard I found injured in the yard. I heard on the news that he'd died in hospital. Poor bugger. You shouldn't die just doing your job.' He chuckled. 'But I don't have to tell police officers that, do I?'

'Did you know Mr Ralston personally?' D'Angelo asked.

Anderson shook his head. 'No. Security is provided on a shared basis by the Car City management as part of the fee we lot holders pay to locate our yards here.'

Larsen took a small notebook from her jacket pocket. 'So, tell us how you found Mr Ralston.'

Anderson looked at the floor for a moment, collecting his thoughts. 'I arrived around seven and saw the security firm's vehicle parked out front with frost over the roof and bonnet as though it had been there for some time. I opened the office and turned off security inside. I then went for my normal stroll around the yard to inspect if any damage had been done to vehicles overnight, and that's when I found the guard on the ground unconscious.'

'Can you show us where you found him?' D'Angelo asked.

Anderson nodded towards the door then led the detectives to a section of the yard right of the main path up to the office. The ground was covered in white quartz pebbles, not the ideal surface to be walking in stilettos. Larsen rued not getting changed. The dealer's son was away to the left, discussing the merits of a late-model black Nissan Patrol with a burly middle-aged man. The female and the boy were abandoned. Anderson pointed to a gap between two late-model sedans. 'He was just down there. There was blood all over the stones, but the forensic people gathered up most of those and placed them in a plastic bag.'

'Was there any blood on the cars?' Larsen asked.

'A few smears on the Rodeo. The police removed them with a swab. I've had both cars washed and polished since.'

Larsen pulled the hem of her skirt above her knees so she could squat down to closely examine where the body had lain, all the time feeling the fabric tighten across her rear and knowing that's where D'Angelo and Anderson's eyes were focussed. Neither man made comment or exchanged glances. Among the stones, and slightly under the Rodeo 4x4, Larsen recovered a square pebble of rubber, or nylon, or plastic, she wasn't sure which. When she rose to her feet, both men were looking away into the distance, to her a sure sign that both had a guilty conscience.

Larsen placed what she had found in the palm of her hand. 'What do you reckon this is?'

'It's a rubber marble,' Anderson replied. 'You see them on car racing tracks. It'll be from a tyre on one of the vehicles that have gone through this yard. Probably picked up in the tread when it was out on the road.'

D'Angelo took the fragment with two fingers of his left hand. 'I don't reckon it's rubber. It looks more like nylon or some type of composite material. I think the lab should have a look at it.' He pulled a small evidence bag from his trouser pocket and slipped the pebble inside.

'Did you provide any first aid to Mr Ralston when you found him?' Larsen asked.

'I know bugger all about that sort of stuff,' Anderson replied. 'But I checked his pulse to see if he was alive then rang Triple O. The only blood I could see was on his face from a big gash, but it wasn't gushing out.'

'How long before the ambos arrived?' D'Angelo asked.

Anderson shrugged. 'Ten minutes tops. They checked his vital signs, if that's what you call it, and loaded him onto a stretcher. The police came about the same time and took a statement from me. Basically told them what I've told you this arvo.'

'Do you have CCTV of the yard?' Larsen asked.

'We do, but it hasn't been working for a week or so. The company has been to check it out, but they're still waiting for a part to fix it.'

D'Angelo shook his head, exhaling loudly in exasperation. 'That'd be right.'

'And you found nothing stolen?' Larsen asked.

'Nope. And no damage to any vehicles that we can see. The security guard did his job, I guess.'

'I bet his family are happy about that,' Larsen responded with an edge.

Anderson dropped his eyes to the ground and didn't reply.

Larsen wasn't about to cut him any slack. 'Have you contacted them to express your sympathies?'

Anderson hesitated just long enough to reveal it hadn't crossed his mind. 'Planned to do that this morning after I heard that he died, but haven't got there yet.'

'Too busy, I guess,' D'Angelo said in a sarcastic tone.

An elderly man entered the lot and strode straight to a Subaru Outback in the middle of the yard. 'Look, I'm going to have to leave you to it,' Anderson said quickly. 'It's the third time that bloke has come to look at that car.'

Larsen didn't like Anderson, or his attitude, and she was tempted to keep asking questions just to frustrate him. She didn't get that chance.

'Well, we'll leave you to your customers,' D'Angelo said. 'When we get the post-mortem results, we might need to come back to check a few things.' He handed a business card to Anderson. 'Give us a ring if you think of anything else.'

Anderson pocketed the card and was already halfway to his customer before he replied over his shoulder. 'I'll do that. Always happy to help.'

'Wanker!' Larsen mumbled to D'Angelo as they walked from the yard.

CHAPTER 5

'Your old mate Delaney can make all the accusations he likes, but in my mind, it makes zero sense that Vincent Norton murdered that woman,' Holmes said as they merged onto the Western Freeway.

'You'll get no arguments from me on that one, Sherlock. If Norton *had* killed her on Wednesday, there is no way he would have then reported finding her body this morning. What was to be gained? Nothing. The body was hidden from public view, and normally his rounds don't take him up near there. In this kind of weather, the reserve would have had bugger-all visitors, and it could have been weeks before the remains were discovered, well after him dropping in on the Wednesday became a distant memory. And you saw the state he was in this morning. He's either another Tom Hanks, or today was the first time he's set eyes on the body. My money is on the latter.'

Holmes wound up his window as the car accelerated to the 110 kph speed limit. 'Delaney's theory doesn't make sense to me either,' he said. 'He reckons Norton has reported finding the body to deflect blame. Portray himself as the poor bugger who made the gruesome discovery.' He chuckled. 'I don't know about you, mate, but if I'd murdered someone in a place open to the public where there are likely hundreds of potential suspects, I'd stay as far away from any investigation as possible. I certainly wouldn't be placing myself front and centre.'

Bowker shrugged. 'I agree entirely.'

'So why is Delaney so gung-ho about Norton? To clear the books? Because a quick investigation is a good investigation? Is he covering for someone? Or simply trying to intimidate Norton into confessing if by chance he *was* guilty?'

'Any or none of the above. But I think getting rid of me is as important as anything.'

Holmes raised his eyebrows. 'You reckon he's capable of fitting a bloke up?'

Bowker pulled into the right lane to overtake an old Bedford truck carrying a load of snorting pigs in a homemade wooden cage. 'Hell, yeah. Seen it when I worked in Ballarat as a connie. Not murders, but robberies or break-ins, that sort of stuff. Delaney, Flynn and their little cabal. Claimed it was justice. Argued the blokes they charged probably got away with other crimes they hadn't solved. Besides the personal stuff with Rachael, it was the main reason why all hell broke loose with me at that station, and why I was transferred to the Mallee. Delaney and his crew thought they'd had a win, but for me, it was the best move of my life.'

* * *

When Bowker and Holmes arrived back at their Spencer Street base, Larsen and D'Angelo were sitting opposite each other at a large table looking through crime scene pictures. Bowker picked up a photo as he pulled up a chair. 'Another new case?'

D'Angelo nodded. 'Security guard rolled at a dealership at Car City out at Ringwood late Wednesday night, early Thursday morning. Died at the Alfred last night from his injuries.'

'Interrupted a robbery, you think?' Holmes asked, sitting down beside Larsen and squeezing her thigh under the table.

D'Angelo shrugged. 'That's our guess, but there's no sign of vandalism or anything being stolen.'

'We're assuming the guard cut short any plans the intruder, or intruders, might have had and they fled the scene once he hit the ground,' Larsen added.

Bowker dropped the photo back on the table. 'Have you looked at the CCTV? I'd assume all the yards out there have it.'

D'Angelo smiled. 'Good news is they do. Bad news is it wasn't working at the business where the guard was rolled. Waiting for a replacement part, apparently.'

'Convenient,' Holmes said.

Larsen shook her head. 'Nah. It's ridgy-didge, Darren. Marco checked with the mob who supply and service the gear. There was a short on one of the circuit boards. They're waiting on a replacement from China.'

'What about neighbouring yards? Or cameras on the street?' Bowker asked.

Larsen nodded. 'We're working on that now, Greg. There must be a thousand cameras out there, which is promising. But it'll take a while to sort through the footage, especially when we haven't got an accurate time for the original assault.'

Bowker leaned back, arms folded. 'Well, you're both a mile in front of me and Sherlock. We have no idea who our victim is, how she got to where her remains were found, or even what day she was killed.'

Holmes grinned. 'In other words, we're all over it.'

This brought a chuckle from the others.

'We'll check with missing persons and see if they have a woman about the right age who's been recently reported missing,'

Bowker continued. 'We're hoping the post-mortem and forensic report might give us something we can follow. Identifying her would be a start.'

* * *

That afternoon, when Bowker walked through the back door of his Balaklava Road home in North Caulfield, his first thought was that his wife Rachael must still be at work at her kindergarten. Normally, she would bound into the kitchen, throw her arms around his neck and peck him on the lips. They would brew a coffee and unpack their day.

Bowker knew Rachael hadn't been herself lately but was not prepared to find his wife curled up on the lounge room couch, covered by a rug and sound asleep. This just wasn't Rachael. She woke when he tapped her shoulder and asked if she was okay. She removed the rug and sat up, yawning and rubbing her eyes with the backs of her hands. Bowker had never seen her this way in their many decades of marriage. Normally, she was a ball of energy, either on her way to some physical activity or suggesting one at home. But she hadn't played sport for weeks and had handed over her dance classes to her assistant.

'How long have you been lying here?' Bowker said gently as he sat down beside her.

Rachael put her hand on his knee. 'I had to come home from work at lunchtime. I felt so weak I could hardly stand up.'

'This bullshit has to stop, Rach. I'm not going to sit here and watch you go downhill.'

'It's probably just a virus. Once I get over it, I'll be back to my old self. I haven't been like this long enough to call it chronic fatigue or anything like that.'

Bowker eyeballed her. 'Virus or no virus, I'm making a medical appointment. We need to sort this out right now.'

Rachael looked away. 'There's nothing a doctor can do for a virus. You just have to ride it out.'

Bowker stood up. 'There's antiviral medication if it *is* a virus. Let's get a diagnosis before we assume anything.'

He was stunned by Rachael's reply. 'You're the boss, Greg.'

She must be crook, he thought. Number one, she was as tough as nails, and leaving work would have been a last resort for her. Number two, she wouldn't normally have acquiesced to his demands so gently.

'See if you can get an appointment time out of kinder hours,' Rachael said quietly.

'You're not going to work until we get this sorted,' Bowker shot back as he dragged out his phone and left the room.

* * *

With little to go on in terms of forensics, Larsen and D'Angelo's first port of call the following morning was the partner of Jeremy Ralston, the murdered security guard. The house where the couple lived was a modest rental in Tamarisk Drive, Frankston. Behind its low white-brick-and-wrought-iron fence was an overgrown garden, a lawn that would be better described as a cow pasture, and a disparate collection of trees and shrubs that had needed pruning several years ago. A single carport to the side of the unkempt dwelling contained an ancient maroon Holden Commodore, its rear left quarter panel caved in and the word 'ouch' roughly handwritten over the damage in yellow house paint. Larsen checked her notes and confirmed that the rego of the vehicle matched the address.

There was little evidence that the grass-covered path leading to the front door was ever used. Cobwebs cocooning the entrance and glistening in the morning sunshine convinced the detectives that the back door would be the most likely place to determine if anyone was at home. At the rear of the carport was a long farm gate with a six-foot-high panel of steel mesh wired to its frame. An assortment of plastic ride-on toys and junk decorated the badly overgrown backyard. The arrival of a snarling black German Shepherd explained the need for the gate. As the dog threw itself against the steel mesh, its teeth bared and saliva dripping, a sliding window overlooking the carport noisily opened and the head of a pinched-faced woman appeared. 'Whatever you're sellin', we don't want none! So piss off before I let the dog out.'

D'Angelo took out his ID and held it close to the window. 'I'm Detective Sergeant D'Angelo, and this is Detective Senior Constable Larsen. Is this the residence of Jeremy William Ralston?'

'It was until Craig fuckin' Bosnich killed him,' the woman shot back. 'Have you arrested the bastard yet?'

'Can we come in for a quick chat?' Larsen asked quietly.

'Not a chance. Whatever you've got to say, you can say from where you are.'

Both officers suspected the inside of the house was probably worse than outside. There was also a possibility that something untoward was being hidden, but without a warrant — for which they had no grounds — their options were limited.

'Fair enough,' D'Angelo replied. 'Can we have your name for our records, please?

'Do I have to give it to you?' the woman replied.

'At this stage, it would be a very good idea,' Larsen warned with a forced smile.

The woman shook her head but after a few seconds complied. 'Raelene Walker. Raelene Deborah Walker.'

Larsen flicked to a new page of her notebook and jotted down the name.

D'Angelo slipped his hands into his pockets. 'And you and Mr Ralston were romantic partners since when?' he asked.

'When you live like we do, there's not much romance. But we've been together since about six months ago.' A small child cried in the background. Walker turned her head from the window and yelled. 'Shut the fuck up, Brittany! Braeden, stop your sister from bloody cryin'. Give her a Tim Tam from the fridge.' She looked back at the detectives. 'Bloody kids! Who'd have 'em?'

'How many have you got?' Larsen asked.

'Only two, thank God. Braeden's father is in the Barwon prison and the bloke who rolled Jezza is Brittany's old man.' She shook her head and exhaled loudly. 'The last six months is the first time in my whole sad life I've lived with a bloke who hasn't got himself into trouble with the coppers. First time the money we live on is legit. Earned properly, you know. Not nicked from somewhere or got from fencing stolen stuff. Always had the dole, of course, but who can live a decent life on that?'

Larsen looked up from her notebook. 'What makes you think that Mr Bosnich killed Jeremy?'

'Because he said he was going to do it,' Walker replied quickly. 'Said he knew where Jezza worked and the places he checked on his rounds each night.' She sighed. 'I thought he was just full of shit. But he's proved me wrong for once, hasn't he?'

D'Angelo remained po-faced. 'So, jealousy would be his motive?'

'Absolutely. When I met Jezza, I told Craig not to come over anymore. He carried on about Brittany needing a father and bullshit like that. But I know it had nothing to do with her. It was about missin' out on a root every night. Jezza would be getting it, not him. Don't think he could handle that.'

The detectives exchanged sly glances, trying desperately to suppress smirks. 'Where does Mr Bosnich live?' Larsen asked.

'With his deadshit mate in Dandenong.'

'Have you got an address?' D'Angelo asked.

Walker shook her head. 'Nope. But I'm sure you'll have it somewhere. He's lived in the same place for years with that other dickhead when he's not doing time for somethin' stupid. The only other place you might find him is at his brother's place in Essendon. He occasionally goes over there.'

'Do you have an address for his brother's place?' Larsen asked.

'Nope. But it's really close to the Red Lion pub, apparently. That's where they meet for a drink.'

D'Angelo thanked her for her time and advised her that they would in all probability need to speak to her again, particularly if she was right about Craig Bosnich being involved in her partner's death.

When the detectives returned to their vehicle, D'Angelo made a call to police records and secured the address of Craig Bosnich. 'How can people live like that?' he asked when he'd written down the details.

'Maybe there's no other option,' Larsen replied. 'No income, no assets, probably no family support.'

'They could at least keep the yard clean and tidy. That wouldn't cost money.'

'Probably grown up in similar conditions and don't notice their surrounds like we do.' Larsen shrugged. 'I'd say their landlord must be one of those slum lords. Doesn't look like the place has had a lick of paint in decades, the trees need lopping and pruning, the carport is half falling down. It's not the tenant's job to do that sort of maintenance.'

'Vicious cycle,' D'Angelo replied.

'Yeah. A cycle that's nearly impossible to break for millions of people.'

'And in a country like Australia.'

'Bloody disgrace.'

The German Shepherd growled his farewells as the pair walked back to the street.

CHAPTER 6

The Dandenong property where police records showed Craig Bosnich to reside made Raelene Walker's dilapidated Frankston rental look like a palace. Jammed between two small factories, it had no front garden, just a patchwork of small concrete slabs, many starting to lift, with thistles growing in the cracks. A brick garage filled the gap between the house and side fence, its rusty roller door permanently jammed three-quarters of the way up. An assortment of junk was piled against the walls, allowing a small space to walk through to a door at the rear of the structure. An ancient Mitsubishi sedan sat on blocks in the drive behind an unregistered Toyota Camry. Parked on the overgrown nature strip was an early-model blue Ford Mondeo, its duco peeling to reveal grey undercoat over patches of roughly applied body filler. Its bonnet was a creamy yellow, likely a replacement after an accident. Two tracks of bare ground at either end of the car linked it to the bitumen of the street. It was obviously the household car of choice.

The front door of the hovel sat behind a caged-in porch. D'Angelo tried the handle on the heavy security door. Locked. He knocked forcefully, causing the whole structure to rattle. There was no response from inside. After vigorous banging on the weatherboards beside the porch, a short, fat man in baggy shorts, rubber thongs and a blue shearer's singlet appeared in the porch and unsnibbed the security door.

'Yeah?'

D'Angelo flashed his ID and introduced himself and his partner. 'Are you Craig Bosnich?'

Thong Man shook his head. 'Nope. Shaun Mortimer.'

'Does Craig Bosnich live here?' Larsen asked.

Mortimer shrugged. 'Off and on.'

Larsen had played this game before. 'Is he here now?'

Mortimer shrugged again. 'Might be. He bunks in one of the back rooms when he's around. Didn't see him when I went to bed last night. Haven't seen him this morning.'

D'Angelo was losing patience but tried not to show it. 'Do you mind checking if he's home? Send him out for a chat if he is.'

Mortimer flicked an invisible fly from his forearm. 'He doesn't like being woken up this early if he's had a late night.'

Larsen consulted her watch. 'Eleven-fifteen! Must have been a real late one.'

Mortimer was becoming edgy. 'Look, I'd prefer you come back when he's up and about. Or when you have a warrant to enter the property.'

Larsen had had enough. 'Is that marijuana smoke I can smell coming from inside, Detective Sergeant?'

D'Angelo twigged straight away and feigned sniffing the wind. 'I think you're right.' He looked at the man in the doorway. 'Now, if you'll stand aside, Mr Mortimer, we believe a crime may be in progress, and it's our duty to investigate. No need for a warrant in this case.'

Mortimer exhaled loudly in frustration. 'I'll go and get him,' he groaned as he disappeared inside.

D'Angelo chuckled. 'He knows the marijuana line is bullshit, but he's not willing to risk us barging in regardless. I'll bet my bum there's things in there he'd prefer we didn't see. Just as likely to be cooking meth.'

Larsen nodded. 'Leave that one for the drug squad, don't you reckon?'

'Yeah.'

After a minute or two, a tall and skinny man with the head and face of a rat exited the house and stood on the porch step, hands on hips. He was fully dressed in black – jeans, a tee-shirt featuring pictures of skulls and firearms, and soiled sports shoes. His eyes were narrow above a pointy nose, his thin face unshaven, but a long scar on his cheek was still visible. *What Raelene Walker saw in him must be hidden from view*, Larsen thought. He was chewing gum with his mouth wide open, allowing loud noises to escape. Two of his front teeth had black decays. 'You looking for me?' he demanded aggressively.

'If your name is Craig Bosnich, we are,' D'Angelo shot back.

'That's me,' Bosnich replied with an air of arrogance. 'Whatever you're here to talk about, I didn't do it.'

'You know Raelene Walker?' Larsen asked.

'Yeah, I know the bitch. What about her?'

'Do you know a Jeremy Ralston?'

Bosnich shook his head, blowing a bubble with his gum that popped before he answered. 'Never heard of him. Who is he?'

'He was a security guard at Car City,' D'Angelo explained.

Bosnich showed no reaction. 'Still never heard of him. What's he got to do with me?'

'He was killed a few nights ago,' Larsen said, dodging the question.

'That's bad luck,' Bosnich replied, and he blew another bubble. 'But like I just said, what's that got to do with me?'

D'Angelo fought a strong urge to flatten the gum against the smart arse's face the next time he blew a bubble. 'Raelene told us you were mouthing off about how you knew where Ralston went on his security rounds. How you would kill him if he didn't move out.'

'And why would I do that?' Bosnich asked smugly.

Larsen smiled. 'Because Ralston had moved in with Raelene and your daughter. Apparently, you were jealous.'

Bosnich laughed out loud. 'Jealous of that bitch! Get real. You've seen her, right?'

And I've seen you too, mate, Larsen thought but didn't say. 'Where were you Tuesday night, early Wednesday morning?'

Both detectives caught the slight twitch below Bosnich's left eye. They had hit a nerve.

'I was here,' Bosnich replied. 'You can ask Shauno. He'll vouch for me.'

D'Angelo raised his eyebrows. 'What if I told you that your prints were all over the scene at the car yard?' he lied. 'Pretty slack for someone who's always in trouble with the law and has spent a bit of time inside.'

Bosnich called his bluff. 'If that was the case, you'd have been around here well before now. You're grasping at straws, Detective.' He blew and popped another bubble. 'I've never been to Car City, and I've never seen fuckin' Ralston except around at Raelene's place a couple of times. That's it. Full bloody stop. Now if you don't mind, I need to make myself some breakfast.' He blew and popped one last bubble before turning away.

'I thought you said you'd never heard of Jeremy Ralston?' Larsen asked quickly.

Bosnich stopped and looked back. 'Maybe I'd seen him at Raelene's, but I never actually knew him, okay?'

'We'll be in touch,' D'Angelo said as Bosnich closed the steel door and walked back into the house.

* * *

Bowker and Holmes were making no progress at all on the Pykes Creek Reservoir case. They'd trawled through hours of vision from security cameras at the Melbourne-bound freeway service centre between Ballan and the reservoir, but without anything specific to look out for, it was a futile exercise, a Hail Mary that something may catch their eye. Without the victim's name, or the day she was murdered, the detectives weren't looking for a needle in a haystack, they were chasing said needle in a fully packed hayloft the size of Victoria.

The first solid facts came when Bowker received a phone call from Erin O'Meara, his direct contact inside the police forensic centre in the northern Melbourne suburb of McLeod. Physically, O'Meara was a wreck of indeterminate age. Heavy smoking and hard drinking had taken their toll, and for the last decade no one had given her more than a year to live. But she continued to endure, easily identified by her emaciated frame, her skinny face with wire-rimmed glasses propped on her long pointy nose, and the cigarette smell that pervaded every space she inhabited. She had broken the mould of a quiet, subservient and unambitious female scientist to rise to the upper echelons of the organisation. Over the years, she had helped Bowker solve many a crime with her lateral thinking and strong grasp of modern technology. Her personal life was a complete mystery, although Bowker believed she had never married or borne children. There were rumours she had once been the partner of a union official who'd been murdered on the wharves. She was a no-nonsense, call-a-spade-a-shovel person who took no prisoners when doing her job.

While she alienated many with her gruff style and intolerance of incompetence, she got on well with Bowker and often accelerated his cases through the system. Bowker occasionally showed his appreciation with a gift of fine whisky. When queried by colleagues about the gifts, she insisted they were birthday presents. Many wondered privately just how many birthdays O'Meara enjoyed each year.

'Gregory, my love, how are you on this fine morning?' O'Meara said when Bowker answered his phone.

'Erin O'Meara. It's been a while, and I don't know what the weather is like at McLeod, but it's pissing down here in the city.'

'It's wet here too, Greg, but any day I actually wake up alive is a fine morning in my view.' O'Meara laughed then burst into a fit of coughing before Bowker heard her spit into a tissue. He hoped it was a tissue, anyway.

'Don't try to be a comedian, Erin. You know it sets off your coughing. I don't want to be on the end of the line when you finally kark it.'

O'Meara chuckled carefully. 'Couldn't think of a better person to be in conversation with when I finally take my last breath. Speaking of which, how's your missus? Still going strong, unfortunately?'

Bowker knew this was O'Meara's normal schtick, pretending she was in the wings if anything were to happen to Rachael, so he was careful not to react negatively, given that she could have no knowledge of his wife's deteriorating health. 'Actually, she hasn't been herself for a few weeks,' he said quietly. 'Lost all her normal zing, spends half her time asleep, sore throat, high temperatures, you name it.'

'Hell, sorry about my shit-stirring, Greg,' O'Meara responded in a serious voice. 'Get her to a doctor, ASAP. I don't like the sound of her symptoms. Could be a dozen things, none of them too flash.'

'She's booked in this afternoon.'

'Make sure you go with her. She sounds like the kind who'll tell a doctor half what they should know and make light of the things that are wrong with her.'

Bowker nodded to himself. 'I'll be there. You've summed her up to a tee.'

There was silence for a long moment before O'Meara spoke. 'I've got the results of the forensics and the autopsy on the woman found at Pykes reservoir.' She paused for a moment. 'Look, if you're concentrating on your wife's health, do you want me to go through this stuff with Darren Holmes? I'm assuming you're working this case together.'

'Yeah, we are, but give me a rundown on what you've found. I can walk and chew gum at the same time.'

Bowker heard O'Meara's rasping cough, followed by her blowing her nose. 'Okay,' she said. 'Obviously a woman. DNA not on file, unfortunately. Height one-eighty-two centimetres, weight at time of death we estimate at approximately seventy kilograms. That's more a guestimate, given that animals had interfered with the body and there would have been the usual loss of fluid over time.'

'Age?' Bowker asked as he jotted down details, disappointed that DNA did not identify the victim.

'Late twenties, early thirties is our best guess.'

'Time of death?'

'Hard to pin it down exactly, but we reckon around four days before her body was found. Five tops. The weather's been cold, so the rate of deterioration would be a lot slower than if it was the middle of summer. In her remains, we found maggots in their early stages of development. It only takes twenty-four to forty-eight hours after a fly lays eggs for them to hatch. The oldest of them point to her body being initially infected in the time period I just mentioned.'

Bowker was impressed but had one question. 'Isn't it a bit cold for flies?'

'There's always a few around, Gregory,' O'Meara replied. 'Now you're probably interested in cause of death?'

'You're one step ahead of me, Erin.'

'As always,' O'Meara replied with a controlled chuckle. 'Death resulted from a massive head injury caused by the impact of a cantaloupe-sized rock. The forensic team searched the area for the murder weapon and found the right-sized rock with traces of blood and hair, which we've since been able to match to the victim. A section of the rock was darker and damper than the rest, indicating it had recently been lifted from the ground. Its rough surface precludes finding usable prints, unfortunately. After a bit more searching, the team identified where the rock had originally been embedded in the ground, and they were able to make a plaster cast of the hole. It matches the rock's damper surface.' She emitted another stifled chuckle. 'Of course, it would have helped if the uniformed sergeant there hadn't stubbed a ciggy in the same hole while he was waiting for the team to finish.'

Bowker threw his head back. 'Fuckin' dumb-shit Delaney, if you'll excuse my French.'

'Not the Brian Delaney who used to be in Ballarat?'

'That's him.'

'Well, this is not the first time that wanker has compromised a crime scene over the years, I can tell you.' O'Meara exhaled loudly enough for Bowker to hear her lungs rattling. 'Anyway, back to Pykes. Not far from where the rock originated, there was a patch of blood in the grass. Once again, matches the victim. I think we can assume that's where the murder occurred. A search of the beeline between this point and where the body was discovered found small traces of blood that would indicate the poor woman was dragged to her final resting place. Drag marks on her clothes would reinforce that theory.'

'Any other injuries?'

'Not that we found, but there was a lot of damage done to the body by animals, birds and insects. Here's the bit that might help you solve this mystery, Greg. Traces of semen were identified in her vagina. Normally, a woman's immune system gets rid of sperm after a few days, but of course if she dies, all these systems die with her. Even nourishment for the sperm collapses on her death. But residues remain, which we can collect and analyse.'

'Were you able to extract DNA from the semen?' Bowker asked enthusiastically, hoping there might be a quick resolution of the case after all.

'The answer to that question is *yes,* we were able to extract DNA,' O'Meara replied. 'The answer to your next question is *no,* the DNA does not match anything on the national database.'

Bowker was disappointed, but the answer was half expected, since only a small fraction of the population had their DNA on file. 'In your opinion, did the victim have sex around the time she died, or could it have been in the days earlier?'

'There were traces of semen in her knickers, so it's more than likely it occurred while she was wearing those clothes, which would point to that day, you would think. But we can't be totally sure. Maybe she didn't change her undies every day. So, did the sex form part of the whole murder scenario, or was it totally unassociated? That's for you to work out, Gregory.'

Bowker continued to jot notes. 'Forensics find anything else?'

'Stomach contents indicated she'd eaten within a couple of hours of her death, although animal damage makes analysis difficult. And acid keeps working post-mortem, of course, but the remnants of food had not progressed further down the digestive tract.'

'Were you able to ascertain what she's eaten?'

'As I said, animals had taken most of what we'd normally analyse in these cases, but from the miniscule traces we *did* find, we guess she'd eaten a sandwich or a roll. Ham and salad, by what we were able to salvage. She also consumed an orange-flavoured drink.'

'When we don't know who she is, or where she lived, it's hard to know whether she stopped somewhere for a bite to eat or had a snack before she left home.'

O'Meara chuckled. 'We're good, but not *that* bloody good.'

'Yeah, I know. I was just thinking aloud. Anything else?'

'All the vegetable matter or soil samples collected from the victim's clothes match the area around where her body was found. And apart from the massive head injury, there was no wound that can't be explained by animal interference, post-mortem. Certainly no bruising.'

'Suggesting she probably wasn't assaulted or knocked down elsewhere before being brought to the reservoir and killed with the rock?' Bowker asked.

'That would be my slant on it,' O'Meara replied. 'But it doesn't mean she wasn't brought there against her will, just that she wasn't handled roughly prior to being killed.'

'Any evidence of rape?'

'Nothing. The animal damage to her clothes, and body in general, makes definitive judgements difficult. But there was none of the bruising we normally find.'

Bowker thought for a moment. 'Is there any possibility the woman slipped over and smashed the side of her head on the rock?'

'Nope. The blood and hair found on the rock were on the section that was buried in the ground. So unless the rock was pulled out of the ground before she fell on it, that wouldn't fit the evidence.'

Bowker chuckled. 'I think we can discount that.'

'You're the detective, not me,' O'Meara replied with a laugh before descending into another coughing fit.

Bowker's face wrinkled. 'Are you seeing a doctor about that cough, Erin?'

'I've seen a dozen doctors, and they all give me the same diagnosis.'

'And that is?'

'I'm fucked. They say to give up the ciggies, but what's the point? I'd prefer to die happy than live an extra six months gasping for a smoke.' She was quiet for a moment. 'Oh, one other thing. The forensic team found two stubbies, a UDL can and some KFC paraphernalia in the bin. They lifted prints from the stubbies. Same person handled both, but no match to anyone on our database. They also salvaged some DNA from the can. Female, but again matching nothing on file. Prints and DNA on the KFC box and drink cup are too smeared in grease to retrieve anything usable.'

'Probably not related to the case anyway,' Bowker replied.

'Maybe not. I'll email you the full report when it's all typed up. I'll CC Darren as well.'

'Thanks, Erin. I'll talk to you soon.'

'Yeah. Look after that wife of yours, okay?'

'Will do.'

Bowker disconnected and walked across to where Holmes was filling out paperwork from an earlier case. He pulled up a chair from an adjacent desk and sat down. 'Just had a call from Erin O'Meara.'

Holmes leaned back in his chair. 'She still alive?' he asked with a grin.

Bowker smiled back. 'She's been dead for ten years, but every time the Grim Reaper comes knocking, she knees him in the balls.'

Holmes laughed. 'Did she tell us anything useful in between coughing up tennis balls of phlegm?'

'The victim was a woman in her late twenties, early thirties. No DNA on file, so we're no closer to IDing her. Tall with athletic build. Killed close to where she was found. Cause of death a rock to the skull. Appears there was no physical assault prior, but she'd had sex that day, most probably. Whether that was associated with the attack, it's impossible to tell at this stage.'

'And you don't need to tell me. No DNA on file for her sexual partner either.'

'Correctamundo, my friend.'

'We're getting nowhere fast. Still don't know the identity of the victim, or where she comes from, or how she got to the reservoir, or whether she was raped or had consensual sex either there or somewhere else, or whether the sex was with the man who killed her or someone not associated with the murder. Nothing.'

'Her body was found with her belt and fly undone,' Bowker said, leaning back in his chair. 'If she was raped then killed, it would seem a strange way to leave the body. With that sort of crime, the perpetrator normally leaves the body in the same state as when he'd raped and killed her. Never heard of a killer pulling up the victim's knickers and jeans after murdering her. If he did decide to do that, why not do it properly, zip up her jeans and buckle her belt?'

Holmes placed his hands behind his head. 'You're thinking it's more likely the victim was redressing herself when the killer decided to cave in her head?'

'Yeah. There's more to this case than meets the eye.'

CHAPTER 7

The Bowker family doctor was a senior partner in a popular general practice clinic in South Caulfield. Housed in a red-brick American bungalow, the clinic comprised seven GPs, all with their own minor specialities. The Bowkers had been with Doctor Liz Conlan since they'd moved to the area from the Mallee more than thirty years prior. She was just a graduate doctor then, but the Bowkers liked her, and they had stayed with her through the birth of their kids, who now used her as their GP as well. As usual, Conlan was running late, in big part due to her meticulous care of her patients. Bowker didn't mind, knowing they would get the same care as the people who were holding them up. He stared at the pictures on the wall, which captured the area when Caulfield was merely a settlement on the outskirts of the city of Melbourne. The local swamp was a popular place for drovers to rest their stock overnight on their way to the Newmarket saleyards on the other side of the city. As he perused the pictures more closely, he appreciated the intricacy of the drawings that predated photography. On other walls were posters informing visitors of various diseases, their symptoms, and their treatment. But remaining front of Bowker's mind was his wife, who sat beside him, head in hands, her breathing heavier than he'd ever heard it before.

A slim, neatly dressed woman in her mid-fifties appeared from a corridor, gently escorting an elderly man to the receptionist's counter. She smiled at Bowker. 'Greg and Rachael.' She led the couple into a room towards the rear of the building, where she ushered them to a pair of fabric-covered chairs beside her large desk. On one wall was a set of shelves containing an assortment of books and other items. On another hung a print of van Gogh's *Sunflowers* above her examination table. Doctor Conlan eased down in her plush office chair and with a clatter of computer keys brought up the Bowkers' medical history on her screen. She turned back to look at the couple. 'This is a bit strange, having you both here at the same time. A bit worrying, really.'

Bowker was keen to break the ice. 'We'd like to discuss options for IVF,' he blurted out, straight faced.

Conlan was stunned before Bowker put her at ease, for a moment or two anyway. He raised both palms in apology. 'Sorry, Liz, I shouldn't joke. We're here about Rachael's health. You know how fit she normally is… well, check her out now.'

Conlan faced Rachael. 'What's the go, Rachael? You do seem very pale.'

Rachael took an eternity to lift her head. 'I'm just stuffed 24/7. No energy. I've had to cancel my dance classes. I haven't played sport for nearly a month, and I'm struggling to make it through a day at work.'

Conlan swivelled back to her keyboard and began typing. 'What else?'

'Feel as if I'm burning up. I'm so hot. Coughing. Sores in my mouth. You name it. I'm a physical wreck. A month ago, I assumed it was just a virus, but I can't seem to shake it. It just keeps getting worse.'

Conlan didn't respond, her eyes locked on the screen, before she stood, taking a tympanic thermometer from her top drawer and placing its point in Rachael's left ear. When the instrument beeped, she checked the digital readout, her brow wrinkling. 'Temp's a bit high, that's for sure.'

'How high?' Bowker asked quickly.

'Thirty-eight point one. She's definitely running a fever.' Conlan proceeded to conduct a series of tests utilising the simple instruments most doctors kept in their consulting rooms. 'You're pretty anaemic, as well.' She scribbled down a few notes on an A4 sheet before using a stethoscope to monitor Rachael's heart, her chest, and her breathing. More notes went down on her page.

The suspense was proving too much for Bowker. 'So what do you reckon, Liz?'

Conlan shrugged. 'She's running a high temperature, she's anaemic, her breathing is a bit off. But that could be the result of a thousand things.' She looked at Rachael. 'Can you climb up on the examination table, please? I'd like to feel your abdomen.'

'What are you looking for?' Bowker asked quickly.

'At this stage, I'm just gathering information.'

It took some effort for Rachael to climb onto the table, a task that a month ago would have taken no more than a step up and a quick flip of her body. Bowker and Conlan exchanged glances but said nothing. The doctor palpated Rachael's abdomen for an extended time, concentrating on the area at the base of her ribcage.

'Okay, Rachael, you can sit up now.'

Rachel complied slowly before walking gingerly back to her chair.

'It's obvious you're not well, but we'll get some tests done to be more specific. I'll order a full blood analysis for a start, plus we'll test your urea and your liver function. When the bloods come back, we may need to do a CT scan of your chest, abdomen, and pelvis regions depending on what they show. We need to get to the bottom of this, quick smart. In the meantime, you're off work until we get things sorted. I'll prescribe you something for iron deficiency.' She sat at her desk and hurriedly typed information into her computer. Bowker tried hard, but he was too far away to read the data being entered. The printer suddenly sprang to life and several pages were disgorged. She folded two and handed them the Bowker. 'One is for the pharmacist; the other is for pathology when you go for the blood and urine tests.'

Bowker thanked Conlan for her time and thoroughness, at the same time suspecting she had a strong notion of what ailed his wife but was unwilling to disclose those thoughts. This worried him. If her diagnosis had pointed to a minor malady, he was sure she would have been quick to share it.

As the Bowkers stood up to leave, Conlan had one more question. 'In the last few weeks, have you cut or scratched yourself?'

Rachael turned up the palm of her left hand to reveal a cut at the base of her thumb. 'Just where I sliced myself with the vegetable knife about a fortnight ago. It seems to be taking an eternity to heal.'

Conlan took Rachael's hand and looked closely at the cut. To Bowker, her sympathetic smile seemed a little forced. 'I think it will be gone in a few days,' she said.

Bowker wasn't so sure.

* * *

Suspecting Bosnich was involved in the killing of Jeremy Ralston was one thing; proving it was going to be difficult. With nothing to go on except Raelene Walker's word that Bosnich had made threats to kill her new partner, D'Angelo and Larsen sought to place him at Car City on the night Ralston was attacked. They'd already viewed hours of CCTV footage from various car dealers hoping for a breakthrough, but so far had no success. Thankfully, the task was simpler than in many cases they'd worked, since most of the video available was captured late at night, contained little action, and could be skimmed through quickly. Where dealership footage showed the Maroondah Highway in the background, the occasional car passed by, but none had stopped in a camera's frame of view. Now that the detectives had seen the Bosnich household's blue Mondeo with the yellow bonnet and checked it was registered to their number one suspect, they at least had something specific to look for. Unfortunately, neither recalled seeing the Mondeo drive past, let alone stop, in any footage captured between the time the centre closed and the time Samuel Anderson said he'd found the injured security guard.

The vision from a dealership at the entrance to the complex had just arrived at police headquarters, and D'Angelo decided to view this first. If they found nothing, then they'd need to relook at footage they'd already watched, hoping they may have missed the Mondeo the first time through.

Today, Larsen sported tight jeans, a pale blue silky top and high-heeled ankle boots. Normally D'Angelo hated checking CCTV footage. It was boring, and in most cases fruitless. But sitting close by Larsen the way she was dressed made the exercise more than tolerable, although her perfume – or was it her shampoo? – made it difficult for him to concentrate on the video. The screen was divided into quadrants, each square displaying the feed from one of the four cameras. One captured the yard, looking back from the showroom towards the highway; a second showed the reverse angle from a lofty elevation, most probably from one of the poles that supported bunting across the front of the lot;

a third captured the view to the side, including the entrance to Car City itself, and the fourth displayed the inside of the showroom with the offices in the background. D'Angelo scrolled through the footage at six times the normal speed. The period between lock-up and 12 a.m. gave them nothing, but when the time stamp on the vision displayed 00.16, Ralston's security vehicle arrived. A remote control slowly opened the compound's heavy gates, and the security vehicle entered. The gates closed behind it.

A couple of minutes passed with no further action before one of the cameras picked up a small white sedan pulling into the kerb in front of the yard.

'Stop it there,' Larsen called out, pointing towards the screen.

D'Angelo paused the playback, and both detectives leaned in for a closer look at the car. Larsen's focus was on the image in front, D'Angelo's on the feeling of Larsen's shoulder against his own.

'What *is* that? A Toyota Corolla?' Larsen asked.

D'Angelo forced himself to concentrate on the screen. 'Looks like one, but it could be a Hyundai. The picture's not the sharpest I've seen. When we're finished, we'll send it over to the tech boys. Maybe they can confirm the make.'

'Can't see the plates from this angle,' Larsen said. 'Run it back a few frames and see if we get a better look.'

D'Angelo complied. He shook his head. 'Nah. Still too side-on.'

He advanced the footage at a slow speed. After a few seconds, two figures emerged from the sedan and entered the front of the car yard before exiting again via the side fence and disappearing out of frame in the direction the security vehicle had travelled. Both intruders wore oversized hoodies obscuring their faces. One was carrying an Adidas sports bag in their right hand. Despite a dozen slow-motion views and rewinds, their identity was as much a mystery as the car they had arrived in.

Fifteen minutes further into the footage, the hooded figures returned, still carrying the sports bag, but this time running. They retraced their path through the car yard and back to their car, which drove off at high speed. Again, the rego plates were not visible. Until the gates were opened by the caretaker and dealers began arriving, there was no sign of the security vehicle leaving the compound.

D'Angelo turned off the video player and leaned back in his chair, hands behind his head. 'I think we saw our killers,' he said quietly, 'but it was no help IDing them.' He turned to face Larsen, who was sitting arms crossed. 'Could be Bosnich and Mortimer in the hoodies. Or maybe another mate we haven't met yet.'

Larsen shrugged. 'Car doesn't fit, though, does it? It was a big step up from the clapped-out Ford Mondeo we saw outside their place in Dandenong.'

D'Angelo rubbed the bristles on his chin. 'Perhaps it was stolen earlier in the night. Maybe it belongs to one of Bosnich's other friends. Someone with a bit more spending power?' He chuckled. 'I hate to suggest this, but now we know there were two individuals wandering around the complex, I think we need to review the footage from the other yards. At least we can narrow our search to the time we know the action took place. We also have a rough idea of the car we're looking for. Perhaps we might luck in and get a look at its plates.'

Larsen unfolded her arms and put her hands on her knees. 'I'd be inclined to start a bit earlier. If Bosnich *was* involved, there's a possibility he was casing the car yards waiting for Ralston to arrive. Seems a bit too coincidental that the two vehicles showed up within minutes of each other when it was so quiet for the rest of the night.'

D'Angelo nodded. 'Yeah. Good move.'

Larsen thought for a moment. 'I'd like to know whether that beat-up old Mondeo went anywhere on the night Ralston was attacked. Bosnich lives a stone's throw from the Eastlink tollway, and I reckon if he was travelling anywhere that night, Eastlink would be the road he'd use. And keep in mind that its northern end goes through Ringwood, just up the road from Car City.'

D'Angelo screwed up his face. 'But we've seen no sign of the Mondeo on any of the videos from Car City.'

'Maybe he met someone in the area with a less conspicuous car.'

D'Angelo shrugged. 'Can't hurt to check, I s'pose. I'll contact ConnectEast and find out if the Mondeo went through any of the toll points that night.' He shook his head. 'Can't see a bloke on his sort of income paying tolls, though, even if he did head up towards Ringwood. More likely to take public roads, I'd say.'

'Be a bastard to get there if you didn't take Eastlink,' Larsen replied. 'There's nothing remotely direct, and you'd be hitting one traffic light after another. It would cost you more in petrol than the toll.'

D'Angelo shrugged again. 'Okay, let's find out for sure, eh?'

* * *

Bowker and Holmes sat on the other side of the squad room, becoming increasingly frustrated by their lack of progress in the Pykes Creek Reservoir case. Not knowing the identity of the victim was their greatest obstacle. No one had come forward in the last fortnight reporting a woman of the right age missing, and publishing a photo of the victim's face was impossible due to the animal damage she had sustained. A digital impression had been published in the dailies, but with no response. The detectives had visited the several houses that sat on small acreage in the vicinity of the reservoir seeking any sort of a lead. Nothing out of the ordinary had been noticed. Residents had remembered the inclement weather but little else about the days in question. Certainly, there had been no raucous gatherings, loud cars, or unusual activity that garnered their attention. Bowker left a business card with each household just in case something extra came to mind, but neither he nor Holmes felt confident that would occur. For one of the few times in their long careers, the seasoned officers had run out of ideas.

CHAPTER 8

Only a little over twelve hours had passed since the Bowkers were last sitting in Liz Conlan's room at her South Caulfield clinic.

'Thanks for coming in on such short notice, but I thought it best to go through the test results in person, rather than over the phone,' Conlan explained as the three took their seats.

'That sounds ominous,' Bowker said quietly. Rachael stared at the floor. Her condition was worsening by the day.

'I'll be honest with you both,' Conlan said, folding her hands on her lap. 'Some of the results are worrying and will need further investigation.'

Bowker swallowed heavily. Rachael raised her eyes to the doctor.

'So what *do* they show?' Bowker asked hesitantly.

'Rachael is anaemic, as we expected, but her platelets are way down, as are her red blood cells. Her lymphocytes are very elevated, which is the most worrying.'

Bowker frowned. 'Lymphocytes?'

'A type of white blood cell.'

'What causes them to be high?' Rachael mumbled.

'Any number of things,' Conlan replied. 'Severe bacterial or viral infections, stress, medications. I don't want you to jump to any conclusions, but as a worst-case scenario, it can also indicate blood cancer.'

'Leukemia?' Bowker shot back.

'Yes, but again, let's not jump the gun,' Conlan replied. She looked at Rachael. 'I'm going to order a CT CAP, which is a scan of your chest, abdomen and pelvis. It's totally non-invasive, but it will give us information about your internal organs and lymph nodes, whether you have a tumour or clusters of white blood cells, lots of things. I am also referring you to a haematologist – a blood specialist, if you like. In my referral, I'll mention that I've already ordered the CT. It should be done by the time you get to see her.'

Suddenly, the Pykes Reservoir killing couldn't have been further from Bowker's mind.

* * *

Back at Police headquarters, D'Angelo, dressed in another of his ill-fitting charcoal-grey suits, sat at his desk disinterestedly working through his long list of emails, most of which comprised administrivia or messages that didn't relate to him or his work. However, one particular item had him suddenly sitting up straight and paying more attention to his screen. He read it twice before calling to Larsen, who was at a filing cabinet ten metres away. Today, she wore tight, shiny black leggings, black stilettos and a light grey sleeveless top. Her blond hair was tied back in a ponytail. She wandered over and sat down beside D'Angelo, close enough to read his computer screen.

'ConnectEast has got back to us about Bosnich's use of their tollway. Just like you suspected, he took that route to head north on the night in question. The old Mondeo passed through a heap of tolling points. The first one around eight fifteen.'

Larsen smiled. 'All the way up to Ringwood, I bet, but a fair bit earlier than I expected.' After a moment, her smile disappeared and she looked at her partner. 'But he didn't stop at Ringwood, did he?'

D'Angelo shook his head. 'Nope. He drove through the tunnel and kept going onto the Eastern Freeway, I presume. No tolls on that road, so we've lost him from there on unless we chase up VicRoads' vision. Where he was headed is the big question.'

'Not to Ringwood, that's for sure,' Larsen replied. 'Although it's early enough for him to get back there if that was the plan.'

'If he did, then he didn't take the tollway. Not before the time the guard was attacked, anyway.' D'Angelo scrolled further down. 'But he did take it around eight the next morning,' he said, pointing to a spot on his screen. 'Tolled at the start of the tunnel and followed EastLink all the way back to Dandenong. Non-stop.'

Larsen shrugged. 'There's no guarantee Bosnich was the one driving the Mondeo, of course. Mortimer could have borrowed it. Or one of his other mates, if he's got any.'

D'Angelo nodded. 'Yeah. And when it boils down to it, the little white car's our vehicle of interest, not the Mondeo.'

Larsen walked back to her desk and retrieved her notebook. D'Angelo looked away just in time to avoid being caught ogling her backside. She flipped through the notebook until she found the page she was after. 'Raelene Walker said Bosnich's brother lives in Essendon. Somewhere near the Red Lion Hotel, where they drink together, apparently. If it *was* Bosnich in the Mondeo, maybe he was on his way over there.'

D'Angelo looked puzzled. 'Then why didn't he tell us he had an alibi for the night Ralston was rolled? Why come up with that half-arsed story about being home with his mate?'

'Maybe he didn't want to be placed at his brother's place on that night either.'

D'Angelo nodded slowly. 'Feel like a run out to Essendon for a squash at the Red Lion?'

Larsen stood up and straightened her top. 'Why not? It may not lead to our killer, but it could eliminate a prime suspect.'

As the pair walked towards the doorway, Holmes entered the room carrying a steaming hot coffee.

'I'll catch you downstairs, Marco,' Larsen said. She wandered over to Holmes's desk as he placed the coffee down and blew on his fingers. D'Angelo waved casually over his shoulder, hoping to disguise the fact that he'd give anything to swap places with Holmes.

'Where are you off to?' Holmes said, ensuring the room was now empty before placing his hand on Larsen's backside, stroking the shiny fabric.

'Leave that for later, Detective Holmes,' Larsen said, smiling and removing the hand from her rear. 'We're heading out to Essendon to check a lead on a suspect for the Car City murder.'

Holmes grinned. 'Keep an eye on D'Angelo, he's got the hots for you. But I bet you knew that already.'

'I'm as safe as houses. Marco's all work, work, work. I doubt he even realises he's been partnered with a woman.' It was time to change the subject. 'Where's Greg?'

The smile left Holmes's face. 'He's taken Rachael to the doctor. He reckons her health's going downhill big time. I know he's worried sick.'

'Remember the night the four of us had dinner a month or so ago? I thought she looked like shit *that* night.'

Holmes nodded. 'Yeah, we talked about it when we got home.' He shrugged. 'Anyway, that's where he is this morning. He said he'll be in after he takes Rachael home.'

'Why doesn't he take leave until it's all sorted?'

Holmes upturned his palms. 'I've suggested that, but he reckons work stops him from going crazy with worry.' He chuckled. 'Not that there's much to think about with the case we're working on. We've hit a brick wall.' He slapped Larsen playfully on the rump. 'Better get going. You don't want to keep the Italian stallion waiting.'

Larsen punched him lightly on the shoulder and walked towards the door, knowing Holmes's eyes had never left her.

With Larsen gone and his heart rate returning to normal, Holmes logged into his computer. He opened the forensic report sent by O'Meara, hoping something would spark an idea. Anything to give him a lead. He was halfway through the second page when his mobile vibrated. He checked the screen. It was Bowker.

'G'day, mate. How's Rachael?'

'Not too flash, Sherlock. And still going downhill, unfortunately.'

'The doc any help?'

'Tests came back showing we need more tests.'

'Shit. Sounds serious. They got any idea what the problem might be?'

Bowker took a long moment to answer. 'Could be any one of a dozen major infections.' He hesitated again. 'But we've been warned it might be leukemia.'

Holmes's mouth dropped. 'Leukemia. Fuck!'

'Yeah, fuck.'

'So when will you know for sure?'

'When the new tests come back. Rach and I are driving around getting them done now. They're taking more blood this morning, then an emergency CT scan late this afternoon. I won't be into work today, unfortunately.'

'Is there anything Kirsten or I can do?'

'Nothing at this stage, mate. Just keep all this under your hat, if you don't mind. You can tell Kirsten, of course, but I'd prefer it not to be the talk of headquarters. The only other people we'll let know are our kids.' Holmes heard Bowker inhale loudly. 'Not a conversation I'm looking forward to, that's for sure.'

'Well, just forget about work, Greg. Things are under control here.' He feigned a chuckle. 'That's if you call the absence of a lead having things under control.'

'That's the other reason I'm touching base. I had a call from one of the owners of those houses we canvased at Pykes Creek Reservoir. Remember I left a card in case they recalled anything else?'

'And one of them did, obviously?'

'Sort of. The lady of the house closest to the reserve wasn't home when we called. But when she heard we'd been asking questions, she informed her husband that she'd followed a one-tonner with a canvas-covered tray into the reserve on one of the days we suspect our victim likely met her death. A *Bradley Murdoch truck*, she called it.'

Holmes nodded to himself. 'Like from the Peter Falconio case up in the Territory?'

'Yeah. Got it in one.'

Peter Falconio was a British tourist who disappeared in July 2001 after his vehicle was stopped in a remote part of the Stuart Highway in the Northern Territory. Falconio was travelling with his girlfriend, who managed to escape the scene and flag down a road train. Falconio's body was never found, but in 2005, Bradley Murdoch was convicted of his murder and sentenced to life imprisonment.

'Bit of a longshot, Greg. Could have been any number of vehicles in that reserve over the time period we're talking about.'

'This is the first one we have any description for. Besides, we've got nothing else, have we?'

Holmes leaned back in his chair. 'I suppose not,' he conceded.

'If you're doing nothing else, it might be worth a trip back to the servo near Pykes to run through their security footage. Keep an eye out in case that canvas-covered ute stopped there. You might get lucky and see its rego.'

'Bloody needle in a haystack.'

'You can narrow it down. The woman spotted that vehicle entering Pykes Reservoir reserve at around two in the arvo on the Thursday before her body was found. That gives you a ballpark time to check if the ute used the servo.'

Holmes wasn't so sure it was worth the trip. Probably one vehicle in fifty, or maybe in a hundred or more, drove into that service centre. But since he wasn't doing much else, it wouldn't hurt to take a drive in the sun. 'I'll head off after lunch.'

'And I've been thinking about that KFC rubbish that Forensics found in the bin. I'll bet my left knacker that it was purchased at the servo and taken to Pykes to eat. The techs said the chicken box wasn't a big family box, more like a medium-size one that a single person or perhaps a couple might buy. If you've got time, fast forward through any vision they have and if you see someone carrying a likely box to their vehicle, jot down the rego.'

'That could take days, mate,' Holmes replied, careful not to put more pressure on his friend, who he knew was preoccupied with his wife's deteriorating health.

'What could take days?' Bowker asked patiently.

'Going through a week's vision looking for who bought takeaway fried chicken. There could be a thousand people who did.'

'Just go through the half hour after the time on the receipt,' Bowker replied.

'What receipt?'

Bowker was quiet for a moment. 'Sorry, mate, in all the fuss about Rach I've obviously forgotten to tell you. Erin O'Meara rang me to apologise that they'd accidently left something off their report. Or one of their newbies had, anyway. The KFC rubbish was stuffed back in the chicken box before it was deposited in the bin. Under all the bones and grease-covered paper, there was a receipt for the purchase. It was a cash sale, so no leads via credit or debit cards, but it does give the day and time the purchase was made. If you check your inbox, O'Meara has probably sent it through by now.' Holmes heard background mumbles that he assumed was Bowker speaking to his wife. 'Listen, I'll have to leave you to it, mate. We've just arrived at pathology.'

Bowker disconnected before Holmes could wish him good luck, but Holmes knew his partner would assume his best wishes anyway. He scrolled through his emails until he found the unread message from the forensic centre. He smiled as he perused the time and date on an attached copy of the KFC receipt. It matched the period he'd be scanning the service centre's video for the Bradley Murdoch ute. *Sometimes you just get lucky,* he thought as he contemplated the alternative – hours and hours glued to a video monitor.

CHAPTER 9

The Red Lion in Essendon was one of the iconic hotels of Melbourne, a licenced establishment that stood on the site since before the Victorian gold rushes of the 1850s. Built on what was once called Firebrace Street in the then-township of Hawkstead, now Pascoe Vale Road in North Essendon, the pub, along with its competitor the Cross Keys Hotel, was frequented by travellers to and from the goldfields. The road outside served as the main highway between Melbourne and Sydney in those early times. The original weatherboard and corrugated iron hotel was rebuilt in the 1930s, with several renovations since. The present iteration comprised a mixture of one and two-storey buildings with a carpark at the rear. A large sign adorned the front and featured two rampant lions facing one another.

D'Angelo and Larsen left their vehicle in a carpark and made their way to the rear entrance of the hotel. D'Angelo pointed in the direction of a large green playing field further down the back street. 'You're probably too young to remember, Kirsten, but Jason Moran and one of his underworld mates were gunned down just down there. Moran was watching his son play football and *bang*, *bang*, all over red rover. In 2007, I think it was. I was just a fresh-faced connie, but it was the talk of the force at the time. And the media couldn't get enough of it.'

Larsen nodded. 'I've heard the name, probably from watching *Underbelly* on television. But 2007? I would have still been at school.'

D'Angelo suddenly felt old. But her live-in partner Darren Holmes was another ten years older again. *How does* he *feel about the age gap?* D'Angelo asked himself.

Inside the cavernous venue were a dining area, a function room, a sports bar and an extensive pokies den. The dining room was heavily patronised with a noisy lunchtime crowd and most tables were occupied. The detectives walked through to the bar, with D'Angelo covertly showing his ID to the young woman replenishing a tub of ice. Aged in her twenties, she wore a black tee-shirt and slacks and had a pretty face, with long dark hair held back with diamante hair clips. Her smile disappeared when she saw the visitors were police.

'We'd like a word with one of your managers, if they're about,' D'Angelo said quietly.

The barmaid remained po-faced. 'You here about the robbery of the old girl on Wednesday night?'

Larsen gave nothing away. 'Just checking our facts. Were you working that night?'

The young woman shook her head. 'No. One of my two nights off.' She shrugged. 'But it doesn't take long for word to get around among staff.'

'So what's the version you've heard?' D'Angelo asked, following Larsen's lead.

'Jean Gawler – she's one of our regular pokie players – pulled a jackpot. Not a big one, but it would mean a lot to her. She comes here nearly every day but has never won much before.'

D'Angelo nodded, knowing that whatever the woman had won, she was probably still a mile behind. He understood many people loved to gamble, but he couldn't imagine why anyone would select a poker machine as their mode of choice. The machine was programmed to retain a set percentage of takings, and for the player, there was absolutely no skill involved. A punter merely pushed a button and hoped the machine's algorithm may have reached a point where it would deign to return money. At the races, you could pick your nag or dishlicker. Most times it didn't win, even if you were a close follower of racing or had inside knowledge, but at least you had some input into your bet. 'How much did the machine pay?' D'Angelo asked after a moment.

The woman tucked a few strands of hair behind her ear and readjusted her hairclip. 'Bit over three grand, I think. But to her it was like she'd won a million, apparently. Yelling and screaming. Finished up getting a big round of applause, according to the wait staff I was talking to.'

'And they told you she was robbed?' Larsen asked.

'On her way home. That was backed up by the police who came back here asking questions. Had her bag snatched by two men wearing hoodies.'

'She drive or walk?' D'Angelo asked.

The woman screwed up her face as she thought. 'Walk, I think. Somebody said she lives up in Wallace Crescent.' She pointed to the north. 'Just over Woodland Street. Only a few blocks away.'

D'Angelo slipped his hands into his pockets. 'Is there a manager around we can talk to?'

'The duty boss is in his office. I can go get him if you like.'

'That'd be great.' D'Angelo smiled. 'We'll hold the fort while you're away.'

The barmaid exited through a door at the back, leaving the detectives alone except for an elderly beer-gutted patron who placed three glasses on the bar a few metres away. He looked around for staff as if his life support system was about to be turned off. 'Where'd Alice go?' he asked.

'Had to pass on a message to the manager, I think,' Larsen replied.

Beer Guts shook his head. 'They have one bloody job!' he mumbled half to himself, drumming his fingers on the bar.

'You know what's running through my head, Kirsten?' D'Angelo asked quietly.

'If Bosnich did come over here to meet his brother, did he not mention it as an alibi because he rolled that old lady for her pokie winnings?'

'Exactly. But we better make sure he was here before we jump to any conclusions.'

Less than twenty seconds later, the woman they now knew was Alice returned with a shortish but well-built man who D'Angelo judged was in his mid-forties. He wore a collared white shirt with a grey striped tie. He had a full head of hair and a well-trimmed moustache, sparkly blue eyes, and a strong chin. He confidently shot a hand over the bar as he approached the detectives. 'Simon Davies,' he said by way of introduction.

D'Angelo and Larsen introduced themselves as Alice walked to the end of the bar to serve Beer Gut before he wasted away.

Davies folded his arms. 'Alice tells me you're here about the robbery?'

'Not exactly,' D'Angelo replied. 'Is there somewhere we can talk in private?'

Davies frowned as if surprised this was becoming more formal. 'Yeah. My office. Go back to the foyer and I'll meet you there.' He disappeared through the door behind the bar.

The manager's office was neat and tidy, a few folders and loose documents piled atop a filing cabinet to the side. Davies unstacked two chairs from the corner and placed them opposite his desk.

'What can I do you for?' Davies asked with a smile after they'd all taken a seat. 'I think we've passed on all the information we can to the previous detectives who visited.'

D'Angelo took the lead. 'Actually, we haven't come about the robbery, Mr Davies. Detective Larsen and I are with the homicide squad.'

Davies looked puzzled. 'I don't understand. There's nobody been killed around here.' He shrugged. 'Not to my knowledge, anyway.'

'We're here hoping to establish the movements of a person of interest in relation to a murder that took place on the other side of the city,' D'Angelo explained. 'He's known to frequent this hotel. We'd like to look at your CCTV footage for last Wednesday night.'

Davies raised his eyebrows. 'To confirm an alibi?'

'Just following up loose ends,' Larsen replied.

D'Angelo removed a photograph from his jacket pocket and slid it across to the manager. 'You ever see this bloke around here?'

Davies leaned forward and perused the picture before sliding it back. 'Not a weekly regular, but I've seen him in here a few times. He's usually with another bloke. Smaller and built like a piece of fencing wire. They sit in the corner of the sports bar and have a few pots. Maybe have the odd bet on the trots or the dishlickers. Whether they were here last Wednesday, I couldn't tell you. I didn't work that night.'

'That's why we're keen to check your security footage,' Larsen replied.

Davies stood. 'Be my guest. Follow me.'

He led D'Angelo and Larsen through to a small room that had probably once been used for general storage. On the shelves was an array of high-end electronic monitoring equipment, various lights flickering as data was collected from around the site. Davies pulled up a chair to the video monitor and typed in a password, which activated a series of menus. The Red Lion Hotel complex hosted a myriad of cameras capturing every area of the facility, external and internal, from every available angle. A series of screens, each one divided to provide multiple mini-screens, displayed the vision captured from each camera. Davies delivered a quick tutorial for the detectives on how to switch from one screen to another, how to isolate each camera, and how to progress forward and backwards at which speed they required. Most security systems worked in a similar way, and the officers had spent many hours searching CCTV footage from a variety of set-ups, from high-end cutting-edge to the comparatively ancient. They'd seen several similar to this; still, they sat patiently until the lesson had concluded.

'Thanks, mate. We'll give you a hoy when we've finished,' D'Angelo said cordially. 'Could be a while, though,' he added, leaving the manager in no doubt that his presence was no longer required.

It took Larsen an hour of fast-forwarding and camera-swapping before the officers found what they were looking for. Craig Bosnich and a shorter man were captured on video walking through one of the rear glass entrances. They both wore hoodies with the hood down and their faces were clearly recognisable. The vision was time-stamped 21.12.

Larsen paused the footage and leaned back in her chair. 'Bingo! And the time fits pretty well with the Mondeo's East Link journey, especially if we assume he went somewhere briefly to pick up his mate. There's a definite likeness, so I reckon the other bloke is probably his brother.'

D'Angelo nodded. 'Before we track them through the building, let's see where they came from.'

Larsen scrolled through exterior vision from the rear of the pub.

By switching between cameras, they were able to ascertain that Bosnich and his mate had walked up Pascoe Vale Road from the south, crossed the carpark and entered through the rear entrance where they were first spotted. 'They're on foot and there's no sign of the Mondeo, so we have to assume Bosnich left it at his mate's place and they walked to the pub.' She smiled. 'Must live just around the corner. I don't think Bosnich's the sort who'd willingly walk a hundred yards if there was an alternative.'

D'Angelo chuckled. 'You never know. They anticipated having a few beers, so it's very responsible behaviour not to drink and drive.'

Larsen remained po-faced. 'Yep. Upstanding citizen, our Mr Bosnich.' She leaned forward and turned her attention back to the video screen. 'Let's see where they went inside the building.'

It wasn't a complicated exercise to track Bosnich past various cameras until he and his mate sat down at a small table towards the rear of the sports bar. Under brighter lighting, it was possible to gain a better view of their subjects of interest. There was little doubt Craig Bosnich's offsider was his brother. His murine features mirrored Craig's; even the way he waved his hand about as he spoke was identical. Larsen scrolled through the vision at high speed. For most of the evening, the two men chatted, one occasionally visiting the bar for replacement drinks, or taking a brief trip to the toilets, or walking to the TAB counter to place a bet. Their reaction to greyhound racing on a big screen strongly suggested their wagering was less than profitable, with many a tote ticket being screwed up and angrily thrown to the floor. At around 11.30, with patronage starting to thin, an elderly woman who the detectives assumed to be Jean Gawler entered the room enthusiastically celebrating her big win on the poker machines, whooping and holding money above her head. Many patrons stood and clapped; a few hugged her enthusiastically. A few minutes later, she exited the sports bar heading towards the main entrance off Pascoe Vale Road. Another thirty seconds passed before Bosnich and his brother stood, skolled what was left of their drinks and followed the same path as the jackpot winner.

'Look at that,' D'Angelo said enthusiastically, pointing at the screen. 'No Backdoor Johnnies this time. Let's try the camera over the Pascoe Vale Road entrance.'

Larsen manipulated various controls, eventually finding the corresponding time on the footage from four cameras mounted outside. In the bottom left quadrant, the detectives watched the vision of Jean Gawler coming out the main hotel doors, handbag over her right shoulder. She turned north and walked slowly towards the intersection with Woodlands Street, no doubt heading back to her home they'd been told was in Wallace Crescent. A few seconds later, Bosnich and his brother exited the hotel, looking both ways before walking south in the opposite direction to Mrs Gawler.

D'Angelo shrugged. 'There goes that theory,' he said quietly as Larsen allowed the footage to run. 'But at least we've established that Bosnich was in Essendon the night Ralston was attacked at Car City. And there's no way he could have been back in Ringwood a little after midnight.'

'So why not just tell us he was here drinking with his brother where CCTV would validate his story, instead of that bullshit about being home with his dumb mate who wouldn't know how to lie straight in bed?'

'There's your answer,' D'Angelo said, indicating the vision in the top right quadrant. It clearly showed Bosnich's beat-up old blue Mondeo with the yellow bonnet heading north on Pascoe Vale Road – in exactly the same direction as Jean Gawler had walked a few minutes before.

CHAPTER 10

Bowker squeezed into a tight parking space at the rear of the pathology centre. Rachael hadn't said a word for the twenty-minute drive, her face now appearing even paler than at the medical clinic earlier in the morning. Bowker helped her from the car and onto her feet. She was unsteady at first, prompting Bowker to suggest chasing down a wheelchair. Rachael forced a smile and assured him that she'd be fine to walk once her head stopped spinning.

Inside the centre, Bowker assisted Rachael to the crowded waiting room before presenting the relevant paperwork to a middle-aged woman at the reception desk. She perused the forms before handing Bowker a white plastic square with a black number printed on both sides. He returned to the waiting room, sat beside his wife, and gave the dozen others who were waiting a cursory glance. Several were chatting to each other, while others stared at the floor. None looked as sick as Rachael. He prayed some of those waiting were like himself, there for support, not in the queue to be tested. He counted eight plastic squares besides his own. Obviously, there would still be a significant wait.

After thirty-five minutes, Rachael's number was finally called and a short, plump woman in her thirties with tied-back bleached hair wearing a pathology company smock ushered her and Bowker into a small room. The woman, whose name tag identified her as Belinda Thorne, welcomed them both and indicated Rachael should take a seat in an ironed-framed vinyl-covered chair with wide padded armrests. In the corner was a young man who Bowker estimated was in his late teens or very early twenties. *Tyler Wills, Student Nurse* was printed on a university name badge.

'My name's Belinda,' the woman said in a friendly voice. She pointed towards the young man, who was standing nervously, hands clasped behind his back. 'This is Tyler, he's with us for a few days learning the dark art of taking blood. So far he's just been observing, but I've assured him it won't be long before we set him loose on some unsuspecting victim.'

Belinda checked the pathology request form, raised her eyebrows but made no comment. Bowker caught the look and hoped Rachael hadn't spotted it. She hadn't. She continued to stare at the floor. Belinda collected a handful of plastic blood tubes from a drawer, carefully peeled barcoded labels from an A4 sheet and attached one to each small cylinder. *How much blood is she going to take?* Bowker asked himself but said nothing. When all the equipment was carefully laid out on a sterile patch of synthetic material, Belinda donned a fresh pair of rubber gloves with a *snap* for each. She applied and tightened a tourniquet on Rachael's left arm before checking inside Rachael's elbow, searching for a suitable vein to extract the blood. She tapped Rachael's arm with two fingers and smiled at Bowker.

'A fit athlete, your wife. Got blood vessels like a racehorse.'

Bowker nodded. 'Normally I'd agree one hundred percent, but right now she's not feeling too fit.'

Rachael smiled weakly. 'He's not wrong.'

'Well, the sooner we get this blood to the lab, the sooner we can get you on the road to recovery.'

As she picked up the butterfly needle to make the insertion, the door opened quickly and the woman from the reception desk walked in, shaken and white-faced. 'Sorry to interrupt, Belinda, but Mrs Williams has just collapsed in the waiting room.'

Belinda took a deep breath and looked at the student nurse. 'Now's as good a time as any to have a go. This lady has veins like rope. You can't miss.' She left the room in a hurry. Tyler clumsily dragged on gloves and took Belinda's place beside Rachael.

Bowker was concerned with the switch. 'Have you done this before, son?' he asked quietly, not wishing to put the young man under any extra pressure.

'A couple of times,' Tyler replied uneasily.

'He'll be right.' Rachael murmured. 'Let's get this over so I can lie down somewhere.'

Bowker looked at Tyler with a forced smile. 'Okay, mate, she's all yours,' he said.

Despite Rachael's prominent veins, Tyler had trouble inserting the butterfly needle. The first two attempts missed completely; the next two passed through the vein, with the needle coming out the other side. Bruising was beginning to appear around the puncture marks. Droplets of sweat were forming on Tyler's brow, and his hands shook. Bowker debated whether he should suggest the young nurse abandon his efforts and wait for the return of the expert. That decision was taken out of his hands when Belinda re-entered the room.

'Storm in a teacup,' she said. 'Mrs Williams gets a bit light-headed after we take blood, but no harm done.' She spotted the bloodied mess on Rachael's arm and the empty tubes on the bench. 'For goodness' sake!' she blurted out as she pushed Tyler away with the sweep of a hand. Within thirty seconds, the tourniquet was on Rachael's other arm, the needle inserted, vacutainer connected, and blood was filling the vials one after another.

If this was the beginning of Rachael's path to recovery, it wasn't a promising start, Bowker thought.

* * *

The service centre on the Western Freeway between Ballan and Bacchus Marsh was much more than a petrol station. The servo itself retailed a large array of food and beverage items, as well as a small selection of overpriced groceries and automotive needs. Sharing the cavernous structure was a takeaway food business, plus a KFC outlet at its south-eastern end. Half a dozen double-sided fuel bowsers catered for light vehicles under roofing connected to the main building. Off to the north-east was a separate covered area catering for trucks, motorhomes or cars towing caravans.

The weather had turned showery as Holmes climbed into the Pentlands and onto the central highlands plateau, with semitrailers and B-doubles throwing up clouds of oily mist. It was a long journey just to check out a Bowker hunch, but with no other leads forthcoming, there was nothing to lose. And only a fool would ignore his partner's hunches, as they had come up trumps on more than one occasion in the past. It was a pity Kirsten was busy with the Car City case, Holmes thought. She'd have been good company on the two-and-a-half-hour round trip, and a valuable second pair of eyes when checking the video at the servo. He smiled as he admitted to himself that half the attraction of bringing Kirsten would have been the skin-tight shiny leggings she was wearing as she headed off with D'Angelo earlier. He consoled himself with the knowledge that she'd still be wearing them when she arrived home after work. But not for long, if he played his cards right.

After purchasing a Coke and a packet of Twisties, Holmes was escorted to a small room containing the video surveillance equipment. Following a quick tutorial that he didn't need, he consulted his notes and navigated a series of directories to the date and time Bowker felt was relevant to the investigation. The weather that day was also diabolical, with sleety rain and high winds. The servo was busy, and the exterior CCTV cameras chronicled an unending progression of rugged-up patrons hurrying from the petrol pumps into the shelter of the centre. Holmes scrolled through to the time quoted on the KFC receipt found in the rubbish bin at Pykes Creek Reservoir. CCTV for the interior of the fried chicken outlet was recorded on its own system, but the ground plan of the service centre required customers for all retail areas to enter and exit through two central doors. These were monitored by several of the cameras Holmes now had access to. He decided to check these first.

Shortly after the time printed on the KFC receipt, Holmes spotted a tall, broad-shouldered male exiting the building carrying a tall paper cup and a red-and-white striped box of takeaway chicken. He watched the man disappear from the camera's field of view but let the vision run for a few minutes to ensure he had the person he was after. Several others with KFC products left through the exit, but none carried a box described in the forensic report or matching the item detailed on the receipt. Holmes reversed the footage then saved the relevant section on a memory stick. He then switched cameras to vision that picked up his person of interest as he made his way towards the large carpark to the southeast. A sleety shower passed over as he walked quickly between two cars, leaving the bowser area. From out of the camera's field of vision, a figure dressed in jeans and medium-heeled boots who, by size and gait, Holmes was sure was female, approached his subject and engaged him in a one-sided, animated discussion.

The jean-clad victim's remains at Pykes Reservoir immediately were front and centre of Holmes's mind. He quickly reminded himself that a high percentage of women wore jeans, particularly in weather like was captured on the video. The boots weren't of help, as no footwear was found at the murder scene. He paused the video and looked closely at the couple. It was impossible to know what clothing the woman wore on her upper body, as a long coat covered everything from her neck to her knees. She had her back to the camera, so her face was obscured, unlike the male's, which was clearly visible. He appeared around forty, with thick eyebrows and a full, out-of-control beard. After thirty seconds, the female clasped her hands together in a begging motion, whereupon the man shrugged and led her to a vehicle that he unlocked remotely. It was a dark blue Toyota Landcruiser with a canvas cover over the tray.

Holmes leaned back in his chair as he watched the pair climb into the vehicle, its number plate obscured by one of the bushy shrubs growing on the divide between parking areas. As he watched it leave in a mist of spray, the rego refused to reveal itself no matter how many times he rewatched it. Holmes copied the relevant vision onto the thumb drive then moved to the cameras that monitored the petrol bowsers. He began viewing footage fifteen minutes before the time on the KFC receipt. After two minutes, he hit the jackpot. The Landcruiser entered the bowser area, the same male alighting from the driver's side. The passenger seat was empty. This time, the front number plate was clearly visible, so Holmes stopped the replay and jotted the rego number in his notebook. He restarted the vision. After filling the vehicle with diesel, the driver walked into the building. Switching cameras, Holmes saw him pay with a credit card. Bingo. After the Toyota's rego, this would provide another mode of identification, particularly crucial if the vehicle wasn't registered to the driver. As he walked back out into the cold to move his vehicle to a parking area, Holmes spotted the woman he now knew had later left with him in the Landcruiser. It was ten minutes earlier, and she was in conversation with a younger man. Again, she appeared to be begging for help, and again, her face was obscured. The young driver shook his head, mouthed a sorry, and walked into the servo. Holmes now felt certain the female was pleading for a ride.

Just to double-check that the KFC box recorded on the receipt found in the bin at Pykes was actually the one the Landcruiser driver carried to his vehicle, Holmes sought and gained access to the KFC security camera records. After a few minutes of scrolling through vision, there were no doubts that Mr Landcruiser had made the purchase. His face was captured on video as he paid cash for his chicken box at the exact time indicated on the receipt. Again, Holmes copied the footage to his memory stick.

Bowker had asked Holmes to peruse the servo's CCTV for two reasons. The first was to seek new information surrounding the KFC receipt found in the bin at Pykes Creek reserve. The second was little more than a Hail Mary that the canvas-topped vehicle which a resident had seen at Pykes might have stopped at the servo for petrol and thus could be identified. As Holmes copied the latest vision of interest, he leaned back in his chair, smiling. Never in his wildest dreams had he believed Bowker's two questions could be resolved on the same combination of camera footage. His first urge was to call and congratulate Bowker on his instincts, but as he fumbled for his mobile, he was suddenly cognisant that his friend and partner was likely embroiled in more important personal issues. As he removed his hand from his pocket, his phone rang, and as if by some sort of mental telepathy, it was Bowker on the line. Holmes couldn't hit the accept button quickly enough.

'G'day, mate. How's Rach?'

'Not flash,' Bowker replied quietly.

Holmes sighed sadly. 'Sorry to hear that, mate. Where are you now?'

'Outside a medical imaging joint. Rachael's inside having a CT scan of her chest, abdomen and pelvis area. It'll be a while, I think.' He paused for a long moment. 'You still at Ballan?'

'Yeah. At the servo. Just finished going through their CCTV footage like you suggested.'

'Anything?'

'We've finally got a lead, I think.'

Suddenly, Bowker's tone carried more positivity. 'What did you find?'

'Believe it or not, the KFC receipt and the canvas-covered Landcruiser are connected. The vehicle stopped for fuel, just a driver, no passengers. The driver went in and bought the box of fried chicken detailed on the receipt. Got his face on my memory stick and the rego of the vehicle. And as a bonus, he paid for the fuel by card, so we can contact the banks and get some personal details.'

'Well done, Sherlock,' Bowker replied quickly. 'Maybe at last we're getting somewhere.'

'You haven't heard the best bit yet. There was a woman at the servo, who I'm sure from her body language was looking for a lift. The cameras caught her approaching at least one other driver, but she finally drove off in the Landcruiser with Chicken Man.'

'Does she fit the description of our victim?'

'Never got a look at her face. It was pissing rain and she was wearing a heavy coat, but she did have jeans on, and she's about the right build.'

'Run the rego and the credit card and see who we get. And if you're doing nothing else, run the servo footage further back and see if you can get a line on how the girl got to the servo in the first place. Might even get a look at her face.'

If I'm doing nothing else?! My plan was to arrive home in time to get Kirsten out of those tight leggings, Holmes thought but didn't say. 'I'm on it,' he muttered instead.

CHAPTER 11

After leaving the Red Lion Hotel, D'Angelo and Larsen travelled south down Pascoe Vale Road to the Moonee Ponds police station. There, they briefed the local detectives, Tristan Hayward and Caroline Costello, both young officers, who were investigating the robbery of the poker machine money. Hayward was tall and thin, his hair cut close to his scalp, clean-shaven with a well-fitted charcoal suit. Costello was short and stocky, wearing baggy slacks teamed with a white collared shirt, a tweed jacket that roughly matched her slacks, and flat lace-up shoes. Her mousy brown hair was cut short, with a fringe covering her forehead. Her partner's eyes rarely left Larsen. He was almost caught out a couple times when his gaze wandered down from her face.

D'Angelo explained their original interest in the movements of Craig Bosnich on that particular night, and how they had developed their theory concerning the robbery after viewing security footage. From her folder, Larsen took out a photo of the older Bosnich brother with his address scrawled beneath it. Costello perused the photo and showed it to her partner.

'We checked this bloke's movements on the CCTV video,' Hayward said. 'He and the other bloke left pretty much straight after Mrs Gawler left the pub with her winnings. But we dismissed him as a suspect because the footage showed him and his mate walking away in the opposite direction.'

Larsen nodded. 'We did the same, until we fluked seeing his car whiz past the pub a minute or so later. There was no way you could've known the Mondeo belonged to him. It was just one of fifty cars that would've driven past at that time.'

D'Angelo shook hands with both local officers. 'Keep the photo. Bosnich's address is on the bottom, as well as his car registration number. We'll leave you to follow up the robbery. With the key suspect over here on the night of our murder, we're back to square one, so we've got plenty on our plate.'

'Good luck,' Larsen said with a smile as she and D'Angelo turned and walked to the door.

Costello waved a hand in front of Hayward's eyes. 'If you stare any harder, you'll burn a hole in her arse,' she said before turning away.

*　*　*

When Holmes finally found video footage of the mystery woman entering the Ballan service centre, his eyes widened in surprise. He'd expected she would arrive as a passenger in a car or riding pillion on a motorcycle, or perhaps hitching a lift with a truckie. Never did he think that she would just walk up the entrance road from the freeway. Did her car break down somewhere, was she dropped off, was she forcibly ejected from her ride thus far, or had she been hitching prior to the servo? He stopped the vision while he pondered the possibilities. If her car *had* broken down, surely she would've phoned for help. There was no evidence on the CCTV that she'd used a mobile, although she may have done that on the freeway. Holmes was sure she hadn't used a servo phone. If she had used a mobile at the scene of a vehicle breakdown, why did she hitch a ride with Chicken Man and not wait for help to arrive? More questions were being raised than answered.

Holmes copied any vision that captured the woman and the half a dozen motorists she'd spoken to. On several occasions, her face was clearly visible. Was she the woman who would later be murdered at Pykes? Holmes couldn't be certain. The victim's face was badly mutilated, but there were similarities in cranial structure and certainly height and build. He placed the memory stick in his coat pocket, thanked the servo staff for their cooperation and headed back to Melbourne. As the miles whizzed past, his mind jumped between the leads the servo expedition had opened up and Kirsten's tight black shiny leggings.

* * *

D'Angelo and Larsen returned to Homicide headquarters with their investigation totally stalled. Craig Bosnich, their chief suspect, was now in the clear, although they felt sure he and his brother would go down for the aggravated robbery in Essendon. When D'Angelo checked his emails, there was one slight positive. He called to Larsen, who had just sat down at her desk to go through Ralston's post-mortem for the tenth time. She wandered over and dragged up a chair. D'Angelo pointed to a message on his screen. 'The techs have enhanced the Car City CCTV vision of the white car and the two hooded individuals.'

Larsen nodded. 'Good news, I hope.'

D'Angelo shrugged. 'I'm not getting too excited. Not much to help us identify the persons involved, but one intruder's height is estimated at approximately 187, the other is bit shorter at around 180. On the positive side, the car's been identified as a 2017 Toyota Corolla.'

Larsen chuckled sarcastically. 'Only a few thousand of them

would have been sold in Australia. That should narrow it down.'

'No help with the rego either, unfortunately.'

'We'll need to check if a 2017 Corolla has been reported stolen. That might give us a start.'

D'Angelo turned back to his computer and began making enquiries. He scrolled through the list of stolen vehicles. He shook his head before looking back at Larsen. 'A couple of Corollas are listed, but no white ones.' He shrugged. 'Where to now? You're the brains of this partnership.'

'Go through the CCTV vision again, I guess. We've got nothing else.'

'You're probably right,' D'Angelo replied in a resigned tone as he set about retrieving the video files from the police mainframe. Much of police investigation nowadays followed a digital path. CCTV cameras captured most aspects of an individual's public life, and a person's movements could be accurately tracked via a trail left behind by credit or debit card transactions, or via their phone pinging various mobile phone towers as they moved around the country. Although face recognition software was available in Australia, it was publicly frowned on and rarely used, and at this stage, it was only a minor weapon in a detective's armoury. Conversely, in countries such as China, face recognition was omnipresent, in a scenario accurately predicted by George Orwell's frightening novel *Nineteen Eighty-Four.* Orwell's Big Brother era had taken longer to arrive than the 1980s, but here it was now, and in all the eerie detail he had foreseen.

While accepting that a high percentage of crimes were now solved via digital evidence, Larsen had a soft spot for the days when most were eventually cracked by good old-fashioned detective work – interviews, hunches, collection of physical evidence, and plenty of legwork. She had heard Greg Bowker's account of solving a murder case in a remote one-copper town in the Mallee in the 1980s. No mobile phones to track, no credit card records to follow, no CCTV to establish a person's whereabouts, no DNA analysis to place a suspect at the scene of a crime. That sort of investigation appealed to Larsen, even though she'd grown up with modern methods. To her, all the new-fangled aids seemed like cheating in the game of cat and mouse played by coppers and crims.

'The video techs have made a composite of material recorded by several car yards along the route our suspects were taking,' D'Angelo said as he cued up the vision. 'Might give us something we haven't noticed before.'

He and Larsen watched as the intruder's progress was tracked from the time they entered Car City until they arrived at Anderson's yard, where CCTV had not been operating.

'Nice bit of editing, but it doesn't show us anything new, unfortunately,' D'Angelo said as he stopped the vision.

'Not so far, but let it run, please,' Larsen replied.

D'Angelo complied. The footage resumed and showed the suspects leaving via the route they had come.

'Stop it there for a moment,' Larsen said.

D'Angelo paused the footage.

'The time gap where we lost vision on them is around four and half minutes,' Larsen surmised. 'If they were the ones who attacked Ralston, then that's when they did it.'

'Four and a half minutes is a long time. More than enough to belt him, even if they had an argument and a bit of push-and-shove first.'

'Yeah. That's what I'm thinking.' Larsen pointed at the sports bag one of their suspects was still carrying. 'What's in the bag, you reckon?'

'Bit of pipe, maybe. Something to belt Ralston with.'

Larsen shook her head. 'I'm not so sure. Up until we visited Essendon, our theory went that Bosnich had a jealous grievance against Ralston over shacking up with his ex-girlfriend. That led us to suspect that Bosnich and a mate followed Ralston to the car yard and attacked him. But we now know that Bosnich was on the other side of the city, so that theory is out the window.' Larsen eyed D'Angelo. 'If we'd never heard of Bosnich, what do you think our assumption would have been about the attack?'

D'Angelo smiled. 'That Ralston had disturbed intruders in the car yard.'

Larsen nodded. 'Exactly. I reckon they were about to break into the showroom, maybe looking for cash or something valuable.'

'Why go all the way around to Anderson's yard? They'd walked past plenty of others. Why pick that one?'

'Out of the way around the back, perhaps? Intel that the CCTV wasn't working or the safe was easy pickings? Maybe it wasn't money they were after. We both saw the display of Bathurst 1000 memorabilia Anderson had in there. Worth a pretty penny on the petrolhead black market.' She shrugged. 'Or maybe they wanted to pinch things off specific cars. The yard had some pretty fancy brands. Maybe they were looking to knock off a mirror or bonnet ornament. Or grab a souvenir from the Monaro.'

'That could possibly explain the sports bag,' D'Angelo replied quickly. 'Maybe it contained a few tools. Just about everything is portable and battery-powered nowadays. A small angle grinder or drill would be handy.' He thought for a moment. 'But Anderson reported that nothing appeared to have been touched, and there was no evidence of an attempted forced entry into the building.'

'After they'd belted Ralston unconscious, surely they'd cut their losses and shoot through,' Larsen replied.

D'Angelo leaned back in his chair. 'You'd think so. So where does that leave us?'

'Why don't we interview Anderson again and see if anyone was sniffing around the yard in the days leading up to the attack? Anyone who seemed a bit dodgy. Especially someone taking particular notice of the Bathurst display.'

* * *

Senior Detective Holmes arrived back at Spencer Street headquarters as D'Angelo and Larsen were preparing to depart for their chat with Sam Anderson at Car City. 'Any closer to getting your man?' he asked, all the time fighting the urge to embrace Larsen and get both hands on her backside.

'Well, if clearing our only suspect is getting closer, then yes, I guess we've made progress,' Larsen replied with a smile. 'What about you?'

'Finally getting somewhere, I think,' Holmes responded. 'CCTV at the Ballan servo showed a bloke picking up a female hitchhiker who roughly fits the description of our victim. The vehicle he was driving was later seen entering the Pyke Creek Reservoir reserve. We've got the rego, which gives us some sort of a lead. I've come in to do some follow-up calls.' He looked at D'Angelo. 'What are you guys up to?'

'Now that our main suspect is in the clear, we're working on the theory that our victim disturbed intruders and got whacked for his trouble. We're taking a run out to Car City to talk to the owner of the yard just in case we missed something when we spoke to him last time.'

Holmes nodded and his eyes shifted to Larsen. 'I'll probably beat you home, then. What do you want to do about dinner?'

Larsen smiled. 'I'll leave that in your capable hands. You know what I like.'

D'Angelo caught the innuendo and for the umpteenth time wished he was Holmes.

* * *

It only took a few minutes for Holmes to establish Bernard David Laidler as the registered owner of the Toyota Landcruiser caught on CCTV at the Ballan service Centre. His address was in Murray Road Preston, a suburb in Melbourne's north. Holmes then accessed the LEAP database to check if Laidler had any priors, leaning forward quickly when the information appeared on his screen. Three counts of sexual assault over the last five years, the latest one costing him six months behind bars. Holmes immediately phoned Bowker to give him a heads-up. The call went to voicemail. Rather than leave a convoluted outline of what he'd just found, he left just one sentence. 'I think we might have the bastard.'

Holmes leaned back in his chair and assessed his next move. Should he take a run out to Preston in the hope Laidler was home, or wait until he'd heard from Bowker to ascertain his availability and garner his advice? As Holmes closed his eyes and pondered his options, his phone rang.

'Sorry I missed your call, Sherlock,' Bowker said. 'Just getting Rachael settled back at home.'

'How is she?'

'Pretty tired, as you can imagine. She's had a big day of tests.' There was a slight pause as Bowker dragged his thoughts away from his wife's condition. 'So you reckon you've nailed our killer?'

'Strong possibility. The bloke in the canvas-covered Landcruiser has got priors for sexual assault. Spent six months in Barwon.'

Bowker whistled into the phone. 'Certainly fits the profile of the person we're chasing. Where's he live?'

'Murray Road in Preston. Just debating whether to drive out there and see if he's home. Ask a few questions.'

'Can you wait until the morning, mate? I'd like to go with you.'

'Who's going to look after Rachael?'

'Our daughter Jacinta's coming for the day.' He sighed loudly. 'I really need to get out and about for a few hours and get my mind onto something else. Just sitting around here watching Rach go downhill is doing my head in. I'm nearly in tears half the bloody time, and that does Rachael no good at all.'

Holmes felt desperately sad for his good friend. He'd never seen a couple so devoted to each other and feared what might become of Bowker if the unthinkable happened to his wife. 'No need to rush in the morning, Greg. How about we meet here at nine thirty, if that fits with Jacinta's schedule?'

'Nine thirty it is, unless you hear otherwise.'

* * *

Sam Anderson was speaking with a customer when D'Angelo and Larsen arrived at his car yard. His cheesy smile evaporated when he spotted the detectives walking up the concrete path towards his showroom. He muttered something to his customer, tapped him on the arm, then beckoned to his son, who was attaching a 'Low Milage' sticker to a Nissan Patrol at the front of the yard. His son wandered across as Anderson met the officers at the showroom door.

'Sorry to interrupt the closing of a deal,' D'Angelo said with a smile as he shook Anderson's hand.

'Tyre kicker,' Anderson replied. 'You get them in here all the time. Part of this game, unfortunately. He asked me what I'd take for the silver Porsche inside.' He nodded towards his customer, who was now in deep conversation with his son. 'Look at him.

Arse out of his pants. He couldn't afford the tyres on one of those babies.' He shrugged. 'Anyway. What can I do for you? Here to tell me you've solved the case, I hope.'

D'Angelo shook his head. 'I wish we were. But I think we're getting closer,' he lied.

Larsen pointed through the open showroom door. 'That Bathurst memorabilia you've got in there. Who's that belong to?'

Anderson touched his chest with his thumb. 'Yours truly. That and the Monaro. Brings in a few rubberneckers who I'm hoping might spot something in the yard they like.' He chuckled. 'Hasn't happened yet, mind you, but it's early days. The stuff's been on display for less than a fortnight.'

'Have you noticed anyone paying particular attention to it?' Larsen asked. 'You know, somebody you thought looked a bit dodgy.'

Anderson shrugged. 'A lot of petrolheads have come in. You know, old Brocky fans who used to camp up on Mount Panorama on the race weekend. But no one stood out as being dodgier than others.'

D'Angelo slipped his hands into his pockets. 'What's the collection worth?'

Anderson screwed up his face. 'A lot less than when I bought it, I know that.' He then smiled. 'It's insured for what I paid for it, so I'd be more than happy for some bastard to knock it all off.'

D'Angelo shot a look at Larson.

'How long had you been without CCTV before the night of the incident?' Larsen asked.

Anderson thought for a moment. 'A couple of days, probably. Maybe three.'

'And you'd have stored vision of the week leading up to when the system went down, I'd presume?' Larsen asked.

'Yeah. And a week or so before that as well.'

Larsen nodded then removed a memory stick from her jacket pocket. 'We might take a copy of that vision, if you don't mind, Mr Anderson.'

Anderson nodded. 'Be my guest.' A well-heeled couple entering the yard and showing a keen interest in a late-model BMW caught the dealer's eye, and he nodded in their direction. 'Look, if there's nothing else, I need to attend to these customers. My gut tells me they're serious buyers.'

Larsen held up the memory stick. 'Can we do this first?'

Anderson called to his son, who had finally dispatched the Porsche tyre kickers. 'I'll get Simon to copy it for you. He's the electronics whiz.' He smiled. 'Shit car salesman, though.'

CHAPTER 12

When Holmes and Larsen arrived at Spencer Street headquarters the next morning, Bowker was already sitting at his desk staring at a file, a cup of black coffee to one side. The time had just turned eight thirty. Larsen hung her handbag over the back of her chair before following Holmes towards Bowker.

'You're here bright and early, mate,' Holmes said as he approached his partner. 'Daughter sleep over or just arrive at sparrow fart?'

'Arrived at six. I phoned her last night to tell her I was keen to work today. Said I'd like to be in by nine. Traffic was light, so I made it ahead of time.' He looked at Larsen. 'Morning, Kirsten. Sorry I've been out of circulation for a few days.'

'Not your fault, Greg. How's Rachael?'

Bowker shrugged. 'Pretty much the same. We see a haematologist later this morning who'll give us the results of all the tests she's had. That should tell us where we head next.'

Larsen smiled weakly. 'Hope it's good news.'

Bowker folded his arms across his chest. 'Yeah. But I'm not confident. The faces on the medicos tell me they fear the worst. But I'll wait and see before I get totally depressed.' He sighed audibly before getting down to business. 'Any progress on the car yard attack?'

Larsen pulled up a chair and sat down. 'Our chief suspect has an alibi, so that avenue is a dead end. We've moved our motive from a jealous lover to a robbery gone wrong. The car yard has a number of high-end vehicles, plus a big display of Bathurst 1000 memorabilia in the showroom. There's one of Peter Brock's winning Monaros in there as well.'

Bowker unfolded his arms. 'And security cameras give you nothing?'

Larsen shook her head. 'The crucial one wasn't functioning on the night.'

Bowker chuckled. 'Unfortunate coincidence.'

'Yeah, that's what we thought. Especially when the memorabilia is insured beyond its current value. I also did a bit of digging when we got back from Ringwood last night, and Anderson's business is in a bit of financial trouble. An insurance payout may have been the fillip it needs.'

Holmes frowned. 'But didn't the tech mob who service the CCTV confirm there was a fault on one of the circuit boards and they were awaiting a replacement?'

Larsen nodded. 'Yeah, but apparently the fault was a short of some description. And the owner of the yard couldn't give us any more details. Said his son was the tech whiz. The more I think about it, the more I think maybe Marco and I should take another run out there and talk to the son in private.'

Bowker stood. 'Worth a try.' He skolled the last of his coffee then looked at Holmes. 'You right?'

'Yep. Let's do it.'

* * *

Bernard Laidler's residence in Preston was a modest rental on Murray Road. A carport to the side of the small brick house sheltered an old-model maroon Kia Festiva from the light rain that was beginning to fall. Dark clouds building ominously to the city's west were a portent of more serious weather on the way. Two cars were parked in the street near Laidler's house. Neither was a Toyota Land Cruiser with a canvas-covered tray. Holmes pushed hard to open the rusty wrought-iron gate giving access to an overgrown, weed-infested front yard. A cracked concrete path led to a faded white front door that had long needed painting. Remnant timber and contrasting paintwork evidenced that a verandah had once adorned the home, but obviously no attempt had been made to replace it after its demise. Holmes pressed the cobweb-covered doorbell button that he expected didn't work. Hearing no chimes from inside, he looked at Bowker, raising his eyebrows in mock surprise. He then knocked loudly on the weatherboards beside the door frame. A few moments passed before a middle-aged woman hesitantly opened the door a few centimetres and peered through the crack.

'Whatever you're selling, I'm not interested,' she said quickly before attempting to slam the door shut.

Holmes held up his ID just in time. 'Can we come in? It's getting a bit wet out here.'

The woman opened the door fully, its base scraping the worn carpet inside. She was diminutive in stature, her hair bleached with dark roots becoming obvious, her face pinched and heavily lined. She led them no further than needed to avoid the rain. A passage ran to the back with timber-trimmed wall panels of old-fashioned plaster painted with well-worn calcimine. Two uncovered light globes hung on cords from spider-colonised ceiling roses.

'He's not here. Gone fishing on the Yanco. He'll be up there for a week.'

'What makes you think we're looking for your husband?' Bowker asked.

'For a start, he's not my husband. Not in a formal sense, anyway. Secondly, there's only the two of us who live here, and I know police wouldn't be looking for me.' She sniffed loudly. 'Bernie, that's a different matter.' She took a deep breath and closed her eyes. 'He hasn't been touching up more women, has he? He promised me he'd turned over a new leaf.'

Bowker wasn't interested in elaborating. 'Where on the Yanco does he fish?' he asked. 'It's a long river.'

The woman shrugged, disappointed she wasn't given more details surrounding the reason for the detectives' visit. 'All I can tell you is that he talks about having the choice between the Yanco and the Billabong creeks without having to move camp, and grabbing a few beers at the Conargo pub. Not here with me is the way *I* describe it.'

'What's his mobile number?' Holmes asked as the rain became heavier, drumming on the corrugated iron roof.

'Won't do you much good,' the woman replied. 'No mobile reception up there.' She exhaled loudly. 'And Lord knows how many times I've tried to contact him.'

'We'll grab his number anyway,' Holmes replied, suspecting lack of reception was an excuse Laidler used for not answering his phone when she called.

The woman reeled off the ten digits as though she'd dialled them on a million occasions. Holmes jotted them down in his notebook. 'And your name is?'

'Sally Price.'

'We might be in touch.'

'Are you gonna tell me why you're looking for him? Is he in big trouble again?'

'We think he might be able to help us with an inquiry, clear something up for us. More a witness than in trouble,' Bowker replied, fudging the truth a little. This seemed to put Price's mind at ease, and she smiled weakly.

'Does he catch any fish?' Holmes asked to lighten the conversation.

Price shrugged. 'Sometimes when they're biting, he'll get a few yellowbellies. Most times not. Just an excuse to get away with his useless mate is my opinion. Occasionally he'll come back with a few ducks they've shot along the river. Leaves me to pluck the bloody things when he gets home, mind you.'

'And his mate's name?' Holmes asked, pen poised.

'Red Dog. No idea of his real name.'

'Mr Laidler doesn't have trouble getting time off work?' Bowker asked.

'He hasn't got a permanent job,' Price replied. 'He occasionally runs a few spare parts up to a garage a mate runs in Ballarat, who slings him a few quid under the table so it doesn't affect his dole.'

The detectives nodded their thanks and jogged back to their car, puddles now forming on the bitumen.

'Looks like a trip up to New South if we're to move this case along,' Holmes said as he pulled his car door closed.

'You and Marco will have to go. I can't leave Melbourne the way things are with Rachael.'

Holmes screwed up his face. 'Not bloody D'Angelo! How about I take Kirsten instead? She's a lot smarter, and she'll be better company than Marco.'

Bowker exhaled audibly. 'You know my answer on that one, Sherlock. It's better that you and Kirsten don't work together as partners. The Port Fairy case proved that personal feelings can compromise an investigation.' He smiled. 'Besides, a road trip will give you a chance to get to know Marco a bit better. I know he's not at the top of your Christmas list.'

'Not on it, actually.'

'I'm still not sure what he's done to annoy you. He comes across to me as a nice enough bloke.'

'I reckon he's got the hots for Kirsten,' Holmes responded without looking at his friend.

'But Kirsten has the hots for *you*. That's all that matters.'

'Yeah. I know. But what if someone better comes along?' Holmes asked, half to himself, as he turned to look out his side window.

Holmes's insecurity when it came to Kirsten Larsen never ceased to surprise Bowker. In every other aspect, his friend was a self-confident go-getter. Bowker put it down to the seventeen-year age difference between him and Larsen. Holmes saw himself drifting into late middle age while Larsen remained in her prime. The fact that she was regarded by most men as a stunner, and always dressed to kill, didn't help Holmes's peace of mind. Rather than rejoicing in the fact that a woman like Kirsten saw him as her soulmate, Holmes regarded every other male as a potential replacement. And this had complicated the investigation they had conducted together with local officers in Port Fairy.

It was time to lighten the mood. Bowker grinned. 'You never know. After a few hundred k's together, you might get to like D'Angelo and develop a bond. One of those bromances people talk about. You might come back and ask to be paired with him permanently and give me the arse.'

Holmes shook his head and was quiet for a few moments as he stared at the raindrops hammering against the windscreen.

'Have you ever been to Conargo?' Bowker asked to break the silence.

Holmes turned in his seat. 'Nope. You?'

Bowker shook his head. 'Look it up on your phone.'

Holmes removed his mobile from his jacket pocket. His fingers danced across the screen. He read for a few seconds. 'It's north of Deniliquin on the Billabong Creek, downstream from its junction with the Yanco. Bugger all in the town, according to Wikipedia. Pub, primary school, general store and a few houses. Pub burnt down in 2014 but has been rebuilt.' He chuckled. 'Originally, the town had three pubs, but there's only ever been one general store.'

Bowker chuckled as well. 'Shows their priorities. Or how bloody hot it is up there. What distance from here are we talking?'

Holmes swiped to a different app and tapped the screen. 'Three hours, fifty-two minutes by the most direct route up through Rochester, Echuca and Denny.' He shook his head. 'Four hours plus in the car with D'Angelo. Eight hours when you count the trip home. Can't wait!'

Bowker smiled but said nothing. He had more important matters on his mind.

* * *

'What do you want to talk to him about?' Sam Anderson asked when D'Angelo requested to see his son. 'He wasn't even at work when I found the bloke injured in the yard.'

'Just a few routine questions,' Larsen replied. 'Mainly concerning your security system. You said he's the whiz-kid when it comes to technology.'

Anderson appeared edgy. 'He's good with computers, but I doubt he knows any more about our CCTV setup than I do. We hire a specialist company to handle our surveillance needs.'

'All the same, we'd still like to talk to your son,' D'Angelo insisted.

Anderson threw his hands in the air. 'Suit yourself.' He pointed through the showroom. 'He's out the back detailing a vehicle that's just come in. I'll get him for you.'

D'Angelo wasn't having Dad talk to his son first. He touched Anderson on the arm. 'Don't worry, Mr Anderson, we'll find him.' As he walked into the showroom, a late-model Audi caught his attention. It had taken pride of place from the Monaro. The other Bathurst 1000 memorabilia had also been removed. D'Angelo walked back to where Anderson was closing the door behind Larsen. 'Where's all the Bathurst gear?' he asked, sweeping his arm across the room.

'Sold it. The car, the trophies, the whole bloody lot,' Anderson replied. 'Finally got a decent offer. Nowhere near what I paid for it, but at least it's off my plate. Passionate Peter Brock fan has been at me for years to sell him the stuff, and finally I've relented. Sick of waiting for better money.'

D'Angelo nodded but didn't respond before walking back to Larsen. 'Sounds a bit coincidental to me,' he said quietly to his partner. 'CCTV camera down, security guard attacked in the yard for no apparent reason, then Anderson disposes of his precious memorabilia within days.'

Larsen folded her arms. 'An insurance scam goes horribly wrong, and he decides to cut his losses. That what you're thinking?'

D'Angelo shrugged. 'Sillier things have happened.'

Larsen tilted her head and screwed up her face. 'It'd be a bit obvious, though, wouldn't it? If we find the CCTV was sabotaged, I'll be more convinced. But you might be right.'

Anderson's son was vacuuming the driver's-side floor of a 2019 blue BMW when the detectives walked through to a service area behind the showroom. With the loud hum of the cleaner, he didn't hear them arrive, and it took a tap on his back from D'Angelo to catch his attention. He turned off the machine and pointed back towards the showroom. 'The old man's out the front somewhere. Surprised you didn't see him on the way in.'

D'Angelo slipped his hands into his pockets. 'It's you we'd like to talk to today, mate. It's Braeden, isn't it?'

Anderson the younger was taken aback. 'It's Baden. No "r".'

'You're a whiz with computers, we're told,' Larsen said.

Baden tried desperately to suppress a smile. 'Who told you that?'

'Your father,' D'Angelo replied.

'That's a first. I thought he reckoned I was hopeless at everything.'

Larsen leaned against the Beamer. 'But you *are* good with computers, right?'

Baden scratched the bum fluff on his chin that he hoped others would see as a fashionable goatee. 'Probably better than most. That's the area I'd like to work in. Not selling cars, which by the way, I hate and am useless at anyway. But the old man rules the roost at our place.'

D'Angelo removed his hands from his pockets and folded his arms across his chest, taking a more businesslike stance. 'Ever done any work on the CCTV system?'

Both detectives looked for a tell, but neither spotted anything.

'Only resetting the bloody thing a few times.'

'Ever pulled it apart?' D'Angelo asked in a matter-of-fact tone.

The young man appeared genuinely puzzled. 'Why would I do that?'

'To fix it when one of the cameras stopped working,' Larsen shot back.

Baden shook his head. 'Not a chance. I know nothing about the circuitry inside that thing, and we weren't given any schematics of the technical stuff. Just the operating manual. Besides, the whole system is still under warranty. Once the access plates are removed, that becomes null and void.'

'So when the camera went down, you just contacted the supplier to come out and fix the problem?' D'Angelo asked as light rain started to fall.

'The old man did,' Baden replied. 'Made a big song and dance about the system being virtually brand new and how he'd be looking for compensation if any vehicles were stolen while the camera wasn't working.'

'So you're saying you didn't touch the system?' Larsen asked.

Baden shook his head. 'I checked there was power to the camera, that's all. It uses Bluetooth to talk to the main unit.' The young man was still puzzled. 'Why are you so interested in me and the system?'

D'Angelo leaned in closer. 'Because the camera being offline the very night a security officer was attacked seems like a big coincidence to us. Maybe something was going to happen that night that was best not captured on CCTV.'

Baden shook his head. 'Go ask the company who supplied the surveillance equipment if the unit had been opened. That will give you your answer. But I can tell you this – I didn't touch anything.'

Anderson Senior materialised behind them. 'Find what you're looking for?' he asked with an edge.

D'Angelo turned, placing his hands on his hips. 'Maybe. Maybe not. To be honest, Mr Anderson, coincidences worry me.'

'And what particular coincidence would you be referring to?' Anderson shot back quickly.

'Your CCTV camera being down on the very night a security guard disturbs intruders in your yard.'

Anderson shrugged. 'Shit happens.'

'Yeah, it does sometimes,' D'Angelo replied as he walked past Anderson and out through the showroom. Larsen nodded her goodbyes as she followed her colleague.

The rain was falling heavier and the wind picking up from the south as the detectives scurried to their vehicle. Once inside, Larsen brushed droplets from her clothes. 'Did the tech company say anything about the seals when you spoke to them?' she asked.

D'Angelo shrugged as he started the car. 'Nothing that I remember. And I didn't know the seals existed, so obviously I didn't ask. I was more interested in what had gone wrong with the system and was told it was a short circuit.'

Larsen nodded. 'You'd think if the unit had been opened, he would have mentioned it.'

'The young bloke is telling the truth. Is that what you're saying?'

'That's my gut feel.'

D'Angelo pulled up at a red light and turned his wipers to a higher speed as the rain became heavier and wind buffeted the car. 'So we rule out another motive?'

'Yeah, I reckon. But let's check with the tech mob to be sure.'

CHAPTER 13

As D'Angelo took the ramp onto the Eastern Freeway and joined the stream of city-bound traffic in a swirling mist of rain and spray, Larsen's phone rang. The caller was Tristan Hayward, one of the young detectives they had met at the Moonee Ponds police station.

'G'day, Tristan,' Larsen said after Hayward had identified himself. 'What's news?'

'We nailed Craig Bosnich and his brother for the robbery near the Red Lion pub,' Hayward reported proudly.

Larsen smiled and covered the phone with her hand. 'Moonee Ponds arrested Bosnich for rolling the old lady in Essendon,' she whispered to D'Angelo, who raised his eyebrows, nodded, but didn't comment.

'How'd it go down?' Larsen asked Hayward. 'He's not the type to confess to anything.'

The young detective chuckled. 'Denied any involvement until we found the victim's handbag on the back seat of his old Mondeo. He then claimed one of his mates must have thrown it in there. Problem was, his prints were all over it, along with his brother's. The victim made a positive ID from a set of photos we showed her.'

'Congratulations,' Larsen said brightly. 'Coppers one, crims nil.'

'Credit to you guys,' Hayward replied quickly. 'Without your involvement, Bosnich would have been no more than another patron at the pub. So thanks a million.' He chuckled. 'Our boss out here gets a bit twitchy when unsolved cases start to mount up.'

'I'll pass on your thanks to Marco.' She laughed. 'He's busy negotiating traffic in zero visibility. There's a big semi in front of us that keeps changing lanes and sending cars in all directions.'

'So you're not on speakerphone?' Hayward asked tentatively.

'No. Why?'

Hayward hesitated for a moment. 'I thought you might like to catch up for a drink. You know, discuss the case.'

'We're a bit flat out at this end chasing an alternative to Bosnich over the Car City attack.'

'I wasn't including Detective D'Angelo,' Hayward replied sheepishly. 'Just you and me.'

A half smile crossed Larsen's face. 'Thanks, but no thanks. I'm spoken for at this stage.'

Larsen could hear the disappointment in his voice. 'Worth a try, I guess. If anything changes, just give me a ring.'

'Bye, Tristan,' Larsen replied gently as she disconnected the call.

D'Angelo looked across as they stopped at a red turning arrow. 'What was that about? The last bit, I mean.'

Larsen didn't make eye contact. 'He asked me out.'

D'Angelo was annoyed. 'Bit out of his league, don't you reckon? The little upstart thinks he can have one conversation then put the hard word on you?'

'I'm not sure a drink is the hard word.'

'I know how these young blokes function, don't you worry about that. Not willing to put the effort in.'

Car horns started tooting, and Larsen pointed through the windscreen. 'The lights are green, mate.'

'Shit!' D'Angelo said as he accelerated to close the gap with the car turning in front of him, denying room for a white VW from the next lane trying to slot in. One thing that really bugged him were motorists who couldn't wait their turn and sped to the front beside a queue of traffic and expected to be let in. Deep down, he felt he was at the top of Larsen's queue if things fell apart between her and Holmes. And there was no way he was letting anyone else jump in front of him.

* * *

Doctor Alana Jamieson's rooms were on the third floor of the Peter MacCallum Cancer Centre on the corner of Melbourne's Grattan Street and Flemington Road. She was in her early forties but looked younger than thirty with her long blond hair, attractive looks and athletic build. She ushered Bowker and his ashen-faced wife into her office and invited them to sit on easy chairs placed around a small coffee table. A window to the side overlooked Grattan Street below, but neither Bowker nor Rachael took in the view.

Following introductions and small talk, Jamieson got straight down to business. 'The tests have come back, Rachael, and unfortunately they confirm what we suspected.'

Bowker's heart sank but he tried not to let his despair show. Rachael remained unmoved – too sick to muster a reaction.

Jamieson continued. 'It's acute myeloid leukemia, often referred to as just AML. It's an aggressive type of blood cancer in which the bone marrow makes a large number of abnormal blood cells.' Neither Bowker nor his wife made comment, so the doctor continued. 'Normally, the bone marrow makes immature stem cells that become mature blood cells over time. The type of cell we're interested in here is called a myeloid stem cell. These normally develop into either an oxygen-carrying red blood cell, a white blood cell that fights infection, or platelets that stop bleeding.'

'But this is not happening with Rachael, I take it?' Bowker asked quietly.

Jamieson shook her head slowly. 'Unfortunately not. In Rachael's case, the myeloid stem cells are not maturing into healthy white blood cells and are building up in her blood and bone marrow so there is less room for healthy cells and platelets. And when this happens, infection, anaemia and other conditions can occur.'

'So what did I do wrong?' Rachael managed to ask, now staring out the window without seeing.

'I'd say absolutely nothing, Rachael,' Jamieson replied. 'You carry none of the major risk factors. You're not male, you don't smoke, you're getting older, of course, but you're not elderly, and you have no previous history of exposure to radiation or being treated with medical radiation or chemotherapy. You've looked after your body very well, so it seems like you fit into the mystery category that possibly has hereditary roots.'

Bowker inhaled deeply, attempting desperately to digest the information. 'Can the cancer spread outside the blood?'

Jamieson nodded. 'Yes. The leukemia cells can spread to other parts of the body, such as the skin, gums, or brain and spinal cord, or form solid tumours called myeloid sarcomas.' When she saw Bowker close his eyes and throw his head back, she moved quickly to qualify her answer. 'But at this stage, scans indicate our main issues are confined to Rachael's blood.'

'So what's the treatment?' Rachael asked, not making eye contact.

'Chemotherapy. Try and kill all the cancer cells. If that fails, we can try chemotherapy in conjunction with a bone marrow transplant.'

Rachael frowned. 'Bone marrow transplant? Will that return

everything back to normal?'

'Your blood will have a different DNA to the rest of your body, but that won't create any major problems.'

'Aren't there difficulties finding suitable donors?' Bowker asked wearily.

'Can be,' Jamieson replied. 'I won't lie to you, sometimes finding a match can be almost impossible. It depends on the rarity of Rachael's marrow tissue.' She smiled weakly. 'But how about we cross that bridge if we come to it? There are other things we can try first.'

Bowker was visibly shattered and couldn't help mentally projecting forward to a life without Rachael. They'd been soulmates for nearly forty years, and outside his work, he had no world without her.

'What are my chances?' Rachael asked quietly.

'Pretty good,' Jamieson replied with a half-smile. 'It's not the best cancer to have, if there is such a thing, but it's not the worst either. Our treatments are improving by the day. There's a lot of research being done in this area.'

Bowker clutched Rachael's hand, knowing there was a long, hard road ahead.

CHAPTER 14

'Interested in cricket?' Holmes asked D'Angelo as their unmarked police car pulled out from Spencer Street headquarters. 'The first test starts this morning.'

D'Angelo shook his head. 'Not really, Darren. Football's my game.'

Holmes smiled. 'Who do you barrack for? Bloody Carlton, I bet. Lygon Street is called little Italy, isn't it? Plus the Silvagni dynasty and all that.'

'Not Aussie Rules. *Football*. The Beautiful Game. I'm a member of Melbourne Victory, and I follow Napoli in the Italian Premier League. They won the championship earlier this year. Did you know that?'

Holmes shook his head. 'That's soccer, mate. Not football. I see the highlights on the news sometimes. They show the goals.' He chuckled. 'That's if there *are* any. It's about all that's worth watching, except for the comedy act when a player hits the deck like he's been shot after he's knocked down by the wind from a bloke running past.'

D'Angelo wasn't sure whether Holmes was baiting him or just indulging in good-natured banter. 'It's called football in every country except here and the States.' He shrugged. 'But I suppose at least in Aussie Rules, the ball does touch a player's foot.

In gridiron, you're lucky to see one or two kicks per game.'

Holmes waited till he'd slipped by a slowing tram before he responded. 'We've earnt the right to call our game football, mate. The first set of rules to be drawn up for any team sport was for Australian Rules *Football*. I've looked it up – 1859. First sign of rules for Association Football, or *soccer*, wasn't till 1863 at the earliest.'

'Suit yourself,' D'Angelo replied as he looked out his window at the crowds milling at Southern Cross Station. 'I call my game football. You call yours the same. Who cares? A lot of people follow both. If I had to pick an AFL team, I'd probably *would* pick Carlton. Blue strip, just like Napoli and Melbourne Victory.'

'AFL players wear jumpers or guernseys, not a strip,' Holmes shot back.

D'Angelo shook his head. 'They wear similar colours, then. Happy with that?'

Holmes didn't reply as he continued along Spencer Street. It was midmorning, and the traffic was light. The plan was to have a late lunch at Rochester in northern Victoria and arrive at Conargo by midafternoon, hoping to find their suspect's campsite with plenty of daylight to spare. Motel accommodation had been booked in Echuca for the way home, with Bernard Laidler safely locked in the local police cells if he failed to explain the fate of the woman he'd transported away from the Ballan servo.

'Why do you follow Napoli?' Holmes asked as he waited to do a right-hand turn into Dudley Street.

'That's where my grandparents come from. Family tradition, I suppose.'

'That's Naples, isn't it?'

'Yeah. But to everyone in Italy, it's Napoli. Just like Rome is Roma.'

Holmes made the turn onto Dudley Street. 'Isn't Naples prime mafia country?'

'Big areas of the Napoli region are still run by organised crime, that is true. But they're called Camorra. The mafia operates further south in Calabria and Sicily, mainly.'

Holmes looked across at his makeshift partner. 'Any of your rellies involved in that?'

'Most probably back a few generations,' D'Angelo replied. 'Certainly, they would have cooperated. If not, they wouldn't have survived, and I wouldn't be here today.' He chuckled and looked out his window at the castled façade of Witches in Britches, a well-known themed restaurant.

'And now you're a cop?' Holmes said, deadpan. 'Poacher turned gamekeeper.'

D'Angelo was visibly taken aback. 'I've never been a poacher, Darren, and neither have my parents. They came to Australia as children.'

'Wasn't implying you were, mate,' Holmes replied. 'Just an old saying that seemed funny to me, but obviously not to you. Sorry for any offence,' he added insincerely.

D'Angelo knew Holmes didn't like him and suspected this stemmed from his close working relationship with Kirsten Larsen. Deep down, he wished that Holmes really *did* have something to be jealous about. But one thing was for sure – he didn't plan to sit in the passenger seat for the next three hours and cop pot shot after pot shot from his senior colleague. 'How about we whack on the radio and listen to the cricket for a while?' he said as he reached down and pushed the 'on' button.

* * *

Rochester was situated on the Campaspe River around one hundred and eighty kilometres north of Melbourne and twenty-seven kilometres south of the former Murray River port of Echuca. The town had a population of around three thousand people and serviced the agricultural areas surrounding it, the main industry being dairying. The detectives reached Rochester as the test cricketers adjourned for lunch in Brisbane. Within the town limits, the Northern Highway morphed into Moore Street, with D'Angelo spotting a bakery just short of the main drag. The temperature had risen significantly since departing Melbourne, and the day the detectives found in Rochester was as close to perfect as anyone could wish. The sky was pale blue with just wisps of clouds high above them. A light zephyr barely moved the fronds on the tall palms in the lawned area beside the bakery, where pop-up sprays provided a gentle shower for a quartet of noisy magpies. If only Bowker had allowed him to bring Kirsten, then the day would've been complete, Holmes thought. Instead, he had bloody Marco D'Angelo, with whom he shared nothing in common except the work they did. And lusting after Kirsten Larsen.

'What do you feel like?' Holmes asked as they scanned the bakery's offerings. 'Not sure they serve spaghetti,' he added with a smile that D'Angelo wasn't sure how to take.

'Focaccias look nice,' D'Angelo replied, determined not to let Holmes's smart-arse comments deter him from one of his favourite foods.

'Might join you with one of those,' Holmes said. 'It's my shout, so go your hardest.' He smiled. 'Actually, it's *Vicpol's* shout, to be more accurate, so go even harder.'

As they sat at a table overlooking the gardens outside, awaiting their meal, Holmes asked, 'So how do you like working with Kirsten?' with all the nonchalance he could muster.

D'Angelo expected Kirsten's name to be raised at some point on this trip but did his best to respond as if it was off-the-cuff. 'She's great to work with. Smart and has a good detective's instinct. Bit different to the last bloke I was partnered with.'

'Better-looking too, don't you reckon?' Holmes asked, attempting to paint D'Angelo into a corner.

'Absolutely,' D'Angelo replied. He smiled. 'But then again, she's your better half, so I'd be a fool to answer any differently, wouldn't I?'

'Don't feel guilty about saying she's easy on the eye, Marco. You wouldn't be a man if you didn't find her attractive.'

D'Angelo wasn't sure where this was heading but was determined to play a dead bat. 'She's a work colleague, mate. I judge her on her police skills, like any other officer I've been teamed up with. Kirsten being a woman is no different. If she worked somewhere else and I met her at a barbecue, I might run an eye over her. But at work, that is a no-go area.' He stared Holmes in the eye. 'You know how that goes, Darren, I'm sure.'

Holmes looked away, aware D'Angelo had taken away the high moral ground. He decided to change the subject but still scout around where his concerns lay. 'You got anyone special in your life? A little lady hidden away somewhere?'

'Was engaged once. But it was more to satisfy my parents than from any great romantic attraction. She was nice enough – Italian girl, daughter of one of Dad's mates. But she didn't make my heart flutter, if you know what I mean.' *Not like Kirsten does*, he wanted to add, but kept his counsel and flipped the discussion one-eighty degrees. 'Someone said you were married once. Church ceremony, big wedding breakfast, the whole box and dice.'

Holmes stared out the window. 'Yeah, I was. And in the early years, Cassie did cause my heart to flutter.' He shrugged. 'But time wearies everything, I s'pose. We had a son and a daughter, good jobs, but bugger-all else in the end.'

'So where'd you meet Kirsten?' D'Angelo asked, even though he knew the answer.

'Benalla. She was a junior detective at the local station when Greg and I investigated a murder up there. Instant attraction, I guess.' Holmes smiled. 'Not only my boyish good looks, but my ability to make her laugh.'

D'Angelo remained po-faced. 'You and Kirsten worked on the case together?'

'Sort of,' Holmes said, finding himself replying defensively. 'Greg and I did the main inquiries, and Kirsten was the local rep on the team.'

D'Angelo smiled and nodded as their focaccias arrived. 'How old are your kids?' he asked as they attacked their meal.

'Son's twenty-two, daughter just turned twenty.'

'Your daughter's the same age as my youngest sister. From the time puberty hit, she's given Dad all sorts of angst. Hung around with some deadbeat skinhead for a couple of years. Now she's being squired around by some sleazebag who'd have to be in his mid-thirties at the youngest. Dunno which is worse. I know the old man is having kittens.' D'Angelo looked at Holmes. 'Kids, eh?'

Holmes didn't answer. Was he getting touchy, or was D'Angelo rattling his chain?

* * *

It was another two hours before the detectives were parked outside the Conargo Hotel. Their progress had been slowed by a truck roll-over near Echuca and by roadworks north of the river a few kilometres short of Deniliquin. Consequently, the hours left in the day to locate and interview Bernard Laidler had been squeezed, although the time of year, combined with the sunny day, left more than sufficient daylight, provided his campsite wasn't totally secluded.

The local pub was located on Conargo Road, the Billabong Creek a hundred metres to its rear. Although the temperature was well short of the summer maximums, the inside of the hotel was still cool by comparison. While Holmes knew the historic watering hole had been rebuilt after a recent fire, the interior still surprised him. Bush pubs were normally rambling, bespoke affairs, with wood-panelled walls covered in memorabilia, photos, or junk that only the locals knew the significance of. Floors were usually well-worn, windows small to keep out heat. Public areas often had a ceiling fan, a welcome addition made possible with the coming of electricity. But in this incarnation of the 1853 Conargo Hotel, things were much different. A brick feature wall framed long windows; clean plaster finishes on other walls gave the interior a light and airy feel. A long pinewood bar, featuring highlighted vertical panelling, stretched from the public bar area into the lounge next door. Unfortunately, due to the fire, there was minimal memorabilia. The little pub would need to start again, to create its own history, a job many times more difficult with an ever-dwindling population, and with it, the disappearance of most of its sporting teams.

The hotel was quiet when the detectives entered. Three local men sat at the end of the bar attacking pots of beer, most likely the drivers of farm vehicles parked outside. At a table in the corner, an elderly couple sipped mixed drinks, a motorhome under a tree across the road being their probable mode of transport. A middle-aged woman with dark hair and a weathered face approached on the other side of the bar, smiling as she waited for a drink order from her new customers. Holmes opted for a Diet Coke,

D'Angelo a lemon squash. Holmes dragged out his identification with his credit card and quietly introduced himself. The barmaid seemed taken aback, especially when she saw the officers hailed from Victoria.

'You blokes are a long way from home,' she said as she retrieved two frosty glasses from a fridge. 'Must be here on business if you're showing me your ID.'

'Trying to track down a missing person. A bloke whose wife is worried sick about him,' Holmes replied, fudging the truth. 'The last place he'd been seen was in Echuca, but one of his mates we spoke to down there said he was coming up here fishing.' Holmes shrugged. 'We'd already driven from Melbourne to the border, so we thought a few more miles wouldn't hurt if it meant we could confirm he was alive and well.'

'What's the bloke's name?' the barmaid asked as she finished pouring the Diet Coke. She passed the drink to Holmes. 'Might know him. This pub's the only watering hole for miles.'

'Bernard Laidler,' Holmes replied. 'Name ring a bell?' He took a sip from his glass.

The barmaid handed a lemon squash to D'Angelo. 'That'd probably be Bernie.' She nodded. 'Yeah. He and his mate come in here for a beer and to stock up on stubbies. Usually stop for a counter tea one night on each trip. They're up here a lot. I'm surprised Bernie's missus wouldn't have known that.' She shrugged. 'Perhaps he spins her a yarn about where he really heads off to.' She smiled knowingly. 'Then again, we get plenty of people through here who don't want to be found.'

D'Angelo wiped a dribble of squash from his chin with the back of his hand. 'Any idea where he camps?'

The answer came from further along the bar. 'They drive through my place to get up to where the Yanco empties into the

Billabong Creek,' said a rotund, bald, weather-beaten man who'd obviously been listening. 'They come up pretty often and go to the same place each time. All I ask is that they shut the gates, but on their way home they normally drop me in a few yellowbellies if they've had some luck, or a couple of ducks they've shot. Nice fellas, as far as I can tell.' He grinned. 'In spite of being Victorians.'

Holmes didn't react. 'What are they driving?'

'Toyota Landcruiser,' the local replied. 'Got a canvas cover on the back.'

Holmes nodded, confirming in his own mind they had the right bloke. 'Can you give us directions to where they camp?' He removed a pencil and notebook from his pocket and slid them further down the bar. 'A rough map would be handy, mate.'

The local scribbled on the blank page Holmes had presented. 'Pretty easy to find, actually. Hardest bit is locating the bridge on my place that gets you over the Billabong and onto this sort of island where the two creeks come together. Follow the main track across the paddock and you should see it. Bernie and his mate normally camp in a bit of bush beside the Yanco, fifty yards or so up from where the creeks meet.'

With the notebook returned to his pocket, Holmes thanked the farmer and the barmaid for their help, skolled his drink and led D'Angelo out into the sunshine.

'That missing person stuff sounds like bullshit to me, Dianne,' the local said as he stared through the window and watched the detectives return to their vehicle.

'Me too, Ripper,' the barmaid replied. 'Two senior Victorian detectives in suits checking on the whereabouts of a bloke because his wife is worried?' She shook her head. 'They must think us country people came down in the last shower.'

CHAPTER 15

Larsen sat at her desk with little of great urgency on her plate. With her homicide squad partner away with her partner in life, and the pair not due back until the following evening, she couldn't help but smile to herself. How she'd love to be a fly on the wall as the two males with an intense dislike for each other struggled to find enough in common to carry a conversation for more than five minutes, let alone a car trip of more than ten hours. That would provide a challenge way beyond them both.

Her reverie was broken by the chirp of the fixed-line phone on her desk. The call was about to break her case wide open.

'Detective Constable Larsen,' she said casually, half expecting a crank call.

'It's Sam Anderson from Car City. From the yard where the security guard was attacked the other night.'

'Yes, Mr Anderson, I know who you are. What can I do for you?'

'I've just received something in the mail that has me totally confused. I'm not sure it has anything to do with the case you're investigating, but I thought I should let you know.'

'Any extra information can't hurt,' Larsen replied unenthusiastically, expecting the useless trivia that most cases threw up. 'What have you got?'

'An invoice from Transurban. You know, the company that owns the City Link tollway. The invoice is for tolls incurred by a car registered to my business, one for sale in our yard. A 2019 grey Hyundai Kona. It hasn't been on the road for a good six weeks. Obviously, I checked if the vehicle was still in the yard, and it was. The engine and chassis numbers match up, so it's the right car. But here's the thing, Detective – it has different number plates attached, front and rear.'

Larsen smiled and leaned back in her chair. She knew this was the break they had been waiting for.

'Are you still there, Detective?' Anderson asked, misinterpreting Larsen's silence.

'Oh, I'm here alright, Mr Anderson,' Larsen replied, her smile morphing into a wide grin. 'Can you give me the rego number presently on the vehicle?'

Anderson recited the details. Larsen jotted them down and read them back for confirmation. 'What date did the car pass through the toll point?' she asked.

Anderson took a moment to respond, and Larsen heard him shuffling papers. 'A day after the guard was attacked. Surely it's not worth the risk of stealing plates just to avoid paying tolls.'

'The plates were stolen to disguise another car of the same make and model, I would suggest, Mr Anderson. Someone is likely driving around in a stolen car and doesn't want to be picked up by police or number plate recognition cameras. It's a simple solution if everything goes to plan. Just swap plates with a clean car.' Larsen paused for a moment. 'But they'd have to be pretty stupid to go through a tolling station.' She chuckled to herself. 'Unless they thought they were being super clever by never having to pay the bill.'

'So you think maybe the security guard disturbed them

exchanging number plates that night?' Anderson asked, suddenly catching on.

'It's as good a theory as any. The crim checks the listings online, searching for a car identical to the hot one he's driving, then heads out and knocks off the plates. With a bit of luck, the swap to the car in the yard isn't noticed, or the vehicle isn't sold for a while. The stolen car has been laundered, if you like.'

'If our plates have been put on a stolen car, how does it help you catch who killed the guard? You're just adding theft of a motor vehicle to their charge sheet without having an idea who you're looking for.'

'It gives us somewhere to start. I can trace the rego numbers back to the real owner of the other vehicle. That's where the likely string of events began.'

'Do you want me to remove the plates from the car in the yard?' Anderson asked.

'Touch nothing,' Larsen shot back quickly. 'I'll send out a forensic team to do that, and to dust for prints on the car. Plus they'll print you and your son for purposes of elimination. In the meantime, don't let anyone go near that vehicle.'

'What if someone is interested in buying it? A sale is a sale. Business hasn't been great of late.'

'I don't like repeating myself, Mr Anderson,' Larsen responded with annoyance. 'No one goes near that car until after my team has finished their work. Sale or no sale. Besides, it is currently missing its genuine number plates. And if you mention fitting trade plates, I'll really lose my cool.'

Larsen hung up, debating whether to contact D'Angelo with the latest news. In the end, she decided against complicating his mission with Holmes. Some preliminary research needed to be done first, anyway.

Her first point of call was to ring Transurban requesting they email the photo capturing the vehicle as it passed through the toll point. Next, she consulted the stolen motor vehicle database and was surprised when the registration details didn't come up. Something didn't seem right. She then logged into the VicRoads registration database and located the vehicle. As she suspected, the car was the same make, model and colour as the sedan now carrying its plates in Anderson's yard at Car City. A 2019 grey Hyundai Kona. Its owner was listed as Katrina Anne Cassidy from Stawell in the state's west. She opened Google Maps on her phone and requested the distance from Melbourne to the country town. Two hundred and thirty-four kilometres. A touch over three hours by car. She glanced at the current time displayed in the top corner of the screen. It was way too late to head off today. In fact, the more she thought about it, the more fruitless a drive it could likely turn out to be. She rang the station at Stawell and requested officers make a visit to the registered address in the hope of locating the owner and finding the whereabouts of her car.

As she finished her call, Bowker walked into the office carrying a coffee in his right hand. He looked pale and washed out. 'Heard from Sherlock?' he asked as he pulled out a chair and sat beside her, placing his drink on the desk.

Larsen angled her seat to face him. 'Not yet.' She looked at her watch. 'Haven't been up there that long, I suspect.'

Bowker nodded. 'Yeah. You're probably right. My whole sense of time is out of whack at the moment.'

'I'm not surprised. How's Rachael?'

'Not good. We've just come from the haematologist. She has an aggressive blood cancer.'

Larsen wasn't sure what to say. She placed her hand on Bowker's knee. 'I'm so sorry, Greg.' She paused for a second, as she noticed moisture forming in her boss's eyes. 'Where is she now?'

'Home. Our daughter is there.' He picked up his coffee and took a sip. 'I just needed a few minutes of fresh air.'

Larsen withdrew her hand. 'Modern medicine does wonderful things. Miraculous things, sometimes. Did they say how they were going to treat her?'

Bowker nodded. 'Yeah. Chemo. Bone marrow transplant, if it gets to that.' He leaned back in his chair and took another gulp of his drink, eager to change the topic. 'Has anything happened in here that I should know about?'

'We might finally have a breakthrough in the Car City case,' Larsen replied, happier to be on more comfortable ground. 'Transurban tolled the rego for a car that hasn't moved from the Car City yard for weeks and now carries a different set of plates.'

Bowker's detective brain clicked in. 'Someone has switched plates to disguise another vehicle, most likely stolen.'

Larsen nodded. 'Yeah. I've run the plates, and they belong to a car of the same make, model and colour. No report of it being stolen, though.'

Bowker raised his eyebrows. 'Must be an old heap then. Not worth reporting as missing.'

Larsen shook her head. 'Just the opposite. Virtually brand new. It's registered to a woman in Stawell. I've contacted the station up there and asked them to check out an address I gave them. See if they can locate the owner and suss out what the story is. If she lived in Melbourne, I'd go see her myself, but I don't want to drive halfway across the state just to find she's away somewhere.'

'No phone?' Bowker asked, taking another sip.

'None listed. Not surprising. Like most people nowadays, she probably uses a mobile. A Stawell officer visiting the address is quicker than me ringing every provider trying to track down a number. There's no guarantee she doesn't have a pre-paid SIM, anyway.'

'Bloody mobile phones,' Bowker growled. 'In some ways, they help us track people, but in others they take away that element of surprise we had in the old days when communication between dirtbags wasn't so easy. Have you put out an APB on the vehicle quoting the new plates?'

'That was my next job,' Larsen replied, before turning in her chair when her computer announced the arrival of a new email. She opened the Transurban communication then downloaded and printed a photograph of the grey Hyundai passing through the toll gate. She perused the picture then handed it to Bowker.

'There's our car, Greg. Looks like a dent near the headlight on the driver's side. Might make it easier to identify if the plates get switched again.'

Bowker looked at the photo then handed it back. 'Well done. Finally, you've got a decent lead in your investigation. With an ounce of luck up at Conargo, Sherlock and Marco might knock our case on the head as well. Good day all round.' He paused as Rachael's situation flooded his mind. 'For policing, anyway.'

CHAPTER 16

Holmes and D'Angelo quickly found the dirt road entrance they were looking for, and following the most established tracks across the paddocks led them to the private crossing of the Billabong Creek. As the farmer had described, they were now on an island, the two creeks and their confluence forming three sides and a dry washaway gully closing the loop. The large paddock that was formed was sown down with barley. As D'Angelo closed the gate at the island end of the bridge, he stopped abruptly. The sound of a shotgun echoed along the creek. Two shots, then another two.

'Somebody firing a shotty not far away,' D'Angelo said as he climbed back into the car.

'I heard,' Holmes replied. 'Four shots. Not enough time between to reload, so it's either two guns or an auto. Probably our mates knocking down a duck or two. Or trying, anyway.' He thought for a moment. 'Now we know they have guns out and about, I think we need to be a bit more careful here, Marco. I don't fancy getting my head blown off if we bowl in unannounced.'

'You'll get no argument from me,' D'Angelo replied quickly. 'So, what's the plan?'

'We split up. Both of us shouldn't walk into their camp together, that's for sure. If Laidler did kill the girl at Pykes Creek

Reservoir, there's no guarantee he wouldn't put a couple of shots into us if he thought we were onto him. And the mate who's with him… who knows?'

'How do we work it?'

'You jump out here and follow the creek through the scrub. I'll drive slowly around the edge of the crop until I see the camp then pull up close so there are no surprises and wait to give you time to get into position. I'll get out of the vehicle and act lost if they spot me. Then I'll casually wander into the camp, looking as unthreatening as possible.'

D'Angelo wasn't totally convinced. 'Are you sure you want to do that?'

Holmes shrugged. 'No. But what are the alternatives?'

D'Angelo opened his door. 'Still don't like it.'

Holmes glanced across at his colleague. 'Make sure your weapon is loaded. If they look like shooting me, then drop the bastards.'

'Having the shotguns out certainly complicates things,' D'Angelo replied. 'I'd imagined we'd just drop in on them for a friendly chat.'

'Me too.' Holmes inhaled audibly. 'Look, I'm probably overreacting. Laidler has no reason to believe anyone would be searching for him, but it's better to have some sort of plan than none at all.'

'Should we call for backup?'

'Backup from where, Marco?' Holmes shot back with annoyance. 'Echuca is two hours away. We can't call the New South Wales coppers, otherwise we have to explain why we're carrying out an operation on their turf. Besides, it would take us all day to brief them on what's going on and why we're here. It'll be dark way before then.'

D'Angelo shrugged. 'You're the boss.'
Holmes nodded but didn't reply.

* * *

D'Angelo was a city boy, born and bred. He had no interest in the Australian bush or any aspect of rural life in general. To him, *Geelong* was the back of Bourke. Making his way through the scrub along the creek didn't come as naturally to him as it would for a Mallee boy like Holmes. He was twice startled by a kangaroo jumping to its feet from the shade and bounding away into the bush. Even a hawk circling overhead made him nervous. A two-metre tiger snake blocking his way gave him serious cause to consider abandoning the cover of the trees and risk being spotted on the perimeter of the crop. His next thought was to deploy his service weapon and shred the reptile. It wasn't the fact that snakes were protected that changed his mind, but the need to avoid warning Laidler and his mate. D'Angelo eventually took the sensible option and circumnavigated the obstacle that gave no indication of ever surrendering its position. His pulse rate slowed, despite approaching more dangerous and unpredictable creatures somewhere in the bush ahead.

The odd honeyeater worked the flowers in the surrounding scrub, and a flock of noisy cockatoos settled in the trees across the creek as D'Angelo spotted the camp thirty metres ahead. A weeping eucalypt gave him the cover he needed. He squatted behind its trunk, the vee in its lower branches providing an ideal platform for his weapon. An army of ants marched in a tight line up and down the tree trunk beside his face, totally indifferent to the events of a world of no concern to them.

Holmes drove slowly around the perimeter of the crop, flanked on his left by scrubby trees adjoining the creek. He occasionally caught sight of D'Angelo angling his way through the bush. When he saw D'Angelo reach where the two creeks met, he knew they were within fifty metres of the campsite. Through the scrub ahead, he picked out Laidler's Landcruiser in a small clearing. Fifteen or twenty metres further along, a makeshift toilet had been constructed from sheets of old corrugated iron. Holmes stopped the car and climbed out. He placed his hands on his hips and turned slowly in a circle, feigning being unsure of his location. When he estimated D'Angelo had surely taken up a position out of sight and within firing range of the camp, he decided it was time to speak to Laidler.

Despite the temperature, Bowker slipped on his jacket to hide his service weapon. He strolled into the camp. It was deserted. Three sawn logs formed a triangle around a shallow fire pit, and the grill shelf from an old fridge balanced on rocks, supporting a blackened kettle and frying pan. A nearby plastic tub contained empty stubbies. An esky plugged into a DC outlet on the tray of the Landcruiser contained trays of meat and more beer, as well as two gutted undersized yellowbellies swaddled in cling wrap. The bank of the Yanco Creek was only a few metres away, with a steep drop down to the low water, which glistened in the sunlight. Under the canvas in the back of the Landcruiser was a mattress with two pillows and a grubby doona. Obviously, Laidler and his mate didn't mind sleeping in close proximity. Holmes saw the vehicle's keys in the ignition as he opened the front driver's door and checked the interior. As he reached across to open the glovebox, he felt the shotgun against his spine.

'What the fuck are you up to, mate?' came the voice from behind. 'Now back yourself out slowly and turn around so I can see you.'

Holmes did as requested, keeping his hands high in case his

assailant panicked. Was it Laidler or his mate? Either way, he had to play this cool. 'I'm a police officer,' he said as he turned slowly and saw it was Laidler holding the shotgun, a Browning five-shot automatic like his father owned back in Murrayville.

'Pull the other leg, it plays *Jingle Bells*,' Laidler replied, his gun pointing at Holmes's chest.

Upwind, behind the tree twenty metres away, D'Angelo could hear nothing of the conversation. Down the barrel of his weapon, he could see Laidler with his shotgun barrel against Holmes's chest. It was an easy shot. He moved the barrel slightly to the right. Holmes was an easy shot, too. If he pulled the trigger, things would get messy for him, but ultimately explainable as a shot gone wrong when one partner tried to protect the life of the other. Kirsten would no doubt be distraught, but when things settled down, she'd need a new soulmate, someone from the force who knew the risks and who had put himself in danger to save a comrade.

'My name is Detective Senior Sergeant Darren Holmes of the Victoria Police,' Holmes said nervously. 'I'll show you my ID.'

Laidler thought for a long moment. 'Slowly, okay? But one false move and I'll pull the fuckin' trigger. I've worked too hard to buy all this gear only to have some arsehole turn up and knock it off while I'm down the creek fishing.'

Holmes slowly slipped his ID from his back pocket, opened it and displayed it to Laidler.

Behind the tree, D'Angelo saw Laidler read Holmes's identification then slowly lower the barrel of the Browning. D'Angelo's bead was still on his fellow detective, and if he was to pull the trigger, now was the time.

With Laidler's gun now pointing at the ground, Holmes exhaled loudly and looked straight at the man in front of him. The Pykes Creek Reservoir questioning could wait a few minutes until the situation was more under control. 'Shit, mate. You can't go around threatening people like that. Even if I was knocking off your stuff, is it worth killing someone?'

Laidler feigned a chuckle. 'I wasn't going to kill you. Just scare you.'

'What if the gun had gone off?' Holmes shot back. 'Wouldn't be the first time that's happened when someone points a gun at another person.'

Laidler turned the shotgun on its side. He pulled back a lever designed to eject unfired cartridges. 'Not loaded. See for yourself.' He handed the Browning automatic to Holmes.

With the shotgun now in his partner's control, D'Angelo bent his elbows, raised his weapon skywards and applied the safety. His heart raced as he contemplated the stupidity of what he had given thought to. Not just the stupidity of murder, but the stupidity of believing he'd get away with it, and the *utter* stupidity of assuming he'd somehow end up with Kirsten, a woman who'd shown absolutely no interest in him outside their work. He wiped the sweat from his forehead with the back of his wrist. With still no sign of Laidler's mate Red Dog, he resolved that this wasn't the time to break cover. He was there to protect a colleague, and that's what he'd do.

'What's a Victorian copper doing in New South?' Laidler asked with a hint of trepidation. 'Or more importantly, why are you here in my camp on private property?'

Holmes smiled, happy to string Laidler along. 'Looking for you to have a quick chat. You *are* Bernard Laidler of Murry Road, Preston?'

Laidler frowned. 'That's me,' he said. 'What do you want to chat about?'

Holmes ignored the question. 'Where's your mate Red Dog?'

'You've been talking to Sally, have you?'

'Yeah. She told us where you were, and said you camp up here with some bloke called Red Dog.'

Laidler looked at the ground and kicked at the dust with the toe of his elastic-sided work boot. 'Normally, I do. But this time I snuck up here without telling him. So what's this about?'

Holmes again ignored his question. 'Wanted a bit of time on your own to think?'

Laidler shrugged. 'You could say that, yeah.'

Holmes nodded over his shoulder towards the Landcruiser. 'That your rig?'

'Yeah. Bought it a few years ago, fair and square. What's this all about, Detective?'

'You drive it up and back to Ballarat?'

'Sometimes. Got a mate up there who runs a garage. When he needs parts from Melbourne, I take them up. He pays me for the trip. Cheaper than using a courier. Win-win.'

'On September 16, you stopped in at the Ballan servo for diesel?'

Laidler's face carried an increasingly puzzled look. 'Quite possibly. I sometimes get juice there if I'm running a bit low. Or something to eat on the way home.'

'On the particular day I'm talking about, you gave a young woman a lift.'

Laidler shook his head slowly, as if he was searching his memory but coming up empty. 'I wouldn't think so. I'm not in the habit of picking up hitchhikers.'

'I can assure you that you did, Mr Laidler.' Holmes took his phone from his trouser pocket, manipulating its apps until he had the vision from the servo's CCTV on his screen. He turned the phone so Laidler had a clear view. 'I think that's you, mate. And there's your Toyota. Same rego. So who's the woman?'

'Why the hell would you copy that video? I've done nothing wrong.'

'Who's the woman?'

Laidler took a moment to assemble his thoughts. 'I'd forgotten about her until you showed me the video, alright?'

'But you remember her now?'

Laidler nodded. 'She was desperate for a lift back to the city. She had a blue with her boyfriend, and he dumped her on the side of the freeway beside the servo and told her to find her own way back. I saw her ask a couple of people for a lift with no luck. She was in my ear and pleading for help. I was in a hurry, so I just told her to jump in the Landcruiser and I'd take her as far as the Deer Park Railway Station, where she could catch a suburban train to wherever she lived.' He looked directly at Holmes. 'Look, mate, it was a shit day and I was in a shit mood because I'd missed one of the pickups in Melbourne and left my mate high and dry in Ballarat.'

'Why didn't you drop the woman at the Bacchus Marsh or Melton stations?'

'Like I said, I was in a hurry. Going to those stations meant getting off the freeway and driving into the centre of town. That takes time.'

Holmes's expression didn't change. 'But you had time to stop at Pykes Creek Reservoir a few miles up the road to eat your KFC.'

Laidler's mouth dropped. 'What makes you think I had KFC, or even went to Pykes?' he bumbled out. 'I wouldn't think there'd be CCTV cameras in there.'

'We found a KFC box in the bin with a receipt inside it. Had a date and time stamp. We checked the time on KFC's CCTV, and guess what we found?' Holmes smiled. 'I can show you the vision, if you want.'

'Alright. I bought KFC and ate it in the carpark at Pykes. And I gave the girl a ride back to Deer Park Station. I still don't know why you've come all this way to talk to me about my trip that day. I have absolutely no idea what going on. I've done nothing wrong. Broken no laws. Nothing.'

'Then why are you being so evasive when I asked you a few simple questions?'

'Because I've been stitched up a couple times by some of your mates. Pays to give away nothing, I've found.'

'The woman you gave a lift. Did she give you a name?'

Laidler thought for a minute. 'Ruth, I think she said. Lived near Dandenong somewhere.' He shook his head in exasperation. 'What the hell's all this about, Detective?'

Holmes placed his hands on his hips. 'What this is about, Mr Laidler, is a woman was found murdered at Pykes Creek Reservoir with her face and half her body chewed off by animals. We haven't been able to identify the victim as yet, but her stature and clothes are a pretty good match for the woman you gave a lift to at the Ballan servo. And you being placed at Pykes sort of fits our scenario. Plus, the fact that you've served time for molesting women puts a cherry on top.'

Laidler took two long steps backward, struggling to speak. 'I didn't kill Ruth, okay. The truth is, I *did* take her home. All the way to Keysborough, and she thanked me for the lift, big-time, if you know what I mean. But I don't want any of this to get back to the missus. I'm already hanging by a thread there.'

Holmes cocked his head and smirked. 'So you can give me an address to check on the woman's welfare?'

Laidler pointed towards the creek, where a woman in her thirties wearing wet shorts and tee-shirt topped the bank carrying two dead black ducks by the neck. 'I fished them out, Bernie,' she called before dropping the shot birds on a camp table and wandering over to the two men.

Once he saw her face, Holmes knew he and his partner had made the long trip north for nothing. He whistled to D'Angelo, who broke cover and joined the group. 'This is Detective D'Angelo,' Holmes said as his partner holstered his weapon. 'Marco, this is Bernie Laidler and the lady friend he picked up from the Ballan servo that rainy day.'

D'Angelo wasn't sure what to say. He just nodded.

'Surely there's no need for this to go further, Detective?' Laidler asked without the slightest hint of smugness, keen that his partner in Northcote not know the details of his latest trip north.

'Nope. No need at all,' Holmes said. 'Treat your lady well and everything will be sweet.'

Laidler nodded, understanding the thinly veiled message.

'One other thing before we go, Bernie,' Holmes said. 'Was anyone else at Pykes while you were there eating your lunch?'

Laidler shook his head. 'No one else would be stupid enough to sit around in that sort of weather.'

Holmes and D'Angelo walked slowly back to their vehicle, the senior officer knowing the Pykes Creek Reservoir murder investigation was effectively back to square one.

CHAPTER 17

It was late afternoon when Kirsten Larsen received Senior Sergeant Creswell's call from Stawell. 'Nobody home at Cassidy's address, Detective. I talked to a neighbour. An elderly woman. I asked if anybody else lived in the house, and she said no, but there was a boyfriend who visited a fair bit and often stayed over. She believed their relationship must have been a bit rocky, since loud arguments often came from their house. I asked around the station, and one of the younger coppers went to school with her here in Stawell. Her recollection is that the girl has big psychological issues. Prone to flying off the handle for no apparent reason and had more boyfriends than you could poke a stick at. She'd be all over a bloke one minute and at war with him five minutes later. Quite a few of the local lads cut their teeth with her, if you know what I mean.'

Larsen jotted notes. 'When was the last time the neighbour saw her?'

'She's a bit vague on that one. She thinks it was about ten days ago but can't be sure. The days all run together, she reckons.'

'Did she have any suggestions about where Cassidy might have gone?'

'I asked her that, but she had no idea. Cassidy was brought up by a grandmother here in Stawell, who died a few years ago.

So obviously we'll get no help there. We're still trying to track down the boyfriend. The neighbour doesn't know his name but thinks he might live on the land. He drives a Toyota one-tonner, and it often has farm stuff on the tray when he comes to visit. We'll keep asking around, and if we have any luck, I'll let you know.'

Larsen thanked Creswell for his assistance and ended the call. This case wasn't giving up its secrets easily. She was confident that being caught switching number plates had been the motive for the Car City attack and that identifying who owned the stolen vehicle would lead to details of a robbery and likely those involved. But without the whereabouts of Katrina Cassidy, the investigation had the potential to again grind to a halt.

*　*　*

Holmes finally obtained decent mobile reception halfway between Conargo and Deniliquin. His call to Bowker was picked up quickly.

'Sherlock. Did you track down Laidler?' Bowker asked, bypassing needless pleasantries.

'Yeah, Greg. We found him,' Holmes replied in a flat tone.

'Have you got him safely locked away in Echuca?'

'He's not our man, mate. The woman he picked up at the Ballan servo is on the river with him.'

'You're joking?'

'No joke, except on us. Apparently they hit it off on the trip back to Melbourne that day, and now they're up on the Yanco playing nooky-nooky.'

'Bloody hell! That means we're back to square shit.'

'Looks that way.'

Bowker feigned a chuckle. 'I s'pose it avoids the sticky situation of arresting a bloke outside our jurisdiction. His lawyer would've had a field day, not to mention the New South Wales coppers.'

'Yeah, that scenario worried me too. If Laidler turned out to be our man, I'd have called in the Deniliquin cops to do the arrest. They'd have been the closest to Laidler's camp. No police station in a place the size of Conargo, of course. We could have expedited him later and things would have been sweet. But that's all moot now. Big long trip for nothing, as it's turned out.'

'Did you get your Conargo Pub sticker?' Bowker replied with a lilt. 'Every hotted-up ute in Australia seems to have one.'

'Nah, and it's too late to grab one now. We're halfway back to Denny. Pity their annual ute muster isn't on. Would've been worth a look, I reckon.'

'You could've done some circle work.'

Holmes chuckled. 'That would've been a sight in this unmarked unit. Good PR, though, if we told them we were coppers.' He paused for a moment before his tone became more serious. 'How's Rachael?'

'About the same, mate. Starts chemo in the morning, and she's not looking forward to it. A cousin of hers went through it, and it made him feel worse, if that's possible.'

'Worth it if it fixes her, though. How'd the cousin fare?'

There was a pause before Bowker replied. 'Died, mate. Unfortunately.'

'Shit, Greg. Sorry I asked.'

'No need to be sorry, Sherlock, you weren't to know. Anyway, the cousin had a different type of cancer. Stage four in his bowel.' There was a short pause before Bowker continued. 'Are you on speakerphone?'

'Yeah, mate.'

'Marco? Can you hear me?'

'Loud and clear, Greg,' D'Angelo replied, nodding, before registering that Bowker couldn't see him.

'Been talking to Kirsten today,' Bowker said. 'Seems you've got a breakthrough in your case out at Car City.'

D'Angelo grinned widely, and not simply because of a potential breakthrough. The thought of cracking his case before the big dogs solved theirs was appealing. 'So what gives?'

'The car dealer received a toll invoice for a car that's sitting in his yard and hasn't been near a road for weeks. When he checked it was still there, he found its plates had been changed, most likely swapped with another vehicle's.'

'Disguising a stolen car?' Holmes suggested.

'Yeah,' Bowker replied.

'So all we need to do is track the replacement plates back to the owner, which should lead us to the theft, and then hopefully to the murder of the security guard,' D'Angelo fired back enthusiastically.

'Unfortunately, things haven't turned out quite so simple, Marco. The car hasn't been reported stolen, even though it's a late-model Hyundai. We've got the name of the owner, a woman in Stawell. Kirsten has the local coppers tracking her down as we speak. She should be able to shed a bit of light on the whereabouts of the car. Something doesn't feel right about the whole thing, though.'

'We're booked to stay in Echuca tonight,' Holmes replied. 'Do you want us to come home via Stawell tomorrow, and Marco can talk to the woman there?'

'It's a fair bit out of your way, mate. Let's wait and see what Stawell comes up with and decide if there's any point making a big detour like that. I'm sure Kirsten will ring you tonight, Sherlock, and she can fill you in on any new developments. See you blokes tomorrow.' Bowker disconnected the call after the travellers had said their goodbyes.

D'Angelo stared out his window at nothing in particular. The thought of Kirsten and Holmes saying their nighty-nights in his presence made his stomach turn. When she rang, he would take a walk outside in the cool air. Luckily for him, that scenario was averted when Holmes suggested a change of plans.

'What about we cancel the motel in Echuca and head home? If we had Laidler to put in the lock-up there, it would be a different matter, but it seems a waste of time to bunk down just for the sake of it. I feel pretty bright-eyed and alert. Having a gun shoved in your back tends to have that effect.'

And having one aimed at your head without knowing it, D'Angelo thought but didn't say. 'Suits me,' he replied instead, relieved he wouldn't have to tiptoe around the subject of Kirsten Larsen for an extra half day. 'Sounds like there's now work to do on the Car City case, so it'd be handy to be back ready to go on that tomorrow morning.'

'Good,' Holmes replied. 'We both get to see Kirsten a bit earlier than we thought, so that can't be bad,' he added with a smirk.

Bit of difference, D'Angelo thought. *You'll slide into bed with her, and I'll show up in the morning and discuss a murder case.* He chose not to risk a reply, not totally sure whether Holmes was baiting him. 'I might see if I can get some shut-eye, mate. Give me a yell when you need a break with the driving.' He closed his eyes and shut down the conversation.

* * *

The following morning, Bowker held Rachael's hand as they entered the Peter MacCallum outpatient clinic to begin her course of chemotherapy. Bowker felt sure her complexion was paler than the days before, when he'd thought it impossible for her to look more anaemic. Today, even the olive skin tones passed down from her mother's Portuguese heritage had disappeared, the fluorescent lights rendering her skin almost translucent. Late yesterday, she had visited her dentist to confirm she carried no oral infections that would run riot when her body's immune system was compromised. Earlier, their daughter Jacinta had taken her for tests to ensure that her liver, kidneys and heart functions were ready to begin treatment. Injecting poisons into his wife's body was an anathema to Bowker, even though he knew this was probably her only realistic chance of survival.

Chemo drugs targeted and killed cancer cells, which were typically fast growing. Unfortunately, many of the body's healthy cells were also fast growing, the most observable being hair cells, which were also attacked during the treatment. The Bowkers had been advised of the side effects and had done their best to prepare physically and mentally. Nausea, vomiting, constipation or diarrhoea, bleeding, bruising, mouth sores – the list seemed endless. Looking down at his wife, now on the bed with her eyes closed, Bowker wished he could exchange places with her, not because he could handle the situation better – he knew he couldn't – but because he'd do anything to spare her from what she was going through.

A fling of the sliding privacy curtain exposed a nurse pushing an IV pole and a trolley carrying various equipment and medications. She took Rachael's wrist and inspected the blood vessels on the surface of her arm. 'I think we'll start with an IV line straight into a vein,' she said without looking up. 'Depending on how the treatment goes, we might need to put a port in under the skin. But that's further down the track, and only if things drag on.'

Within ten minutes, the IV line was in Rachael's arm and deadly poisons were flowing into her bloodstream. Bowker read the label on the IV bag – daunorubicin. Its crimson colour worried him. Was this the Red Devil people spoke about, the chemo drug that caused horrific side effects? He asked the nurse.

'That's doxorubicin. Different drug altogether,' she replied casually.

'But it ends in the same letters. Is it related?'

'The "rubicin" part relates to its red colour, nothing more. It'll still have side effects, but nothing as bad as doxo.' She patted Bowker on the forearm. 'Just try and relax. This is the first step in a long journey. You won't be much help to your wife if you exhaust yourself with anxiety.' She smiled and left the room.

Easy for her to say, Bowker thought. Right now, he saw his world balancing on a knife's edge, yet outside the window, birds continued to sing, the sun continued to shine, and the four million residents of the city went about their daily business, virtually all of them oblivious to the microscopic battles that were beginning within his wife's body.

A patch of red light centred on Rachael's chest, the sun's rays focussing through the liquid lens of an IV bag. Bowker was not a superstitious man, but found himself thinking this was not a good omen.

CHAPTER 18

'That just about sums up where we are at present, Marco,' Larsen said, elbows on the table at Homicide headquarters. 'The good news is that finding the Hyundai probably holds the key to solving Ralston's murder. *Bad* news is we can't even find the owner, let alone the car,' she added with half a smile.

D'Angelo took a sip of his hot coffee. 'Only a matter of time. Now we know the replacement rego Cassidy's car is carrying, it'll be picked up on a camera somewhere. Car thieves tend not to be too bright.' He took a second sip.

'Yeah, I s'pose.' Something was playing on Larsen's mind. 'From the moment Anderson told me about the switched plates, I've assumed Cassidy's car was stolen.' She leaned back and folded her arms. 'But if it hasn't been reported as stolen, there's always the chance the owner still has it and the plates' swap is to cover something she's been up to, or plans to get up to. From what Stawell have been able to ascertain, she's a bit of a loose cannon.'

'Well, if she is up to something, she must have help,' D'Angelo replied. 'There were definitely two people on the Car City CCTV the night the security guard was killed. One might have been Cassidy herself.' He shrugged. 'But who knows? It was dark, and they both wore hoodies.'

Larsen nodded. 'A lot of questions need an answer, that's for sure. The sooner we can track Ms Cassidy down, the sooner we'll know which direction to head.' She began packing up the notes in front of her.

D'Angelo stood. 'Darren tell you what went down in our little escapade up in New South yesterday?'

'Eventually. I'd been in bed for a couple of hours when he arrived home out of the blue. But in the end, I got the full story.'

D'Angelo didn't make eye contact. 'You were a bit sleepy, I guess.'

'Something like that,' Larsen replied, trying to hide a smile. D'Angelo picked it up. He grabbed his jacket from the back of the chair and strode to his desk.

When Larsen's mobile rang with a Stawell Police Station label running across its screen, she called D'Angelo back to the table. 'Stawell,' she whispered as she accepted the call.

'It's Liam Creswell from sunny Stawell, Kirsten. What's the weather like in our state capital?'

'Believe it or not, it's sunny and warm down here too, Liam. I've got my partner Marco D'Angelo beside me at the table. Do you mind if I put you on speaker?'

'Go for it. Morning, Marco.'

'Morning, mate,' D'Angelo replied. 'I hope you've solved things for us?'

Creswell chuckled. 'Not quite, but we've been able to run down a few bits and pieces that might help you folks sort it out.'

'My pen is poised,' Larsen replied.

'I'll email you all the details when we finish the call, but this is what we've got. Most disappointingly, we haven't found Katrina Cassidy, and according to her neighbour, she hasn't been back to her house. We contacted the agent who looks after the property, and they've given us some information that might help track her down. Her next of kin is listed as a sister who lives in Frankston. The address and contact details are in the email. That might give you somewhere to start, anyway.'

'That's a big help. Thanks,' D'Angelo replied.

'We also have Ms Cassidy's banking details, although the real estate agent said she always pays by cash. He said he wished he'd set up a direct debit arrangement for her, because she's well behind in her rent. She's been sent her final warning before the eviction procedures are set in motion. Her bond will pay the arrears, but the property owner will miss out if repairs need to be made.'

'I've heard that happens a lot these days,' Larsen lamented. 'A bad tenant knows they won't get their bond returned, so they stop paying rent leading up to when they plan to leave. In effect, they receive their bond back via nonpaid rent. And in most of these cases, it's not worth the owner pursuing them legally, because they have no saleable assets.' She chuckled. 'Sorry, Liam, that happened at my sister's investment property, so I'm a little bit over it.' She paused for a moment before returning to business. 'Anything else on Katrina Cassidy?'

'We went to her workplace. She's not very popular with either the managers or her fellow workers. I know it's not politically correct, but they described her as *schizo*. Friend one minute, enemy the next. Her employment hangs by a thread, according to the manager on duty. She's already been moved away from roles involving contact with the public. They've apparently lost a few customers when Cassidy has *gone nuts*, as it was described.'

'Sounds like she's very unstable,' D'Angelo suggested. 'It's hard enough to locate a person who acts logically, let alone one who's unpredictable.'

'*Unpredictable* is the very word used by the so-called boyfriend when we finally tracked him down,' Creswell replied. 'He's a farmhand who lives on a property out near Navarre, to the east of Stawell. Clayton McInerny is his name. Bit rough around the edges and keeps company with a few dickheads in Stawell when he comes into town. Been in trouble with the law down in Ararat a few times. Assault, that type of thing.' Creswell paused for breath. 'Anyway, he claims Cassidy isn't really a girlfriend, just someone he drops in on when he needs a little bedroom action.'

'Nice,' D'Angelo grumbled.

'McInerny gave us the same story we got at her work. Cassidy's erratic and unstable. He also used the term *schizo*. He said she could change moods in two seconds. Even during sex, apparently. You'll have to excuse my language here, Kirsten, but McInerny called it the *bronco root*. Happy one moment, trying to buck him off the next.'

'Don't apologise, Liam,' Larsen replied, trying desperately to suppress a smile. 'In this job I've heard a lot worse.'

'McInerny said she could change back just as quickly. Accusing him of rape one minute, wanting more the next.'

'Any chance he knows where she is now?' D'Angelo asked.

'Claims he doesn't,' Creswell replied. 'But I'm not sure I'd trust him to always tell the truth. By the same token, the way he described Ms Cassidy tallies with what others have said.'

Larsen scribbled a note. 'Mobile?'

'Was quoted the same number by her work, real estate agent and McInerny. Pay-as-you-go. Been inactive for months, according to all three. If they needed to contact her, they visited her home. We rang the number, and it was dead. It's in the email.'

'Good stuff,' Larsen replied. 'Anything else?'

'No, that's about it. But if something else comes up, I'll be straight on the phone. I'll email that information down now.'

D'Angelo leaned back in his chair. 'Thanks, mate. You've done well.'

'Yeah, thanks, Liam,' Larsen said as she ended the call. She stood, tugging down the hem of her silky blue top. D'Angelo's eyes never left her tight blue jeans as she returned to her desk.

* * *

Creswell's email arrived five minutes later. It listed Katrina Cassidy's banking details, the contact information for her sister in Melbourne, and material pertinent to Clayton McInerny, her farm worker friend.

D'Angelo raised the receiver on his desk phone as he called across to his partner. 'I'll ring her bank and ask for a printout of any transactions on her cards over the last fortnight. Where she's used them might give us a clue to where she is now.' He frowned. 'Pity we don't have a current mobile phone number so we could check which towers it's been pinging. That would give us an even better clue to her whereabouts. Hell, she might even answer it!'

By the time D'Angelo had been shunted through half a dozen departments at Cassidy's bank to gain access to her records, it was late morning, and the detectives were on their way to Frankston. A simple phone call may have been able to establish whether Cassidy's sister was home, but Larsen in particular was keen not to give prior notice of their intended visit. If Katrina Cassidy had indeed disguised her own car with swapped plates, there was no guarantee she wasn't staying with her sister, or possibly even in cahoots with her. Larsen's detective instincts still told her Cassidy's car had been stolen, but at this point it was important not to become tunnel-visioned – to keep all avenues of the investigation open.

Frankston was a Melbourne suburb, forty-odd kilometres southeast of the CBD. It had long been a destination for holiday makers due to its pristine beaches and proximity to the city. Once a rural town, it was now subsumed within Greater Melbourne, along with fellow former Port Phillip Bay holiday resorts – Rosebud, Rye, Sorrento and Portsea.

'My grandparents went to Frankston on their honeymoon,' Larsen said with a smile.

'Wouldn't go there now,' D'Angelo shot back. 'I've heard it called *Shankston* or *Skankston*.'

'Yeah, by people who don't live there, I bet. By people who wouldn't know the place if they fell over it. Same as they refer to High Point as *Knife Point*, or Brimbank as *Grimbank*, or Brighton as *Whiteton*.'

D'Angelo smirked and raised his eyebrows. 'Or Dandenong as *Dandebong?*'

'Got it. Derogatory names given by smart-arses trying to put down communities where other people live.'

'You'd have to admit that crime figures are pretty high in Frankston, though,' D'Angelo suggested.

'No worse than many other parts of Melbourne,' Larsen fired back. 'They're actually better than where *you* live, Marco.'

D'Angelo shrugged but didn't respond as they followed the Nepean Highway into central Frankston and turned left, as instructed by their GPS. They came to a halt at a stop sign as a scruffy young couple crossed the street in front of them, both with a cigarette in hand.

D'Angelo smirked. 'How do you tell the difference between a Frankston bloke and a Frankston girl?'

Larsen didn't acknowledge the question. D'Angelo was going to tell her anyway. According to Holmes, she enjoyed a laugh. 'The girls have a higher sperm count.' He chuckled. 'Pretty funny, eh?'

Larsen remained po-faced. 'Nope. Totally inappropriate,' she replied. 'And a bit out of character for you.'

D'Angelo didn't reply, instead pondering how he managed to get things so wrong with this woman.

Larsen checked the GPS and pointed ahead. 'I think this is Findlay Street up here on the left.'

A sea breeze freshened as D'Angelo parked the car outside a modest red triple-fronted brick-veneer house set back from a knee-high wrought iron fence. The garden was minimalist, with three mature shrubs close to the house and a dead tree fern beside the concrete steps leading to the front door. Two wheelie bins sat beside the steps, convenience obviously being valued more highly than aesthetics. The grass in the front garden and around a well-established currajong tree on the nature strip was long and unkempt. There was no grey Hyundai in the drive or the garage at the back. In fact, there were no cars on the property at all, full stop.

As D'Angelo and Holmes walked through the open gateway, an elderly man watering the garden outside the old fibro house next door called out. 'Nobody home,' he said, 'so you're wasting your time if you're selling anything. Or preaching anything.'

D'Angelo slid his ID from his back pocket and held it where the neighbour could see. The old man flicked a small plastic lever on his hose fitting. The water slowed to a trickle then stopped. 'If you're looking for Bella, she works at the solicitor's in the main street. Vince mixes paint at Bunnings.'

'Anybody else live here?' D'Angelo asked, pointing a thumb over his shoulder.

'Couple of primary school kids,' the elderly man replied. 'Sienna and Wilbur.'

Larsen nodded. 'Anybody staying over that you've noticed in the last few days?'

The neighbour shook his head. 'None that I've spotted.'

'Haven't noticed a late-model grey Hyundai parked nearby?'

Again, the neighbour shook his head. 'They in trouble or something? Wouldn't have thought them the sort.'

'Absolutely not,' Larsen assured him. 'We're looking for a missing person and thought the Jefferies might be able to give us a clue.'

'Like I said,' the elderly man replied, 'Bella works at the solicitor's in the mall, Vince works at Bunnings. That's where you'll find them.'

Both detectives nodded and returned to their car. Within five minutes, they were in the offices of the only solicitor in the mall. Thirty seconds later, they sat in a conference room with Annabel Jefferies, a filing clerk with the firm. She wore a conservative skirt and top, in keeping with the atmosphere of a legal office, and had her hair tied up in a French roll. She had a plain, friendly face with a pallid complexion and wore simple tan-rimmed glasses. D'Angelo outlined their search for her sister's car and ultimately for the woman herself.

Jefferies seemed genuinely perplexed. 'I have absolutely no idea where she might be, Detective. We don't have much to do with each other these days.' She hesitated before continuing. 'She does have serious mental challenges, but I guess you've gathered that if you've spoken to other people who know her.'

D'Angelo nodded but didn't reply.

'I think there's a bloke she spends a bit of time with,' Jefferies said. 'He might know where she is.'

'Our Stawell colleagues have had a word with him,' Larsen replied. 'Apparently, he doesn't know where she is either.'

'Is there a special place your sister might retreat to if she's under pressure?' D'Angelo asked. 'A bolthole, if you like?'

Jefferies shrugged. 'Not to my knowledge, but who can be sure? She's unpredictable, verging on irrational.'

D'Angelo rubbed the back of his neck. 'Is it possible she could be tied up in something illegal?'

'Anything is possible with Katrina, detective,' Jefferies shot back.

'Do you now hold concerns for her, in light of what we've just told you, Mrs Jefferies?' Larsen asked.

'I always hold those concerns,' Jefferies replied. 'Not that I spend a lot of time worrying about it. I've tried to help her in the past, but I think she's incapable of accepting assistance. Or advice, for that matter.' She hesitated. 'To tell you the truth, when you arrived this morning and asked if I was Katrina's sister, I felt sure you would tell me that she'd taken her own life.' She smiled weakly. 'So news that she's gone missing is an improvement on that.'

* * *

Katrina Cassidy's bank records were on D'Angelo's desk when he and Larsen returned to Spencer Street headquarters. He picked up the two printed and stapled sheets without sitting down. 'Didn't think we'd get these so quickly. Things must be slow in the world of finance.' He scanned their contents. 'No recent withdrawals from her savings account. All Stawell purchases are on her credit card. Last one was at a Stawell servo on the morning of September 16. Eighty-two dollars sixty. Unless she bought a basket-load of overpriced crap, then you'd have to assume she's filled her tank.'

'Then nothing,' Larsen said, reading over his shoulder.

'Worries me, Kirsten,' D'Angelo said, breathing in Larsen's subtle perfume and wishing she would stay there forever.

'Me too, Marco. I can understand her being difficult to find, but not accessing her bank for, what?' She looked at her watch to retrieve the date. 'Eight days? Maybe there's a more worrying reason why she hasn't reported her vehicle stolen.'

D'Angelo rubbed his chin. 'This case is doing my head in. Every time we look like finding an answer, we uncover more questions.'

'Still the same equation, though. Find her and we find the car. Find the car and we find the security guard's killer. I'll give the Stawell petrol station a ring and ask them to check their records for September 16. Let's confirm what she actually bought. If she filled up with fuel, plus purchased items you'd normally grab for a road trip, it might indicate she left the Stawell area that morning.' She walked back to her desk, pulled out the chair and sat down, crossing her long legs. She consulted Google, seeking contact details for the servo.

D'Angelo inhaled deeply to clear his head as he walked to his desk and slumped into his chair. An incoming email caught his eye.

CHAPTER 19

'How's Rachael?' Erin O'Meara from the forensic centre asked by way of introduction amid intermittent coughing.

'I'm assuming that's Erin O'Meara,' Bowker replied, sitting beside his sleeping wife on the colourful striped couch in their sunroom. She looked pale and insipid in her pink towelling dressing gown, the absolute antithesis of her normal vibrant self.

'How'd you guess?' O'Meara replied, hacking up phlegm. Bowker heard her expectorate – he hoped into a tissue or hanky. Knowing the woman as he did, there was a good chance the mucus could have ended up anywhere within a couple of metres of where she was sitting. 'Is Rachael doing okay?' she asked again as her breath returned.

'We just started chemo, Erin. She said she feels shithouse. More shithouse even than before. She's sound asleep beside me here on the couch, thank goodness. She'll need all the strength she can muster to make it through what's in front of us.'

'Well, give her all my best when she wakes up.'

'Will do,' Bowker replied, visualising the chicken-framed, chain-smoking alcoholic sitting at the other end of the phone. Life seemed so unfair at times, he thought. Here was Rachael on death's door, a woman who had never smoked, had always been in peak physical condition, and only drank socially, normally limiting herself to one glass. Erin, on the other hand, was fifteen years older and had staved off the grim reaper for decades despite being a physical basket case who had smoked and drank to excess for most of her life. Bowker wished his forensic colleague no ill-will, but at the same time felt his wife had been cheated. He was thankful for Rachael's healthy lifestyle. If she had strayed down O'Meara's path, he may have lost her decades ago. 'Is this just a social call, or have you busted a case wide open for us?'

'Social and business, Greg. Are you still working the Pykes Reservoir case, or are you on compassionate leave?'

'I'm still working, but there are times I need to be here with Rachael. Sherlock's been doing most of the legwork. What have you got?'

O'Meara coughed for a few seconds, then Bowker heard her blow her nose. 'You familiar with the Car City case? Security guard attacked and died in hospital?'

'I'm across most of it. Marco D'Angelo and Kirsten Larsen are working it. Running into as many dead ends as Sherlock and I are with the Pykes case.'

O'Meara sniffed loudly. 'Apparently some registration plates were swapped in the car yard. Larsen sent them in for fingerprinting. We've just sent the report to D'Angelo.'

'Yeah, I knew about the plates,' Bowker replied. 'Don't keep me in suspense.'

'Fingerprint division ran them against the national database. No match, unfortunately.'

'You rang me for that?' Bowker said in a disappointed tone.

'No, I rang you because I thought you'd be interested to know something else. Most of the prints on those rego plates match the unidentified prints on the stubbies you found at Pykes Creek Reservoir.'

* * *

D'Angelo read the email twice before he relayed the news to Larsen. 'Forensics have matched the prints on the rego plates from Car City.'

Larsen hung up her phone midway through dialling the service station in Stawell. 'Who do they belong to?' she asked quickly.

'They can't tell us that, but the prints matched those lifted from two stubbies found during Greg and Darren's investigation of the murder at Pykes Creek Reservoir.'

Larsen frowned. 'You thinking what I'm thinking?' she replied after a moment.

'That the mystery victim at Pykes is Katrina Cassidy? Absolutely.'

'If that's the case, the four of us have been working the same investigation without knowing it.' Larsen leaned back in her chair and raised her eyebrows. 'Ironic, eh?'

D'Angelo wasn't thinking *ironic*; his feeling was more disappointment. With the Car City case, he had Larsen all to himself – well, during working hours, anyway. Now Bowker and Holmes would become involved, and with Bowker's first priority being the health of his wife, it would principally be Holmes they'd be working with. With that, D'Angelo saw himself relegated to second place, both in seniority and in Larsen's attention.

'Presumably Greg's been told the news,' Larsen said, snapping D'Angelo out of his self-absorption.

'I'd assume so. I suspect we'll hear something soon about combining the investigations. You make that follow-up call to the Stawell servo. If we're going to work with the big dogs, we better have all our bases covered.'

* * *

It was a drowsy Rachael who suggested that her husband meet with his colleagues to analyse the game-changing information Erin O'Meara had delivered. Bowker phoned Holmes, who was re-watching CCTV footage on his laptop, then waited until Jacinta arrived from her nursing shift before making the half-hour journey to his Spencer Street headquarters. Holmes was already present, chatting with his colleagues across a square table in the centre of the room. He and D'Angelo had opened folders in front of them. Bowker smiled. 'Got it sorted?'

'How's Rach?' Larsen asked before the others could respond.

'Pretty crook,' Bowker replied. 'What else can you expect when your body's chock-a-block with poisons? But the anti-nausea drugs help.' He pulled up a chair. 'So, obviously we've all had a chance to digest the news from Forensics. Give me your theories.'

Holmes flashed a glance around the others before leading off. 'I think we're pretty much in agreement, Greg. Our crimes have to be connected. It's stretching coincidence way too far for the same prints to be left at two murder scenes.'

'Agreed,' Bowker replied. 'Let's see if our timelines gel.'

'We know Katrina Cassidy, the owner of the car we've been chasing, bought a tank of petrol, a round of sandwiches, and some lollies at Stawell on September 16,' Larsen replied. 'Despite our best efforts, we haven't been able to locate her, or to place her after that. Her bank accounts haven't been touched, and her sister hasn't heard from her. Next time her name surfaces is as the owner of a car whose rego plates were switched with an identical vehicle's in a car yard where a security guard has been murdered. Marco and I are assuming he disrupted the switching of the plates and lost his life for his trouble.'

'If her plan when she left Stawell was to travel to Melbourne, she would have passed Pykes Creek Reservoir in the same ballpark period the plate switcher's prints were left on the stubbies,' D'Angelo added.

Holmes folded his arms. 'September 16 fits nicely into the coroner's estimation of time of death for our victim at Pykes.'

Bowker ran his fingers through his hair. He looked across the table at D'Angelo and Larsen. 'You guys interviewed the sister in relation to Katrina Cassidy's disappearance, right?' They nodded their agreement. 'Okay, let's get a DNA swab from her and establish whether the body found at Pykes *is* her sister. If that turns out to be the case, then we have a decent starting point. Not knowing the identity of the victim has limited my and Sherlock's progress in this investigation.'

Larsen went to her desk, rang Forensics, and requested a DNA sample be gathered from Annabel Jefferies.

Bowker took a deep breath. 'So, if the body belongs to Cassidy, how did it all go down?'

Holmes shrugged. 'She stopped at Pykes for a break, or maybe lunch, and she's raped and murdered there. Her car is stolen and that ultimately leads to the sequence of events at the car yard.'

Larsen returned and sat down. 'In that scenario, there would need to be at least two perps. One to drive their own car and one to drive away Cassidy's Hyundai.'

'There *were* two intruders at the car yard,' D'Angelo said before hesitating a moment. 'But we need to keep in mind that Cassidy was a loose cannon. Totally unstable and unpredictable, we've been told. She could have easily picked up a passenger who then rolled her and took her vehicle.'

Holmes acknowledged what D'Angelo theorised with a nod. 'Plus, according to Forensics, there was only one type of semen recovered from the victim. Not that this precludes one or more others being present.'

Bowker raised both hands, palms facing out. 'Let's just get the DNA comparison before we go too far down that track. We're probably looking at Monday before that comes through, so how about we all take the weekend off? Help clear the mind.'

'Works for me,' Holmes said with a chuckle. 'Kirsten's brother owns a beach house in Anglesea that he's been on us for months to use. Might be a good time to take up the offer, I reckon.'

'Sounds like a dirty weekend to me,' Bowker retorted quickly with as big a smile as he could muster knowing he and Rachael were a long way off a dirty weekend, if indeed they were destined to have another one.

'I hope so,' Larsen replied.

D'Angelo stared at the tabletop, so jealous he felt his face must have looked green, hoping his colleagues wouldn't ask his agenda for the weekend. He was out of luck.

'What about you, Marco?' Larsen asked. 'Big plans you now don't need to put on hold because of work?'

D'Angelo shrugged sadly. *Nothing like a weekend rolling in the hay by the beach with you*, he wanted to say but instead explained his sad reality. 'Probably watch the nephew play Under Twelve soccer tomorrow morning. Sunday lunch with Mum and Dad will pull me up. Excitement plus, eh?'

'I'll swap,' Bowker said quietly. 'Rachael and I have chemo both days.'

* * *

Bowker hurried home to relieve his daughter, checked on his sleeping wife, then rang Erin O'Meara.

'Question, Erin. We can now read DNA off fingerprints, right?'

O'Meara stifled a cough. 'Yes and no, Greg. If you have prints that have lots of sweaty ridges, then you can retrieve good DNA. But the risk of contamination is enormous, as you can imagine.' She hacked up mucus. Bowker heard her spit. 'I think what you're really asking me is whether we were able to gather DNA from the number plates or the stubbies.'

Bowker laughed. 'Read me like a book.'

O'Meara blew her nose. 'Unfortunately, the stubbies and the plates had been exposed to shitty weather for quite a few days. And to tell you the truth, mate, our techs were pretty proud of themselves for salvaging *any* decent prints.'

'But they obtained DNA from the UDL can in the same bin.'

'The can being sheltered by other items would be my explanation.'

Bowker thanked O'Meara and signed off before readying himself for Rachael's daily induction chemo. As he understood it, induction was the first phase of treatment and the most harrowing. It would be short and intensive, usually lasting around a week. The aim was to clear the blood of leukemia cells and reduce their number in the bone marrow. Consolidation chemo targeting any remaining leukaemia would come after Rachael had recovered from the induction stage. This new phase would be less full-on with days of recovery in between. Bowker felt physically ill merely contemplating what his wife would need to endure.

At the chemo clinic, Rachael was again connected to an intravenous cocktail of poisons. Bowker wondered what a time traveller from the next century would think of this treatment. He suspected they would have a similar reaction to the one modern humans do when they read about the brutal medical procedures of centuries gone by. Bowker was reminded of an episode of *Star Trek* where its central characters were swept back in time to a late twentieth-century hospital. *My God, Jim!* the time-travelling doctor exclaimed to his captain. *They're cutting people open!*

Although of limited help to Rachael in her present predicament, the science of genomics was evolving at an exponential rate, where individual cancers were being treated with specific programs gleaned from an expanding database of successful therapies. Bowker had researched all the emerging treatments, but time was running out for his wife, and despite all the encouraging new discoveries, chemo still promised her the best chance of survival. Right now, his eyes never left his wife's face, except for the occasional glance at the ever-flattening IV bag, as drip by red drip the fluid designed to kill in order to save invaded her body. He saw some parallels with the tasks he performed on a daily basis – chasing down and eliminating threats to personal and societal safety. But *his* methods were more selective; he didn't kill the innocent in his quest to banish the guilty. But mankind hadn't always been so discerning, he knew. Mass killings to ensure one's enemies were destroyed had occurred on numerous occasions throughout history.

Bowker's philosophical musing was interrupted by a nurse pulling back the sliding curtain. 'I think we're done,' he said, examining the IV bag. 'I'll take some blood for analysis, and that will be it for the day.' He smiled at Bowker. 'Bring some work with you tomorrow, or something to read. Sitting there watching grass grow doesn't help anyone.'

There is no way Rachael's playing second fiddle to anything while she's here, Bowker thought but didn't say. He just smiled weakly.

CHAPTER 20

Bowker stared out his kitchen window as rain tumbled down in his backyard. Water pooled on the lawn, and the fronds on his tree ferns bowed under the weight of a million droplets. Leaden clouds hung low over the city, with a forecast of worse to come over the next few days, an outlook he hoped wouldn't be mirrored in the report due from their haematologist in the afternoon. Bowker decided he needed to clear his work slate first.

'Erin O'Meara rang this morning, Sherlock,' Bowker announced into his mobile. 'We now have a name for our victim at Pykes.'

'Katrina Cassidy from Stawell?' Holmes asked quickly.

'Yeah, the sister's DNA proves that beyond doubt. So I think the scenario we sketched out last week is probably accurate. She stops or is stopped at Pykes, is raped and killed by a person or persons unknown, who then take her car and subsequently roll the security guard at Car City.'

'Do you want to start asking a few questions up at Stawell?'

'Eventually we'll need to go up there, but right now her Hyundai holds the key to this whole thing. As Kirsten said about the Car City case, find the car and we find our killer. I think we can now expand that to the Pykes murder as well.'

'Not as easy as it sounds, though, is it, Greg? They've been chasing that vehicle for a week with no success.'

'But they've mainly been checking toll points and CCTV in Melbourne because its plates turned up in Ringwood. I think their assumption that the car was probably in Melbourne was understandable, given the limited information they had to go on. Now we know Cassidy was from Stawell and was killed at Pykes, I reckon we need to go back a few steps further.'

'Back along the highway, you mean?'

'Yeah. Back to the start of her journey. Kirsten has already established that Cassidy bought fuel in Stawell on the sixteenth. I think we can assume she met her fate at Pykes on the same day. We need to track her car from the moment she left that servo in Stawell. Track it to Pykes, and then try and pick it up again when it left there without her. Maybe we get lucky, and it stopped somewhere like a McDonald's or another servo. Establishing the time that happened may lead us to the use of a credit card that we can track.'

'The victim's cards haven't been used since Stawell,' Holmes shot back. 'Marco got a printout from her bank.'

'I'm not talking about Cassidy's cards, mate. If they did stop somewhere, maybe the perp used his own card.'

'Big ask if you're suggesting we work our way down the Western Highway from bloody Stawell. It's not like the metropolitan area, where there's a camera on every corner. Finding CCTV will be a job in itself.'

'Yeah, I know it won't be easy. But there'll be some on the freeway. In Ararat or Beaufort, there's bound to be the odd camera outside a business that might pick up traffic passing by on the highway. And there should be plenty in Ballarat.'

'She most likely wouldn't have driven into Ballarat if she followed the bypass like most through traffic does,' Holmes surmised. 'And there's no businesses along that part of the highway.'

'Yeah, you're right. But I'm sure we passed under Western Highway speed cameras between Ballarat and Pykes. That would give us a time, and we could calculate whether she detoured into Ballarat.'

Holmes hesitated a moment, as if not totally convinced. 'Okay. I'll get on the blower and suss out where there might be other cameras along the highway.'

'Get onto VicRoads, they've got traffic cameras everywhere,' Bowker replied. 'If the car came into Melbourne via the Ring Road, it should've been picked up there.'

'Unfortunately, VicRoads footage isn't recorded, Greg,' Holmes replied. 'It's for live traffic flow information only.'

'I'll bet my left knacker that some of their cameras do record. Especially at intersections and entry or exit ramps to establish who's at fault if there's a bingle.'

'I'll see what I can find out. I'll get Kirsten and Marco to give me a hand, if that's alright with you.'

'Fine, providing a new case doesn't land at our feet.' Bowker replied. 'It's hard to justify four detectives working the one investigation if something new comes up.'

Well, not really four detectives, Holmes thought. It was more like three and a half, given his boss's need to be with his wife.

* * *

The weather had worsened and streetlights were on when Bowker drove to the hospital in the early afternoon. Rain hammered on the carpark's asphalt surface, creating fleeting miniature fountains as droplets bounced off the ground in a random pattern. Bowker did his best to position his raincoat above his wife as she gingerly made her way to the shelter of the building's portico roof. A trail of droplets followed the couple as they trudged the polished lino-floored corridor towards the treatment cubicles. A dark-haired, overweight nurse with tattooed flowers on her forearms smiled widely, pulling back a curtain. With the heavy overcast sky outside, there was little natural light within the room as Rachael slowly mounted the bed for her daily dose of poison.

'Your latest bloods are back,' the nurse announced as she pushed in a trolley and turned on the florescent lights.

'I hope they're better than the last ones,' Rachael said weakly, shielding her eyes with her right hand.

Bowker watched the nurse's face, praying for a look that might precede positive news. She gave nothing away as she lifted a clipboard from the trolley. 'Good news is your organs are coping well with what we're doing to them.'

'And the cancer?' Bowker blurted out.

'Still too many abnormal leucoblasts. Red blood cells and platelets are down.' The nurse looked up and forced a smile. 'But it's still early days, and we can give a blood transfusion if we need to.' She shrugged. 'Talk to Alana. She's the haematologist.'

Bowker felt increasingly depressed. 'When will Rach's bone marrow be tested?'

'In the next fortnight, probably. If the chemo hasn't knocked over the leukemia cells there, then she might need more rounds, or maybe a marrow transplant to replace the faulty stuff that she's making herself.'

Bowker dropped his head. This wasn't going well.

* * *

D'Angelo and Larsen travelled to Stawell to collect vision from the service station where Katrina Cassidy had refuelled before beginning her fateful trip south. As a courtesy, they visited the Stawell police station first, a double-storey red-and-cream brick building in Patrick Street. Dwarfing it to the right was the arched nineteenth-century magistrates court. If ever one needed a stark comparison of the wealth and architectural values of two eras, this was where it could be found. Side by side.

A female constable showed the detectives through to an office where Senior Sergeant Liam Creswell was at work at his desk. Creswell looked up when the trio entered the room, his eyes drawn immediately to Larsen in her tight leather skirt, high-heeled boots and pink short-sleeved top. *Bloody hell*, he thought, *I'm in the wrong part of the force.* The young policewoman retreated to her post as Creswell climbed to his feet and shook hands with his Homicide colleagues.

'You're a long way from home,' Creswell said as he nodded towards two chairs. 'Come up to see if you have better luck finding Katrina Cassidy than us local yokels?' he added with a smile.

D'Angelo didn't rise to the bait. 'Unfortunately, we *have* found her,' he replied as he sat.

Creswell dropped back into his chair. 'That doesn't sound promising.'

'DNA has identified her as the victim in a separate case Homicide has been working on,' D'Angelo continued, unconsciously folding his arms across his chest.

'Shit,' Creswell muttered. 'So are you up here chasing anyone in particular?'

Larsen shook her head. 'Not at this stage, Liam. The evidence seems to point to her being killed at Pykes Creek Reservoir the other side of Ballarat.'

Creswell nodded. 'Near Ballan. The freeway dips down over a bridge.'

'Yeah. There's a little picnic reserve there,' Larsen replied. 'At this stage, we have no idea whether she was followed there.' She shrugged. 'Perhaps from up here. Or whether she was taken there, or pulled in there herself and was randomly attacked.'

'Our boss wants us to track her car after she left the servo down on the highway,' D'Angelo explained. 'Work out the timings to calculate whether she might have stopped anywhere, or perhaps met someone on the way. My opinion is that we're chasing shadows doing that. If we were in Melbourne, we'd have a chance, but not out in the middle of the countryside where we might get a glimpse of her car every now and then. That's if we're lucky. Let's face it, she could stop somewhere for a few minutes, and we wouldn't have a clue.'

'If she was killed the same day she left Stawell, then we know someone else must have driven her car when it left Pykes,' Larsen explained. 'If we can follow it from there, it'll take us a lot closer to solving the murder.'

Creswell leaned back in his swivel chair, hands folded behind his head, exposing patches of sweat on the underarms of his shirt. 'Anything we can do up here?'

'Keep an ear to the ground is the main thing,' D'Angelo replied. 'Once her death becomes public, theories will race around Stawell like crazy. You never know what useful information you might pick up. We'll stay in touch.' He stood.

'Where to now?' Creswell asked.

'Down to the servo to view their CCTV footage,' D'Angelo replied as he returned his chair to its original location.

Larsen followed his lead. 'Then to Ararat, then Beaufort, then Ballarat. Chasing wild geese all the way back to Melbourne.'

Creswell stood up and again shook their hands. 'You never know your luck in a big city. Or a small town,' he said with a smile.

* * *

The highway service station was less than five minutes away. Larsen copied the CCTV footage of Cassidy filling her tank and ultimately turning onto the highway towards Melbourne. Cassidy wore a pink fiddler's cap with jeans and a brown polar fleece top over a high-necked blouse. Larsen allowed the vision to run for several minutes after Cassidy had driven out to check if any vehicles followed. None did. And except for two B-double trucks, there was no traffic within eyeshot of her leaving the servo. This was the easy part. But it was a start. They had established the Hyundai's time of departure, allowing them to calculate when the car would likely reach Ararat, Beaufort, Ballarat and ultimately Pykes Creek Reservoir.

The city of Ararat sat thirty-one kilometres to the southeast of Stawell on the other side of the Great Dividing Range, which by this easterly point was little more than a chain of hills. The most promising CCTV cameras the detectives could identify belonged to a car dealership in High Street, which carried the Western Highway traffic through the town. The officers quickly identified the Hyundai passing the business at precisely the time they had predicted.

Their next stop was Beaufort, a small community of around fifteen hundred people that promoted itself as the last highway town before Melbourne. Its main street was part of the Western Highway and was dotted on either side by takeaways and other eating establishments. The town had long been earmarked for bypass, but progress had been stymied by its surrounding geography. To its south was a lake and to the north the Pyrenees Ranges. Plans had lain in the 'too hard' basket for decades.

For the detectives, a quick scope of the main street failed to identify a CCTV camera that would be of help in tracking

Cassidy's Hyundai, but it did convince them that the town was as good a place as any to stop for lunch. Given the pleasant sunny weather, a table in a small park beside an historic rotunda seemed the ideal place to consume their takeaway sandwiches. Birds flittered and chirped in the leafy trees above, and the whole town had a relaxed feel about it. So far during the day, conversation between D'Angelo and Larsen had centred on police business, particularly matters surrounding the Cassidy case. Watching Larsen raise the hem of her tight skirt to manoeuvre into the narrow space between the wooden seat and picnic table sent D'Angelo's mind wandering onto more personal matters.

'What's your verdict on the brother's beach house?' he asked casually.

'Better than I thought it might be. The big bro is a bit slapdash, and I half expected a cheap fibro shack in one of the town's back streets.' She smiled. 'But he's done himself proud this time. Big open-plan kitchen and living area with an open fire on the second floor overlooking Bass Strait. The master bedroom is on the same level, with a massive window framing the ocean. Darren and I couldn't believe the luxury. You just wake and look out over the water without needing to get out of bed.' She smiled again as she began unwrapping her sandwich.

The mental picture rendered D'Angelo speechless. He busied himself opening the folded top of his iced coffee.

'If you're interested, I could see if the brother could swing you a weekend down there,' Larsen continued matter-of-factly. 'Maybe when it's quiet and there's no big demand from his family or paying customers.'

'Would you be interested in coming too?' D'Angelo blurted out before his mind had a chance to censor his words.

Larsen chuckled. 'Darren and I would only cramp your style,

Marco. It's the sort of place more suited to a couple. Get naked in front of the fire with a nice wine. A man like yourself must know a lady somewhere you'd enjoy a few days with by the beach.'

Yeah, she's sitting across the table from me, he thought but dared not say. Did Kirsten not pick up his thinly veiled proposition, or was she saving him the embarrassment of confirming she preferred the affections of a man old enough to be her father? 'Work keeps me pretty busy,' was the best he could come up with as he took a gulp from his milk carton. A thin rivulet dribbled down the front of his shirt. He flipped it off with the brush of his hand. 'Don't socialise enough to meet someone who's not part of my extended family.'

'I'll give you some advice for free. Kick up your heels while you're still young, mate.'

Before D'Angelo could muster a reply, Larsen's mobile rang. It was Holmes seeking information relating to Cassidy's departure from Stawell.

'We've got her leaving the servo at eleven sixteen,' Larsen advised. 'Hold on while I put you on speaker.'

'You in the car?' Holmes asked.

'Nope. In a park in Beaufort eating lunch.'

'Any CCTV you can use in the town?'

'Not that we can see, Darren,' D'Angelo replied. 'There are cameras at the service station, but they point the wrong way. We did pick up the Hyundai passing through Ararat, though. Showed up in the background of a car dealer's CCTV. Same dent near the driver's side headlight.'

'And it was right on the time we predicted, so she was keeping to the speed limits,' Larsen added. 'If she kept that up and didn't stop, we reckon she would have been in Ballarat around midday and at Pykes Creek Reservoir by around twelve thirty.'

'This is where things become a bit confusing,' Holmes replied after a short pause. 'I've been scanning traffic footage on fast forward since seven this morning. Finally spotted the car on the highway at Melton at time stamp five twenty-two in the afternoon of September 16. If you're right about her being due to reach Pykes around twelve thirty, then that leaves nearly five hours before the car is picked up again just thirty-one kilometres further along.'

Larsen gave D'Angelo a puzzled look then returned to the call. 'So what are our possible scenarios, Darren? Cassidy detoured somewhere and arrived at Pykes much later than we're speculating? Or, heaven forbid, she was held there for hours before she was killed and her car stolen?'

D'Angelo leaned in closer to the phone. 'Or maybe we're dealing with an extremely callous bastard or bastards who have killed her, hidden the body and just hung around while they plotted their next move. It was a shitty day. Probably didn't think anyone else would turn up in that weather.'

'It's a theory, Marco,' Holmes replied. 'But usually, once a murder is committed, those involved flee the scene ASAP.'

'So where to now?' Larsen asked.

'It would be great if you guys could confirm when she cleared Ballarat,' Holmes replied. 'If she was on time there, I can't see her detouring between then and Pykes. I'll check any cameras closer to Melbourne. At least I've got a ballpark time the car should appear if it didn't turn off somewhere soon after Melton. If it did, that'll mean legwork in the town itself. But for the moment, I'll assume the car was heading for the city.'

CHAPTER 21

The next morning dawned icy cold with an Antarctic southerly blasting an overcast city. Holmes, D'Angelo and Larsen met with Bowker at headquarters prior to his daily sojourn with his wife for her next round of chemo. Rachael sat at her husband's desk, head propped on hands, doing her best to control the nausea that passed over her in waves. In terms of policing, yesterday afternoon had produced positive results contrary to the pessimism expressed in Holmes's phone call with D'Angelo and Larsen. Holmes had lucked in, locating two highway cameras between Melton and the start of the Western Ring Road. The first captured the grey Hyundai at the time predicted it should appear based on when it passed through Melton. The second hadn't caught the car at all, despite Holmes allowing the footage to run for an hour after its anticipated arrival time. There was no doubt in his mind that the vehicle had left the highway short of the Ring Road, but he could find no vision to confirm this had happened, or where that diversion had taken place.

In another slice of good fortune, D'Angelo and Larsen had spotted the Hyundai on CCTV footage from a business on the outskirts of Ballarat, again at a time consistent with their calculations. Now, with all the traffic information arranged in sequence, there was little doubt that Cassidy had driven to this point without stopping for any significant amount of time, if indeed she had stopped at all. In keeping with Holmes's practice, a still photograph of each sighting was produced with the car in centre frame. By the time each detective had explained their discoveries from the day before, six glossy pictures lay strewn on the table between then.

'The long and the short of it,' Bowker said, 'is that we have vision of the car leaving Stawell and making its way through Ballarat, almost certainly without stopping anywhere. It then disappears off our radar until it's picked up on camera in Melton around four hours after it was due through there, assuming of course that the victim was travelling directly to Melbourne. It's then captured again closer to Melbourne twenty-five minutes later before disappearing altogether.' He shrugged. 'So what happened during those four hours we can't account for?'

D'Angelo leaned back in his chair, folding his arms across his chest. 'Obviously she was murdered at Pykes and her car was stolen.' He screwed up his face. 'But accounting for the missing time has got us all stumped, I presume. If she pulls into Pykes at around twelve thirty as we predict, does she eat her sandwiches, then drop off for a snooze for a few hours before getting murdered? That would seem more likely than her being killed soon after she arrives, with the perpetrator, or perpetrators, hanging around for a few hours before shooting through with her car.'

Before the discussion moved further, Rachael slowly arrived at the table and placed her hand on Bowker's shoulder. 'I think we might need to go, Greg,' she said quietly.

Bowker looked at his watch then stood up abruptly. 'Shit! Time has got away. Sorry, Rach.'

Rachael stared at the photos strewn on the table. 'Is this the car Greg said you've been tracking?'

'Yeah, Rach,' Holmes replied, devastated by how sick his friend looked.

Rachael pointed at two photos. 'Were those taken at the same place?'

Holmes shook his head. 'No. One is at Melton. The other is closer to Melbourne.' He frowned. 'Why do you ask?'

Rachael had helped her husband solve a couple of cases before with her keen eye and sharp intellect. But today she was so ill that Holmes didn't expect anything helpful.

'There's a motorbike behind the car in both pictures. It's a bit harder to see in one of them because there's a four-wheel drive hiding half it. I reckon it's the same bike. Big handlebars, a high backrest and a bright red fuel tank.'

Holmes picked up both photos and perused them closely. A single rider was astride what looked like a modified Harley Davidson. 'Can't see the plates, but I reckon you're right, Rachael. It seems a bit too coincidental that the same bike is right behind the Hyundai when there's so many k's between where each photo was taken.'

Rachael looked at Bowker. 'We really need to go, Greg. I hate being late.' She smiled weakly. 'Even to my daily poisoning.'

'Our priority is now that bike,' Bowker said as he turned and took Rachael's hand. 'See if you can find vision of it prior to Melton.'

The others remained seated, staring at the photos. They were all thinking the same thing. How could four seasoned detectives have missed what a woman wracked with cancer had spotted?

* * *

There was little alternative but for D'Angelo and Larsen to return to Ballarat and re-examine the private CCTV vision that had captured the Cassidy vehicle on its trek towards Pykes Creek Reservoir. The weather on the way up was diabolical. As they climbed into the central highlands, misty rain gave way to sleet, with light snow falling near the Gordon exit. The weather hadn't improved as they reached the outskirts of Ballarat, and it was with a sense of relief that they entered the business housing the CCTV vision they'd come to review. The manager was most obliging, inviting them to stay as long as they needed and providing each with a mug of warm coffee. Larsen took charge of the keyboard and quickly found the appropriate camera and time of day. She reversed the vision to an hour before Cassidy's car was captured, just in case the bike had come through earlier and stopped for significant time somewhere between this point and Melton. Using fast forward, they were back to Cassidy's car within a few minutes, but without any sign of the motorcycle.

Larsen tucked a lock of blond hair behind her ear. 'How far do we have to go forward, you reckon?'

D'Angelo thought for a moment, then consulted his notebook. 'The Hyundai with the bike behind was caught at five twenty-two passing through Melton. That's around seventy kilometres from here. If we allow for the Harley pushing the speed limit a little, that's forty minutes minimum. So the latest the bike could have come through here is four forty-two. Let's run the video on fast forward from when Cassidy's car came past. If we don't spot the bike by four forty-two, then I reckon we can assume it didn't come this way and must have joined the highway further along.'

As the traffic on the vision flew past at high speed, Larsen paused the footage from time to time and rewound it to examine a passing motorcycle. None matched the one they were looking for. Few words were exchanged, but as the time stamp flashed by 4 p.m., they were close to admitting their trip to Ballarat was a waste of time.

'Stop it there,' D'Angelo suddenly exclaimed.

Larsen had seen the same thing. She paused the footage then reversed it slowly until the motorcycle was centre screen in the background.

'That's it, I reckon,' D'Angelo said as he leaned in closer to the screen. 'High backrest and handlebars. Red fuel tank.'

'But it's carrying a pillion passenger. In Darren's photos, there was just a rider.' She thought for a moment and faced D'Angelo. 'Passenger drove the Hyundai later on, do you reckon?'

D'Angelo shrugged. 'Would fit, I guess.' He pointed towards the time stamp on the screen. 'But the bike passed here at four oh-two. If it stopped at Pykes, it should have been at around four thirty. We calculated that Katrina Cassidy most likely arrived there at twelve thirty. If she was killed by the riders of this bike, what was she doing at Pykes for four hours?'

'*Was* she at Pykes for four hours?' Larsen replied. 'We have her passing here, then vision of her car is picked up as it passes through Melton. Her body was found at Pykes, but there's no proof she spent the afternoon there. She might've gone into Ballan or one of the little places along the way, like Gordon, Wallace or Bungaree. Maybe she has a friend on a property in the area.'

D'Angelo rubbed his chin. 'Let the footage run a few frames. Maybe we'll get a look at the licence plate.'

Larsen did as asked, then leaned in so her head was close to D'Angelo's. She didn't notice, but *he* did. 'The bike's a long way from the camera, Marco. But I think I can just make out a couple of letters. An O, and perhaps an S.'

D'Angelo leaned back to avoid his primal instincts taking over, tricking him into a move on Larsen that he knew would destroy their relationship. 'Copy the vision, and we'll give it to the tech people to look at,' he said. 'Sometimes they can convert shit into strawberry jam.'

* * *

A day later, the strawberry jam arrived in D'Angelo's inbox. Using sophisticated imaging equipment, the boffins in VicPol's technical laboratory were able to discern three characters from the motorcycle's registration plate. Checking these against the make and year of the bike enabled them to identify the owner. D'Angelo scribbled the details on a small pad before beckoning Larsen and walking across to Holmes, who was elbow-deep in paperwork.

'The techs identified the Harley we suspect might have a connection to the Cassidy case,' D'Angelo said. He glanced at his notepad. 'Domonic John Standish, Unit 2, 48 Vipont Street, Footscray.'

Holmes leaned back in his chair, his face carrying a wide grin. 'Thank you, Rachael Bowker.' His grin collapsed a little. 'That's if there's a connection with the Hyundai, of course.'

'Has Standish got form?' Larsen asked.

'Haven't checked yet,' D'Angelo replied. 'Just got the email and thought I'd pass it on.'

Holmes turned back to his desk and logged into the LEAP database. 'Name and address again, Marco?'

D'Angelo again consulted his notebook and recited them slowly. After a clacking of keys, Holmes shook his head. 'Nothing.' He rubbed his chin. 'No real surprise, though. The prints left on the number plates at Car City and on the stubbies at Pykes weren't on file, so if Standish is our man, it's logical he wouldn't be on LEAP.'

'You want Kirsten and me to whip out to Footscray and see if we can find him?' D'Angelo asked.

Holmes screwed up his face before replying. 'Greg will be in after Rachael's chemo, so maybe he and I should do it. It'll be good for him to get his mind onto something else.' He looked at D'Angelo. 'Besides, it's our case now we know that Cassidy was the victim at Pykes.'

D'Angelo wasn't happy to hand over all their hard work but tried to hide his annoyance. 'The security guard killing is tied up in this too, and that's *our* case.'

Holmes held up his palms. 'I know, Marco. I know. But if there are two teams working the same patch, we're going to finish up stepping on each other, or even worse, fucking up the other's case.'

D'Angelo was far from convinced and wasn't about to give up their investigation without a fight. 'We've done a shitload of work on this, Darren. How about you work the Pykes end, and we'll work Car City?' He looked at Larsen. 'What do you think, Kirsten?'

Larsen immediately felt wedged. She knew Holmes was probably right, but wasn't keen to abandon D'Angelo, particularly given her personal relationship with Darren. She tried to steer a middle course. 'I don't want to give up our case either, but Darren has a point. The two cases have converged. There's a very strong possibility the same person or persons are responsible for both killings. One of our teams needs to step back.'

D'Angelo was having none of it. 'We're the best team to handle this case. Greg's not even at work half the time, and when he is, his mind is miles away.'

Bowker strode into the room behind them. 'So I can't walk and chew gum at the same time? Is that what you're saying, Detective Sergeant?'

D'Angelo turned, red-faced. 'I'm not saying you can't handle it, Greg. I'm just thinking you have more important things on your mind than chasing crooks. We're more than capable of doing that and leaving you to support your wife.'

Bowker placed his hands on his hips. 'I'll be more support to Rachael if I'm not sitting on my arse at home becoming increasingly depressed and pessimistic.' He inhaled deeply. 'Any update on the motorcycle?'

'Thanks to the lab techs, we have the owner of the bike,' D'Angelo said. 'Domonic John Standish.'

'How do we want to handle this?' Holmes asked, hoping Bowker would agree with his earlier plan. 'In practical terms, the whole box and dice revolves around the Pykes Creek Reservoir murder investigation.'

'Yeah. But I'd like to keep Marco and Kirsten involved,' Bowker replied. 'They have all the facts around the Car City attack down pat. Plus, if things go horribly bad with Rachael, we'll need more than just you working the case, Sherlock.'

Holmes shrugged. 'Your call, Greg.'

Bowker consulted his watch. 'Eleven twenty-two. Sherlock and I might take a run out to Footscray and see if we can find Mr Standish.' He looked at D'Angelo and Larsen. 'You guys check the internet and social media sites and see if his name comes up anywhere. Ring Stawell police and see whether they've come across him, especially in relation to Katrina Cassidy. If there's history there, I'd like to know about it.'

D'Angelo jotted down notes, disappointed that he wasn't part of an interview with Standish, but happy to still be working the case.

CHAPTER 22

Vipont Street was an attractive short thoroughfare divided at intervals with shady trees down its centre. Most of its original housing had been replaced with blocks of flats, many of them slaves to utility rather than aesthetics. In recent times, the whole suburb of Footscray had been gentrified, its industrial and multicultural flavour gradually being pushed further west. Gone were the greengrocers and specialty food shops that used to line the streets, replaced by ubiquitous coffee shops and other venues popular with the hipster crowd. Vipont Street itself was close to the site of the original punt service over the Maribyrnong River that in the early nineteenth century served as the only connection between Melbourne and Geelong. Within easy walking distance was the Pioneer Hotel, established in the 1840s as the Punt Hotel, serving drovers bringing sheep and cattle to Melbourne from the rich western district squatters' runs. The discovery of gold in the 1850s was a boon for the pub, as tens of thousands of fortune-seekers passed its doors. By the early twentieth century, the rich region of streams, lakes, swamps and lagoons that had served the Indigenous people so well was subsumed by industry, housing and the sprawling Flemington Racecourse on the eastern side of the river.

'Shit day,' Holmes said as misty rain driven by a cold southerly slapped against the windscreen.

'Yeah, mate.' Bowker wiped condensation off his side window. 'Pull in here. That's Number 48. That brown brick building. The one that looks like a big square dog's turd.'

Holmes chuckled as he slapped on a blinker, did a U-turn and pulled into the kerb. 'Unit 2 is downstairs on the left, by the looks of it.'

'Hopefully someone's home,' Bowker replied as he unsnapped his seatbelt and climbed from the car. 'On a weekday, that's got to be doubtful, though.'

Bowker and Holmes jogged quickly to the door of Standish's unit and into the shelter of a small portico supported by two faux-Greek columns. Holmes rang the doorbell several times before banging heavily on the wooden door. There was no answer, nor any sounds of life coming from inside. Bowker walked back into the rain and down a path between the building and the aluminium side fence. He knocked on the sliding glass door at the back, but again there was no answer. He cupped his hands on the glass and peered inside. There were no signs of movement, and all the lights were off. By the time he had satisfied himself that no one was home, Holmes had arrived in the backyard and stood beside a folding clothesline. He held out the end of a dripping tradie's polo shirt so his colleague could read the printing on its back. *West Footscray Tyres.*

Once back in the car and out of the rain, Bowker googled West Footscray Tyres on his phone and found the business was less than a ten-minute drive away. Whether Standish was an employee there or had acquired the polo shirt through other means would hopefully be answered by a visit to the business.

At the listed address, they found a prefabricated concrete building with a small showroom and office behind a large glass window to the right of two opened roller doors, each revealing vehicles on hoists.

'Yeah, Dom works here,' a middle-aged woman sitting behind an office desk stacked with papers replied with a puzzled look. 'What's he done?'

'Nothing, as far as we know,' Bowker replied. 'We're just following up a missing persons report. All routine.'

The woman looked at a clock on the wall featuring a hammer and a screwdriver as hands. 'He's probably on smoko at the moment. Do you want me to go get him?'

Bowker shook his head. He'd like to confront Standish cold. 'You just point us in the right direction, and we'll find him.'

The woman shrugged. 'Suit yourself. The boys will be in the lunchroom, but I think you'll find Dom in the loading bay out the back sucking on a ciggie. The boss is a reformed smoker and can't handle the smell around the workshop.' She pointed with multicoloured nails over her shoulder. 'Through that door behind me and follow the corridor to the back.'

The detectives nodded their thanks.

'The loading bay is under cover, so you won't get your lovely suits wet,' she added with a smirk that threatened to crack the heavy makeup on her face.

The loading bay was a concrete ramp at the back of the building that was accessed via a heavy steel gate off a laneway to the rear. Domonic Standish stood leaning against a brick wall under the cover of the metal roof. He stared out into the sodden yard stacked with bald tyres. Standing around one eighty centimetres, or a little under six foot in the old, he wore a full beard, with dark hair pulled back in a ponytail under a battered Nike cap. He was wiry in stature, his face weathered, his eyes green and penetrating. A small scar ran horizontally above his left eyebrow. The fingers on his right hand were badly nicotine-stained, and tattoos ran up both arms. The rain had become heavier and the wind chillier. The day had darkened under leaden skies, Standish's cigarette glowing orange when he took a long draw. He didn't look around when he heard the door behind him open.

'Fuckin' shit of a day,' he said absently.

'Amen to that,' Holmes replied, glad the wind was whipping away the stench of cigarette smoke.

Standish turned quickly at the sound of the unfamiliar voice. 'The office is at the other end of the building, mate,' he said as he dropped his cigarette butt into a tin bucket at his feet.

'Been to the office, and the lady said we'd find you out here.' Bowker flashed his ID as he introduced himself and his partner. 'You Domonic John Standish of Vipont Street?'

Standish looked puzzled. 'Yeah.' His eyes darted between the detectives. 'What's this about?'

'Probably nothing.' Bowker took a notebook from his pocket, flicking through it to a particular page. 'You own a motorcycle with this rego?' he asked as he showed Standish his scribble.

Standish took a moment before answering. 'Yeah. Have I been nabbed speeding or something?'

Bowker shook his head. 'Nothing like that. Now, two Thursdays ago on September 16, your bike was captured on CCTV travelling the Western Highway between Ballarat and the beginning of the Ring Road. Were you the rider of the motorcycle on that day?'

Standish frowned. 'Captured on camera? I thought you said I wasn't doing anything wrong?'

'Were you riding the motorcycle?' Bowker persisted.

Standish nodded. 'Yeah, it was me. I had the day off, so me and my girlfriend went to Ballarat to check out some Harley parts advertised on Gumtree. Turned out to be a heap of shit.'

'What's your girlfriend's name?' Holmes asked quickly, removing a notebook and pencil from the inside pocket of his suit coat.

Standish turned up both palms in a *'What's all this about?'* gesture. 'Narnia. Narnia Simms. Why?'

'She live with you?' Holmes asked.

'Not yet. She lives with a couple of chicks in Maribyrnong.'

Holmes had his pen poised. 'Address?'

'Sixty-five River Street,' Standish replied, shaking his head in the frustration of not knowing where this was all heading.

'So you and Narnia travelled to Ballarat to look at motorbike parts, then returned to Melbourne later in the day?' Bowker asked.

Standish was becoming increasingly agitated. 'Yeah, that's right. If the parts had've been any good, I would've borrowed a mate's ute to pick them up the next weekend.'

'What's a bit confusing to us, Domonic,' Bowker countered, 'is that we have vision of your bike passing through Melton with just one rider. No pillion passenger.'

Standish pulled a cigarette box from his pocket, removed the last Benson & Hedges it contained and dropped the empty box into the tin below him. He retrieved a lighter from his other pocket and lit the ciggie. Bowker was sure he was stalling, hoping to invent a plausible response.

'Mr Standish?' Bowker prompted.

Standish feigned a weak smile and pointed at his temple. 'If I had another brain, it would be lonely,' he replied with a contrived chuckle. 'I forgot that we pulled off the highway and rode into Ballan for a beer. Narnia started flirting with some local dropkick, so I pissed off and left her to it. I was bloody angry. She got home on the train that night.' He feigned another smile. 'I've dumped her. There's plenty more fish in the sea.'

Bowker and Holmes were thinking the same thing. If Standish and Simms did go into Ballan, that would explain the missing time before the motorcycle was spotted again at Melton further towards Melbourne. But they both found it hard to believe that Standish wouldn't have immediately remembered that he'd dumped his girlfriend in Ballan when first asked about his trip on the sixteenth. Surely it wasn't such an everyday occurrence that it had skipped his mind. Neither detective saw this as the moment to challenge his explanation. It was time to let him talk and see how consistently his story would unfold.

'So you left the young lady in Ballan and rejoined the highway on the Melbourne side of the town?' Bowker asked.

'Yep,' Standish replied as he took a long draw on his cigarette and blew the smoke out into the rain.

'Did you go into the Pykes Creek Reservoir reserve for any reason?' Holmes added.

Standish pulled a puzzled face. 'Pykes? Why would I? Especially on a day like that.' He paused for a moment. 'Can you please tell me what all this is about?'

'We're trying to track a car,' Bowker replied. 'You may be our last hope,' he added, attempting to relax Standish a little. Except for his delay in informing them about the detour to Ballan, everything else he'd explained could be fitted within the parameters of what they knew of his bike's movements that day. 'There's a young woman gone missing,' Bowker went on. 'She was driving a grey late-model Hyundai. The reason we're talking with you is that we have that car captured on CCTV with your bike in the background. Twice, in fact.'

'And those cameras were quite a few kilometres apart,' Holmes added.

Standish shrugged. 'I have no idea what car you're talking about.

Once I left Ballan, I just went with the traffic flow. I was shitty with Narnia and kept debating whether I should go back and pick her up.' He thought for a moment. 'From memory, I didn't try to pass any lines of traffic and certainly didn't weave in and out of lanes like I sometimes do if I'm in a hurry.'

Bowker thought his story unlikely, but had himself passed cars in other lanes many times only to see them reappear beside him further down the road as lines of traffic ebbed and flowed. 'Where'd you leave the Ring Road?' he asked.

Standish shook his head. 'I didn't take the Ring Road.'

'You weren't captured on any CCTV on Ballarat Road,' Holmes replied. 'I've looked.'

'That's because I dropped in on my brother in Caroline Springs,' Standish shot back.

Holmes smiled. 'There was nothing on the cameras at the Christies Road intersection where people turn to go into Caroline Springs.'

'I left the highway at the interchange just past McDonald's on the other side of the road. I followed Neale Road into the back of Caroline Springs, where my brother lives in Clarke Road.'

'What number in Clarke Road?' Holmes asked.

Standish hesitated for a moment. 'Twenty-six, I think it is. Shitty old farmhouse on the edge of town, but the rent's cheap.'

Bowker took a step backwards as the wind whipped rain further under the flat roof. 'How long were you at your brother's?'

Standish shrugged. 'We grabbed a pizza and played a few games on his Xbox. Wouldn't have got home till after ten, I reckon. Maybe even eleven.' He folded his arms. 'Why is that important? I thought you were tracking a car.'

'Was the car still in front of you when you turned off at Neale Road?' Holmes asked.

Standish was becoming frustrated. 'I don't know what fuckin' car you're on about. I believe you when you say it was pictured near my bike, but I have absolutely no memory of seeing it. A wanker in a blue Subaru WRX, yes, but not a grey Hyundai.' He took a last suck on his cigarette and dropped it in the bucket with a hundred other butts. He looked at a battered watch on his left wrist. 'Look, smoko's over and the boss will come looking for me. He's as tight as a fish's arsehole, and he'll dock my pay if I go over on a break.' He glanced from Holmes to Bowker. 'So if there's nothing else, I'll leave you to find your own way out.' He turned and disappeared through the door behind.

Bowker watched him leave and was about to address Holmes when he saw that his partner was half a step ahead, already donning a rubber glove and retrieving the Benson & Hedges box and the still partly alight cigarette from the tin bucket.

* * *

'What do you reckon?' Holmes asked as he pulled his door closed and did his best to flick droplets of water off his clothes.

'What he says is plausible. It all fits with what we know,' Bowker replied, snapping home his seatbelt.

'Too well, if you ask me, Greg. And would you have spat the dummy with Rachael if she was flirting with another bloke? Not that she ever would, of course. But you know what I mean.'

'Yeah, but people are different, Sherlock. Hell, you know that. Some blokes belt women, while most see it as the gutless act it is.' Bowker shrugged. 'Maybe he did abandon her in Ballan, knowing she could always get a train home.'

Holmes started the car and pulled away from the kerb. 'Do we interview the girlfriend and the brother?'

'We might get Kirsten and Marco to do that. Just to keep them in the loop. But I suspect any prints and DNA on the cigarette butt and packet will tell us more than any interview. By now, Mr Standish will have rung Miss Simms and his brother to fill them in on what we've spoken about.'

CHAPTER 23

The house at 65 River Street, Maribyrnong was the quintessential 1970s western suburbs home, a triple-fronted cream brick veneer with aluminium-framed windows, a brown tiled roof and a front yard covered in large swaths of concrete. At the front, three steps took a visitor to a heavy security door that was sheltered by a semicircle of concrete overhead. The property had no front fence nor garden, and the double strips of bare dirt bore witness to the lawn serving predominantly as a carpark. A mulberry-coloured Mitsubishi Mirage was parked out front. D'Angelo had run Narnia Simms through various databases. LEAP showed no criminal convictions. VicRoads records listed her as the owner of the car that sat out front. There was a good chance that she was at home.

A petite female no more than five feet in height answered the door, hovering behind the security screen until the detectives displayed their ID and introduced themselves. Simms sported dyed-green hair, a nose ring, and multiple metal studs in both ears. Tattoos covered her forearms, and an inked image of barbed wire circled her neck.

'Can we come in for a quick chat?' D'Angelo asked.

Simms nodded, turned, then led them into a cluttered lounge room. Larsen and D'Angelo sat tentatively on an old couch with its back to a gas heater enclosed within a brick fireplace. Simms sat down opposite.

'We'd just like to grab a few details surrounding a trip you took to Ballarat with Domonic Standish on Thursday September 16,' D'Angelo said. 'You remember that day?'

'Course I remember it,' Simms replied a little too quickly. 'Bloody Dom left me in Ballan, didn't he?'

Larsen nodded. 'Tell us about the trip.'

Simms folded her arms defensively. 'Not much more to tell, really. We went to Ballarat so Dom could look at some Harley parts advertised on Gumtree. They turned out to be a load of crap. On the way home, we detoured into Ballan for a few beers at the pub in the main street. This young bloke on the table beside us starts giving me cheek about my tatts. We get into a bit of a conversation about what they all mean, and whether I'd advise him to get one on his dick. Dom turns all precious and accuses me of flirtin' with the kid, then storms out, leavin' me to make my own way back here.' She shrugged. 'That's the long and the short of it. Ask Dom. He'll probably give you a different version where's he's the hero and I'm a fuckin' slut. But that's what happened.' She paused for a quick moment, and the level of her voice dropped. 'I gave him the arse after he left me in Ballan. Originally only got it on with him because he offered to pay my rent here. Then he wanted me to move in with him, but I was happy here with the girls. Didn't need to be with him 24/7. Didn't need to be his housemaid, cleanin' up after him.'

Larsen glanced around the room at the dirty mess Simms now lived in, and wondered what she saw as the job description of a housemaid. 'Which pub did you go to?'

'The one in Ballan. I told you,' Simms replied tersely.

'Which one?' Larsen persisted. 'There's three.'

Simms shrugged. 'Dunno what it's called. The one near the roundabout. Sort of modern for a country pub. There's a carpark out front where Dom left the bike. It's got a drive-through bottle shop on the side.'

Larsen maintained eye contact. 'What's the inside look like?' she asked.

'Fancy. Wooden bar and old-fashioned tables and chairs.'

D'Angelo leaned back on the couch and folded his arms across his chest. 'How'd you get from Ballan to here?'

'Train.'

'V/Line train from Ballarat?' D'Angelo asked.

Simms nodded. 'Got off at West Footscray and walked up Gordon Street. Bloody tired when I got home, I'll tell you that.'

D'Angelo smiled. 'V/Line trains don't stop at West Footscray, Narnia.'

Simms shrugged. 'Must have been Footscray, then.' She thought for a moment. 'Yeah, Footscray Station. That's right. I walked up Barkley Street, then into Gordon Street.'

Following a few further questions, D'Angelo and Larsen stood and walked to the front door, thanking Simms for her time.

'One last question,' D'Angelo said as he pushed open the security door. 'Does Domonic's brother have a job? The one who lives in Caroline Springs?'

'He works at a panel place in a street just off Ballarat Road. Right up near the Caroline Springs turn-off.'

'Do you know what it's called?'

Simms shook her head. 'No idea, sorry. Dom just pointed down a side street one day and said Warren worked at a panelbeater's down that way.'

* * *

'What do you reckon?' Larsen asked once the detectives were back in their car and heading south down Gordon Street.

'Dunno. She's hard to read. Getting the railway station wrong may have been a genuine mistake. And she seemed to have a good handle on the pub in Ballan. But maybe she's been there before, or is just bullshitting, hoping we wouldn't check.'

'Or she's looked up a pub on the internet. I did that this morning, and the description she gave would be easy to glean from the photos for one of the Ballan pubs I googled.'

D'Angelo angled into the right turning lane for Ballarat Road. 'Is she that smart?'

'Well, she's street smart, I'll guarantee that,' Larsen replied with a smile. 'Maybe Standish gave her details for a cover story after Greg and Darren came calling.'

The red traffic arrow changed to green, and D'Angelo turned right onto Ballarat Road. 'While we're out this way, it might be worth zipping up to Ballan and seeing if someone there remembers a bikie with a green-haired companion.'

Larsen shook her head. 'That pub isn't open today. I checked opening times when I googled the Ballan hotels. Hoped maybe to catch out a lie if the pub they referred to wasn't open on a Thursday when they claimed to have visited. But that day was a goer.'

* * *

'The blood results are not encouraging,' haematologist Alana Jamieson said with a hint of disappointment discernible even over the phone.

Bowker stared at his mobile on the table, unable to look at his wife sitting opposite. 'Okay, that wasn't the news I was praying for.' He inhaled audibly. 'So where to now?'

'Bigger doses of chemo and see if that has any impact.'

'And if that doesn't work?' Rachael asked wearily.

'Bone marrow transplant would be our next option,' Jamieson replied.

Our last option, Bowker knew. Rachael was already struggling to cope with the chemo, and he wondered whether she'd survive the increased doses. But before the leukaemia had taken hold, she'd been super fit and seemingly immune to any ailments that struck down those around her. If others had survived this new chemo, surely Rachael would do the same.

'When do we start the new doses?' Rachael asked.

'Tomorrow, when you come in.'

'Can't wait,' Rachael said, smiling weakly at her husband.

'Quite a few patients respond to the higher dosage; that's why we use it as the next line of treatment,' Jamieson said. 'So we've still got a few weapons up our sleeve. Talk to you soon,' she added and closed the call.

Bowker stood and walked to his wife, leaning down and hugging her from behind. He knew this nightmare wasn't about to end.

* * *

After visiting panel shops in the area Narnia Simms had described, Larsen and D'Angelo eventually located Domonic Standish's brother in a cul-de-sac close to the Christies Road intersection. *Outer West Panels* was painted in gaudy pink across a background of blue and yellow on the prefabricated workshop. CCTV cameras surveilled the building and yard. A heavy tow vehicle with a crane and a flatbed tilt truck were parked to the side. The concrete-covered grounds, back and front, were stacked with vehicles with various degrees of panel damage. The whole compound was surrounded by a high chain-wire fence. A freshening wind swirled in the alcoves of the building, raising spirals of dust and loose litter in small clouds.

Dressed in badly soiled coveralls, steel-capped boots and heavy gloves, Warren Standish was a similar height to his brother, with a pinched face, short-cropped hair disguising a growing bald patch, and a bushy moustache. He sat on a bench in the lunchroom as he spoke with D'Angelo and Larsen.

'Dom arrived at my place around sixish,' Standish recalled. 'I wasn't long home from work, so I got him a beer while I had a shower.'

'What did you do after that?' D'Angelo asked, leaning against a bench on the other side of the small room.

Standish shrugged. 'Not much. Went down the street and bought pizzas, then played the Xbox and drank the odd stubby until about ten, or a bit after.'

'Cash or card for the pizza?' Larsen, who sat at a chair at the table, asked.

'Cash. It was my shout,' Standish replied. 'The boss usually pays me in cash if I work a few hours overtime. Saves on my tax.' He smiled. 'Probably shouldn't tell the police that, eh?'

'We're not the Taxation Department, mate,' D'Angelo replied without emotion. 'What did your brother tell you about his trip back from Ballarat?'

'Mainly that he was done with Narnia. He said she was flirting with some yokel in Ballan, so he fucked off and left her. Then finished up dumping her for good, apparently.' Standish shook his head. 'Dunno what he saw in her, to tell you the truth. I know she bangs like a dunny door, but there's plenty of chicks who do that and have a personality at the same time.'

With nothing untoward in Warren Standish's account of his brother's movements on September 16, there was little to delay

D'Angelo and Larsen's return to Spencer Street headquarters. With the exception of Narnia Simms's confusion regarding a railway station, both their interviewees' accounts matched that given to Bowker and Holmes by Domonic Standish himself. Either they were all telling the truth, or they were all telling a consistent lie. Forensic reports from Domonic Standish's cigarette and its packet would help split those alternatives.

CHAPTER 24

Whether Bowker's touchy mood flowed from his wife's modest response to several days of increased chemo or the annoying wait for the forensic results that had the potential to break their case open was hard to tell. Likely it was a combination of both. By midmorning, he decided to ring Erin O'Meara to ascertain how far the analysis of Standish's cigarette butt and packet had progressed, and hopefully move the process along. He knew the forensic centre was understaffed, but if you didn't push your own case, you'd often find yourself shoved to the end of the queue. Normally Bowker was front of that queue, not through intimidation – which wouldn't work with O'Meara anyway – but his friendly relationship with her, which had been developed over many years and seen them solve many tough cases together. O'Meara didn't just churn out technical information but had an instinct about cases that often sent investigators down new paths that typically led to successful outcomes.

'We were just about to send out that report, Greg,' O'Meara said after pleasantries had been exchanged and Bowker had stressed the importance of the forensic analysis to his investigation.

'Then the cheque's in the mail, so to speak, Erin?' Bowker replied.

O'Meara read his frustration, but in light of his wife's health, she was more forgiving than normal, when she would have enjoyed a verbal joust with her favourite detective. 'DNA takes a lot longer to retrieve and analyse than lifting fingerprints.'

'Yeah, I know you're all doing your best. Sorry for being a shithead.'

'No need to apologise, mate. I know what you're going through.' There was a pause as she suppressed a cough. 'Look, I've just brought up the report in front of me if you're interested in a summary.'

'Sounds good. I'd appreciate that.'

'Okay. Some good news for your case.' O'Meara broke into a long fit of coughing, keeping Bowker on tenterhooks. The coughing finally subsided, and he heard her clear her throat and spit out the result. He was glad he wasn't there in person.

'Are you alright, Erin?'

'Yeah. Big lump of phlegm went down the wrong way. But you can relax, it's in my rubbish bin now. Absolute monster. I can send you a picture, if you like.' As she broke into laughter, she needed to retch again to clear her throat. She was quiet for a moment.

'What's the good news?' Bowker asked. 'That you're still alive?'

'Yeah, I'm still here. But I'm not sure whether that's good or bad news for the world.' She paused for a moment as she caught her breath. 'The prints on the cigarette box match those on the stubbies at the scene and on the plates that were swapped at Car City.'

Bowker whistled out loud. 'The owner of the cigarette box said he didn't go near Pykes Creek Reservoir.'

'Well, he's lying, unless someone else dumped the stubbies there and didn't leave any prints of their own.'

'My gut says he was there. Well done. What about DNA on the cigarette butt?'

O'Meara sniffed then blew her nose. 'We got a good sample

and were able to sequence it.'

'Sounds promising.'

'Unfortunately, Greg, it doesn't match anything on file. And that includes DNA from the semen found inside the victim. Doesn't mean he's not your killer, but he certainly didn't have sex with her around the time of her death.'

Bowker was quiet for a moment, trying to digest what he had been given. 'And the only other DNA retrieved from the scene was on the UDL can, and that was female.'

'Yep. And in all my years in this job, I'm yet to come across female semen,' O'Meara replied with a chuckle.

* * *

Bowker assembled his team at a large table in the centre of the homicide squad room and relayed O'Meara's summary of the new forensics.

'So Standish *was* at Pykes,' Holmes said after a moment. 'The Ballan pub stuff is just bullshit to account for his girlfriend not being on his motorbike as it approached Melbourne.'

Bowker nodded. 'That's my reading of it.'

Larsen looped a stray lock of blond hair behind her left ear. 'And if she's not on the back of his bike at Melton, and she hasn't been abandoned at a Ballan pub, then there's every chance she was driving Cassidy's Hyundai when it was picked up on CCTV in front of Standish's bike.'

Holmes grimaced. 'There's something not quite right here, Greg,' he said.

Before Holmes could explain his concerns, D'Angelo butted in. 'It all fits to me,' he said, leaning back. 'Standish and Simms are on their way back from Ballarat and stop in at Pykes Creek Reservoir, where he consumes a couple of stubbies, and she downs a UDL vodka mix. They encounter Cassidy at the same reserve, roll her, possibly not meaning to kill her, then steal her car. Simms drives it back to Melbourne and Standish follows solo on his Harley. They know the car will be hot, so they find an identical model for sale at Car City and swap plates. They're interrupted by the security guard, who dies of injuries incurred during some sort of struggle.'

Holmes rolled his eyes. 'The coroner found semen in Cassidy's reproductive tract. Semen that didn't belong to Standish.'

D'Angelo wasn't swayed. 'Forensics couldn't tell exactly how long that semen had been there. She could've had sex that morning or the night before, or had a quickie on the way before she reached Pykes. We know she was a bit whacky.'

'Your scenario still has more holes than a colander,' Holmes shot back, always keen to discredit the man he knew had romantic designs on Larsen. 'Number one, we have absolutely no proof that the UDL can belonged to Narnia Simms. Presumably, we'll acquire prints and a DNA sample from her to prove that one way or the other. Number two, what motive would there have been to kill Cassidy? Surely not to steal a car.'

'It may have turned violent when Standish and Simms tried to knock off her vehicle,' D'Angelo shot back. 'We know she was a wildcat.' He thought for a minute. 'Or maybe Cassidy had gone for a walk along the shoreline and they tried to pinch the Hyundai on the quiet but she returned and they didn't want any witnesses.'

Larsen folded her hands on the table. 'I'm happy with the theory that they stole her car, but I can't come at them doing it if they'd killed her first. If it was me, I'd be getting as far away from her body as possible, and I certainly wouldn't want to risk being caught with something that could tie me to a murder. A second-hand Hyundai is not worth that.'

Bowker nodded. 'The timing still worries me,' he said. He consulted his notes. 'According to CCTV captures and our subsequent calculations, if Cassidy planned to visit Pykes, it would have been around midday or a bit after. Using the same methods, we calculate Standish arriving at the reservoir at four thirty. That's four hours after we think Cassidy got there. And her car is spotted even later with Standish's bike heading through Melton.'

Holmes rubbed the back of his neck. 'So Cassidy's either detoured somewhere before arriving at Pykes, or she's stuffed around at the reservoir for four hours, or–'

Larsen cut him off. 'Or she's already dead when Standish and Simms arrive.'

D'Angelo shock his head and held out both palms. 'But they still take the car. A moment ago, you said Standish and Simms wouldn't want to be associated with a murdered person.'

'Cassidy's body was found hidden from normal view,' Bowker replied. 'It's possible that Standish and Simms arrived at Pykes with nobody around and found the Hyundai with the keys in the ignition. Stealing the car was totally opportunistic.'

D'Angelo still wasn't convinced. 'Bit of a coincidence if they had nothing to do with Cassidy's murder but went on to commit another killing within days.'

'Coincidences happen, Marco,' Bowker said before straightening the papers in front of him. 'Okay, this is where we go from here. Kirsten, can you ring the pub in Ballan that Simms says she and Standish visited on their way home from Ballarat? From your description, Simms sounds like someone who'd be difficult to forget. If an employee remembers seeing a green-haired, leather-clad woman there on the sixteenth, then we might need to go to Ballan with a photo.' He chuckled. 'It'll certainly throw a spanner in our theories if Simms and Standish were there as they say.

If the pub has no recollection of them, I'm willing to assume they're lying about visiting Ballan. In which case, Sherlock and I will head out to Footscray and arrest Domonic Standish on suspicion of both murders. Maybe there is doubt about the Cassidy killing, but I don't think there's much surrounding the security guard. We'll accuse him of both and see what he has to say.' He looked across the table at D'Angelo and Larsen. 'At the same time, you two will bring in Narnia Simms. Print her and have a DNA swab done. Don't interview her until we've had a chat to Standish.' He glanced around the table. 'And we don't allow any mobile phone communication from either of them, okay?'

Bowker's colleagues nodded their understanding. Larsen walked to her desk, consulted the internet for the hotel's phone number, then made the call. A woman answered, and Larsen introduced herself before asking about the presence of the bikies.

'I'll need to check the diary to see who worked the bar that day,' the hotel employee replied. It was thirty seconds before her voice returned. 'What was the date, you said?'

'September 16. Afternoon,' Larsen replied, hearing pages being turned. 'It was a Thursday. I checked on the internet that you open on that day of the week.'

'Bad news, I'm afraid. We do open on Thursdays, but on the sixteenth, there was a big funeral in town and most of the staff wanted to go, so we didn't open until six o'clock. Sorry, I'm not much help to you, I'm afraid.'

Larsen thanked her and hung up. The woman had been more help than she could have imagined.

CHAPTER 25

'Take a seat, Mr Standish,' Bowker said as he and Holmes ushered their suspect into an interview room. Bowker closed the door behind him and took a seat beside his colleague. He then read Standish his rights, including his right to silence and to have a lawyer present. 'We're also recording and videoing this interview. Is that clear?'

Standish was shaken by the events of the last hour. Bowker and Holmes had arrived at his work and stuffed him into the back of a police vehicle without any clear explanation of what was happening, or more importantly, why it was happening. *All will be revealed when we get to Spencer Street* was all they would tell him. Was he being arrested or just taken for an interview? He was aware they should tell him something, but wasn't familiar enough with the law to know where his protests should be directed. As a result, he resolved to sit in silence and let events unfold, hoping he could answer any question to the detectives' satisfaction. 'At this stage, I don't want a lawyer,' he said, hands folded like a schoolboy called to the principal's office. 'I don't even know why I'm here. Aren't you supposed to tell me that?'

'We did,' Holmes pointed out with a smile. 'You were informed that we'd like to talk to you about your movements on

September 16. The day you and Narnia Simms took a motorbike ride up to Ballarat.'

'I told you all I could remember when you talked to me at work,' Standish said, upturning his palms.

Bowker shrugged. 'We'd like you to tell us again in here, where we can record and film your story. Miss Simms is in a room just up the corridor, and we're keen to see if your accounts match.'

Standish threw back his head. 'Why are you so interested in that day? Aren't you Homicide detectives?'

'That's right, Mr Standish, we are,' Bowker said, leaning forward. 'But we'll get to that later.' Bowker turned on the recording devices and looked at his watch. 'For the purposes of the audio recording, the time is now fourteen twenty-one. I am Detective Inspector Greg Bowker and with me in the room is Detective Sergeant Darren Holmes. The interviewee is Domonic John Standish. Mr Standish, we'd like to hear about your movements on September 16. The day you rode your motorcycle to Ballarat and back.'

Standish inhaled deeply. 'As I said before, Narnia and I rode up there to check out some Harley parts advertised on Gumtree. But they were worn-out rubbish. No way could you use them as spares. I thanked the bloke for wasting my fuckin' time, and we headed back to Melbourne.'

Bowker contemplated grabbing the name of the parts seller but decided that information was superfluous. Video had captured Standish and Simms leaving Ballarat, and that was the crucial piece of information they needed.

'And you rode straight back to the city?' Holmes asked, knowing this would provoke an objection.

'No, I told youse the other day. Me and Narnia went to a pub in Ballan for a few drinks on the way home. We were there for a while before Narnia started flirting with this young dickhead about tattooing his cock, so I cracked it and left her with him. I rode home. She got back to Maribyrnong on the train, I think.' Standish leaned back and folded his arms across his chest, content that he'd got his story right.

'Which pub did you stop at?' Bowker asked.

Standish shrugged. 'The newer one. Not sure what it's called. The something Western, I think.'

'It has the carpark between the entrance and the street?' Holmes prompted.

Standish's face revealed the hint of a smile. To him, part of his narrative was confirmed. 'Yeah, that's it. Parked the bike in the corner bay.'

'And that was in the afternoon of September 16?' Holmes pushed.

'Absolutely,' Standish shot back. 'You can ask Narnia.'

'We will,' Holmes retorted quickly.

'What if I told you that your hotel was closed on the afternoon of the sixteenth?' Bowker pressed.

Standish shook his head smugly. 'No, it's open on Thursdays. Check the internet if you don't believe me.'

'Normally it is, Mr Standish,' Bowker replied. 'But on the sixteenth, it was closed so the staff could attend a funeral.'

Standish leaned forward, hands flat on the table. 'Bullshit,' he said firmly. 'You're just making up crap. Don't know why, but you're trying to pin something on me.'

Bowker took out his mobile and placed it on the table. 'You can ring the pub yourself if you want to. You can even look up its number so you don't think I'm setting you up.'

Standish pushed away the phone. 'I must have the wrong pub, then. I'd had a few that day. Perhaps I'm confused.'

'So then you went straight back to Melbourne afterwards?' Holmes asked.

Standish emitted a small sigh, relieved that his confusion about the pubs might pass muster. 'Absolutely. On my own, straight back to the city. No doubts there.'

'And you didn't drop into Pykes Creek Reservoir?' Bowker asked.

Standish feigned frustration. 'What's all this bullshit with Pykes? I told you before that I didn't go there.'

Bowker nodded as if giving some credence to what Standish was saying. 'Then how do you explain your fingerprints being on two stubbies we found in a bin at Pykes?'

Standish was dumbstruck for a moment. 'That's bullshit too,' he finally shot back with as much sincerity as he could muster. 'I've never had my fingerprints taken. Never!'

'Afraid you have, mate,' Bowker replied with a smirk. 'From the cigarette packet you dropped in the bin when we visited you at work. Got your DNA from the cigarette butt you discarded, too. It was still burning, so we knew it was the one you dropped before you went back to your work.'

Standish was shocked and looked at Holmes. 'Is that even legal? I didn't give my permission.'

Holmes smiled. 'It's legal, mate, otherwise we wouldn't have bothered collecting your trash.'

'Why deny you were at Pykes?' Bowker asked.

Standish thought for a moment, assessing his options. 'There was a story on the tellie about a woman being found dead there. I don't want you blokes to think I was tied up with that, because I wasn't.'

Holmes raised his eyebrows. 'No? So what were you doing at Pykes?'

Standish shrugged. 'I was pissed off with Narnia at the pub, so I stopped there to down a couple of stubbies before heading home. Didn't see anyone else.'

Bowker shook his head slowly. 'But you never went to the hotel in Ballan.'

Standish looked at the tabletop. 'I told you I got the pub mixed up,' he said, this time without conviction.

'Cut the crap, Domonic,' Holmes said quickly. 'We know you didn't go into Ballan.' He glanced at Bowker. 'And we know Narnia was with you at Pykes.'

'Oh yeah?' Standish replied defiantly. 'How'd you figure that one out?'

'Prints and DNA on a UDL can,' Holmes retorted, stretching the known facts. 'Two other detectives working the case grabbed samples when they interviewed Miss Simms at her home.'

Standish took a big breath. 'Okay, Narnia was there with me at Pykes, and we didn't go into Ballan. Are you happy now?'

'Oh, what a tangled web we weave when first we practice to deceive,' Holmes said, leaning back in his chair, hands folded behind his head.

Standish frowned. 'What the fuck does that mean?'

'It means the more you lie, the more unbelievable your story becomes,' Bowker explained. 'So, now we have you and Narnia at Pykes. Why?'

'We stopped to have a drink, and that's the absolute truth,' Standish replied, then held up two fingers on the wrong hand. 'Scout's honour. The weather was shitty and cold, so we didn't stay more than a few minutes.'

Bowker smiled. 'For what it's worth, I believe you, Domonic,' he said.

Standish visibly relaxed. 'Good,' he said quickly. 'The dead girl is the only reason I didn't come clean from the start.'

Standish's comfort was short-lived.

Bowker was keen to keep their suspect off balance. 'But wasn't the Ballan fairytale meant to explain why Narnia wasn't on your bike when it was caught on CCTV going through Melton? So if you both went to Pykes, how did Narnia get home?'

Standish thought for a moment. 'I think I need a lawyer,' he said quietly.

'I think you might,' Bowker replied with a smile.

* * *

Narnia Simms was picking at her sparkling, multicoloured fingernails when Bowker and Holmes entered the interview room and sat opposite her. Bowker delivered the same spiel about her rights and set the recording equipment in motion before identifying those in the room for the benefit of the audio. After listening to similar objections to those raised by Standish, Bowker asked Simms to describe the events of September 16. Her account was effectively a word-for-word facsimile of that given by her ex-boyfriend.

Bowker held up both palms. 'Okay, I'm going to save us all a bit of time here, Miss Simms. We know you didn't visit the hotel in Ballan, as it was closed for a funeral that afternoon. We also know that you attended Pykes Creek Reservoir with Domonic Standish. He's confirmed this, and I'm positive the fingerprints and DNA swab you've just had taken will match samples lifted from a UDL can our forensic team recovered from a bin at Pykes Creek Reservoir. In summary, there is no doubt you were there. It is our contention that the Ballan hotel story was invented to explain why you weren't a pillion passenger when CCTV vision twice captured Mr Standish's Harley between Pykes and Melbourne.'

Holmes leaned forward, forearms on the table. 'So, how did you *really* get back to Melbourne, Miss Simms?'

Simms stared into space, mulling her options.

'Do you want to call a lawyer?' Bowker asked quietly.

Simms slowly shook her head. 'No. I just want this to be over.'

Bowker raised his eyebrows. 'Okay. So, tell us what happened when you arrived at Pykes.'

Simms gazed at the ceiling, assembling her thoughts. 'We stopped at Pykes for a drink while this heavy shower passed over. The weather was terrible, and conditions on the highway were dangerous. Dom found it difficult to see the road and his visor kept fogging up. We pulled into the Pykes Creek reserve and parked under the shelter of a big tree. Dom downed a couple of stubbies, and I drank a UDL.'

'Was anyone else there?' Holmes asked.

'No. The place was deserted. But there was a grey Hyundai in the carpark. Dom walked past it to have a leak, and on his way back, he saw that it was unlocked and the keys were in the ignition. He suggested that we knock it off and drive it back to Melbourne. He thought maybe he could flog it off, or get it repainted.' She looked at Bowker with sad eyes. 'I was dead against it, but he said if I didn't drive the car back to the city, he'd leave me at Pykes.'

Bowker folded his arms. 'So, you drove the car, and he followed on his Harley?'

Simms nodded.

'Back to his brother's place in Caroline Springs?' Holmes suggested.

She shook her head. 'No. We did go into Caroline Springs the back way, but we went straight through to his place in Sunshine, and I parked the car in the street a block or so away.'

'Domonic run you home from there?' Bowker asked.

'Yeah. On his bike. When we got to my place, he was hanging around, hoping for a root, I'd say. In the end, I told him I didn't want to see him again. I'm not a criminal, and he'd forced me into stealing a car.' She smiled weakly. 'Plus, it was a good excuse. I was getting sick of him anyway.'

Bowker scratched his chin. 'But you've been in contact over recent days?'

Simms again nodded. 'He said you'd been to see him at work and we needed to get our stories straight, otherwise we'd both be going to jail. He came up with the idea of saying he left me in Ballan to explain why I wasn't on his bike when the CCTV filmed him.'

'Where's the Hyundai now?' Holmes asked.

Simms shrugged. 'No idea. I haven't seen it since that night I drove it back from Pykes.'

Bowker and Holmes looked at each other, wondering the same thing. They were confident Standish was present at Car City exchanging plates because his prints were there, but if it wasn't Simms with him on the CCTV footage, then who was it?

'Were you surprised when the security guard approached you and Domonic at Car City? You know, on the night when Mr Standish exchanged the licence plates with another vehicle's?' Bowker hoped her reaction would give him answers.

It did. Simms was totally bewildered. 'I'm not sure what you mean. What's Car City?'

'A big car yard where the number plates from the car you stole were exchanged for those of an identical car,' Bowker replied. 'A security guard arrived and was attacked. He died in hospital a few nights later. It's in your interests to come clean if you know anything about that incident.'

Simms was shaking her head vigorously. 'I don't know what you're even talking about.'

'Mr Standish was there that night,' Holmes said. 'We found

his prints all over the number plates he exchanged. He entered the car yard with another person – we know that from CCTV footage. Are you sure the other person wasn't you?'

Simms stood up indignantly. 'No, it wasn't me!'

Bowker and Holmes knew she was telling the truth. They had seen the CCTV footage, and both intruders were roughly the same height. Simms was way shorter than Standish, but they hoped she might volunteer a name to clear herself.

'Sit down, please, Miss Simms,' Bowker said. She complied. 'If it wasn't you, then who would you guess did it? Who are his mates?'

Simms shrugged. 'He's got a few friends, I think, but I don't really know their names. I've never socialised with any of them. One mate is from his work, and there are a couple he played footy with until he thought he was too cool for sport. Or too lazy.'

Holmes nodded. 'Is he close to his brother?'

'S'pose,' Simms replied. 'Bit of a dickhead, though.'

'The brother's name is Warren, right?' Bowker asked.

'Yeah. But everyone calls him Wazza.'

Holmes wrote it down. Bowker removed a blank sheet of paper from the manilla folder in front of him, took a pen from his shirt pocket, and pushed both across the table to Simms. 'Can you write down your mobile phone number and those of Domonic and his brother, please?'

'I'll need my phone to look them up,' Simms replied. 'The lady detective wouldn't let me keep my mobile while I was in here waiting for you.'

'I'll go grab it,' Holmes replied, and he stood up and left the room.

'Am I in a lot of trouble?' Simms asked as she watched Holmes leave.

'Not as much as you will be if we find you're lying to us.'

'I haven't been. I've told you all that I know.' Tears welled in her eyes. 'Will I go to jail for stealing the car?'

'Depends on how cooperative you are. You might be able to convince a judge that you drove the stolen car under duress from Standish, but that won't hold much water if you stuff our investigation around.'

Before Simms could respond, Holmes returned and placed the phone on the table in front of her. She scrolled through her contact list then wrote and named three mobile numbers on Bowker's sheet.

'That's a good start,' Bowker replied with a smile as he took back the paper.

* * *

'What's the go?' D'Angelo asked when Bowker and Holmes returned to the homicide squad room.

'We'll keep Standish locked up while we make a few further enquiries,' Bowker replied. 'There's no doubt he's the key to solving the security guard's killing.'

'What about the girl?' Larsen asked, wandering across to her colleagues.

'We've set her loose,' Holmes replied. 'I think the only thing she's guilty of is driving Cassidy's car back to Footscray. And it sounds like that was probably done under duress. I don't think she's a flight risk. We know where to find her if we need to talk to her again.'

'So how does it all fit with Katrina Cassidy's murder?' D'Angelo asked.

Bowker shrugged. 'I'm not sure it does, Marco. I suspect the only thing that links the two investigations is the grey Hyundai. I reckon Cassidy was already dead when Standish and Simms arrived at Pykes. Her car was there abandoned with the keys in the ignition, and Standish decided to knock it off, forcing Simms to drive it back to Melbourne. After that, we pretty much know what happened at Car City.'

'Someone else must be tied up in the whole thing as well,' Holmes said. 'Standish had help when he switched the plates. Simms is too short to match either figure caught on the Car City CCTV.'

'His brother, maybe?' Larsen asked.

Holmes slipped his hands into his pockets. 'Could be. Apparently, he has a couple of mates he used to play footy with. Might be one of them.'

'Sherlock and I will chase them up tomorrow after Rachael's chemo,' Bowker added.

D'Angelo turned away and walked back to his desk, annoyed that the case he and Larsen had worked hard on was being hijacked so close to its solution.

CHAPTER 26

By the time the first fire truck arrived, the car was well ablaze. The windows had already exploded, and flames from the interior engulfed the body of the vehicle, sending plumes of black smoke into a cloudy night sky already tinged orange by the city lights less than ten kilometres to the south. Once crewmembers of the first tanker were satisfied that no people were inside the Hyundai, they concentrated their efforts on preventing the fire from spreading into grassed paddocks on either side of the country road. Within an hour, the flames were extinguished, and arson squad detectives were on the scene to examine the smouldering wreck. It came as no surprise to them that the vehicle carried no licence plates. Burnt-out cars were normally stolen for use in a subsequent crime, more often than not a major robbery or a targeted shooting. Their hope was that the chassis or engine numbers hadn't been erased before the car was set ablaze.

* * *

As Rachael rested with eyes closed, receiving her latest dose of toxins, Alana Jamieson entered the darkened room and pulled up a chair beside Bowker, who sat at the bedside holding his wife's hand. After pleasantries were exchanged, Jamieson nodded towards the printout she carried.

'Not good news, I'm afraid. The bloods show a slight improvement, but I think we need to prepare for a bone marrow transplant. If things suddenly pick up, then we're no worse off; if they don't, then we've got a head start on acquiring a donor.'

Bowker's need to remain calm and controlled for his wife's sake kicked in before he exploded and punched in a wall or screamed out loud at the unfairness of her condition. He spoke slowly and with as much optimism as he could muster. 'So where do we start looking? Presumably at someone with the same blood type as Rach.'

Jamieson placed the printout on the bed. 'Unfortunately, it's a bit more complicated than that, which is why finding a donor is often so tricky. It's all a bit technical.'

'I'd still like to know,' Bowker replied. 'After all, it's Rachael's life we're talking about here,' he added with an edge.

'Okay,' Jamieson said, folding her arms. 'Donors and recipients are matched using things called human leukocyte antigens, or HLA. It's a term you'll hear a lot of as we move forward. And matching HLA is a lot more complicated than just blood type itself. All cells in an individual carry the same combination of these markers, but they vary from person to person. It's the way our immune system recognises cells that belong in a person's body, and the ones that are alien. The alien ones are attacked and eliminated. If we transplant marrow cells that Rachael's immune system identifies as invaders, these cells will be rejected and the transplant will fail.'

'So why is matching these HLAs often so hard?' Bowker replied, risking his deep need to understand obstacles to his wife's recovery being seen as pedantic.

'Your HLA type is made up of many genes, but when it comes

to matching, we are most interested in only six of them. Each one of these has two different versions, making twelve in total. You inherit one version from your mother and one from your father. If all twelve match with a donor, it's called a 12/12, or a perfect match. If eleven match, it's an 11/12 match, and so on down. It's important that we find the best possible match, because this will give Rachael's body the best possible chance of accepting the donor's cells.'

'Where do we start looking for a donor?' Rachael asked weakly, eyes still closed.

'Your family is our best bet. As I just mentioned, you inherited half your HLA from your mum and half from your dad, so by definition, you have a 6/12 match with each of them. But 6/12 is not close enough, although a few transplants have been done with the aid of special drugs and in circumstances that are not relevant in your case. In very, very rare cases, one of the parents may be a complete match, but I wouldn't get my hopes up there. The odds are about the same as winning TattsLotto.'

'What about her sister?' Bowker asked hopefully. 'Same mother, same father.'

Jamieson nodded. 'She's our best chance. Each offspring receives two parts of HLA from each of their parents; however, only one from each is combined to make the child's HLA. That means there are four possible combinations. A patient will have one of those four, as will each other offspring from those parents. In percentage terms, there is a twenty-five percent chance an individual sibling has a matching HLA. Naturally, the larger the family, the more likely at least one brother or sister will be a match.'

'I have one sister, and that's it,' Rachael said quietly.

'So there's a one-in-four chance she'll match. Twenty-five percent,' Jamieson replied with a faint smile.

'Or a seventy-five percent chance she won't,' Bowker said half under his breath.

'If we can't get a familial match, we'll search the databases both here and overseas. After that, our next best chance is looking at ethnicity. HLA is passed down genetically, and some types are very common in certain genetic groups.' Jamieson looked at Rachael. 'Do you know where that beautiful olive complexion came from?'

Rachael smiled weakly. 'Mum's parents are Portuguese.'

Jamieson patted her on the leg. 'Well, there's a good start if we draw a blank with your sister.' She looked at Bowker. 'But it may not even come to a transplant. The chemo may do the trick.'

Bowker said nothing, fully convinced that in the next few months, he would be involved in the most important manhunt of his life.

* * *

Bowker called his team together that afternoon at the Spencer Street headquarters to outline the change of plans he was forced to make in the light of Rachael's disappointing prognosis. Before he had a chance to address the new circumstances, D'Angelo's festering frustration boiled over.

'Before we start, Greg, I'd like to express my disappointment and annoyance at Kirsten and I being sidelined on the security guard murder investigation. We've been with this case from the start, and just when we're about to start laying charges, you and Darren take it over. If the Katrina Cassidy killing is independent of Standish and Simms stealing her car, then there's still a case to solve there. Why don't we stay with our original investigations?'

Holmes wasn't impressed. 'It's not a bloody competition, Marco! It's a team effort. The two cases are intertwined, so it makes no sense for us all to go back to working independently.'

'I tend to agree, Marco,' Larsen said quietly, knowing D'Angelo wouldn't be happy. 'It was Cassidy's car they stole. All the timings and crime scene details cross over.'

D'Angelo threw his hands in the air. 'Thanks for the support, Kirsten. What do they say? Blood's thicker than water.'

'What's that supposed to mean?' Larsen shot back.

'That you'll always support the bloke you're sleeping with in preference to the officer who's watching your back,' D'Angelo retorted.

'Watching her arse, more like it,' Holmes said loudly, standing up.

Larsen rolled her eyes. 'Come on, Darren. Cut the bullshit.'

'I'd just like to know what the old man's implying here,' D'Angelo blurted out, standing on his toes to reach somewhere near Holmes's height.

'I'm not implying anything, D'Angelo,' Holmes shot back. 'I'm just putting the truth on the table. You've got the hots for Detective Larsen, and I'm not sure that's a healthy working relationship.'

'Darren, stop imagining things,' Larsen replied in as calming a tone as she could muster.

D'Angelo wasn't listening. 'I've heard when men pass their prime, they start suspecting other blokes of cutting their lunch.'

'I'll cut your lunch in a minute, pal,' Holmes retorted. 'I'll start with a knuckle sandwich!'

Larsen held up her hands. 'If this is about who runs this case, then we'll withdraw from the investigation.'

Bowker slammed both palms on the table. 'Cut the bullshit, the both of you!' he shouted. 'I've got enough on my bloody plate without having to referee a schoolboy pissing competition. Kirsten, has Marco made any advances towards you?'

Larsen shook her head. 'Absolutely not.'

Bowker stood up straight. 'Alright, that's end of story. Everybody sit down.' He took a long, deep breath. The others avoided eye contact with each other. Bowker slowly sat. 'Now, just to put everything in perspective, the haematologist can't see any improvement in Rachael's condition, despite upping her chemo doses. She'll more than likely need a bone marrow transplant as a last resort. The path she's heading down is scaring the shit out of me, to tell you the truth.'

There was immediate contrition among his colleagues. 'Shit, mate, I'm so sorry,' Holmes said. D'Angelo and Larsen endorsed his sympathies.

'I've got no time, and frankly no inclination, to umpire personal issues,' Bowker declared after a moment. 'If they affect work, then I'll do what I need to do, but I don't intend to intervene in private matters. I'm not your bloody father, for God's sake.' Holmes and D'Angelo stared at the tabletop. Holmes in particular felt he'd let his good friend down. 'Now, Marco, if you hadn't barrelled me first-off, we could have avoided this embarrassment. I actually called this meeting to advise that I've had a change of mind about Sherlock and I working both investigations. With Rachael's condition deteriorating and the probable need to track down bone marrow donors, I'll effectively be here part-time at best. That would leave too much work for Darren. So, Marco and Kirsten, I want you to stick with the security guard murder investigation, and *we'll* concentrate on finding who killed Katrina Cassidy. With the few leads we've got on that case, I think Darren can handle the investigation with whatever help I can give. In summary, it's all back to the future, if you like.' Bowker looked around the table. 'We all happy with that?'

They nodded.

'Sherlock?' Bowker asked. 'You were the one pushing for a combined inquiry.'

'What you say makes sense, Greg,' Holmes replied with a mixture of acquiescence and acceptance of his boss's logic. 'If we agree the theft of her Hyundai probably had nothing to do with her death, then we're effectively back to square one with Cassidy. And there's still a fair bit of work left to do tying Standish to the security guard killing and establishing if others were involved. The Cassidy case *does* deserve a dedicated investigation.'

Bowker rubbed his chin. 'Okay, then. Marco and Kirsten, can you interview Standish's brother and see if you can find his football mates? The brother might give you a heads up on that.'

D'Angelo nodded as he and Larsen stood.

'And this is my last word on this,' Bowker said sternly. 'If any personal animosities show their heads again, I'll break up the teams. I've got two or three young turks who'd give their eyeteeth to get involved in cases like these.'

* * *

When D'Angelo and Larsen had departed, Holmes wandered sheepishly to Bowker's desk. He dragged up a chair beside his boss. 'Sorry about that outburst, Greg. That bastard rubs me the wrong way. Having a go at Kirsten was more than I could take.'

Bowker turned in his chair. 'You have to get over this jealousy, mate. If D'Angelo does have a thing for Kirsten, doesn't mean it's reciprocated. And if she does have feelings for him, which I thoroughly doubt, you acting like a dick won't change that.'

'I s'pose you're right.'

'Course I'm bloody right. Knowing Kirsten, if things were headed that way, she'd tell you straight up. She's not the sort of person to go behind your back.'

Holmes sighed. 'Yeah, I know. But I just don't like him sniffing around, that's all.'

'Kirsten is a striking woman, Sherlock, and of course men are going to be attracted to her.' Bowker smiled. 'You can't threaten to deck all of them.'

Holmes chuckled. 'I feel like it, sometimes.'

'Unless Marco makes unwanted advances towards her, you've got no right to have a dip at him.' Bowker paused, waiting for Holmes's response. None came. 'Okay. The Katrina Cassidy murder. What have we got if we remove Standish and Simms as suspects?'

Holmes folded his arms. 'Jack nothing, Greg. Everything we had was based around her car, and now that connection is gone. The stuff left in the rubbish bin all related to Standish and Simms, and the KFC box belonged to Bernie Laidler of Yanco Creek fame. The only evidence collected at the scene that's left unexplained is the piece of car trim, and that could have been there for days or even years and most likely has nothing to do with our case.'

Bowker nodded as he thought for a moment. 'I reckon we have a real blitz on Crime Stoppers.'

Holmes shrugged. 'We've done that before and got nothing except a few kooks with conspiracy theories.'

'I'm suggesting we go harder on the TV stuff. Maybe get a story in the dailies or online about the case. You never know what can jog a person's memory. Maybe someone in the public might remember something they saw on the highway, or something that happened in Ballarat that day. You never know your luck in the big city.'

'We're not talking about a big city here, though, are we? We're talking about a lonely reservoir in shit weather.'

Bowker upturned his palms. 'All the more reason that something abnormal might stand out.'

* * *

D'Angelo and Larsen were halfway to Warren Standish's workplace near Caroline Springs before the elephant in the room was addressed. 'I didn't appreciate that *blood thicker than water* comment you made when I supported running the two cases together.'

D'Angelo lifted his fingers on the steering wheel. 'Yeah, I apologise for that. It's no excuse for having a go at you, but I was shitty that after all our work, it seemed like Bowker and Holmes were grabbing the glory of solving the case. *Our* case. Especially when now it appears they've made zilch progress on *their* investigation.'

'Well, I didn't appreciate my name being thrown around like a piece of property. I'll be having a word to Darren about that too. I've worked too hard to get where I have. It's difficult enough for anyone to make the homicide squad, let alone a woman. I'm not going to cop what happened this morning.'

D'Angelo's eyes never left the road. 'Sorry, that was my Italian blood boiling over. When I'm accused of something that's untrue, I tend to hit back at the person who said it.'

Larsen had her apology but contemplated pushing further – to settle once and for all whether there was any truth to Holmes's belief that D'Angelo had feelings for her, and to nip those in the bud before something arose that would destroy their working relationship. Her deliberations were cut short when her mobile rang. It was Greg Bowker.

'Hi, Kirsten, information for you and Marco. Are you on loudspeaker?'

'I am now.'

'Look, we've just had a call from the arson squad. They attended a burnt-out Hyundai on a track west of Craigieburn. Haven't had time to go over what's left of the car in fine detail, but they *can* tell us the number plates and compliance plate had been removed. An attempt had been made to file off the engine number, but under magnification, the techs were able to read three digits. And guess what?'

'They were able to match those to the Hyundai from Pykes,' D'Angelo called out.

'Spot on, mate. So someone must have thought we were getting a bit close to finding the history of that car.'

'When was the fire?' Larsen asked.

'Last night,' Bowker replied. 'And I bet I know what you're thinking.'

Larsen smiled at D'Angelo. 'That Standish was in custody when that happened.'

'Spot on,' Bowker said. 'Which means there are more people involved in this than just Domonic Standish.'

'Do you think maybe Simms torched the car when she was released?' D'Angelo asked.

'Didn't look the type. But it must have involved two people. Someone to drive the Hyundai and someone to run them home.' Bowker paused for a moment. 'Anyway, I'll leave you with it. Thought you should know about the car before you talk to Standish's brother.'

Larsen ended the call and looked across at D'Angelo. 'The flot plickens.'

CHAPTER 27

A cooling breeze greeted D'Angelo ad Larsen at Outer West Panels, a pleasant change from the fierce northerly of their previous visit. A short, rotund man with a droopy moustache, bushy eyebrows and paint-spattered overalls introduced himself as Ken Abbott and informed them that Warren Standish had rung in sick that morning. This was particularly annoying, he said, since two new jobs were booked in that day and he needed every man on deck. From his tone, the detectives formed the impression that this wasn't the first time Standish had let the business down.

Clarke Road formed the western boundary of Caroline Springs, open paddocks on one side facing housing developments on the other. Number 26 was an old farmhouse, a remnant of when the whole area was used for agriculture. A straggly hedge fronted the road, with a potholed driveway winding in between an aging weatherboard home and a row of old sheds under half-dead pines behind. D'Angelo brought the car to a stop towards the rear of the residence. There was no fence around the house, and if there had been a garden, it was now extinct under weeds and taller plants gone wild. A later-model white Toyota Corolla sat parked a few metres from the back door.

'White Corolla,' D'Angelo said as he alighted from the car.

'Now where have we seen one of those before?' he asked with a sardonic smile.

'Outside Car City on the night the plates were swapped maybe,' Larsen replied, with a nod.

The back door was sheltered by a bespoke steel-and-corrugated-iron structure above a bare-earth floor. A variety of junk was stacked against the back wall, much of it disused fishing gear and car parts. D'Angelo climbed an old army shell box that now served as a step and knocked on the back door. He stepped back to the ground. After a moment or two, Warren Standish warily opened the door and stood hands on hips in the entrance. He wore jeans and a red checked flannelette shirt with the sleeves cut out. He sported the same cap as when they met him at work, but no shoes or socks. Catching the eye of both detectives was the bandage on his right hand.

'What do you two want this time?' Standish asked by way of pleasantries.

'Just need a quick chat,' D'Angelo replied. 'Can we come inside? Shouldn't take longer than a few minutes.'

Standish shrugged and led them into a kitchen that struck D'Angelo and Larsen as more civilised than they had expected. A few dirty plates were in the old sink, a couple of empty stubbies sat on a table surrounded by three chairs, but the rest of the room was neat and tidy, albeit outdated and in need of a good paint.

'Mind if we sit?' D'Angelo asked.

Standish upturned his left palm. 'Be my guest.'

All three pulled out old-fashioned wooden chairs and sat with hands on the worn tabletop.

'Didn't make it to work today?' D'Angelo asked.

Standish held up his bandaged hand. 'Had to go to casualty last night to get this treated. Wouldn't be much use at work, so I thought I may as well stay home and let it recover. I know the boss is pissed off. Two extra wrecks came in. One of the other blokes had to go get them with the truck.'

Larsen knitted her fingers. 'So what'd you do to the hand?'

'Cut it with a chisel down in the shed,' Standish replied quickly. 'Tryin' to fix the kitchen chair that belongs with this table.'

'When'd this happen?' D'Angelo asked.

'About eight o'clock last night. Should have known better. Accident waiting to happen. The light is shithouse in the shed.'

'What hospital did you go to?' Larsen asked.

'Western and District in Sunshine. Had to wait for bloody hours. Kept pushin' me back in the queue.' Standish paused for a moment. 'What are you out here for, anyway? I told you everything at work the other day.'

D'Angelo smiled. 'Afraid not, Warren. We now know that Domonic didn't come here on his way home from Ballarat. All that stuff about playing the Xbox and buying pizzas is bullshit.'

Standish's gaze dropped to the table for a quick moment before returning to D'Angelo. 'I can assure you that he did come here. Who told you different?'

'Narnia Simms admitted she was driving a car that she and Domonic stole from the Pykes Creek Reservoir carpark, and your brother was following her on his motorcycle,' D'Angelo replied. 'They did get off the Western Freeway and come through Caroline Springs, but they didn't stop here.'

'They went back to Dom's place in Footscray,' Larsen added.

Standish threw his hands in the air. 'And you believe that little bitch? She's only trying to save her own arse.'

'Save her own arse from what?' Larsen shot back with a smile.

Standish didn't answer.

'Save her arse from *what*, Mr Standish?' D'Angelo pressed.

'Nothing,' Standish eventually replied. 'I just said the first thing that came into my head.'

D'Angelo didn't pursue it. 'Your brother is currently in custody and will be charged with the theft of a motor vehicle. But you knew that, didn't you?'

Standish dropped his head before staring up at the ceiling. He needed to change tack. 'Yeah, okay. I knew. He rang, asking me to get him a lawyer.'

D'Angelo sighed. 'Then why fuck us around?'

'He's my brother. It's my job to protect him.'

D'Angelo flashed a glance at Larsen. 'When he rang, did he tell you there's a very good chance he'll also be charged with murder?'

Standish snorted. 'Murder of *who*?'

'A security guard at Car City the night your brother exchanged number plates with another vehicle to disguise the car he had stolen from Pykes,' D'Angelo replied.

Standish feigned a chuckle. 'This is all bullshit. Dom's being set up. He's not a thief, and he's certainly not a murderer.'

Larsen leaned forward. 'We know he stole the car. We have his fingerprints.' She stared Standish in the eye. 'Were you with him the night the guard was killed?'

Standish slammed the chair back and stood up quickly. 'I know nothing about a stolen car or someone killed at Car City!'

'Then why lie to us about your brother visiting here that night?' D'Angelo pressed.

Standish slumped down onto his chair and stared at the tabletop. 'Because he asked me to. Okay?' he mumbled. 'He didn't tell me what it was about, but he was begging me to say he was here if I was asked.' He glanced at both officers. 'I told you. He's my brother, alright?'

There was a moment before Larsen spoke. 'Who are his best mates?'

Standish frowned then shrugged. 'His best friend is probably John Lasgis, or Todd Lloyd maybe. He played footy with them, and they've sort of hung around with each other since.'

Larsen removed a notebook from her pocket and wrote the names. 'Do you have addresses?'

Standish shook his head slowly. 'No idea, really. I know Todd works in his father's printing business in Braebrook. Not sure where Lasgis works. I've only met these blokes a handful of times.'

'So they're not your friends as well?' D'Angelo asked. 'Blokes you could call on to give you a hand with something if you were in a tight spot?'

'Like I said, I hardly know them.'

D'Angelo scratched his cheek. 'Who are *your* mates then, Warren?'

'Stick pretty much to myself. Do a bit of fishing. If I need company, I'll ring up Dom.'

'Live here on your own?'

Standish nodded.

'Got a girlfriend?'

'Nope. Was married until a couple of months ago, when that went belly-up.' Standish looked at Larsen. 'Fuckin' women. I'm staying well clear of them at the moment.'

Larsen didn't react. 'Do you know the name of the printing business Todd Lloyd's father owns?'

'Just Lloyd Printing, I think. It's on Ballarat Road not far up from Braebrook Secondary College. Near the footbridge over the street.'

D'Angelo was keen to keep Standish off balance. 'What did you get up to last night?'

Standish shrugged. 'Cooked bacon and eggs and ate them on toast. Then went down the shed to fix the bloody chair.' He pointed to the stubbies on the table. 'Had a couple of beers when I got back from the hospital with my cut hand.'

Following a further five minutes of questioning, D'Angelo and Larsen were back in their car and heading towards Braebrook and Sunshine.

* * *

Bowker hung up his desk phone and beckoned to Holmes. 'The media department will release a priority Crime Stoppers to TV and radio stations this afternoon. They'll also have something for tomorrow's newspapers. I know we're grasping at straws here, Sherlock, but it's all I can think of to do. We've watched CCTV until our eyes have turned square, and still we've got nothing.'

'We've ignored the Stawell end a bit, don't you reckon, Greg? The local coppers have done a lot of legwork, and good on 'em. But now we know a bit more of what happened at Pykes the day Cassidy was murdered, do you think it's worth taking a run up? Maybe meet Cassidy's next-door neighbour and talk to her supposed boyfriend? He's probably not involved, but he might tell us something that fits with other information we've discovered since the investigation opened.'

Bowker knitted his fingers behind his head. 'I can't leave Melbourne, mate. But I'm more than happy for you to drive up. There's nothing here at the moment that I can't handle between Rachael's chemo sessions. If something breaks, I can always draft Marco and Kirsten back in.'

* * *

Lloyd Printing was housed in a rectangular building set far enough back from the footpath to allow two vehicles to park out front. It had a blue hoarding above a glass frontage that ran the width of the premises. The business was bordered on one side by a sandwich shop, the other by a tattoo parlour. In one sense, D'Angelo and Larson's visit was a waste of time, but in another it placed suspicion squarely back on the shoulders of Domonic Standish's brother Warren. Todd, the son of Lloyd Printing's boss, was travelling in Europe with his good mate John Lasgis. Neither could have been involved in the Hyundai's burning.

The emergency department at the Western and District Hospital was a tougher nut to crack. The triage nurse was in her fifties, short and rotund, and wearisome in attitude. 'We can't give out private information,' she explained tersely when D'Angelo sought details of Warren Standish's visit the previous night.

D'Angelo was about to object forcefully when Larsen stepped forward, quickly appreciating the wizened-faced nurse would not be bullied. 'We understand. Can we ask a general question that won't involve divulging an individual patient's details?'

'You can try,' the nurse replied, her eyes locked on the lengthening queue behind the officers.

'Can you check your records and tell me if a male came in here late last night for treatment for a cut on his right hand, or alternatively, a burn on that hand? No names. No other information. Just if anyone with either of those injuries attended.'

The nurse thought for a moment before turning and addressing a younger male staff member in navy-blue scrubs. She returned to her window and asked the detectives to stand aside so she could deal with a young mother cradling a sniffling baby.

It was a good five minutes before the young nurse returned, unlocked a door and approached D'Angelo and Larsen in the waiting room. 'I've checked the computer. Wasn't overly busy last night. Records show no cut hands, but the staff did treat a male patient for burns on his right hand.' He shot a glance to both detectives and shrugged. 'Sorry, can't give you more than that, I'm afraid. Privacy laws and all. If you come back with the relevant orders, we can probably give you more.'

D'Angelo shook his hand. 'You've given us all we need to know. Thanks, mate.'

The nurse nodded his farewells and returned to duty.

'His brother tipped him off over the phone, and he burnt the car, I reckon,' D'Angelo said quietly. 'The cut hand was bullshit. Now the question's just who helped him.'

* * *

To Holmes, his trip to Stawell was shaping up as a total waste of time. After speaking to local officers, he was able to locate Katrina Cassidy's boyfriend, Clayton McInerny, on the farm near Navarre, a village around twenty-five kilometres to the northeast of Stawell. McInerny was a skinny, scruffy man of around thirty years old. Holmes found him cooperative and open. He answered all questions without hesitation, even those that educed answers that painted him in a less than gentlemanly light. He admitted he didn't have strong feelings for Cassidy, but saw her as an *easy lay*, as he put it. Except for sex, they didn't spend much time together. She was unpredictable and volatile. *Schizo*, he described her. He didn't see her on the day she died, and he didn't know she'd driven out of Stawell. It was shearing time at the farm, and he'd worked in the wool shed all day. Two shearers, another rousie, and the boss cocky could all attest to his presence. In Holmes's mind, everything pointed to McInerny not being directly involved in her death. He did have petty crim mates who possibly could have done the job on his behalf, but from his attitude, Holmes thought that unlikely.

Holmes also visited Cassidy's former next-door neighbour, an elderly woman with a sharp mind and a keen eye for the goings-on in her neighbourhood. She hadn't witnessed Cassidy's outbursts, but she had often heard yelling when McInerny visited. She had found Cassidy a nice enough neighbour who always said hello when the two crossed paths.

Holmes bought fuel, coffee, a salad roll, and a packet of chewing gum at the servo on the highway, at the same time scoping the area where Cassidy had last been seen alive. By the time he finally left Stawell, he was convinced the answer to Cassidy's demise didn't lie in her hometown.

He had just bypassed Ballarat on his way home when Bowker rang.

'Change of plans, Sherlock,' Bowker said in an optimistic tone. 'The daily papers with the Crime Stoppers stuff had barely hit the ground this morning before we got a call.'

'A confession, by the sound of your voice,' Holmes replied.

'Unfortunately, no. But we do have something new to chase up. A woman rang in after reading about the case in the *Herald Sun*. She's been in Europe for six weeks so knew nothing about Cassidy's death until this morning.'

'If she's been overseas for six weeks, then she won't be a lot of help. She'd have departed Australia weeks before Cassidy left that day for Melbourne.'

'What she told me has nothing *directly* to do with Katrina Cassidy. In fact, she's never heard of the victim. But it might lead to a possible connection.'

'Okay.'

'The woman's name is Dearne Ericksen. She's twenty-eight.

Earlier this year, she was driving on the Western Freeway heading to Melbourne when this car came up on her outside. The male driver tooted the horn and pointed towards the rear of her vehicle. He then gestured for her to pull over, which she did out of concern that something was amiss on her car. He stopped his vehicle in front of hers and walked back to her. She wound down her window and asked what was wrong.'

'This is not sounding good, mate,' Holmes said. 'Hope she had her doors locked.'

'He was nice as pie, according to her. Good-looking rooster, she said. Very polite and spoke nicely. Anyway, he asked if she was interested in a quick root. His words were a little less crass, of course.'

'You're *joking?*'

'It's dinkum, according to the woman. She was dumbfounded and declined his offer, as you can imagine. Apparently, he just nodded, apologised for wasting her time, and began wandering back to his car. Curiosity got the best of her, and she stuck her head out the window and asked if he did this on a regular basis. He said he did, but with mixed success. *Win a few, but lose most*, he said. Then he just drove off. She was astute enough to jot down his rego.'

'*Win a few*, the bloke said? In that situation, I would have thought he'd win *none*. Good-looking rooster or not.'

'That was my reaction too, Sherlock.'

Holmes was far from convinced. 'Her call has to be a hoax, surely. You get all sorts of weirdos ringing up either as a joke, or they're putting two and two together and getting five – or fifteen, sometimes.'

'Weird things happen out there on the road, mate. I was driving down Punt Road one day when this bloke pulled up beside me at the lights and held up a little painted sign with *Right brake light not working.'*

'Bullshit!'

'No bullshit, mate. Two traffic lights later, I see him again, two lanes over, and he's holding up a different sign to the driver beside him. This one related to the bloke's left indicator.' Bowker laughed. 'Good Samaritan, or weirdo? You can judge. All I know is when I got home, I checked my right brake light, and sure enough the globe was blown. Saved me having to book myself!' He laughed again.

'I still think the pull-over-for-a-root story has got to be bullshit.'

'That's what I thought, until she told me she dropped in at the Ballan police station and made a report.'

'Okay, that adds a bit of credibility. Her story is verifiable.'

'Yeah. And get this. She said an overweight sergeant filled out some paperwork, which she signed.'

Holmes emitted a short whistle. 'Brian Delaney, you think?'

'Has to be, I reckon. There wouldn't be more than one sergeant assigned to a little station like that.'

'If it's all true, that report should've been front of mind when Delaney attended the Cassidy murder scene at Pykes just down the road.'

'My thoughts exactly, Sherlock.'

'Have you run the plates of our highway Casanova?'

'Yeah, it's a Mercedes wagon belonging to a Michael Ferreira of 12 Morgan Street, Ballan.'

'You want me to stop in Ballan and talk to him?'

Bowker hesitated before answering. 'I've been thinking about that. I'd like to be with you when we speak to him. But how about you go to the Ballan police station and see if you can get a copy of the report Dearne Ericksen filled out? There's nothing on LEAP.

Ask whoever's on duty what they know about this Ferreira bloke.'

'Will do,' Holmes replied.

'How'd you go in Stawell?'

'Waste of time. Cassidy's neighbour just confirmed what we already knew, and the bloke she was shaggin' was shearing on the day she was killed. He knows nothing, I'm sure.'

The two men spoke for a few minutes further before Bowker ended the call and Holmes took the exit to Ballan.

* * *

D'Angelo and Larsen passed the junction of Ballarat and Geelong roads and climbed the bridge over the Maribyrnong River on their way back to their Homicide headquarters. Larsen stared out over the luscious green expanses of Flemington Racecourse.

'Ever been to the Cup?' D'Angelo asked to break the silence.

'Once,' Larsen replied. 'The year Prince of Penzance won at a hundred to one.'

'You back it?'

'Nah. Don't think anyone backed it, except those with a couple of dollars on the female jockey.'

'Bet you won Fashions on the Field,' D'Angelo said casually.

Before Larsen could answer, a car-carrying tilt truck swerved into their lane, cutting them off. 'Dickhead,' D'Angelo said as he touched the brakes.

'Next chance you get, do a U-turn,' Larsen blurted out.

CHAPTER 28

A divisional van parked outside the Ballan police station gave Holmes heart that the station was open and the officers weren't out and about. Constable Nathan Patterson sat behind the reception counter flipping through a copy of *Police Life*. When Holmes entered, Patterson stood, grinned widely, slid open the glass partition and shook hands with his detective colleague.

'G'day, Darren. What brings you to this neck of the woods? Still working the Pykes Creek Ressie case?'

Holmes nodded. 'Yeah. Still running down leads. But the leads are getting skinnier by the day. Listen, does the name Michael Ferreira mean anything to you?'

Patterson raised his eyebrows. 'Mick Ferreira? His parents owned a big farm at Gordon before they were killed in a car accident down in Gippsland somewhere. Collided with a log truck, poor bastards. Before my time here. Mick sold the farm and built a big fancy house on Geelong Road on the edge of town. Keeps a few showjumpers in stables out the back. Was a top footballer in his twenties. Can play any sport. A natural at everything. Popular bloke in Ballan.' He smiled. 'Particularly with the ladies.'

Holmes leaned on the counter. 'A single bloke, then?'

Patterson shook his head. 'Nope. Got a wife and a couple of little kids. Wife's a stunner' – he shrugged – 'but you know what they say – the grass is always greener on the other side of the fence.'

'Came from a squatter family, did he?'

'No. But he does come from money. His parents immigrated from somewhere in Europe and bought the farm many years ago. Sold a big business over there and got out during some sort of revolution, apparently. That's just what I've heard. Could be right or could be total bullshit. You know what small towns are like.'

'Yeah. I come from one a lot smaller than this.'

'So, why the interest in Mick?'

'A woman responded to a newspaper story we released about the murder at Pykes. Said she was waved over by Mr Ferreira on the Western Freeway and asked if she'd fancy a bit of casual sex.'

Patterson's jaw dropped. 'Bullshit!'

Holmes smiled. 'Yeah, that's what Greg and I thought, until she said she stopped in here and made a report.'

Patterson's mouth was still agape. 'Well, *I* didn't take it.'

'She said she spoke to a sergeant. An *overweight* sergeant.'

'That would have to be Brian. He's the only sergeant attached to this station.'

Holmes nodded. *And probably the only fat one*, he thought, but didn't say. 'I'd like to check that paperwork, if we can find it.'

Patterson ushered Holmes through to a pair of filing cabinets in an office at the back. 'I'm not sure what Brian would have classified this under,' he said as he looked in various folders. He snapped his fingers. 'It'll probably be in the crank file.'

Holmes raised his eyebrows. 'You better explain that one, mate.'

'Brian has a file he drops weirdo reports into,' Patterson said as he pulled a folder from the back of the top drawer. 'You know. Stuff that won't need following up, or is resolved with a drive past of the divi van. A resident claiming to have seen a UFO, or complaining about a stray dog, or suspicious that a neighbour is growing marijuana in their backyard and it turns out to be a shrub from the nursery, that sort of thing. The type of encounters you wouldn't record on LEAP.' He put the file on the desk and flipped through its contents until he smiled, picked up a form and handed it to Holmes. 'There we go.'

'So, a report of a woman stating that she was waved over on a public road and asked for sex ends up in the crank file?'

'No laws broken, Detective,' came a deep voice from behind as Senior Sergeant Delaney entered the room. 'No harassment after his offer was rejected. No use of force.'

'Did you interview Mr Ferreira?'

'We had a laugh about it over a beer,' Delaney replied. 'I know Mick well. He has an eye for the ladies, and they have an eye for him. God knows why he'd stray from home when he's got Julia there' – he fanned his face with his hand – 'but who knows what happens behind closed doors.'

Holmes wasn't convinced it was such a trivial matter. 'So you and Ferreira laughed it off?' he asked.

'I told him a woman had reported the encounter, and I suggested what he was doing involved risks.' Delaney suddenly frowned. 'What's all this about, anyway? Surely you don't think Mick had anything to do with the murder at Pykes?'

Holmes held up the report. 'The woman who made this statement must've thought it could be related, because she rang Crime Stoppers this morning when we published another story about Katrina Cassidy's killing.'

Delaney snorted. 'And you drove all the way to Ballan because of that? You must be struggling for leads.'

'I was on my way home from Stawell when Greg rang me and

thought it was worth grabbing a copy of the report.'

'I can put your mind at ease with this one, Detective. Mick Ferreira is the last person I'd suspect of murdering that girl. He loves women, a bit too much for his own good at times, but he's a thorough gentleman.'

'Unless you get on the wrong side of him, Brian,' Patterson interjected. 'Can crack it big time and is more than happy to hold a grudge is my experience. Pulled him over for a breatho one night and he still hasn't spoken to me, unless you count personal abuse.'

Delaney waved away the criticism. 'He's alright most of the time. Most people love him. Everybody's friend, big in the footy and cricket clubs, and does a lot of great things for Ballan.'

Holmes wasn't convinced by Delaney's whitewash. 'Did Ferreira say he'd pulled that stunt before?'

'Around a dozen times, he said,' Delaney replied, then smiled. 'Had a bit of luck with three of them, according to him. Twenty-five percent strike rate, which is pretty impressive. Better than the pub for most blokes.'

Holmes ignored Delaney's envy of Ferreira. 'So he admitted to waving over *twelve* women?'

'We're talking a couple of months ago when we spoke about the woman who made the report.' Delaney shrugged. 'Not sure if he's tried again since our yarn, or how much success he had if he did.'

Holmes raised his eyebrows. 'I can't believe she was the only one to lodge a report.'

'Got to pick your spot, he reckons. Have a quick look at the driver before you decide whether to chance your luck. Look for the tell-tale signs of a female who might be up for it. You know, bright-coloured hair, alternative headwear like a beret or nets of beads, hippy stickers on the car, that sort of thing. And behave like a gentleman. If the lady refuses your advances, graciously accept her decision, apologise for delaying her trip, and wish her well for the remainder of her journey.' Delaney put his hands into his pockets. 'I can guarantee one thing, Detective. Mick Ferreira had nothing to do with your murder at Pykes. That sort of thing's not in him.' Holmes caught Patterson rolling his eyes. 'He's a lover, not a fighter,' Delaney added with a grin.

How about if his target accepted his offer but turned psycho and suddenly accused him of rape? Holmes thought but didn't say. 'I'll grab a copy of that report and be on my way. Greg and I will probably come back for a chat with your local Don Juan.'

* * *

Rachael's chemo session had all but finished when Bowker's phone rang. On the line was Alana Jamieson, who quickly revealed the bad news. 'Rachael's latest test results don't look good, Greg. A marrow transplant is definitely on the cards now.'

Bowker felt shattered but tried not to betray his disappointment to Rachael, who lay with her eyes closed. He climbed to his feet and walked to an empty waiting room up the corridor before he spoke. 'So a donor search now begins?' he said quietly.

'I've already contacted the various marrow banks, Greg. Unfortunately, no matches.'

'What about internationally?'

'None there either so far. But we're still searching.'

'And Rachael's sister?

'We'll test her next. She's probably our best chance, but my staff looked into the banks first because the computer can search them in minutes. I was hoping to have a backup if the sister's not a match.'

'And the odds with her are one in four, you said?' Bowker asked pessimistically.

'Yep. Twenty-five percent chance. The odds are against us, but much better than zero.'

'I s'pose,' Bowker replied.

'Have you got a contact for Rachael's sister? We'll do the rest. I'll gab a contact for her parents as well. We'll test them too in case there is a miracle match.'

'I'll text them to you.'

When the call was finished, Bowker walked slowly back to where Rachael was sitting up, eyes open. 'What was the call?'

'Sherlock. He's on his way back from Stawell. No new leads on the Cassidy murder.'

'So what did *Alana* say? Obviously not good news.'

'It was Sherlock.'

'Rubbish, Greg,' Rachael muttered. 'I can read you like a book.'

There was silence while Bowker contemplated what he should disclose. 'Alana said a bone marrow transplant is looking more likely. She was after a contact for Elise so they can test for a match.'

'Only a one in four chance of that,' Rachael replied in a voice barely above a whisper. 'But I guess we've still got the databases if Elise doesn't match.'

'Yeah,' Bowker replied softly as his wife closed her eyes.

* * *

Back at Outer West Panels, the reception D'Angelo and Larsen received was far from cordial. Ken Abbott, the rotund man they had encountered earlier in the day, was less than impressed when asked for access to the business's CCTV system.

'What the fuck for?'

'Just want to check something. Probably nothing,' D'Angelo replied evasively.

Abbott placed his hands on his hips. 'Shit, officers. I'm flat knacker here. We're one down, as I told you this morning. Customers tend to get shitty when you promise them their car by a certain time and you don't deliver. They'll go somewhere else the next time they have a prang.'

D'Angelo wasn't in the mood to justify their visit. 'Just point us in the right direction and we'll figure it out.'

'Have I got any option?' Abbott asked in frustration.

D'Angelo shrugged. 'You can refuse us access and we'll come back later with the paperwork to do the same job.'

'Only this time we'll insist you help us scan the footage,' Larsen added with a smirk.

Abbott shook his head. 'Fuck me. I'm trying to run a business here. Just trying to do my job.'

'Us too,' D'Angelo shot back.

D'Angelo and Larsen were led to a small room. Lights blinked on units that sat atop shelves, and a video monitor constantly cycled through vision from four cameras outside and one surveilling the office counter area.

'We might be here for an hour or two while we sort this system out,' Larsen said. 'Haven't used one quite like this.'

Abbott rolled his eyes and pulled out a chair from under the bench supporting the video monitor. 'What do want to see?'

'Last night's vision from the front gate,' D'Angelo replied.

'What? All of it?' Abbott exhaled audibly.

'You just set it up from about eight o'clock and show us how to fast forward and stop, and then you can get back to your work.'

Within a minute or so, the footage was queued and ready to run. 'I'll leave you to it. If there's anything I should know about, call me in, but I'll bet you see nothing between daylight and dark. Or the other way around.' Abbott exited in a huff, pulling the door shut behind him.

Larsen took his seat in front of the monitor, with D'Angelo looking over her shoulder. On fast forward, the footage showed the sunlight gradually fading until, by time stamp 21.00 hours, Outer West Panels would have been in darkness if not for two huge floodlights that illuminated the face of the building and its front yard. Except for a couple of possums running along the ridge of the roof, nothing changed in the picture. That altered at time stamp 22.07, when a figure entered the edge of the camera's field of view and unlocked the main gates, swinging both wide open.

Larsen pointed at the screen. 'Warren Standish.'

D'Angelo leaned in so his cheek came close to touching Larsen's ear. 'Yep. If your theory is right, he'll be after the tow truck.' Larsen wound the vision forward. D'Angelo maintained his position close to Larsen's head and breathed in her faint perfume.

The vision showed Standish disappearing down the side of the building. The footage advanced through another fifteen minutes.

'Stop it there,' D'Angelo said urgently.

Larsen had already hit pause. On the screen, the flatbed tilt truck appeared, entering the front yard from the rear, the grey Hyundai on its tray.

D'Angelo pecked Larsen lightly on the cheek. 'You're a bloody genius.'

Larsen stood immediately. 'Do something like that again, Marco, and at the very least our partnership is finished. You're on notice that I'll go to Internal Affairs if it happens again, so take this as your one and only warning.'

D'Angelo backed away. 'Calm down, Kirsten. I was just excited we've made a breakthrough.'

Larsen placed her hands on her hips. 'If I was a male officer, you wouldn't have done that.'

'A male officer wouldn't be wearing a tight skirt and high heels. He wouldn't be wearing perfume.'

'So it's dress uniforms or tweed suits now for female detectives, is it? Spray on half a can of Lynx? Sorry, I forgot.' Larsen turned to leave the room. 'I'm going to the car to grab a memory stick from the glovebox. When I get back, we're professionals again.'

D'Angelo looked at the floor then back at Larsen. 'I'm sorry, alright?'

'I hope so,' Larsen said as she departed the room.

As soon as she'd left, Abbott appeared at the door. 'Wouldn't mind your job, mate. Locked up in the dark with that piece.'

Given what had just transpired, D'Angelo thought it best to ignore the statement and instead pointed at the frozen vision on the monitor.

'What the fuck!' Abbott blurted out. He looked closely at the time stamp. 'That's ten o'clock at bloody night!'

'What's the car on the tray?'

'It belongs to Wazza's brother. It's been out the back for a few days waiting for a dent to be repaired and a respray. Apparently, the brother prefers blue to that grey it is now. If he changed his mind, why didn't he just come and get it? Don't need a bloody truck. And why in the middle of the fuckin' night?' He smiled. 'S'pose that's why you and the babe are here.'

'The other detective, you mean?' Larsen said from the doorway. 'Show some respect.'

D'Angelo attempted to defuse the situation. 'Was the truck here when you arrived this morning, mate?'

'Course it was,' Abbott replied indignantly. 'I do a walk around after I open up.'

'Didn't see the Hyundai was missing?' Larsen said with an edge.

'There're twenty cars out the back, *Detective*. I don't count them.

I check the trucks and any high-end vehicles we're working on. A Hyundai sedan doesn't qualify as either.'

Larsen pushed past Abbott and sat at the monitor. 'We'll take a copy of this section, plus the footage of when the truck was returned.'

'Bloody Standish is skating on thin ice, I'll tell you,' Abbott said as he left the room.

Larsen found the vision capturing the empty truck's return at a little after midnight. 'He was away for a bit over two hours,' she said.

'Plenty of time to drive to Craigieburn, unload and set the car on fire, then drive back here,' D'Angelo replied.

Larsen nodded. 'I bet when we get a look at those hospital records, they'll show him attending at some time between twelve and one.' She copied the relevant footage to the memory stick. 'Where to now, you reckon?'

D'Angelo thought for a moment. 'In my opinion, he burnt the car, and I think it was probably him and his brother who rolled the security guard at Car City. I'd like a good look around at his place, but if we wait for a warrant, things might disappear like the car did here. I say we arrest him on suspicion of arson. That way we can legally search while we're there.'

* * *

As Holmes climbed into his car, his phone rang. It was Bowker again.

'Are you still anywhere near Ballan, mate?' Bowker asked.

'Just leaving the police station.'

'Got the Ericksen report?'

'Yeah. Seems like this Michael Ferreira bloke is a bit of a lad around town. Your mate, Delaney, reckons the whole report is a bit of a joke. Filed it in a folder labelled *cranks*. He said Ferreira told him he'd waved over a dozen women, which netted him a trifecta of roots. Picks his targets, apparently. Females he can spot from his car with alternative hairstyles or headwear. Women who are a bit different to the norm.'

'Like Katrina Cassidy?'

'Exactly,' Holmes replied quickly. 'On CCTV footage, I remember seeing her wearing this pink fiddler's cap at the servo before she left Stawell. Didn't mean anything at the time, but now perhaps it does.'

'What's a fiddler's cap?'

'Like the captain of a ship might wear. But they're usually blue or black, not bright pink.'

'So she fits the profile, you reckon?'

'Yeah, from what Delaney said.'

'And given the right mood, Katrina Cassidy sounds like the type who would've been up for it.'

'Yep. And could change her mind and yell rape just as quickly.'

The call fell silent for a moment.

'Are you still there, Greg?'

'Yeah, I'm here. Mind keeps wandering. Just trying to digest some bad news Rachael and I received this morning. She's going to need a bone marrow transplant, and early indications are that finding a donor won't be easy. Unless we get lucky with her sister, of course.'

Holmes inhaled deeply. 'Shit, mate, I'm so sorry.'

'I don't know when I'll be available to interview your bloke at Ballan, so while you're there, see if you can track him down and have a word. You might catch him off guard before Delaney tips him off that we've been asking about him. What's he do for a quid?'

'Dunno. Delaney didn't say, but I suspect he might be living off his parents' inheritance. He lives on the edge of town in a big fancy place with stables at the rear. Delaney loves him, but his constable reckons he's got a hot temper if things go against him.'

'Whip out and see if he's home. If he's not, perhaps somebody might be there who can tell you where he is. Let us know how you get on.'

'No worries, Greg. All my love to Rachael.'

'Thanks, mate.'

The line went dead.

CHAPTER 29

erreira's home on the outskirts of the town was not difficult
to find. Like a scene from the 1980s series *Dallas*, an
ostentatious house sat on a massive block with sheds and
a row of stables at the rear. Holmes drove up the sealed driveway,
which was bounded by white railed fences on both sides, and
parked near the front entrance on the massive roundabout
encircling hundreds of roses. The sun was warm on his back, and
he could smell the flowers and hear bees working the blossoms as
he knocked on the front door. After a moment or two, it opened
to reveal a tall, stunningly beautiful woman dressed in a white
linen blouse and matching trousers. Long auburn hair rolled
down over her shoulders, and her green eyes sparkled in the
sunlight. Holmes was taken aback. *Why the fuck would Ferreira be
wasting his time waving over cars on the highway when he has this
at home?* he thought as he introduced himself without disclosing
he was attached to Homicide.

'Are you Mrs Ferreira?' he then asked.

'I'm married to Michael Ferreira, but I've maintained the name
my parents gave me. Julia Crowe.'

Holmes nodded. 'Is Michael about?'

'He's down the back with his precious horses,' Crowe replied
with an edge. 'What's a detective want with him? Last I heard,

philandering wasn't a crime.'

He hasn't fooled you, Holmes wanted to reply but just chuckled instead. 'Down the back, you say?' he asked, pointing to the rear of the house. 'Very nice to meet you.' He walked off quickly to avoid further questioning concerning his visit.

The immaculately kept row of stables ran parallel to the back of the house. A wheelbarrow stood on its tyre with handles resting against the stable wall. Alongside were a pair of shovels, a hay fork and an ornate bespoke doorstop made from horseshoes welded together. The stable block contained six horseboxes, five with equine heads protruding over a half door, their eyes fixed on their stablemate being saddled in the cobblestoned yard. Michael Ferreira yanked the girth up tight, then pulled the stirrup back down into place as he spotted Holmes approaching. He was over six feet tall, in great physical condition, with a healthy mop of sandy hair, blue eyes, and a strong chin. He was dressed in riding boots, jodhpurs, a riding skullcap and a white flowing shirt, its sleeves rolled partway up his tanned forearms. He wiped his palms on his jodhpurs as Holmes approached.

Holmes displayed his ID in his left hand as he thrust out his right to shake. 'Detective Senior Sergeant Holmes,' he announced, again not adding he was from the homicide squad.

'Michael Ferreira,' the horseman replied. 'Most people call me Mick. You just caught me. I was about to put this bloke over a few jumps out the back.' He placed his hands on his hips. 'What can I do for you, Detective?'

'Not sure, Mr Ferreira,' Holmes replied, keen to keep the conversation formal. 'I'm following up a report from a woman who claims you waved her over on the Western Freeway and propositioned her about having sex.'

Ferreira was clearly annoyed. 'Who told you that?'

'It's in a report at the local police station. Sergeant Delaney told me he spoke to you about it.'

Ferreira waved a dismissive hand. 'That was months ago. Why all the fuss now? I didn't break any laws. No different to speaking to a woman at a cabaret or a pub and asking if she's interested in a quick roll in the hay. There was no coercion. When the girl said she wasn't interested, I apologised for wasting her time. Perfect gentleman, I was. Can't see why she reported it, really.' He sighed heavily. 'Why is it important?'

Holmes ignored the question. 'How many times have you pulled this trick?'

'What trick?' Ferreira asked with a straight face.

Holmes rolled his eyes. 'Waving women over for sex.'

Ferreira shrugged. 'A dozen times, maybe.' He smirked. 'Hit paydirt on three of those, which is a better strike rate than I have here at home.'

Holmes ignored the comment. 'So when was the most recent time you waved over a woman?'

'Probably the one who submitted the report. Brian Delaney warned me the whole scheme could backfire, so I took his advice and limited myself to the local ladies.'

'You didn't wave someone over on September sixteenth? Someone in a grey Hyundai?'

'No. As I said, I've given up the whole exercise after my little chat with Brian.' A tiny muscle in his left cheek twitched ever so slightly. Holmes saw it.

'Are you sure you weren't on the prowl that Thursday?'

'Stop with the bullshit language, Detective.' He exhaled loudly. 'No. I was here all day. I work my horses on Thursdays. Why are you so interested in the bloody sixteenth?' Ferreira took the horse's reins and swung up into the saddle.

'Because a young lady was murdered at Pykes Creek Reservoir that day,' Holmes replied, looking up at Ferreira. 'Forensics say she'd recently had sex, plus Pykes is near the stretch of road where our informant said you waved her over.'

Ferreira's face reddened. 'I've never been to Pykes Creek Reservoir in my life, so you can fuck off, Detective.' He turned his mount and cantered away.

Holmes stood for a moment and watched Ferreira disappear around the corner of the stables. *I've got a bad feeling about you, mate,* he thought as he turned and walked back down the cobblestoned laneway past the side of the house. As he passed Ferreira's Mercedes wagon, it caught his eye. A small length of chrome strip was missing from the trim on the passenger side door. Holmes dropped to his haunches and surveyed the minor damage. He stared at the ground for an extended moment before returning to his vehicle and retrieving the packet of chewing gum he had purchased in Stawell. He placed the pellets one at a time into his mouth and chewed until his jaws ached. By the time he was back at the Mercedes, he was rolling the ball of gum in his hand, kneading it like putty. He dropped to his haunches again and rolled the gum in the dust to absorb most of its stickiness. He then squashed it against where the trim had broken, before carefully removing the gum and observing the detail left imprinted on the underside. He nodded to himself and smiled at his own ingenuity.

Ferreira's wife appeared behind Holmes as he placed his bespoke mould into an evidence bag before carefully putting it on the backseat of his car.

'Can I ask again why you're out here, Detective?'

Holmes closed the car door. After having quizzed Ferreira about the death of Katrina Cassidy, Holmes felt there was little point in being less than forthcoming with his wife.

'I'm a homicide detective investigating the death of a young woman at Pykes Creek Reservoir a few weeks ago. I thought maybe your husband could shed some light on the case.'

Crowe didn't seem surprised. 'Because he pulls up women on the highway and asks for sex?'

Holmes raised his eyebrows. 'You know about that?'

'Takes a lot to hide a secret in this town, Detective.'

'And how do you feel about it?'

'It disgusts me. Spoilt little rich boy, he is. If it wasn't for our two young sons, I'd be out of here quick smart.'

'Have you heard any talk about Katrina Cassidy? The girl whose body was found at Pykes?'

Crowe shook her head. 'Nothing. I only know what I've read in the papers. Never connected it with my husband until you turned up today.'

Holmes slipped his hands into his pockets. 'Would he be capable of committing a terrible crime like that?'

Crowe shrugged. 'I know he's belted me on more than one occasion when things didn't turn out the way he wanted. I've seen him lose his temper and shoot a horse that kept refusing jumps.' She stared into the distance for a moment. 'But it's a big step from that to murdering someone.'

'There's a saying you hear a lot among police. People who abuse animals finish up abusing people.' Holmes removed a business card from his shirt pocket and handed it to Crowe. 'Call me if you think of something. Even if it's just gossip. And not just about your husband's movements, but about the Cassidy girl's death in general.'

Holmes drove away, watching the woman in his rear-view mirror. She still hadn't moved by the time he'd turned out of the drive and back onto the road.

* * *

D'Angelo and Larsen found Warren Standish constructing a small bonfire at the rear of his property. He had dragged up several fallen pine branches, along with an old timber door, an assortment of cardboard boxes and cartons, and a filthy queen-sized mattress. On the ground beside him was a supermarket bag containing smaller items to be burnt.

'Not Guy Fawkes night yet,' D'Angelo said, surprising Standish, who hadn't seen his visitors arrive.

Standish spun around, at first lost for words. 'Just a general clean up,' he said after a moment. 'Bloody trees are getting old and dropping limbs, and you can't buy anything these days without it being packaged to the shithouse.'

'You're not supposed to burn mattresses,' Larsen said.

'Yeah, well, I'm not taking it to the tip, am I? Cost me a day's wages.' Standish sighed heavily. 'Authorities wonder why they see mattresses dumped on backroads, or in the bush, or beside railway lines. The average person can't afford to get rid of them legally.'

D'Angelo agreed, but he wasn't about to condone breaking the law. 'What's in the supermarket bag?' he asked instead.

'A few items of clothing left behind by the bitch I was married to before she moved out,' Standish replied. 'I think I can assume she's not coming back for them. Chucked the bag in the shed months ago waiting for my next bonfire.'

'Can I take a look?' Larsen asked.

'Why would you want to do that?' he replied defensively.

'Might be something that'd suit me to wear,' Larsen said with a smile. 'Pity to burn it.'

'Won't fit you. The ex was a big fat bitch.'

Larsen picked up the bag and looked inside. She immediately glanced at D'Angelo, raising her eyebrows.

D'Angelo pulled a rubber glove from his coat pocket, wiggled his right hand into it, and fossicked in the plastic bag held open by Larsen. The first item he removed was a pink fiddler's hat, followed by a pair of leather low-heeled shoes, and finally a polar fleece windcheater.

Larsen pointed at the windcheater. 'I think your ex would have struggled to get into this top,' she said with a smile.

Standish shrugged. 'Most likely from her early days. Before she went to seed. Probably why she left it here.'

'Why didn't you burn them with the car?' D'Angelo asked.

Standish feigned surprise. 'What car?'

D'Angelo eyeballed him. 'The Hyundai you burnt last night after your brother phoned to say he was in custody and the car he stole at Pykes Creek Reservoir near Ballan needed to disappear.'

Standish took a step back, shaking his head. 'That's bullshit! I know nothing about a stolen car, and I certainly haven't set fire to one.'

'Must have got careless and burnt yourself,' Larsen said, nodding towards his hand.

Standish rolled his eyes dramatically. 'I *cut* my hand with a chisel!' he replied in a raised voice. 'Don't you listen?'

Larsen chortled. 'We checked with the hospital. You had a burn, not a cut.'

D'Angelo dived into his inside coat pocket, retrieved a thumb drive and held it up. 'On this memory stick is CCTV footage of you taking the Hyundai from Outer West Panels on the tray of a tilt truck last night and returning two hours later with the truck empty. We've got you cold on arson at least.'

'But that may be the least of your problems, Mr Standish,' Larsen added, holding up the bag. 'These items belong to a Katrina Cassidy who was found murdered at Pykes.' She was careful not to disclose that they had already cleared his brother of *that* murder. It was time to let him stew.

Standish dropped to his haunches but said nothing.

D'Angelo placed his hands on his hips and stood over him. 'I think these items of clothing were probably removed from the car when it was stored here prior to being deposited at your workplace awaiting a dent being repaired and a new paint job.'

Standish looked up, all his bravado gone. 'Look, Domonic stole the car, I'll admit that. Bad move. But he had nothing to do with the girl being killed at Pykes. He might be a dickhead at times, but he's not a murderer.'

'Isn't he?' D'Angelo shot back. 'The partner of a security guard at Car City would probably disagree with you.'

Standish stared at the ground. 'Dunno what you're talking about,' he muttered.

D'Angelo glanced at Larsen. 'Yes you do, Warren, because you were there.'

Standish stood up. 'Listen. I know he swapped plates with a car there, but it had nothing to do with me. He told me about it. And he told me about the security guard dying, but it was a separate incident, Dom said. He didn't even see a guard.'

'Detective Larsen and I are not going to stand out here arguing. You'll be formally interviewed about that murder at Spencer Street. For now, I'm arresting you on a charge of arson.' D'Angelo then read Standish his rights.

Larsen pointed to the outbuildings. 'While you're sorting that out, Marco, I'll have a wander back to the shed.'

D'Angelo nodded as he handcuffed Standish. 'I'll meet you back at the car.'

The open-fronted shed was old but well built, once probably housing farm machinery. Spiderwebs lined the rafters, and the roof creaked with the passing of each cloud as the corrugated iron expanded and contracted. A workbench down the side was well organised, in keeping with the way Standish had maintained his house. A shadow board screwed to the wall behind the bench displayed Standish's wide collection of tools. *A place for everything and everything in its place*, Larsen thought before noticing three painted shadows without their respective tools. A claw hammer, a medium-sized shifter, and a pair of multi-grip pliers. A narrow shelf with holes drilled through held an array of screwdrivers, Phillips heads up one end, flat blades up the other. Two from each category were missing. *If I were to remove the number plates from a car without having first inspected the job, what tools would I need?* Larsen asked herself. Screwdrivers, obviously, but also a shifter and pliers if the plates were secured by bolts. A hammer would be handy to punch bolts or screws through, or to lever plates off, if they weren't easily freed. So where were these tools? She started at one end of the bench, searching first above, and then below. *This tight skirt is a pain in the bum*, she thought as she squatted down. A pair of tracksuit pants and runners would have been ideal.

She saw the three parallel white stripes before she had confirmed they belonged to an Adidas sports bag stashed beneath a short sheet of craft wood. The bag fell open when she dragged it out using a pinch bar acquired from the shadow board. There on display were the tools she felt sure were used at Car City.

* * *

Obtaining forensic results for items casually collected by investigating officers took time, with delays caused by the hours required to transport and deposit items at the forensic centre, and the need to maintain a strict and well-documented chain of custody. It was for this reason that Holmes elected to take the

Western Ring Road around to MacLeod rather than travelling directly back to Spencer Street, where he would need to navigate protocols to see his chewing gum mould transported to Forensics. Travel would take much longer this way, but Holmes preferred sitting in his car to filling out forms at Homicide headquarters.

'What has my second-favourite detective got for us?' O'Meara asked between coughs.

Holmes chortled. 'Second to Bowker again. Story of my bloody life.'

O'Meara smiled. 'Look on the bright side, Darren. When Greg calls it a day, you'll move up to number one, just like he did when Jack Moloney pulled the pin.'

'A couple of good acts to follow, I suppose.' Holmes carefully placed the evidence bag on O'Meara's desk. 'I'm pretty proud of this, Erin. Brought it here myself because I was worried it would be squashed.'

O'Meara pushed her glasses back on her nose and looked at the gum closely. 'Okay. Tell me what it is and what's its story.'

Holmes sat down on a chair beside her desk. 'For a start, it's chewing gum.'

'Are you wanting DNA extracted?'

Holmes shook his head. 'You can do that if you want, but you'll only find mine.' He carefully turned the bag over. 'I used it to make a mould of the end of a chrome strip from a vehicle where I saw a short piece had broken off.'

O'Meara leaned back in her chair with a wide smile. 'Clever bastard, aren't you?' she said before coughing up something that she spat into a rolled-up tissue. 'This relates to the Cassidy murder, right?'

Holmes nodded.

O'Meara leaned forward, tapped some keys, and brought up a

fresh screen on her computer. She pointed at the monitor. 'You're hoping the broken end captured by your mould will match this piece of trim the techs found at the scene?'

'Absolutely. It'll be a big breakthrough if it does.'

'So far, that piece they recovered hasn't been much help to us, since most modern cars use similar trims made of identical materials. Probably manufactured at the same factory.' She thought for a moment. 'What my people will do is take your mould and use plaster of Paris to fill the depression and make a replica of the end that's still on the car. When that dries, we'll pop it out and see if the broken end marries up with the bit we collected at the scene. If it does, then we'd be pretty certain the broken bit came from that particular car, and that the car was at Pykes Creek Reservoir at some time. Not necessarily the time of the murder, but *some* time.'

'Give us grounds to take DNA from the owner and see if that matches the semen found in the victim.'

'Good work, Detective Holmes,' O'Meara said. '*Sherlock* might just be the right name for you, despite what people say.' She broke into a fit of coughing before Holmes could respond. He stood to leave when O'Meara's hacking settled down. 'How's Greg's wife?' she asked.

Holmes closed his eyes and sighed. 'No bloody good, I'm afraid. Chemo's not working. They're pinning their hopes on a bone marrow transplant.'

'Fuck.'

'Yeah. All eyes are now on Rachael's sister to see if she's a match.'

'Give them my best. They're going to bloody need it. I'm no medical doctor, but I understand human biology. I don't like their chances. But don't tell Greg I said that.'

* * *

'Call it detective's intuition, call it what you like, Greg, but I reckon Ferreira is our man,' Holmes said back at headquarters as he updated Bowker on his Ballan excursion. 'Do you want me to go back and have a real dip at him? See if he'll crack?'

Bowker pondered the question for a minute, the computer monitor behind him displaying an article on bone marrow transplants. 'Let's wait for Forensics to get back to us,' he said. 'If they match that trim to his car, then that puts him at the crime scene. And since he denies ever going there, that gives him a few tricky questions to answer.'

Further conversation was interrupted by the entry of a jocular D'Angelo and Larsen. 'You two look like the cats who got the cream,' Bowker said.

'We've arrested Domonic Standish's brother for arson, printed him, taken DNA, and locked him up,' D'Angelo said proudly. 'Got him dead to rights.'

Larsen pulled up a chair. 'And we're pretty sure we've found the tools used to switch plates at Car City. They're on their way to Forensics for testing.'

The next thirty minutes were consumed by each team describing in detail what had transpired during their day. It had been a good one for policing. All that was required before heading home was the dreaded paperwork. Finally, Bowker was alone at his desk re-reading the intricacies of marrow transplants and the criteria for donating tissue. Tomorrow was a big day. If the forensic tests went their way, two murders would come close to being solved. But for Bowker, by far the most important test result related to the blood of Rachael's sister.

CHAPTER 30

The next day dawned sunny and mild, with a light zephyr wafting from the west. The sky was clear over the city and the traffic lighter than normal. Bowker prayed these were good omens as he drove his wife to her daily chemo. The results of her sister's blood test hadn't arrived, so Bowker decided against attending work after the session, preferring to be with his wife when that crucial information was phoned through.

The first forensic verdict arrived from McLeod via Holmes's email. The piece of chrome trim found at Pykes was an exact match for Michael Ferreira's car. Holmes immediately phoned Bowker.

'Any results from the sister's tests?' Holmes asked, having already resolved not to bother his boss with a Ferreira update if Bowker had received bad news.

'Nothing yet, mate. I'm so stirry in the guts I can hardly breathe without chucking up.' Bowker exhaled audibly. 'What about your end? Heard anything from McLeod on the Ferreira car?'

'Yeah. The trim they found at Pykes came off his vehicle. Thought I might take a run up to Ballan and have another chat. Put a few facts on the table and see what he has to say.'

'Take a DNA swab kit with you. If he's a match for the semen found in Katrina Cassidy, it's all over for him. Keep me posted.'

Bowker ended the call, and his thoughts immediately returned to his wife.

Within ten minutes, Holmes was in his car.

* * *

Larsen had pulled up a chair to D'Angelo's desk, finalising the paperwork for their arrest of Warren Standish and the search of his property.

'Did you tell Darren about what happened yesterday?' D'Angelo suddenly blurted out.

Larsen leaned back in her chair. 'I presume you're not talking about the case.'

'No. What occurred at the panelbeater's.'

Larsen eyeballed him. 'I didn't. It doesn't affect him, and I know that if I told him, all hell would break loose.'

D'Angelo stared straight into her eyes. 'I'll level with you, Kirsten. If you weren't in a relationship with Holmes, I'd ask you out. I'm very attracted to you.' He held up both hands, palms out. 'But don't worry, what happened yesterday won't happen again. Things will remain professional.' He inhaled deeply. 'I'm just putting my cards on the table in case your personal circumstances change.'

Larsen folded her arms. 'When we finalise this case, I'll be asking Greg if I can partner someone else in the squad, Marco.'

D'Angelo's head dropped. 'I *knew* I shouldn't have told you,' he muttered.

'What you just said has nothing to do with it. I made my decision as we left the panel shop yesterday.'

D'Angelo's brow wrinkled. 'But we work so well as a team.'

'Yes, we do, but I'm not having this little subplot running in the background of every case we investigate. I don't want to second-guess what I should wear to work.' She paused for a short moment. 'Don't get me wrong, Marco. I like you, but nothing more than that. You're a good investigator, and you'll work well with anyone Greg teams you with. Same story with me.'

D'Angelo stood. 'I need a coffee. What about you?'

'Yeah. Thanks.'

D'Angelo had barely left the room when his desk phone rang. Larsen answered and identified herself. The caller was Erin O'Meara from the forensic centre.

'The Standish brothers' prints are all over those tools, Detective,' O'Meara said after clearing her throat.

'So Domonic used them as well.'

'Yep. But what'll be most interesting to you is that we found specks of the security guard's blood on the bag.'

'Bingo,' Larsen said with a wide grin.

'And now for the biggie. Tarantara!' O'Meara retched up sputum before continuing. 'The head of the hammer had minute traces of the guard's blood as well, even though an attempt had been made to rub it clean.'

'And don't tell me. The hammer handle had been wiped of prints as well?'

'Nope. There were prints on the handle, but only those belonging to Warren Standish, who I'd expect washed the hammer. And we matched his prints to those we originally found on the number plates but weren't able to identify at the time. Both brothers were at Car City that night, no argument.'

'Yeah, but unless one of them spills their guts, it'll be hard to prove which one landed the fatal blows.'

'Fair chance both attacked the poor bugger. He passed away in hospital days later from a combination of injuries. I suspect a court will find both brothers culpable of murder.' She coughed briefly.

'I'll email you the paperwork. There's a lot more detail there.' She ended the call as she spat something out. Larsen hoped it was into a tissue.

Larsen replaced the receiver just as D'Angelo returned. She took her coffee and blew over its surface.

'That was O'Meara at Forensics.'

'Shit. Is she still alive?' D'Angelo asked with a forced smile.

'*Just*, by the sounds of her. Details will be in an email, but to cut a long story short, Ralston's blood was found on the hammer and the sports bag. Prints from both brothers found on everything, just about. Warren Standish's prints match those on the plates we couldn't identify originally.'

D'Angelo shrugged. 'They'll both go down, unless one of them squeals on his brother.'

Larsen nodded. 'Either way, they're both looking at lengthy prison time.'

* * *

Holmes found Ferreira at home and irritated with another police visit. 'What is it this time?' he snarled as he stood in his front doorway.

'I'd like to ask you about something,' Holmes replied, happy that his visits were annoying his suspect.

'*What?*' Ferreira snapped back. 'I told you everything I know yesterday.'

Holmes didn't reply but beckoned Ferreira to follow. When they reached the Mercedes now parked beside a Mazda sedan in a gabled double garage attached to the end of the house, Holmes squatted down and pointed to where the piece of trim was missing from the passenger side door.

'Where'd you lose that?'

'Lose what?' Ferreira said, becoming frustrated.

Holmes touched the area he was referring to. 'The three inches of trim that belongs here. You can see it has broken away from the rest.'

Ferreira placed his hands on his hips and stared into the roof of the building. 'Now how the fuck would I know that? Didn't even know it was missing until you just pointed it out. Next time it goes in for a service, I'll get them to order a replacement strip.'

Holmes stood up with a wide grin. 'No need to, Mr Ferreira. We've got the missing piece, and I'm sure the panel place I saw in town will be able to glue it back good as new.'

Ferreira's face tightened. He did his best to remain cool. 'Find it on the ground yesterday?'

Holmes shook his head slowly and melodramatically. 'Unfortunately for you, no. It was found at Pykes Creek Reservoir by a forensic team on the day the woman's body was discovered. Any ideas how it may have got there?'

Ferreira took a moment to answer. 'I occasionally eat lunch there if I'm out on the road.'

'Out on the road picking up women?'

'No. When I'm on my way somewhere.'

Holmes raised his eyebrows. 'I've got two problems with that. One is that Pykes is no more than ten minutes from home, so it seems a bit silly to be eating lunch there during a trip. But my *biggest* problem is that yesterday, you swore black and blue that you've never been to Pykes. So which is it, Mr Ferreira?'

Tiny beads of sweat were forming on Ferreira's forehead. 'Well, I must have been in there at some stage if that's where the trim was found.' He eyeballed Holmes as a way out occurred to him. 'But not in the last six months. Certainly not in the time frame you're looking at for the death of that poor woman.'

Holmes was keen to keep up the pressure. 'So if you wave over a woman who agrees to have casual sex, where do you go to shag her?'

Ferreira was caught off guard and took a moment to organise his thoughts. He shrugged. 'It varies. If it's a nice warm day, I might find a quiet backroad and put a rug down in the grass. If the weather's shit, I put the seats down in this car and we do it in the back.'

Holmes smiled. 'Sounds romantic. Why not just use the picnic reserve at Pykes? There're spaces all over the grounds where you could stop and not be bothered by others.'

'It's busier than you think at times, Detective. There's a playground and a boat ramp.'

'You seem to know a fair bit about it for somebody who hasn't visited there a lot,' Holmes shot back.

Ferreira had heard enough, and his temper was rising. 'This is all bullshit, Detective. Somehow, I've gone from having the odd consensual root along a backroad somewhere to being a suspect in a murder.' He pointed towards the town. 'Check out Ballan and you'll find couples having sex in cars along some road every night of the week. Are they murderers too?'

'They most probably don't wave over unknown women on the highway and proposition them, Mr Ferreira.' Holmes sighed. 'Most of them probably don't turn violent if things don't go their way, either.'

'Who told you that shit? If it was my bloody wife, I'll–'

'Do *what*, Mr Ferreira?' Holmes leaned in closer. 'If I hear you've touched your wife, or any other woman, I'll have you straight before a court.'

Ferreira looked at the ground and didn't answer.

Holmes feigned lightening the mood. 'The good news is that

forensic science can not only prove a person's guilt, but also their innocence. We're going back to my car, and I'm going to fingerprint you and take a DNA swab.'

Ferreira seemed taken aback. 'A DNA swab?'

'Yeah. The lab will sequence your DNA, and if it fails to match the semen found inside the victim, then you're halfway home free.' Holmes smiled. 'For an innocent man, DNA analysis is a gift.'

'What if I refuse?' Ferreira shot back.

'You'll just be delaying the inevitable. We'll apply for a court order to take it. The outcome won't change. You can't alter your DNA, no matter how much time we give you.'

'Waste of fuckin' effort,' Ferreira muttered as he followed Holmes back to the police vehicle, where he was fingerprinted and swabs were taken from the inside of his cheek.

Holmes saw the look on Ferreira's face as he trudged back to the house. He was now certain Ferreira had killed Katrina Cassidy.

* * *

The crushing results from Rachael's sister's blood test came midafternoon. A match always carried the slender odds of just one in four, but it had remained the best chance of finding a compatible donor. International databases were still being checked, but as Rachael's health deteriorated, so did the family's confidence that her life could be saved.

Bowker had always prided himself on his ability to think things through, to find a solution where there seemed none, to pull the right rein when confronted with a difficult choice. But now, here, in the most crucial situation of his life, he was relegated to a mere spectator as his wife's body continued to destroy itself.

CHAPTER 31

Despite hours of intensive interrogation, neither of the Standish brothers would give up the other for the murder of Jeremy Ralston, the security guard at Car City. Consequently, both were charged with murder and with a plethora of lesser crimes, including theft of a motor vehicle and arson.

* * *

Holmes took the call on Bowker's desk phone the next day. It was Erin O'Meara from the forensic centre.

'Greg not there, Darren?' she asked with a wheeze.

'Hasn't been in for a couple of days. Things have gone to shit with Rachael.'

'Chemo still not working?'

'Nope. And the sister's bone marrow, which held their hopes, is not a match.'

'Fuck.'

'Yeah, fuck.'

'The sad part is that there *will* be a match, probably many of them, here in this country alone, but only a small percentage of the population is registered. It would make things a bloody sight easier if HLAs were tested and recorded when a new baby has their heel prick blood test done.' O'Meara paused while she cleared her throat.

'Never going to happen. Civil liberties, Big Brother, all that.'

'Would be handy if they recorded the DNA when they did that test as well. Three quarters of the crimes we take weeks or months to crack could be solved within a day.' Holmes exhaled audibly. 'But I suppose it wouldn't be long before insurance companies would want access, or personnel and recruitment departments.'

'Get hold of the film *Gattaca* if you want to see where that path could take us.' Holmes heard O'Meara cough and spit out the sputum before she continued. 'Anyway, back to practical things. We sequenced Mr Ferreira's DNA from the swab you supplied.'

'*And?*' Holmes asked expectantly, certain there would be a match.

'The semen found in the victim doesn't belong to him.'

'Shit.'

'But it's close. Comes from a brother.'

Holmes was puzzled. 'There *is* no brother in our investigation. Are you sure you're not mixing this up with the security guard murder? Two brothers are involved there.'

'Of course we're not mixing it up!' O'Meara replied indignantly. 'What sort of a disorganised backwoods operation do you think we're running out here, Darren? This is a scientific institution. Not sure how you do things in at Homicide, but for your information, we keep records out here.' Her voice faded as she wretched up phlegm.

'Okay, okay. Point taken. Sorry for that. It's just that there's been absolutely no mention of a Ferreira brother.'

'Doesn't mean there isn't one,' O'Meara replied. 'How many years have you known me, Darren?'

'About ten, I suppose.'

'How many siblings have I got?'

'No idea.'

'Exactly.'

Holmes was suitably chastened and keen to change tack. 'So how does DNA show that it was a brother's semen?'

'The amount of *common* DNA between the swab and the semen tells us they were brothers. The fact that the DNA is *not identical* tells us the swab sample and the semen came from different individuals.'

'Could it mean he's got a secret half-brother? Could his old man have jumped the fence at some stage?'

'Nope. This is a brother with the same two parents. DNA proves it. Absolutely no doubt.'

'I was sure our killer would be Michael Ferreira,' Holmes said in a tone dripping with disappointment.

'Still might be,' O'Meara replied. 'The brother's semen doesn't preclude that.'

'True. But it complicates things.'

'Find the brother and you're halfway there.'

Holmes thanked O'Meara and hung up. He leaned back in his chair, fingers knitted behind his head, as he contemplated his next move. His thoughts were interrupted by the vibration of his mobile in his jacket pocket. He didn't recognise the number.

'Detective Sergeant Holmes.'

'Hello, Detective. This is Julia Crowe from Ballan. You might remember me.'

Oh, I remember you, alright, Holmes thought. 'Yes, Julia, you're Michael Ferreira's wife,' he said politely instead.

'That's right. You might recall giving me your business card in case I needed to contact you.'

'Yep. What can I do for you?'

'You spoke to Michael yesterday, and I haven't seen him since. His car is gone, and I haven't heard from him. I don't think he'd be too worried about me and the kids, but it's unlike him to leave his horses unfed.'

'Has he gone to his brother's?'

'He hasn't got a brother, Detective. What would make you think he has?'

Holmes frowned. This wasn't making any sense. 'Are you sure?'

'Of course I'm sure. I've been married to him for twelve years. I think I'd know if he had a brother.' She paused for a moment. 'You're not implying his father had an illegitimate child.'

'No. No I'm not, Julia. I'm asking if Michael has a brother with the same mum and dad. How long ago did the parents move into the district?'

Crowe didn't answer for a moment, obviously making historical calculations. 'A couple of years before I met Michael and moved up here to be married, I think. They started a business in Melbourne after they immigrated from Europe. That's where Michael was born. In Melbourne I mean.'

'Perhaps they had a child who is significantly older than Michael, who is now estranged and the family don't want to discuss. Or maybe there's a son who stayed in the old country.'

'It's possible, I suppose, although there's only Michael left to answer that question. You probably know his parents were killed in a road accident a couple of years ago.'

'Yeah, Constable Pattison at the local station told me.'

'I was never all that close to the Ferreiras, to tell you the truth. The whole family treated me as if I was trash. From the wrong side of the tracks. Thought I'd trapped their precious boy by getting pregnant. Reckoned I was after the family money.' She chuckled. 'Me getting pregnant had nothing to do with me going after him, let me tell you. They should have been thankful I didn't have the bastard charged.'

'You can still do that, if you want,' Holmes replied. 'There's no statute of limitations on serious crimes in Australia.'

'Wouldn't do it to the kids, Detective. Especially to the older one, who was the product of that episode.'

'Well, the option's there if you change your mind. I'm glad you tipped me off that he's absent without leave. If he returns or contacts you, let me know, okay?'

'If my husband has anything to do with all this, I'll gladly give whatever help I can. If he is guilty of killing that girl, he's not fit to be the father of my boys. The family would be better without him.' She took a deep breath. 'Before you go, can I ask what makes you think Michael has a brother?'

After rapid assessment of his options, Holmes decided to take a punt and disclose more information than he would normally, hoping it may bring Ferreira home, where they could ask him more questions.

'Julia, I'm gonna level with you. Before he disappeared, Michael may have told you that I took a DNA swab for comparison with semen samples retrieved from the victim at Pykes Creek Reservoir.'

'He didn't tell me, but I watched you doing the tests through the loungeroom window.'

'Okay. The first time I visited, you told me you'd heard rumours about his history of waving over women on the highway and propositioning them for sex. Well, those rumours are true. He's admitted that to me, and bragged to the local police sergeant. Pykes Creek Reservoir is just up the road from his hunting ground, if you want to call it that, so he was an obvious person to either rule in or rule out regarding sexual contact with the woman who died.'

'I understand,' Crowe replied quietly.

'When the DNA results came back, they showed no match for Michael, but one for an unknown person who can't be anything but a brother.' Holmes paused. 'Remember to ring me if you hear anything.' He ended the call before she could raise further questions.

The more he thought about it, the more Holmes felt at a loss to explain why Ferreira had disappeared. If Ferreira knew his DNA would match the semen sample, then that would explain why he took off without explanation. To run from arrest. But the DNA *didn't* match, and so proved his innocence – of the sex, anyway. He would have been aware of that before the sample was tested. Did he know his brother was involved and possess sufficient knowledge of DNA to understand his own sample would implicate his brother? Even in that case, the only reason for his disappearance would be finding and warning his brother. Or perhaps the brothers were involved together in something more sinister, for which neither could afford to be caught.

Holmes took a sheet of paper from a shelf above his desk and wrote a list of documents he needed. The main one was a copy of Michael Ferreira's birth certificate from Births, Deaths and Marriages in Collins Street. This would detail any siblings Ferreira had at the time of his birth and his parents' dates and places of birth. Holmes would also contact the Department of Immigration, or Home Affairs as it was now, and seek details of his parents' arrival in Australia and whether any male children immigrated with them. If necessary, Holmes would contact the Ferreiras' home country and ascertain if there was any record of the couple having a son there. If they *did* have a boy before coming to Australia who did not migrate with them, he would need to seek immigration and visa officialdom to check if any such offspring had travelled to Australia, particularly in the current year. Holmes resolved first to acquire Michael Ferreira's birth certificate and his parent's immigration details before wading into the minefield of overseas bureaucracy.

With the resolution of the Car City murder, Holmes's task was made easier when D'Angelo and Larsen volunteered to share the task of locating Michael Ferreira's mysterious brother, more specifically making overseas enquiries and handling paperwork so Holmes was free to work the case from other angles. Given Bowker's regular absence, Holmes was thankful for the help, particularly when it relieved him of his most hated part of the job – tedious paperwork that kept him tied to his desk.

*　*　*

Holmes received a second call from Julia Crowe around midnight.

'Sorry to ring so late, but Michael just called and asked me to feed the horses,' she said. 'He wouldn't tell me where he was or what he was doing.'

'Did you tell him I'd been asking about his brother?'

'Yes. At first, he denied he had any siblings, but once I explained about the DNA proving his brother's existence, he said he'd better come home and sort things out.'

'Call me again when he arrives,' Holmes said before ending the call.

'Ferreira's wife?' Larsen asked, rubbing her eyes and draping an arm across Holmes's bare chest.

'Yeah. Bloody midnight, and I was dead to the world.'

'Well, we're both awake now,' Larsen said coquettishly. 'Interested in an encore?'

'Bloody oath,' Holmes replied as he rolled over and kissed her passionately.

*　*　*

Crowe's next call came midmorning the next day. Holmes was back at headquarters.

'He's home,' she said quietly. 'He's down at the stables checking on the horses.'

'How long ago did he arrive?'

'Half an hour. Brushed me aside when I asked where he'd been. Wanted time to think, he said. Planned to jump a couple of his horses to clear his head.'

'I'll be up there within ninety minutes to have a little chat about his brother. Don't tell him I'm coming.'

Holmes thanked Crowe and ended the call.

Thus far, he'd avoided contacting Bowker since he'd received the bad news surrounding Rachael's sister's blood test. But things had become increasingly complicated since Ferreira's DNA results had come in. Holmes changed his mind twice before electing to call his boss.

Bowker's voice was flat, as Holmes had expected. He listened without interruption as the latest developments in the Cassidy investigation were explained. When Holmes mentioned his plan to visit Ferreira and seek more information concerning a brother, he received an unexpected response.

'I'll come with you, mate. Rachael says I'm giving her the shits just moping around the house. She suggested I should go out somewhere to take my mind off things here for a couple of hours.'

'Love to have you along, obviously. But will Rachael be okay on her own?'

'Jacinta's here, and she's a lot more qualified than me.' There was a pause. 'I'll be at Spencer Street in half an hour, unless the traffic holds me up.'

CHAPTER 32

'I'm not sure how I'll cope if I lose Rachael,' Bowker said softly, eyes moistening.

Holmes stared ahead as he drove through Melton. He wasn't sure how to respond but felt the need to remain positive. 'They'll find a donor, Greg. They're searching the whole world. Has to be a match out there.'

Bowker shrugged. 'That's what *I* thought, but as each day passes, you get another little kick in the guts. If we don't find something in the next week or so, our haematologist is suggesting we stop chemo and put Rach into palliative care.' He looked across at Holmes. 'You know what palliative care is, Sherlock? God's waiting room.'

'I wish I could do something to help…'

'We all do, mate. I've never felt so useless in my life.' Bowker shook his head. 'The hardest thing to cop, especially for Rach, is that her own body is manufacturing the shit that is killing her. If only the brain had the capacity to order it to stop.' He forced a smile. 'This trip isn't quite doing what it was supposed to do, is it? Take my mind off cancer and Rachael's fate. Tell me about this Michael Ferreira.'

Holmes breathed a secret sigh of relief that they were moving to a more comfortable topic. 'I don't like him. Arrogant.

Mistreats his wife. One of those blokes you hear about who men want to be like, and women want to be with.'

Bowker laughed. 'Like you and me, Sherlock?'

It was the first time Holmes had heard a genuine laugh from his partner since Rachael had become sick. 'Can't disagree there.'

* * *

Again, Holmes found Michael Ferreira at his stables, this time just as he was flaying his boots into the ribs of a frightened chestnut gelding that was pulling hard against its headstall. Shoeing tools were on the ground beside him. The horse squealed, its eyes wide with terror, their whites as brilliant as the big white blaze on its forehead. Ferreira was more casually dressed than on Holmes's last visit, wearing jeans, riding boots, and a sleeveless, tight-fitting tee-shirt that showed off his impressive physique. Over the top, he wore a leather farrier's apron. He was in no mood for visitors.

'Go easy, mate!' Holmes yelled.

'Fuck me, are you back *again*?' Ferreira said as he threw the ball hammer he'd been holding into a wooden box of horseshoe nails.

'Yeah, can't keep away,' Holmes replied. 'Brought a friend with me, this time.' He grinned. 'He's a bit of a horseman, like yourself, so you might like to compare training methods. This is Detective Inspector Bowker.'

Neither Bowker nor Ferreira made any attempt to shake hands.

Ferreira folded his arms instead. '*Inspector*. Must be a serious visit.'

'Just getting a little country air,' Bowker replied, already taking a dislike to the man. 'Not impressed by the way you treated that gelding.'

Ferreira ignored the gibe. 'So why the visit this time? I've been fingerprinted and DNA swabbed, which I presume have all proved negative, otherwise you would have already arrested me. I've told you everything about my movements around the time that poor woman was killed.'

'You didn't tell me about your brother,' Holmes said quickly.

'What brother?' Ferreira replied.

Bowker thought it safer to keep his hands in his pockets. 'Don't play games with us, Mr Ferreira. When our forensic people analysed your DNA swab, they were able to ascertain one hundred percent that the semen found in Miss Cassidy belonged to a sibling of yours.'

'My wife explained that over the phone. But I know nothing of a brother.' Ferreira smirked knowingly. 'Unless, of course, my parents had a son before they immigrated to Australia who stayed behind when they came here.' His smirk intensified. 'If that person did come out here on a visit and commit such a heinous crime, I'm sure he'd have fled the country by now.'

Bowker could feel his anger building. Perhaps he was in the wrong frame of mind to be doing these interviews. 'Sounds like a reasonable explanation,' he said with an edge. 'And perhaps your brother needed help making his exit. So can I ask where you've been for the last day or so?'

'Here and there,' Ferreira replied smugly. 'Visiting a few friends I've made out on the road over the years.'

'You didn't tell your wife that you'd be away?' Holmes asked.

'Nope. I knew she'd work it out when I didn't turn up for dinner.'

'I'm not sure I like that attitude, Mr Ferreira,' Bowker said, his face reddening, his hands balling into fists in his pockets. 'Show some respect to your wife. At the very least, she's still the mother of your children.'

'I'm not sure if you're married, Detective,' Ferreira said. 'If you aren't, keep it that way. Get married and you'll rue that decision for the rest of your life. She'll become a millstone you'll never be rid of.'

Bowker had Ferreira by the throat against the wall before Holmes could react, and it took him an extended while to convince his partner to let go. A smudge of blood coloured a cedar board behind Ferreira's head, and two droplets stained the lower sleeve of Bowker's jacket. The horse reared and broke free of its tether before galloping off behind the stables.

'Your career is over!' Ferreira yelled as he straightened his shirt and felt the back of his head.

'Not before I charge you with the domestic assault of your wife, soliciting in a public place, and abetting the escape of a murderer.'

'We'll be in touch,' Holmes said as he and Bowker walked back to their car.

Ferreira was left rubbing a small amount of blood he'd found on his head between his thumb and fingers.

* * *

It wasn't until the police vehicle exited the Ferreira property that either detective spoke.

'Sorry, Sherlock,' Bowker said quietly. 'As soon as he started talking about his wife being a burden when I'm about to lose mine, I saw red. He'd already sent my blood pressure off the chart by the way he treated that horse.'

Holmes nodded. 'Don't worry, I get it. I totally understand why you did what you did. But we should never have put you in that position with the challenges you face at the moment.' He looked at his partner. 'I don't want you to take this the wrong way, mate, but I don't think you're fit for duty at present.'

'It won't happen again. I can promise you that,' Bowker replied.

'No you *can't*, Greg. That's the point.' Holmes took one hand off the steering wheel and upturned a palm. 'Come into work and run the case, by all means. No one in Homicide has a sharper mind. But I don't think you should be involved in the legwork. Not in potentially confrontational interviews like that one, anyway.'

Bowker looked out his window as they passed through Ballan, but didn't answer.

'What do you think of that suggestion?' Holmes pressed. 'Just until Rachael's situation is resolved.'

'Just until she *dies*, you mean?' Bowker mumbled.

'I don't mean that at all, mate. You know exactly what I'm saying. You're on tenterhooks all the time, waiting for the phone to ring with news of a donor, or waiting for the latest blood count. No person can function properly under that sort of pressure. I know I couldn't.'

Bowker turned and nodded. 'You're probably right. Until things become clearer, I'll chain myself to my desk when I'm not at home with Rach. But everything on this case comes back through me, okay?'

'Absolutely. You're still the boss.'

'I'm powerless to help Rachael, so I'd like to feel useful somewhere.' Bowker looked out his side window, but Holmes could tell he was crying.

Holmes placed his left hand on his friend's shoulder. He didn't need to say anything.

* * *

Larsen and D'Angelo had been busy while Bowker and Holmes were away. Larsen had downloaded the relevant police application forms and walked north for a block up Spencer Street. She turned east up Collins Street and found the offices of Births, Deaths and Marriages within a hundred metres. *What did people call it?* she thought as she entered the building. *Hatches, Matches and Dispatches?* Gaining priority treatment, she was back at her desk with Michael Ferreira's birth certificate in hand within an hour. Checking his driver's licence details for his date of birth on the VicRoads database had made the process easy. Only one Michael Ferreira, or Miguel Ferreira, as he was officially named, was born on that particular date. No siblings were listed. Larsen then urgently requested the immigration details for a Carlos and Madalena Ferreira from the Department of Home Affairs. At the same time, D'Angelo had contacted colleagues in the mother country asking that they access relevant authorities for evidence of an earlier child being born to the Ferreiras.

By the time Bowker and Holmes had grabbed a late lunch and had sat discussing a myriad of topics – the Cassidy case, the winding up of the Car City investigation, but mostly Rachael's condition – Larsen and D'Angelo had departed Spencer Street headquarters. Sitting on Holmes's desk when he and Bowker returned was Michael Ferreira's birth certificate. Holmes immediately zeroed in on the box that detailed siblings. It was empty. 'Fuck! What the hell's going on here?' he muttered in frustration as he handed the certificate to Bowker, now seated at the desk next to his. 'No brother on record.'

Bowker's eyes scanned the document, but they only saw one thing. *Portugal.* Both Ferreira's parents were Portuguese. 'You head home, mate. You've had a big day. I'll hang around and tidy up some paperwork that's mounted up while I've been away.'

'Is there anything I can help you with? To help you catch up?'

Bowker shook his head. 'Nah, but thanks. Take an early one. You deserve it. You've been doing two jobs.'

Holmes tapped Bowker on the shoulder and wandered out of the room.

* * *

O'Meara had left work, so Bowker rang the mobile number that only a few of her favourite officers had been given. She answered after three rings.

'Sorry to bother you at home, Erin.'

'You can bother me any time you like, Gregory, but I'm not sure Rachael would approve.' She emitted a combination of a chortle and a cough.

'Actually, it's Rachael I'm ringing about.'

O'Meara was suddenly serious, fearful of what Bowker might be about to announce. 'Okay,' she replied hesitantly.

'You'd know about human leukocyte antigens, right?'

'Yeah, HLAs. A set of proteins on a cell that identifies that cell as part of your body, and prevents it being attacked by your own immune system. This is in relation to potential marrow transplant for your wife, right?'

'Yeah. Is it possible to identify HLAs from a DNA cheek swab?'

O'Meara wasn't sure where this was all heading so played a straight bat. 'HLA genes are on the DNA helix molecule. They're grouped together, so they're not hard to find if you know where to look. Why?'

'You already analysed Michael Ferreira's DNA. I wonder if you can go back and identify his HLAs?'

O'Meara didn't answer for a moment, and Bowker heard her sigh quietly. 'To check if it matches your wife's?' she asked.

'Correct.'

O'Meara's normal reaction would have been to burst out laughing and lambast Bowker about the futility of what he was asking. But right now, she knew she had to tread gently. 'And what singles Ferreira out for a test? Why not just grab a stranger passing by your front gate?'

'Ferreira's parents were both Portuguese, and Rachael's mother's side are all from Portugal. Same city. Braga. Our haematologist said the best chance for a match outside the immediate family was from people with the same ethnic heritage.'

'Has your doctor searched the Portuguese database?'

'I think so. Nothing positive that I know of,' Bowker replied sadly. 'But there's no way Michael Ferreira would have been on it.'

'I don't want to be a wet blanket, Greg, but it's a million-to-one shot,' O'Meara replied, suppressing a cough. 'Ten million to one, more like it.'

'At this stage, ten million to one is the only shot I've got left,' Bowker replied, on the edge of tears.

No words were exchanged for a few moments, but the emotion on the line was palpable. O'Meara broke the silence. 'Have you got a copy of Rachael's HLAs?'

Bowker brightened a little. 'I've got every bit of information ever written on the subject, plus a copy of all Rachael's test results.'

'Look, email me the results and I'll see what I can do. I can't promise anything. The DNA lab we use will wonder why the hell police forensics would be chasing this kind of data. There's a bloke over there I get on alright with, so I'll ask him to do it as a favour.' She chuckled. 'Might have to turn on the O'Meara charm.' Her laughter degenerated into a series of coughs. 'I need a smoke,' she added after the coughing had subsided.

Bowker smiled. 'Can't thank you enough, Erin. I really owe you.'

'A bottle of Johnnie Walker Red should square the ledger.'

'It'll be on its way by lunchtime.'

O'Meara suddenly became serious once more. 'Don't get your hopes up, Greg. Go buy a donkey and run it in the Melbourne Cup. The chances of it winning are better than those of Ferreira being a match. And when I say a donkey, I don't mean a slow racehorse, I mean a real bloody donkey.'

'Yeah, I know I'm grasping at straws,' Bowker replied, 'but if Rachael *is* the die, I don't want any ifs or buts. I want to know that I tried everything to save her, however miniscule the chances were.'

When the call ended, Bowker leaned back in his chair, conceding Rachael's fate was probably sealed, and within a few months at most, he'd be on his own for the first time in thirty-five years.

CHAPTER 33

The wet and windy weekend passed, causing many much-anticipated events to be cancelled or postponed – a music festival in the Yarra Valley, a cup meeting at a country racecourse, a yachting event on Port Phillip Bay, the Head of the River Regatta on the Barwon River in Geelong. For the Bowkers, the foul weather was a mere change of backdrop to their routine of daily chemo visits, a debilitating regimen that seemed more pointless by the day. Rachael was progressively weaker, as were the chances of finding a donor. Alana Jamieson tried hard to create a positive atmosphere, but even her false optimism displayed tiny cracks when Bowker asked about the future. She said good palliative care was available, should it be necessary, and modern drugs could make the last weeks of life pain-free. The mere fact that palliative care had crept into the conversation seemed to the Bowkers a portent of what was to come.

Monday morning was the first time Rachael successfully raised the subject of funeral arrangements. Each time before, Bowker had shut down any conversation immediately, fearful that such talk would have a negative impact on her normal optimism and her natural willingness to fight. However, if he was to be totally honest with himself, he was unable to countenance any suggestion that his wife could die. But with greater and more open discussion of palliative care, Rachael was finally able to convince him they needed to talk.

'I'd like to be cremated, like you, Greg,' she said. 'No big fancy coffin. If they won't allow cardboard, then I want one of those plain pine ones.'

Bowker was taking notes, not because he wouldn't remember his wife's wishes, but because he needed somewhere for his eyes to focus. Looking at Rachael calmly discussing her own death would be impossible to endure.

'And I want half my ashes spread on your old farm at Benalla, just like you. I was born in a country town, and nothing tugs at my heartstrings there.' She smiled weakly. 'Nothing I want to fertilise, anyway.'

'And the other half?' Bowker asked, trying desperately to hold it together.

'Cast it to the wind up at Manangatang. We had the best years of our lives up there in the Mallee. Had the three kids in the Manang hospital.'

Bowker scribbled a few lines. 'Okay.'

'And for music, I'd like *Fields of Gold*. The Eva Cassidy version. No better sight than the ripe cereal crops waving in the breeze, or a paddock of canola in full flower.'

Bowker stared at the table, remembering the times when they were first married, where they'd chase each other through the crops and fall down, looking into the blue sky and watching the odd puffy white cloud billowing above them. They'd pick out ephemeral sculptures before the heavens morphed into another creation of their imagination. 'Who would you want to speak?' he finally asked.

'You, of course. And the kids.'

'I'm not sure I'd be able to, Rach. I'd be a mess.'

'Doesn't matter.' She smiled. 'It's the thought that counts.'

They struggled through another twenty minutes of planning and reminiscence, with Bowker's eyes aching from his effort not to cry when his wife was so stoic. His phone ringing in the bedroom gave him the way out he needed.

* * *

A new email caught D'Angelo's eye when he booted his computer. Sender, Polícia de Segurança Pública – Portugal's civil police force. The message was brief but added to the mystery of the Katrina Cassidy investigation. Portugal's birth records had been searched, with no record of a child being born to Carlos and Madalena Ferreira. D'Angelo printed the email and wandered over to where Holmes sat crouched over his desk, poring over various statements germane to the case. D'Angelo dropped the email in front of him.

'Doesn't help much,' D'Angelo said. 'Or maybe it does. Stuffed if I know.'

Holmes picked up the printout in one hand, leaned back in his chair and scratched the back of his head with the other. 'Stuffed if I know either, Marco. This case is doing my head in.'

'Do you want me to ring Greg?'

'Nah. Not at this stage. We'll wait until Kirsten hears back from Home Affairs.'

D'Angelo placed his hands on his hips. 'If it wasn't for the DNA, you'd have to say the brother doesn't exist.'

'If it wasn't for the DNA, I'd have Michael Ferreira locked up! That's if Greg doesn't kill him first.'

'Kirsten told me there was an altercation. How's Greg doing? You know him best.'

Holmes sighed loudly. 'About how you'd expect. The clock is ticking with Rachael. If she doesn't make it, I'm not sure which way he'll go. He'll either throw himself headlong into his work, or he'll chuck the job in altogether. He's not all that far off retirement age.' He shrugged. 'Then again, I wouldn't be surprised to see him return to the Mallee. He never stops talking about the place. Lots of memories up there. Dropping back to a uniformed senior connie might be his go.'

'To each their own, I guess,' D'Angelo mused. 'Couldn't think of anything worse than living up there in the sand.' He looked at Holmes. 'City boy mentality, I suppose. Think the world ends a mile from where you're born.'

'Not just city people, mate. Lots of country people think that about their front gate.'

D'Angelo's eyes dropped to the floor. 'What do you think are Rachael's chances?'

'Zilch. But don't tell Greg I said that. While she's still breathing, he sees hope.'

* * *

Bowker grabbed his mobile from his bedside table. Erin O'Meara's name jumped from the screen. Almost too frightened to answer, he took a deep breath and tapped the 'accept' icon.

'G'day, Erin,' he said quietly.

'Morning, Greg,' O'Meara said wheezily. 'We ran those tests, and–' She stopped as a tickle in the throat got the best of her and she descended into incessant coughing.

Bowker stared at the ceiling in frustration as her coughing subsided. 'You still alive?'

'I am. What are you doing this afternoon?' she asked.

'Shit, Erin. Why?'

'Thought you might go out and buy a donkey to enter in the Cup.' She chuckled.

Bowker was dumbstruck. 'Are you saying Ferreira is a match?'

'Not perfect, but that was one in a million chance anyway. Its 7/8. I've done some research, and that will work.'

Bowker was beaming. 'I'm speechless here, Erin. Bloody speechless. Thank you, thank you, *thank you.*'

'Don't get carried away just yet,' O'Meara warned. 'Finding the match is only half the story. Your mate Ferreira has to agree to donate.'

'Yeah, I know,' Bowker mumbled.

'I've done my bit, now the rest is up to you. And if I was you, I wouldn't be mentioning anything to Rachael until you get that agreement set in stone.'

Bowker said nothing as he recalled slamming Ferreira's head into the stable wall. Had he effectively slammed Rachael's head into that wall at the same time?

'You still there, Gregory?'

'Last week, I had a scuffle with Ferreira and spit his head open.'

O'Meara wheezed. 'Can I ask why a normally level-headed man like yourself would have done that?'

'He was slagging off women, especially his wife. I'm on a knife's edge, and he's advising me that if I'm not married, I should keep it that way, because I'd be lumped with a woman I'd never get rid of.'

'Ouch.'

'Yeah. Looks a bit ironic now. He holds the key to saving the wife I *never* want to be rid of.'

O'Meara sniffed loudly. 'So what's the plan?'

Bowker shrugged to himself. 'Can you email me your results? I'll forward them to our haematologist. If I have no joy mending bridges with Ferreira, an official approach from a medico might have more success.' He heard the back door slam and his daughter

Jacinta's voice in the kitchen as she and Rachael spoke. 'My daughter just arrived, so I might take another run up to Ballan and crawl up Ferreira's arse.'

'Well, don't tell them where you're going, or why. Rachael doesn't need another kick in the guts right now if Ferreira won't cooperate. But you're a big boy, Gregory. You're old enough to make your own decisions.' Bowker heard her hack up something before spitting it out – somewhere.

'I'll send over a four-litre bottle of cough mixture,' Bowker replied.

'Make it Johnnie Walker. That's my cough mixture these days. I'll slip outside in a moment and suck on a Benson & Hedges. That usually settles the cough.' Her laugh disappeared into a crackle.

Bowker again thanked her profusely and ended the call. He strode through to the kitchen and pecked his daughter on the cheek.

'Who was on the phone?' Rachael asked feebly.

'Forensics. More test results, but we're no closer to finding who killed Katrina Cassidy,' he lied without lying. 'I might go into work and check if Sherlock has made better progress.'

Within five minutes, he was on his way to Ballan for the most important interview of his life.

* * *

Larsen's email from Home Affairs later in the day heaped further mystery on the whereabouts of Michael Ferreira's brother. No offspring of Carlos and Madalena Ferreira had travelled with them when they immigrated to Australia, and there was no record that a passport under the Ferreira name had been used to enter the country. No Ferreira that fitted the parameters Larsen had supplied, anyway.

Once informed of this latest development, Holmes's lingering doubts concerning the existence of a second Ferreira brother percolated to the surface. He was a novice when it came to understanding DNA, but had faith in the knowledge of the experts, and trusted the scientists at the forensic centre. He picked up his phone and rang Erin O'Meara, not realising that Bowker had been in constant contact on more private matters.

'Detective Holmes, what a pleasure to hear your voice. I don't think we've got any results still hanging for your case,' she said, careful not to disclose her earlier dealings with Bowker.

'I just need to pick your brain,' Holmes replied.

O'Meara coughed to clear her throat. 'Well, you'd better hurry, because my brain is dissolving by the minute in whisky and nicotine.'

Holmes chuckled. 'What do you know about DNA?'

'Not as much as the experts, but probably more than most. What's your question?'

'Greg told me their cancer specialist said that if Rachael received a bone marrow transplant, then the DNA of her blood would match the donor's, even though the rest of her body's DNA would stay the same.'

'The doctor is absolutely correct,' O'Meara said, reflecting on the fact that if Michael Ferreira could be convinced to become a donor, Rachael Bowker's blood would forever be a copy of his.

'Then is it possible Michael Ferreira had a marrow transplant himself sometime in the past, and this is confusing our results? Sorry if this sounds like bullshit, Erin, but we're hitting brick walls here.'

O'Meara blew her nose loudly. 'Two problems with that, Darren. His brother would have had to be the marrow donor for his DNA to show up in Ferreira's body. And, let's face it, the presence of the brother's DNA in the semen found in the victim can be explained much easier by him simply putting it there himself.

'But it is possible?' Holmes persisted. 'I'm sure Michael Ferreira is as guilty as sin.'

'Not if you're talking about DNA in semen. If we were trying to explain the DNA difference between *blood* and the semen, you'd be right in suggesting that solution. But in this case, we have a variance between a *cheek swab* and semen. Neither of those are affected by a marrow transplant. There has been one case out of millions where, over time, a donor's DNA has ended up in semen, but it was also detected in most other parts of the body, including cheek cells. In the Ferreira case, both were very distinct.'

Holmes was disappointed. 'So it's only *marrow* transplants that can impact DNA?'

'No. Any transplant will impact the DNA associated with it. You can check Ferreira's medical record, but I'll bet he's had no transplants of any description. And before you ask, it's too risky to transplant prostates or testicles.'

Holmes sighed. 'Thanks, Erin. Sorry to waste your time. It was just a shot in the dark. We've run out of places to find this brother. We've checked birth and immigration records both here in Australia and in the Ferreira family's native Portugal, and there's no evidence that he exists. To be honest, if it wasn't for the presence of his DNA in the semen, I'd be willing to bet my life that there is no brother.' He shrugged to himself. 'But there must be. How else could his DNA have ended up in our victim? We need to keep searching for the bastard.' He exhaled loudly. 'What was that Winston Churchill saying? It's a riddle wrapped in a mystery inside an enigma.'

There was silence for a few moments before O'Meara gave a sudden groan. 'A mystery inside an enigma! Of course! Bloooody hell, you're a dumb bitch, O'Meara!' she blurted out. 'Why didn't I think of this before, when you doubted the existence of a brother? It's as obvious as the nose on your face. Ever heard the term *chimera*, Darren?'

Holmes was puzzled. 'Yeah,' he replied slowly, wondering what this had to do with their case. 'There were chimeras in one of my kids' computer games. They're mythical monsters made up from sections of different creatures.'

'Do you know what the word chimera describes in the real world?' Holmes heard her coughing as she tackered on her keyboard. 'Here we go. Straight from the online dictionary. *A chimera is an organism containing a mixture of genetically different tissues, formed by a process such as fusion of early embryos.*'

Holmes frowned and combed his fingers through his hair. 'So in our case, you're saying that organism might be Michael Ferreira, and he could be composed of different genetic material? Sound like science fiction gobbledygook.'

'Chimeras are not as uncommon as you might believe. I'm kicking myself that I didn't think of it earlier.'

'Okay,' Holmes replied sceptically. 'Explain to me how a human becomes one.'

'They don't become one, they're born one. And they might live their whole life not knowing it.'

'Just remember I'm a dumb-arse copper and my head's starting to ache.'

'Don't sell yourself short, Darren. Greg said you're the sharpest detective he's worked with. You've done your Year Eight biology and the *Males and Females* unit, I'm sure. Class all had a giggle, probably. Covering up the collective embarrassment.'

Holmes chortled. 'Yeah, but it was in Year Ten when I did it. Before the internet. They'd need to teach it in Grade One now!'

'Well, you'll remember being taught that animals develop from a single fertilised egg, so in theory, all cells in the body should have identical DNA. A chimera can arise when two embryos that would normally develop into *non-identical* twins fuse in the womb. Parts of the resulting individual derive from one embryo and parts from another. If Ferreira is a chimera, some of his body will have developed according to one DNA plan and the rest according to a second. So if this scenario is accurate, Ferreira's brother has been hiding in full sight. As parts of Michael Ferreira. A mystery inside an enigma.'

'But shouldn't it be noticeable?'

'Chimeras can appear entirely normal, so it's usually discovered by accident. Occasionally, there are obvious signs like different-coloured eyes or patches of skin that vary in colour. When a person is a mixture of male and female cells, there can be reproductive abnormalities.'

'So, theoretically I could be one and not realise?'

'Most chimeras wouldn't know. It sometimes comes out in paternity cases where the father's DNA doesn't match that of the baby.'

Holmes was on intellectual overload. 'How do we test Ferreira? I don't think he'll fancy wanking into a bottle so we can DNA-test his semen. At the moment, with the tests we've done, he's home free. Why would he jeopardise that?'

'Has he got kids?' O'Meara asked, suppressing a cough.

'Two boys. Both quite young.'

'Assuming Ferreira's wife hasn't been unfaithful, the boys' DNA will tell us accurately whether Ferreira is a chimera. If their DNA is consistent with the sample taken from Ferreira's cheek, then the semen found in Cassidy can't be his, and you'll need to mount a new hunt for his brother. On the other hand, if the kids' DNA shows they were fathered by the owner of the semen, then either Ferreira is a chimera, or the wife has had dalliances with the elusive brother.'

'And if the boys' DNA is consistent with neither?'

O'Meara chuckled. 'Then the wife has been shagging someone outside the family, unless we find another familial connection. The only one I can think to fit that bill might be her father-in-law.'

'He was killed in an accident before the boys were born,' Holmes replied. 'Certainly the second one, anyway.'

O'Meara coughed up phlegm. Holmes didn't hear her spit it out. 'Well, that means the alternatives are pretty cut and dried. Three possible outcomes, only one consistent with Michael Ferreira being the father and therefore the owner of the semen left at Pykes. Since you've found no evidence that a brother even exists, my money is on Ferreira being a chimera.'

Holmes thanked O'Meara and leaned back in his chair, planning his next move.

CHAPTER 34

Julia Crowe, sporting shorts, a singlet top and bare feet, ushered Bowker to an open-plan kitchen in the Ballan Ferreira residence. Sun streamed through skylights and a gentle breeze wafted through open windows. With a cup of coffee in one hand, her husband, dressed in jeans, riding boots and a muscle shirt, sat at a circular table reading the day's edition of the *Herald Sun* newspaper. He placed the coffee on the table and stood when he saw Bowker.

'Back to assault me again, Detective?' he snorted.

Bowker held up both hands, palms out. 'Just the opposite, Mr Ferreira. I've come to apologise for my behaviour. My wife has terminal cancer, and I'm struggling a bit.'

'That's terrible,' Crowe said sympathetically.

Ferreira wasn't as generous. 'There's no bloody excuse for a police officer acting that way. None.'

'I agree,' Bowker replied, conscious that he was grovelling. 'I pride myself on my professionalism. What happened the other day is completely out of character.'

Ferreira rolled his eyes. 'So you've driven all this way to apologise?' he asked sardonically. 'Could have saved your time and your petrol. You can stick your apology up your arse. But don't worry, I won't file a complaint. That'd be a waste of my time anyway, knowing how coppers protect each other. Your mate would back you up and claim I was lying about your attack, so why bother?'

Crowe pursed her lips. 'Come on, Michael,' she said quietly. 'The detective has a terminally ill wife, which would unsettle anyone, and he *has* come all this way to apologise. Surely you can cut him some slack?'

Bowker's hopes of Ferreira donating bone marrow were dissipating before his eyes. But he remained resolute about giving it his best shot. 'My wife has an aggressive form of leukemia that is not responding to chemotherapy. Her only hope of survival is a bone marrow transplant, and that requires finding a donor whose cells are compatible with hers. No matches have been located, and we've searched databases all over the world.'

Crowe placed her hand on Bowker's forearm. 'That's awful, Detective.'

Ferreira turned to leave. 'I don't envy your situation. But my horses won't feed themselves, so I'll leave you with my wife. I'm sure she'll lend a more sympathetic ear than me.'

Bowker took a step forward. 'It's you I need to talk to, Mr Ferreira. We tested your DNA, and your cells are a partial match for my wife's. Close enough to be a donor.'

Crowe's face lit up. 'That's wonderful, isn't it, Michael?'

Ferreira's expression darkened. He ignored his wife. 'Why the hell would you test my DNA for that? It's a special test, I'd presume.'

'You are from Portuguese heritage, as is my wife on her mother's side. Our doctor told us that the best chance of gaining a match was among siblings or from persons of similar ethnic background. My wife has only one sibling, a sister, and she wasn't a match. In the midst of trying to track down your brother, it came to our notice that both your parents were Portuguese. We had your

DNA already, so I requested it be tested.'

Ferreira's face reddened further. 'You didn't have my permission to do specific tests!'

'But it's lucky they did, wasn't it?' Crowe said with a forced smile.

Ferreira eyeballed Bowker. 'You've wasted your trip, Detective. There'll be no bone marrow donations from me. End of story. I'd advise you to find some other Portuguese candidates. Ones you haven't assaulted.'

Crowe had her hands out in front, palms up. 'But you could save a woman's life!'

Bowker closed his eyes. 'I'm begging you, Mr Ferreira. There's nothing to the procedure. Bone marrow is extracted under general anaesthetic from the back of your hipbones via hollow needles. No cuts or scars. You can usually leave hospital that afternoon.'

'You're wasting your time, and whatever time your wife has left,' Ferreira replied coldly. 'Now if you don't mind, I've got horses to attend to.'

Bowker had reached the desperation stage. 'I could pay you. I know paying for organ donations in Australia is illegal. But I'm desperate. I have a house in Caulfield I can sell. It's worth millions.'

'I'm a rich man already,' Ferreira said smugly. 'I could buy ten houses in Caulfield and not blink. But the bottom line is, I'm not having my cells multiplying in someone else's body, and then being blamed for something I didn't commit.'

'Just do the right thing for once!' Crowe shouted out before raising her arm in reflex against being hit.

'Don't you dare talk to me like that!' Ferreira growled through gritted teeth.

Bowker knew that had he not been present, Ferreira would have belted his wife.

'Perhaps if I was guilty of a crime, I could trade for a few favours,' Ferreira said with a smirk. 'But unfortunately for you, I haven't committed the crime you suspected me of, and ironically, my DNA proves that.' He walked out the back door without looking back.

Bowker dropped his head, realising he shouldn't have expected anything better.

Crowe looked at him, her eyes watery. 'I'm so sorry. He's a shit of a man.' She brightened a little. 'But I'll keep working on him. You never know.'

'Don't get yourself belted up,' Bowker replied. 'My wife wouldn't want another woman to die because of her disease.'

Crowe gently touched Bowker's forearm again. 'I'll be careful. And give my best wishes to your wife.'

Bowker smiled politely, wondering how so many impressive women ended up married to pieces of shit. Or, more puzzlingly, why they stayed with them. Kids, probably. 'I'll do that. Thank you.'

He walked through to the front door. 'Have you appointed anyone with enduring medical power of attorney? Someone to make medical decisions on your behalf if you are mentally incapacitated?'

Crowe shook her head. 'Doesn't that automatically go to your next of kin?'

'It does if no one else has been appointed.'

'Do you think I should do something about that?'

Bowker shrugged. 'It will probably never happen, but you don't want to finish up unconscious or in a coma and have your husband judging what treatment, or non-treatment, is best for your health.'

'Thanks, Detective. I'll give it some thought. Some *serious* thought.'

'And your husband is in the same boat, I presume? If he's unable to, you'll make his medical decisions?'

Crowe nodded. 'That's the way I understand it. Yeah.' She laughed. 'That'd be a change. Me getting to make a decision in this marriage.'

Bowker reached out and shook Crowe's hand. 'Keep safe.'

* * *

Bowker and Holmes most probably passed each other on the Western Highway near Bacchus Marsh, but the two lanes of the freeway were so widely separated in many sections, much of it with vegetation in between, that they were unlikely to spot each other travelling in different directions. Holmes and Ferreira also narrowly missed seeing each other, with Ferreira turning into one of the hotel carparks a minute or so before Holmes passed through the main street of Ballan.

When Crowe answered her front door, she was flabbergasted to be confronted by a second detective in the space of an hour. She invited the briefcase-carrying Holmes through to the kitchen, where he accepted an offer of coffee and biscuits. Unbeknownst to Crowe, Holmes had no inkling of Bowker's recent visit, so when he failed to mention it, she made the decision not to bring it up unless he did. After the odd minute of small talk, Holmes addressed the reason for his visit.

'I'm going to put my cards on the table, Julia, because it involves something I need from your two boys.' Holmes held up both palms when he saw the anguish on Crowe's face. 'Don't worry, they're not leaving the house, and it's nothing that will hurt them physically. Or mentally.'

'Okay,' Crowe replied warily.

'When we spoke on the phone after you rang me to report that your husband had disappeared, I asked about Michael's brother.'

'Yes. And I told you he didn't have a brother.'

'Then I explained we had DNA that proved there *was* one, and that semen found in the murder victim belonged to him.' She nodded, so he continued. 'Well, we've searched records both in Australia and in Portugal, where the Ferreiras hail from, and we now agree with you. There *is* no brother.' He sipped his coffee while Crowe digested the first chapter of his story. The next chapter would be harder to accommodate.

Crowe's brow wrinkled. 'Then who did the semen come from?'

Holmes inhaled, choosing his words carefully. 'Have you ever heard the term *chimera*, Julia?'

'It's got something to do with Greek mythology. Creatures that are made up of two different animals. Like a centaur or a minotaur.'

'Okay. Hold onto your hat for this one. Our forensic people believe Michael is a chimera – an individual with two sets of DNA.'

Crowe's mouth fell completely open. '*What?*'

'They're more common than people think. Most of the time the person never finds out, apparently.'

Crowe took a long slug of her coffee. 'So how does it happen?'

Holmes went on to explain non-identical embryos fusing into one and the resultant child having dual DNA. 'We believe this has happened with Michael. That the DNA in his cheek swab is different to the DNA in his semen.'

Crowe placed her hands over her mouth. 'You now believe he killed that girl,' she said in a strained voice.

Holmes nodded. 'We believe he had sex with her, and probably killed her, yes.'

Crowe had turned white. 'What do you want with my boys?'

'Did you ever do RAT tests with them during COVID?'

Her brow wrinkled. 'Three or four times. Why?'

Holmes reached down and lifted his briefcase onto the table. He snapped the locks, opened the lid, and took out two small plastic zip lock bags, each containing a swab stick. 'There's no need for me to be involved. I'm just asking if you'd swab each of the boys like you would for a RAT test. But swab the inside of their cheek, not their nose. You can tell them it's for COVID if you like. They'll like it better than a nose swab, anyway. Seal the swabs in the bag and I'll take them back to be tested.'

'What will you be looking for?' Crowe asked hesitantly.

'One thing, and one thing only. Whether your husband's DNA passed on to the boys matches semen at the scene of the crime. Once that is established, one way or the other, the samples will be destroyed.'

'What if they *don't* match?'

'Then we'll be back to looking for the mystery brother.'

'And if they do match, then the only explanation is that the semen belongs to Michael? That's set in stone?'

'There's only one other explanation, but I don't think you'd appreciate me describing it. I don't think it's likely, anyway.'

Crowe frowned. 'I still want to hear it.'

Holmes shrugged. 'As I said, it's highly unlikely. But the only other explanation would be that Michael does have a brother and he is the father of your sons.'

Crowe chortled. 'I can assure you of something, Detective. I've had sex with no one other than Michael since we were married. Before we were married, actually. Wouldn't have been possible, even if I wanted to. Michael is a control freak. I can't blow my nose without asking him first.'

'Where's he now?'

She shrugged. 'Pub, probably. He never tells me where he's going or for how long.'

'Might be best to do these swabs while he's away.'

Crowe was still uncomfortable. 'Do the boys have to be involved? I could probably get you a sample of semen if I planned it properly. The one thing he'll never refuse is sex.'

'Nope. Too risky, if you get caught trying to smuggle something out. My advice is, once the boys have been swabbed, pack them and yourself up and get as far away from here as possible. Have you got a sibling or parents you can stay with?'

'My brother lives down in Coburg.'

'Sounds good.'

Crowe remained concerned about her sons' welfare. 'The boys' DNA won't be used to match the bone marrow of Detective Bowker's wife, will it? They're a bit young to be donors.'

Holmes was totally puzzled. 'I'm not sure what you're talking about, Julia. Someone has to be eighteen or over before they can donate tissue for transplants. Your boys are way short of that. What's this about Greg's wife?'

Crowe explained Bowker's visit, the request he had made, and the response he was given. Holmes said nothing, but now worried that his good friend had gone rogue on the investigation.

'There's one other thing, Detective.' Crowe opened the pantry, pulled out a drawer and removed a pair of men's socks hidden behind a rack of spices. She handed them to Holmes. 'Yesterday, I emptied our bins and found these in the incinerator with other stuff ready to be burnt. They're quite new, and at first I thought Michael had thrown them out by mistake. But when I unfolded them to check if they were holed, I found this.' She pulled the pair apart, showing Holmes a patch of what looked like dried blood. 'It's probably from one of his horses. But I thought I should show you.'

* * *

With the socks and the Ferreira sons' cheek swabs safely in his briefcase and Julia Crowe packing up behind him, Holmes knew it was time for a serious chat with Greg. No investigation can succeed with its lead detectives running different agendas.

Holmes found Bowker at his desk scribbling on a notepad when he arrived back at headquarters. He dispensed with pleasantries. 'We working the Cassidy case together or not, mate? Just been to Ballan and Ferreira's missus tells me you'd just been out there. Would have been nice to be given a heads-up.'

Bowker leaned back in his chair. 'It was a private matter. Nothing to do with solving the case.'

'Julia Crowe told me why you went, and I'm genuinely sorry about the reception you received. But it would have been handy to know what you were up to. Or even that Ferreira was the tissue match you've been chasing.'

Bowker dropped his pen on the pad and exhaled loudly. 'Yeah, you're right. I'm sorry, Sherlock. I should have let you know, but my mind won't let me concentrate on anything other than Rachael. We're running out of time.' He looked back at Holmes. 'Why did *you* go out to Ballan? I asked everything to be run by me.'

Holmes slowly shook his head. 'Turn on your bloody phone and you'll hear my message. I rang, and it went straight to voicemail.'

Bowker held up both hands, palms out. 'Shit. My mistake. I apologise.' He sighed. 'I'm listening now. Why the trip to Ballan?'

Holmes pulled up a chair, increasingly willing to cut his good friend some slack now he had had his say. He explained the chimera theory and O'Meara's suggestion to collect DNA from Ferreira's sons to confirm it. He smiled when he described the bonus of Julia Crowe rescuing the socks. 'Everything's been sent to Forensics for analysis. If the lab can match Ferreira to the semen, and the blood on his socks turns out to belong to Katrina Cassidy, we've got him cold. Just the semen match would give him wriggle room to argue that he merely had consensual sex with her, like he had with others, possibly also at Pykes. He could claim that when he left, Cassidy was alive and well. But if that *is* her blood on his sock, he's in more shit than a Werribee duck.'

Bowker folded his arms. 'So we wait?'

'Yeah. Until the forensics come back.'

Bowker feigned a weak smile. 'At the moment, waiting is the one thing I'm good at. Waiting for blood test results, waiting for news on donors…' He hesitated. 'Waiting for Rach to die.'

Holmes touched Bowker on the shoulder. 'Hang in there, mate. It's never over until it's over.' He wandered back to his own desk, feeling totally powerless to help one of his oldest friends.

Bowker turned on his phone. Besides the missed call from Holmes, O'Meara had also tried to contact him. She had left a short voicemail requesting he ring her ASAP. He quickly returned the call.

'You been talking to Darren Holmes, Greg?' O'Meara asked in lieu of introductions.

'Just a minute ago. Why?'

'Did he mention anything about chimeras and the possibility that Ferreira might be one?'

'Yeah. He explained it all to me. He said it could crack the case wide open. It would explain how Ferreira could own that semen even though this DNA cheek test said otherwise.'

'The reason I tried to call you earlier was to warn you that if Ferreira is a chimera, it could spell trouble for him being a matching donor for Rachael.'

'They're not looking to transplant semen. They're using bone marrow, and you said the DNA test showed he was a close match.'

The *cheek swab* DNA showed he's a match. But if he's a chimera, the DNA of his all-important *blood* may match his semen rather than the cheek swab.'

'Fuck!' Bowker said half under his breath. 'Not that it matters much. He won't volunteer to donate marrow anyway. But I held out a faint hope that when push comes to shove, he might do the right thing.'

'He could still do that if the blood DNA falls the right way for Rachael,' O'Meara said, feigning optimism.

'Is there any way we can be certain about the blood?'

'We need a sample to test.'

'Yeah, and he's going to give us one of those,' Bowker said sarcastically. 'Not in a zillion fucking years.' He looked down at his outstretched fingers. 'I shouldn't have washed my hands after I belted him.'

Then he spotted them. Two small circular bloodstains on the sleeve of his jacket, which he hadn't noticed in the wake of his physical altercation with Ferreira and all the drama surrounding Rachael. 'Don't move, Erin. I'll be out at McLeod in less than half an hour.'

CHAPTER 35

Two days later, Bowker received the news he'd been dreading via Rachael's haematologist. Bone marrow database searches had been exhausted. Rachael's rare HLA combination could not be matched with sufficient compatibility to allow a transplant. A few donors had come close, but even in the magical world of medical science, with the use of experimental drugs and treatments, *close* was not good enough. Palliative care was the best that could be offered. Alana Jamieson asked if Bowker wanted to break the news to Rachael himself. If he couldn't face that, she would do it, but she wanted him present supporting his wife. Bowker was adamant it was his responsibility. They'd faced a life together, and they would face this together as well. After hanging up, Bowker stared at the notices pinned on the board behind his desk, seeing nothing, his eyes moistening. The nightmare was now a reality. The love of his life would die. In effect, *his* life was over as well.

His phone rang. He picked it up, hoping it was Doctor Jamieson ringing back to apologise, to tell him there'd been a mistake and a donor *had* been found. His shoulders dropped when O'Meara spoke.

'Gregory, Erin here. First off, how's your wife?'

'Not flash. And getting worse.' Bowker replied dejectedly.

'Well, some good news is that our analysis of the blood on your jacket shows that Ferreira's blood carries the same DNA as was found in the cheek swab. So he *is* a match for Rachael.'

Bowker's mood lightened for a moment but then plummeted. 'He won't donate. I didn't tell you when we last spoke that I got desperate enough to say I'd pay him under the table. But he's got so much money, he just threw that idea back in my face.'

'He might change his mind when he thinks about the implications of his decision a bit more deeply.'

'I don't think he's capable of that, Erin. He's a prick of the highest order. Takes pleasure out of other people's pain.'

'Well we've got some news that will take the smile off his face.' Bowker heard her sigh, then cough lightly. 'Do you want me to talk to Darren about this? You've got more than enough on your plate. I'm surprised you're even at work.'

'Rachael would prefer me here than moping around the house. So now I do my moping at work. Give me a verbal report and I'll pass it on to Sherlock. He's gone downstairs for a coffee.'

'You're sure you can be bothered with this?' O'Meara asked gently.

'Yeah, give it to me. I'm supposed to be leading the case, which is a bit of a joke when Sherlock has carried the load.'

'Okay. We'll email a full report, of course, but this is the gist of our findings.' She cleared her throat. 'First of all, both his sons' DNA are consistent with Ferreira being the source of the semen found in the victim.'

Normally, such a breakthrough would've had Bowker over the moon, but today his voice was deadpan. 'So your theory about him being born a chimera was right? Same bloke, two types of DNA?'

'He had sex with Katrina Cassidy, I can tell you that, one hundred percent certain. But our tests on the socks give Ferreira bigger questions to answer. It was human blood we found there, and it belongs to the victim. And there's a lot of it. It's not just on the side, but a big build up along the bottom of the sock where blood has flooded into the shoe. This didn't come from a cut from a stick when they were having a roll in the grass. This came from a very big wound.'

'Rules out an innocent liaison between the two before Ferreira left the scene?'

'Absolutely,' O'Meara shot back.

'Thanks, Erin. I'll look forward to reading the full report. Darren's back with our coffees, so I'll leave you to it.'

'All the best to Rachael, Greg. Look after yourself.'

Bowker disconnected the call and stood as Holmes approached, a takeaway cup in each hand. Bowker pulled his second-favourite suit jacket from the back of his chair and slid into it. 'Grab your coat, mate,' he said as he adjusted his collar and took a cup from Holmes.

'Where are we heading?' Holmes asked as he picked up his coat and followed his boss.

'Back to Ballan. And make sure you've got your weapon.'

* * *

Bowker drove as the Western Freeway disappeared into a gathering storm above the Pentlands to the west. Threads of lightning illuminated the interior of grey anvil-shaped clouds. Vehicles in the city-bound lanes all had their lights on, some with windscreen wipers still waving as they left the tempest behind.

The atmosphere inside the car was also electric. Bowker had outlined the revelations O'Meara had announced in her call, but promised himself no one would be informed of Rachael's prognosis before he had broken the news to her himself.

'There's no need to do this tonight, Greg,' Holmes stressed for the umpteenth time as they climbed the long and steep incline towards the storm. The smell of ozone flowed through the car's vents. 'We could go to Ballan tomorrow when it's earlier in the day and the weather's better. Ferreira will still be there. He thinks he's home free.' He upturned his palms, almost beseeching his partner and friend. 'We could rope in the local uniforms.'

Bowker chortled. 'Delaney would tip Ferreira off before we left Melbourne.'

Holmes folded his arms, knowing he was getting nowhere. Bowker was not in the mood to listen or develop a logical plan. 'Is this about closing out this case, or is it about Rachael?'

Bowker's eyes never left the road. 'What's it got to do with Rachael? He's refused to donate his bone marrow, which is his choice. In practical terms, once that occurred, Rachael became irrelevant to this case. But I'll tell you one thing, Sherlock. When this bastard goes to prison, not only will he have Katrina Cassidy's murder on his conscience, but he'll have Rachael's death as well. That's if he possesses a conscience, of course.'

Holmes eyeballed him. 'So you're *not* going to shoot him? Is that what you're saying?'

Bowker didn't blink. 'Of course I'm not going to fuckin' shoot him. What good would that do? Rachael would still be dead, and I'd be in jail with the prick. Besides, he might have a road to Damascus moment and decide to donate the marrow.' He looked across at Holmes. 'I'm not a total idiot, Darren. The most painful thing I can do to Ferreira is send him to jail, destroy his playboy image and deprive him of the wealth he was handed on a silver spoon by his parents.'

Large raindrops landed like shelled eggs on the windscreen, and lightning lit the interior of the car in a stream of intermittent pulses. The detectives were at the top of the Pentlands and in the heart of the storm.

'Then why this afternoon?'

Bowker blinked quickly, and Holmes could see the lightning reflected in the moisture laminating his eyes. 'Because time is no longer unlimited for me, mate. I can't put off things until tomorrow, because tomorrow Rachael may die, and I need to be with her if she does. I know you and Kirsten or Marco could drive here tomorrow and take in Ferreira, but I want to be the one who arrests the prick. I want to be the one to cuff the bastard who killed my wife.'

A blinding flash and a giant clap of thunder shook the car. The storm was intensifying.

CHAPTER 36

'The Mazda's gone,' Holmes said, pointing to the empty spot next to Ferreira's Mercedes in the garage. 'Hopefully his missus took my advice and shot through with the kids.'

Bowker nodded and pulled the police car in behind the Merc. Unless Ferreira had a ute or another vehicle in one of the sheds, he was going nowhere. That's if he was home and hadn't taken the Mazda himself. Or worse, taken the Mazda with his wife and boys.

The sky remained leaden, and rain continued to hammer down, but the worst of the storm had passed. Lightning flickered out to the east, followed by the roll of distant thunder.

'You go around to the back, and I'll knock on the front door,' Bowker said, feeling his coat to ensure his automatic was still in his shoulder holster.

Holmes nodded. 'Don't do anything silly, Greg. Okay?'

Bowker didn't reply.

Holmes jogged his way to the rear of the house as Bowker approached the front entrance. The heavy wooden door was open, and through the security door Bowker could see Ferreira at the kitchen table, phone in hand, scrolling the screen. His dress was a step down from casual – shorts, muscle shirt and bare feet.

Bowker rang the doorbell. As Ferreira climbed to his feet, Bowker saw Holmes arrive at the glass door at the rear of the kitchen. When Ferreira recognised his visitor, he shook his head vigorously. 'The answer's still no, so you could've saved yourself a bloody trip.'

'It's police business this time, so we need another chat.'

'You've found my wife and kids, have you? Didn't realise Brian Delaney would call the big boys in so quickly.'

'This is about you and Katrina Cassidy's death,' Bowker replied, ignoring Ferreira's reference to his wife and sons, who he knew would be safely ensconced in Coburg.

Ferreira's concern for his family's absence evaporated. He sighed theatrically as he unsnibbed the security door. 'Once you bastards have a bloke in the frame, you won't give up, will you?'

Ferreira saw Holmes at the rear door as he walked back towards the kitchen. 'Thought I was going to do a runner or something?' He snorted. 'Innocent men don't run.'

'We're here to charge you with murder,' Bowker declared almost casually as he unlocked the back door for Holmes to enter.

'Fuck off,' Ferreira replied in an offhand manner, confident that Bowker was merely flying a kite. 'You've got nothing. The DNA said it wasn't me who rooted the girl, so you've got zilch to tie me to that murder.'

'You're right, Mr Ferreira. We *do* have the DNA.'

'Well, if you're looking for my brother, he's back in Portugal. Emailed me to confirm he was home and he enjoyed the trip out to see where the family had moved.' Ferreira tried hard to remain smug. 'So if you're to continue your investigation, I hope your passports are up to date.'

'Don't worry, we've found your brother,' Bowker said. He pointed to Ferreira's groin. 'He's right in there, where he's been from before you were born.'

'Have you lost the plot, Detective?' Ferreira replied, his eyes betraying a hint of panic.

Holmes smiled. 'Unfortunately for you, he hasn't. To cut a long and complicated story short, your mother conceived unidentical twins all those years ago. But the embryos fused together, and instead of two babies being born, there was only one.' He pointed at Ferreira. 'You. But you carry two strands of DNA. One of those matches the semen found in Katrina Cassidy.'

Ferreira was suddenly nervous, but managed to feign a chuckle. 'You blokes have been watching too much science fiction.'

'We didn't believe it ourselves at first, but our lab's confirmed it,' Bowker replied, mentally questioning why they were humouring this arsehole with an explanation. Why not just charge the prick and let his lawyer chase down the details?

Beads of sweat formed on Ferreira's brow. Certainly, the humidity was high, but the closeness he felt was more to do with his plummeting confidence that he would never face charges relating to Katrina Cassidy. 'You're playing me. Feeding me bullshit on the off chance I'll reveal something. Well, there's nothing to reveal.' He thrust out his chest in a false tenor of bravado. 'I've never had my semen tested, so there goes your theory.'

Holmes chortled. 'Didn't need to. We cheek-swabbed your two boys—'

'I didn't give permission for that,' Ferreira blurted out urgently.

'Your wife did,' Bowker shot back.

'She didn't run that by me first!'

'Contrary to the way things are done in your grubby misogynous world, she doesn't have to,' Bowker replied with an edge.

'The boys' tests both show their father was the same man whose semen was found in Katrina Cassidy. I can get the reports from the car if you don't believe me. And before you accuse your wife of being unfaithful, you need to realise the only other person who could have fathered the boys is the non-existent brother who must have visited Australia on two other occasions to impregnate your wife. It was *you* who had sex with that woman at Pykes. That is now beyond question.'

Ferreira pulled out a chair and nervously sat down at the table. Holmes then sat opposite, Bowker electing to remain standing. Silence prevailed, the detectives allowing Ferreira to ponder his options. They still had more ammunition if needed. It wasn't long before it was.

'Okay. I had sex with the Cassidy girl at Pykes. She was driving towards Melbourne, and I waved her over when I saw she was wearing this crazy pink hat and had lairy dyed hair. Thought she was a chance for a quick root at Pykes.' He shrugged. 'She turned out to be an inspired choice. When we finished, I asked if she was okay to continue her journey. She said she was. So I left her there, putting on her shoes, and I headed back home.'

Holmes raised his eyebrows. 'Would've been a lot easier to tell us this when we first spoke to you.'

Ferreira's brow furrowed. 'What? Tell you that I'd waved over a girl on the highway, we'd had sex at Pykes Creek Reservoir and she was later found dead there? You know where that would've ended up.'

'In the same conversation we're having here, but without all the bullshit in between,' Bowker replied.

'Why didn't you fess up when I swabbed your DNA?' Holmes asked. 'You must've known you were dead meat.'

Ferreira shrugged. 'Hoping for a miracle, I suppose. And when you asked about a brother, I thought I'd been granted one.'

'What made you think a piece of shit like yourself was due a miracle?' Bowker growled.

Ferreira ignored him and looked at Holmes. 'You might have me for obstructing an investigation, but you've still got a killer to find. Must've driven into Pykes straight after I left, and before the girl had time to drive away.'

'Cut to the chase, Sherlock,' Bowker said quietly. 'I'm sick of reasoning with this fucker.'

Holmes nodded to his partner. 'We have a pair of your socks. Your DNA is all over the insides, but one was saturated with dry blood. Katrina Cassidy's blood.'

Ferreira didn't argue about the socks, or how they'd come into the police's hands. He had one last roll of the dice. 'It was an accident. Cassidy was some kind of psycho. We had consensual sex, which she seemed to enjoy, then *bang*. She's suddenly a different person. She says she's going to the police to report me for pulling her over and raping her. She grabs me by the throat, and I can't get her off, but I am able to reach down and pick up a rock. I hit her lightly on the head with it to get her off. Blood went everywhere, and she fell to the ground. It was an accident.'

'So you hid her body?' Holmes said.

Ferreira was choking back tears. 'Yeah. I was sure nobody would believe my story if I reported it.'

'You were right,' Bowker replied angrily. 'We don't fuckin' well believe it. You're six-one or two and as fit as a trout. Cassidy was short and built like a reed. There's no way you needed to hit her with a rock to get her off you, if that even happened. And you didn't make a report because it *wasn't* an accident. It was murder. You murdered that girl in cold blood. It was all about your image. A rape charge, proven or not, would've destroyed your rich sportsman playboy persona.'

Ferreira's mouth dropped and he thought for a minute. He looked at Bowker. 'Can we make a deal?'

If this deal entailed what he feared it would, Holmes knew it would represent his worst nightmare. An impossible choice between his friend and everything he held dear in the police force.

'What sort of deal?' Bowker shot back, already knowing the answer.

'I donate the bone marrow you need, and you make this case go away. Stamp it as *unsolved*.'

Bowker looked at Holmes, who looked away.

'Deal of a lifetime,' Ferreira said with a smirk. 'Your wife's life for my freedom. I make the appropriate donation and disappear somewhere overseas.' He nodded towards Holmes. 'No problem with your mate here, I'd assume. Coppers always cover for each other.' When Bowker didn't answer, he added, 'Easy decision, I would've thought, for a man who says he loves his wife.'

Bowker took two angry steps towards Ferreira before he regained control. 'There'll be no deals, shithead.' His eyes moistened. 'The wife I love with every shred of my existence, and whom I would give my life right now to save, would never accept that I could put my best friend in such an impossible position. In practical terms, a deal like that wouldn't work anyway, even if my partner here went along with it. Two detectives from our team in Melbourne know all the details of this case, and our forensic centre has already signed off on your dual DNA and Cassidy's blood on your sock. And do you know what else, Mr Ferreira? I reckon if we set you free, you'd disappear, and we'd never get that bone marrow anyway.' Bowker waved an arm. 'Read him his rights, Detective Holmes.'

Holmes complied and turned to lead Ferreira away and back to the car. The rain continued to pour, puddles forming on the paving on both sides of the house.

Ferreira looked at his feet. 'Can I at least grab a pair of shoes out of the bedroom?'

Bowker nodded. 'You've got fifteen seconds. You go with him, Sherlock, in case he has any stupid thoughts of doing a runner.'

Bowker watched as the two men walked away from him. He contemplated what decision Holmes would have made if he'd agreed to Ferreira's trade. One thing he *was* sure of, however. He'd just passed up his last chance, albeit remote, of saving Rachael's life.

His self-flagellation was interrupted by Holmes sprinting up the corridor. 'The bastard went into his ensuite to grab his shoes. Another door leads to a second bedroom that shares that bloody bathroom. He opened a sliding window and bolted out into the rain.'

'The prick won't get very far. His car is wedged in the garage.'

'No. He didn't head in that direction. I saw him sprinting down towards the sheds and stables.'

Both men ran towards the back door. 'You check the sheds in case there's a ute or quad bike down there that could get him through the paddocks in this weather!' Bowker yelled. 'I'll check the stables in case he takes a horse. Would have to be bareback. Can't see him taking the time to saddle up.'

Holmes quickly checked the sheds. They *did* contain a Nissan one-tonner and a quad bike, but there was no sign of Ferreira. He checked machinery, cupboards, and all conceivable places where their fugitive could be hiding. After ten minutes, he was convinced. Ferreira wasn't in the sheds.

When he walked to the front of the stable block, the chestnut gelding with the baldy face charged out of its box and galloped off into the rain, a bridle half done up on its head, the reins flailing across the ground. Holmes hurried to the open box. Bowker was sitting in the straw, his back to the wall, pushing his mobile phone into his pocket with shaking fingers. Lying on his back, unconscious, with blood seeping from his head and left ear, was Michael Ferreira.

'Is he still alive?' Holmes asked.

'He *was* two minutes ago,' Bowker said with a tremor in his voice. 'I've just called triple zero for an ambulance.'

'What the fuck happened?' Holmes asked, crouching down beside his friend, placing a comforting hand on his shoulder.

'The horse kicked him in the head, as far as I can tell,' Bowker replied. 'Gave him both barrels, by the look of it.'

'Wasn't that the horse Ferreira was belting the other day?'

'Yeah. And in my experience, horses don't forget. Poor bastard was quivering all over when I got here. Nostrils flared, the whole deal. In the end I just opened the door and let him out. A run around the paddock will calm him down in a while.'

'Karma?' Holmes suggested quietly.

'Yeah,' Bowker uttered.

Holmes scanned the stall. Partially covered in straw was the heavy doorstop someone, perhaps Ferreira, had constructed from old horseshoes. 'What's that doing in here?' he asked.

Bowker half shrugged. 'I think I would have copped that if the horse hadn't got him first. It was lying where it is now when I came in. The horse was standing over the top of it.'

'Ferreira should have known it was no match for a bullet,' Holmes said.

'He wouldn't have known I was carrying.'

Holmes moved to Ferreira and felt the pulse in his neck. 'Weak, but he's still alive. I'll go to the tack room and grab some old towels I saw in there. He's not bleeding too badly, but I'll try and stop whatever's seeping out while we wait for the ambos.'

'Go for it, mate,' Bowker said as he climbed to his feet and stared out into the rain.

* * *

The ambulance arrived in good time, and two young paramedics examined Ferreira before calling in the air ambulance to convey their patient to Melbourne. 'We'll send him straight to the trauma centre at the Alfred,' an ambo told the detectives. 'We'll transport him to the footy ground and the chopper can pick him up from there. Easiest place to find from the air, especially on a shit day like this. His vitals are not good, and we're pretty sure he's got a fractured skull in at least two places. The contusions follow the line of the horse's shoe, so the bugger got him pretty flush. Enormous power they have when they lash out like that. Little girl got killed the same way when I was doing my training.'

The paramedics placed a brace around Ferreira's neck and lifted him onto a stretcher. The ambulance was backed up to the stable door, and Ferreira was loaded into the rear.

'We better go inside and lock up, I s'pose,' Bowker said as he watched the ambulance slowly leave the cobblestoned area.

'You do it,' Holmes replied. 'I'll wander back through the garage and get the car started, and I'll pick you up at the front door. There's no way you're driving back after what you've been through. Especially in this weather.'

Bowker held his hands out in front of him. They were visibly shaking. 'You're right, mate. Thanks.'

* * *

Back on the freeway, the weather was improving. It was still raining, but the heaviest of it was now over Melbourne somewhere. Persistent mist and light rain kept the bitumen wet, and vehicles, especially large trucks, threw up maelstroms of spray. If they weren't on a divided road, Holmes wouldn't have passed a single slow-moving vehicle between Ballan and the city. Only a fool or someone with a suicide wish would pull out into that wall of spray.

Few words passed between the two as they began the trip home. Bowker had his eyes closed, but opened them in confusion as the car's indicators continued to click. They were now on the exit to Pykes Creek Reservoir.

'What's the go, mate?' Bowker asked. 'I thought you would've had enough of this place.'

'Only take a minute, Greg.'

Bowker was perplexed, but too tired to request an explanation. Holmes would tell him in his own good time anyway.

Holmes pulled up in the carpark, as close as he could get to where the reservoir narrowed and passed under the freeway bridges. Here the water was at its deepest. He alighted from the vehicle and opened the boot. He removed the horseshoe doorstop. When he looked up, Bowker was standing beside him, but neither man said anything.

Holmes walked to within a few metres of the reservoir's edge than ran and heaved the doorstop to the midpoint of the water. He watched it disappear below the surface in an instant.

When he returned to the vehicle, Bowker was already in the passenger seat. 'Why'd you do that?'

'It's better that it isn't found in that horse box, or anywhere around those stables.'

'Do you believe I whacked him with it? To make it look like he was kicked by a horse?'

'*That* horse hadn't been shod, Greg. That's why Ferreira was belting him the last time we were there.'

'Ferreira would have shod him after we left.'

'Possibly,' Holmes replied without emotion.

'If I was going to whack him, why didn't I finish him off?'

'Maybe you didn't want him dead.'

'Okay, Sherlock. Turn around and we'll go back, catch that bloody horse and check his feet.'

'We're not doing that, Greg.'

'Why not? There's enough light left to find him.'

Holmes started the car. 'I'd rather not know.'

EPILOGUE

Rachael's colour was returning. Another couple of weeks would be needed before her blood could be deemed normal. 'It must have been a tough decision,' she said.

'Not tough at all. You needed the marrow. Without it, you would have died. That, plus the evil that man committed, overrode any other considerations.'

Rachael nodded but didn't respond.

'Besides, as his next of kin, I had the legal right to allow his marrow to be harvested. It happens all the time with brain-dead people.' Julia Crowe placed her hand on Rachael's. 'Perhaps, through you, his DNA can do some good and give the kids something about their father to be proud of.'

Bowker stood in the doorway, not wanting to interrupt the two women, who would forever share a bond. But he knew one thing. Michael Ferreira would always be entangled with the Bowker family, pulsing through Rachael's body, and infecting their thoughts.

Author's Note

The notion that a male motorist would wave over female drivers on a freeway before suggesting casual sex would seem preposterous even for a writer of fiction. But this in fact happened to a friend some years ago. The male in question was good looking, polite and on for a chat. My friend wisely declined his invitation. She then asked if he'd ever been successful. He smiled and nodded in the affirmative. Bowker's tale of the good Samaritan with a stock of painted signs he used to alert fellow motorists of blinker and brake light failures is based on events the author observed when driving along the Nepean Highway some years ago. Sometimes, fact is stranger than fiction.